CHILDREN

OF THE

STORM

Children of the Storm★

The Golden One★

Lord of the Silent★

He Shall Thunder in the Sky★

The Falcon at the Portal★

The Ape Who Guards the Balance★

Seeing A Large Cat★

The Hippopotamus Pool★

Night Train to Memphis

The Snake, the Crocodile & the Dog★

The Last Camel Died at Noon★

Naked Once More

The Deeds of the Disturber★

Trojan Gold

Lion in the Valley★

The Mummy Case★

Die for Love

Silhouette in Scarlet

The Copenhagen Connection

The Curse of the Pharaohs★

The Love Talker

Summer of the Dragon

Street of the Five Moons

Devil-May-Care

Legend in Green Velvet

Crocodile on the Sandbank★

The Murders of Richard III

Borrower of the Night

The Seventh Sinner

The Night of Four Hundred Rabbits

The Dead Sea Cipher

The Camelot Caper

The Jackal's Head

★ Amelia Peabody Mysteries

Elizabeth Peters

WILLIAM MORROW
An Imprint of HarperCollins*Publishers*

CHILDREN

OF THE

STORM

HarperCollins books may be purchased for educational, business, or sales
promotional use. For information please write: Special Markets Department,
HarperCollins Publishers Inc., 10 East 53rd Street, New York, NY 10022.

FIRST EDITION

Printed on acid-free paper

Library of Congress Cataloging-in-Publication Data
Peters, Elizabeth.
Children of the storm / Elizabeth Peters.
p. cm.
ISBN 0-06-621476-9
1. Peabody, Amelia (Fictitious character)—Fiction.
2. Women archaeologists—Fiction.
3. Egyptologists—Fiction. 4. Egypt—Fiction. I. Title.
PS3563.E747C48 2003
813'.54—dc21
2002041083

03 04 05 06 07 WB/RRD 10 9 8 7 6 5 4 3 2 1

To Joan Hess
Pax Ovinica

The day of the children of the storm.
Very dangerous. Do not go on the water this day.

—*Excerpt from an ancient Egyptian horoscope*

Acknowledgments

I am deeply indebted to the Benson Ford Research Center at the Henry Ford Museum and Greenfield Village, and to reference archivist Carol Whittaker for supplying me with detailed information on the use of the Ford Light Patrol Car in the Palestine campaign of World War I and thereafter. Emerson's assessment of this amazing vehicle did not exaggerate its capabilities.

My thanks as well to the amiable friends who read the entire manuscript and made suggestions: Dr. W. Raymond Johnson, director of the Epigraphic Survey of the University of Chicago, Dennis Forbes, editor of *KMT: a Modern Journal of Ancient Egypt,* George B. Johnson, special projects editor of *KMT,* and, as always, my invaluable assistant, Kristen Whitbread. I take full responsibility for any errors that remain despite their help.

Editor's Note

The Editor has been reminded that this present volume is the fifteenth of Mrs. Amelia P. Emerson's journals to appear in print. When she was first asked to prepare them for publication, she knew it would be a formidable undertaking, and so it has proved. The discovery of additional Emerson papers, including a somewhat spasmodic diary kept by her son (Manuscript H), complicated the task even more. There are gaps in the record, since some of the journals are missing; nevertheless, it is an amazing family saga, encompassing three generations, a world war, and thirty-five years of turbulent history.

It began with the first trip to Egypt of Amelia Peabody (as she then was) in 1884. She was accompanied by a young companion, Evelyn Barton Forbes, who, like Amelia, found a career and true love in the Land of the Pharaohs. They married brothers—Amelia accepting the hand of the distinguished archaeologist Radcliffe Emerson, and Evelyn that of his younger brother Walter. Amelia's love of Egypt almost equaled her love for her hot-tempered (but extremely handsome) husband. She joined him in his annual excavations, which, except for a few brief hiatuses, continued for the entire thirty-five years.

Inevitably, as Amelia might say, a second generation of Emersons ensued. Walter Emerson and his wife retired to her family estate in Yorkshire, where he could pursue his study of ancient languages. They became parents of six children (one of whom perished in infancy): Radcliffe Junior, Margaret, Amelia Junior (who insisted on being addressed as Lia to avoid confusion with her aunt), and twin boys, Johnny and Willy. Johnny died in France, serving his country during the First World War.

For reasons Mrs. Emerson declines to discuss (as is certainly her right), the elder Emersons had only one child, a boy named Walter Peabody Emerson. He is better known by his nickname of Ramses, given him by his father because he was "swarthy as an Egyptian and arrogant as a pharaoh." His mother would have said (and indeed, often did say) that one like Ramses was quite enough for any woman. Precocious, prolix, and pedantic, he barely survived a number of hair-raising adventures, but he finally developed into a young man with all the qualities a mother could wish.

Further additions to both families came through adoption and/or marriage. On a trip to an unknown oasis in the Western Desert, Amelia and Emerson (who prefers to be addressed by his last name) discovered a young English girl, Nefret Forth, and brought her back to England as their ward. Ramses and Nefret were raised as brother and sister, and it took Nefret some time to realize that her feelings for him were considerably warmer than that of a sibling. (Ramses was a lot quicker to catch on.) After a considerable amount of misunderstanding, heartbreak, and frustration (particularly for Ramses), they were married and—as we will see in the present volume—produced the third generation of Emersons.

The other adopted child was David Todros, a talented young Egyptian artist, who was working in semi-slavery for a forger of antiquities when the elder Emersons found and freed him. The grandson of their Egyptian reis, or foreman, Abdullah (of whom more hereafter), he became Ramses's blood brother and eventually his cousin by marriage, when David wed Lia Emerson. Lia and David also produced a third generation, a girl named after Evelyn Emerson and a boy named for his great-grandfather, Abdullah.

The Emersons had very little to do with Amelia's Peabody kin, an unattractive lot who produced one of the nastiest villains they ever encountered. The only good thing Percy ever did was produce a child, little Sennia, who was adopted by the Emersons and became very dear to them. However, Amelia considered herself to have a second family in a group of Egyptians who were the blood relations of their reis Abdullah. Abdullah's innumerable relatives worked for the Emersons on the dig and in the household; several became close friends of the Emersons, including Selim, Abdullah's youngest son, who replaced his father as reis after Abdullah's heroic death; Daoud, Abdullah's nephew, noted for his immense strength, amiable disposition, and love of gossip; Fatima, Abdullah's daughter-in-law, who became the Emersons' indispensable housekeeper; Kadija, Daoud's wife, the dispenser of an amazingly effective green ointment; and of course David Todros.

As Amelia mentions, Egyptians are fond of nicknames. So, it would appear, were the Emersons. Ramses and Lia are consistently referred to by those names; Amelia secretly appreciated her flattering appellation of Sitt Hakim, Lady Doctor, though she was equally appreciative of her husband's habit of calling her by her maiden name of Peabody as a demonstration of equality and affection. Emerson detested his given name and preferred to be addressed by his surname or by his Egyptian sobriquet, Father of Curses (which, as his wife admits, was well deserved despite her effort to cure him of using bad language). Nefret was known to many Egyptians as Nur Misur, "Light of Egypt." Her husband's less charming Egyptian name was Brother of Demons. It was meant as a compliment, however, acknowledging his varied abilities in disguise and languages.

One other member of the family had a plethora of pseudonyms. When Amelia and Emerson first encountered Sethos, aka the Master Criminal, aka the Master, they regarded him as a deadly enemy—head of the illegal antiquities racket in Egypt and the Middle East, and Emerson's rival for Amelia's affections. It came as a considerable shock to them (and, the Editor must admit, to her) when they discovered he was Emerson's illegitimate half-brother. During the First World War he redeemed himself by serving as a secret agent, a role for which he was well qualified by his skill in the art of disguise and his knowledge of the Middle East. Ramses, who had similar talents, was also recruited for the Secret Service, and carried out several perilous missions in Egypt and the Middle East. His best friend, David, served with him on one of these jobs; the Editor suspects David may have been involved in at least one other, but unfortunately the journals for several of the war years are still missing. Sethos, much to the surprise of everyone except Amelia (who claimed the credit for reforming him) became a friend and supporter.

And now, dear Readers, the Great War has ended and the family is about to be reunited. The saga continues!

CHAPTER ONE

The encrimsoned sun sank slowly toward the crest of the Theban mountains. Another glorious Egyptian sunset burned against the horizon like fire in the heavens.

In fact, I did not at that moment behold it, since I was facing east. I had seen hundreds of sunsets, however, and my excellent imagination supplied a suitable mental picture. As the sky over Luxor darkened, the shadows of the bars covering doors and windows lengthened and blurred, lying like a tiger's stripes across the two forms squatting on the floor. One of them said, "Spoceeva."

"Russian," Ramses muttered. scribbling on his notepad. "Yesterday it was Amharic. The day before it sounded like—"

"Gibberish," said his wife.

"No," Ramses insisted. "It has to mean something. They use root words from a dozen languages, and they obviously understand one another. See? He's nodding. They are standing up. They are going . . ." His voice rose. "Leave the cat alone!"

The Great Cat of Re, stretched out along the back of the settee behind him, rose in haste and climbed to the top of his head, from which position it launched itself onto a shelf. Ramses put his notepad aside and looked severely at the two figures who stood before him. "Die Katze ist ganz verboten. Kedi, hayir. Em nedjeroo pa meeoo."

The Great Cat of Re grumbled in agreement. He had been a small, miserable-looking kitten when we acquired him, but Sennia had insisted on giving him that resounding appellation and, against all my expectations, he had grown into his name. His appearance was quite different from those of our other cats: longhaired, with an enormous plume of a tail, and a coat of spotted black on gray. With characteristic feline obstinacy he insisted on joining us for tea, though he knew he would have to go to some lengths to elude his juvenile admirers, who now burst into a melodious babble of protest, or, perhaps, explanation.

"Darling, let's stick to one language, shall we?" Nefret said. She was smiling, but I thought there was a certain edge to her voice. "They'll never learn to talk if you address them in ancient Egyptian and Anglo-Saxon."

"They know how to talk," Ramses said loudly, over the duet. "Recognizable human speech, however—"

"Say Papa," Nefret coaxed. She leaned forward. "Say it for Mama."

"Bap," said the one whose eyes were the same shade of cornflower-blue.

"Perverse little beggars," said Ramses. The other child climbed onto his knee and buried her head against his chest. I suspected she was trying to get closer to the cat, but she made an engaging picture as she clung to her father. They were affectionate little creatures, much given to hugging and kissing, especially of each other.

"They're over two years old," Ramses went on, stroking the child's black curls. "I was speaking plainly long before that, wasn't I, Mother?"

"Dear me, yes," I said, with a somewhat sickly smile. To be honest—which I always endeavor to be in the pages of my private journal—I dreaded the moment when the twins began to articulate. Once Ramses learned to talk plainly, he never stopped talking except to eat or sleep, for over fifteen years, and the prolixity and pedantry of his speech patterns were extremely trying to my nerves. The idea of not one but two children following in the paternal footsteps chilled my blood.

Ever the optimist, I told myself there was no reason to anticipate such a disaster. The little dears might take after their mother, or me.

"Children learn at different rates," I explained to my son. "And twins, according to the best authorities, are sometimes slower to speak because they communicate readily with one another."

"And because they get everything they want without having to ask for it," Ramses muttered. The children obviously understood English, though they declined to speak it; his little daughter raised her head and fluttered her long lashes flirtatiously. He fluttered his lashes back at her. Charla giggled and gave him a hug.

The question of suitable names had occupied us for months. I say "us," because I saw no reason why I should not offer a suggestion or two. (There is nothing wrong with making suggestions so long as the persons to whom they are offered are not obliged to accept them.) Not until the end of her pregnancy did I begin to suspect Nefret was carrying twins, but since we had already settled on names for a male or a female child, it worked out quite nicely. There was no debate about David John; no one quarreled with Ramses's desire to name his son after his best friend and his cousin who had died in France in 1915.

A girl's name was not so easy to find. Emerson declared (quite without malice, I am sure) that between our niece and myself there were already enough Amelias in the family. It was with some hesitation that I mentioned that my mother's name had been Charlotte, and I was secretly pleased when Nefret approved.

"It is such a nice, ordinary name," she said.

"Unlike Nefret," said her husband.

"Or Ramses." She chuckled and patted his cheek. "Not that you could ever be anything else."

Charla, as we called her, had the same curly black hair and dark eyes as her father. Her brother Davy, now perched on his mother's knee, was fair, with Nefret's blue eyes and Ramses's prominent nose and chin. They did not resemble each other except in height, and in their linguistic eccentricity. Davy was more easygoing than his sister, but he had a well-nigh supernatural ability to disappear from one spot and materialize in another some distance away. The bars had been installed in all the rooms they were wont to inhabit, including the veranda, where we now sat waiting for Fatima to serve tea, after one such incident: looking out through the open archway I had seen Davy—who had been quietly pilfering biscuits not ten seconds before—pursuing one of the fierce feral curs from the village, with cries that may or may not have meant "dog" in some obscure language. The dog was running as fast as it could go.

Our Luxor home was an unpretentious sprawling place, built of stone and mud brick and surrounded by the flora I had carefully cultivated. The plan was similar to that of most Egyptian houses, with rooms surrounding a series of courtyards, the only unusual feature being the veranda that ran along the front. Open (before the twins) arches provided a view across the desert to the green strip of cultivation bordering the river, and the eastern mountains beyond. A short distance away was the smaller house occupied by Ramses and Nefret and the twins. The arrangement had been somewhat haphazard, with wings and additional structures added as they were needed, but in my opinion the result—which I had designed—was both attractive and comfortable.

The space would be needed, since the rest of our English family would be joining us in a few days for the first time since the beginning of the Great War. Hostilities had ended in November of 1918, but the shadow cast by that dreadful conflict was slow to pass. For those who had lost loved ones in the muddy trenches of France or on the blood-stained beaches of Gallipoli, the shadow would never entirely pass. Emerson's brother Walter and his wife, my dear friend Evelyn, would always mourn the death of their son Johnny, as would we all; but 1919 was the first full year of peace, and I was determined to make this Christmas a memorable one. How good it would be to have them with us again—Walter and Evelyn, their daughter Lia and her husband David, who was Ramses's best friend and an accomplished artist, not to mention their two dear little children.

That would make four dear little children. It would be a lively Christmas indeed.

As I bent my fond gaze upon the twins nestling in the arms of their handsome parents, I decided I would ask David to paint a group portrait. Photographs we had in plenty, but color was needed to capture their striking looks. Ramses's well-cut features and well-shaped form resembled those of his father, but he was brown as an Egyptian, with a crop of curly black hair and long-lashed dark eyes. Nefret's fair skin and gold-red locks were those of an English beauty, and the children combined the best features of both parents.

If we could get the little creatures to sit still long enough. Simultanously both children squirmed out of the arms of their parents and pelted toward the door that led into the house. It opened to admit their grandfather.

I have sometimes been accused of exaggeration, but when I say that my husband is the most famous and respected Egyptologist of all time I speak only the literal truth. After thirty-odd years in the field, he was still as straight and stalwart as he had been on the day we first met; his sapphirine orbs were as keen, his shoulders as broad, his ebon locks unmarked by silver except for snowy streaks at each temple.

"Good Gad!" he exclaimed, as the twins flung themselves at his lower limbs.

"Don't swear in front of the children, Emerson," I scolded.

"That was not swearing," said Emerson. "But I cannot have this sort of thing. An unprovoked attack, and by two against one! I claim the right to defend myself."

He scooped them up and settled into a chair with one on each knee. How much of his nonsense they had understood I would not be prepared to say, but they were both giggling wildly.

Fatima came out with the tea tray.

"Will you pour the tea, Sitt Hakim?" she asked.

Emerson twitched at the sound of my Egyptian sobriquet, "Lady Doctor." He always does, since he has no high opinion of my medical skills. I would be the first to admit they were not the equal of Nefret's—she had actually qualified as a surgeon, no small feat for a woman in those days—but during my early years in Egypt, when the Egyptian fellahin had almost no access to doctors or hospitals, my efforts had been deeply appreciated and—if I may say so—not inadequate.

"Yes, thank you," I replied. "Put the tray here, please."

Fatima lingered for a while, her plain but kindly face warm with affection as she watched the children close in on the plate of biscuits. Like the other members of what I may call our Egyptian family, she was more friend than servant. They were all close kin of our dear departed reis Abdullah, and through the marriage of his grandson David to our niece Lia, kin of ours as well.

We were soon joined by other members of the household: Sennia, our ward, and her two followers, her cat Horus and her self-appointed bodyguard, Gargery. Strictly speaking, Gargery was our butler, but he had taken on additional duties as he (not I) determined them to be necessary. These included eavesdropping, proffering unasked-for advice, and squabbling with Horus.

I must be fair to Gargery; Horus did not get on with anyone except Nefret and Sennia. He followed the child wherever she went, even into the dangerous proximity of the twins. He immediately got under the settee and hid behind my skirts.

Now nine years of age, Sennia was believed by some evil-minded persons to be Ramses's illegitimate daughter, which was not the case. She was living proof of the fact that proper rearing can overcome heredity, for hers could hardly have been worse: her mother an Egyptian prostitute, her father my unprincipled and deservedly deceased nephew. Her coloring was Egyptian, her manners those of a well-brought-up little English girl, and her nature as sunny as that of any happy child. She was absolutely devoted to Ramses, who had rescued her from a life of poverty and shame, and I had been a trifle apprehensive as to how she would react to the babies. If she felt jealousy, she concealed it well; and if she was sometimes inclined to order the little ones around, that was only to be expected.

Having dispensed the genial beverage, I leaned back in my chair and watched the animated, cheerful group with a smile which was not without a touch of smugness. I believe I may be excused for feeling complacent. We had been through troubled times in the past; even before the war involved Ramses in several perilous secret missions, we had encountered a number of thieves, murderers, forgers, kidnappers, and even a Master Criminal. I could scarcely remember a season when we had not faced danger in one form or another. For the first time in many years, no cloud hung over us, no old foe threatened vengeance.

I will not claim that I had not enjoyed some of these encounters. Matching wits with experienced criminals and persons intent on doing one harm lends a certain spice to existence. However, facing danger oneself is not at all the same as having loved ones in peril. A number of my gray hairs (concealed periodically by the application of a certain harmless concoction) had been put there by Ramses. It had been bad enough when he was a child, getting into one scrape after another. Maturity had not made him more cautious, and after Nefret and David joined the family, they were usually up to their necks in trouble too.

But it was different now, I told myself. Ramses and Nefret were parents, and the welfare of those precious little beings (who were trying to climb the back of the settee in order to get at the Great Cat of Re) would surely restrain their recklessness.

FROM MANUSCRIPT H

"Something rather odd happened today," Ramses said.

He and Nefret were dressing for dinner—not in formal evening attire, since his father only permitted that annoyance on rare occasions. However, a change of clothing was usually necessary after an hour with his offspring, since various substances, from chocolate to mud, somehow got transferred from them to any surface they came in contact with.

Nefret didn't answer. Her head was tilted, her expression abstracted. She was listening to the shrieks of laughter and meaningless chatter that floated in through their open window from the window of the children's room farther along the corridor. They were supposed to be asleep, but of course they weren't. Ramses was used to the sounds, but he forgot what he had been about to say as his eyes moved over the figure of his wife, seated before her dressing table. She hadn't put on her frock yet; her white arms were raised, her slim fingers coiled the long golden locks into a knot at the back of her neck. He went to her and replaced her hands with his, running his fingers through her hair. It felt like silk.

She smiled at him, her eyes seeking the reflection of his face in the mirror. "I'm sorry, darling; did you say something?"

"I can't remember."

"Hurry and dress. I want to look in on the children before we go to dinner."

He took his hands away. "All right."

THE SOUNDS OF THE CHILDREN'S voices had died into silence by the time they left the house. It was several hundred yards from the main house, hidden from it by the trees and shrubs his mother had forced to defy the sandy soil and lack of rain. Lanterns lit the winding path that led through the greenery, and the scent of roses filled the night with sweetness.

"I love this place," Nefret said softly. "I didn't expect to, you know. I had originally hoped we could be just a wee bit farther removed from the family."

"It was just like Mother to have the house built without consulting us, but she's stuck to her word to respect our privacy. Even Father doesn't drop in without asking permission first."

Nefret chuckled, a sound that always reminded her infatuated husband of flowing, sunlit water. "Not since the time he popped in and caught us in bed at five in the afternoon."

"He's in no position to criticize. I've lost track of how many times I've sat twiddling my thumbs waiting for him while he and Mother were up to the same thing."

They weren't too late after all. Emerson had just entered the parlor, delayed this time not by dalliance but because he had got involved in his notes.

"Where is your copy of the inscription we found on the wall of that house?" he demanded of his son.

"You might at least say 'Good evening' before you begin badgering him," his wife remarked.

"Good evening," said Emerson. "Ramses, where is—"

Thanks to the interruption, Ramses had been able to recall the inscription to which his father presumably referred. He hadn't thought of it for several months. "If you mean the inscription of

Amennakhte, it's in my notes. Didn't I give them to you? I was under the impression that I had."

He knew he had. No doubt Emerson had misplaced it. His desk was always a disorganized, overflowing heap of material. He could usually lay his hand on any given document at any given moment, but if it didn't turn up immediately he lost his temper and began throwing papers around.

"Hmph," said Emerson.

"Have you lost it?" Nefret asked. "It must be there somewhere, Father. I'll help you look, if you like."

"Bah." Emerson reached for his pipe. "Thank you, my dear, but that won't be necessary. I—er—don't need it just now."

"Yes, you do," said his wife, somewhat acerbically. "Emerson, you promised that article to the *Journal* weeks ago. You haven't finished it, have you?"

Emerson fixed her with a formidable glare and she abandoned the subject. Ramses was pretty sure she had not put it out of her mind, though. She had her own ways of managing her husband.

"Ah well, enough shop talk," she said cheerfully. "We need to discuss the arrangements for our guests."

"It's all settled, isn't it?" Nefret asked. "Sennia has kindly consented to give up her little suite to David and Lia and their brood, and Aunt Evelyn and Uncle Walter can stay with us or on the dahabeeyah, whichever they prefer."

"If I were in their shoes I'd choose the dahabeeyah," Ramses said lazily. "With four children under the age of six in residence, this place is going to be a zoo. I wonder how Dolly and Evvie will get on with our two."

"Badly, I should think," said his mother. "Yours are accustomed to our full attention, and Dolly will be hurt if Emerson neglects him."

"What nonsense!" Emerson exclaimed. "As if I would neglect little Abdullah!"

"You have only two knees, Emerson, and mark my words, they will all want to occupy them simultaneously."

"There you go again, borrowing trouble," Emerson grumbled.

"Anticipating difficulties," his wife corrected. "Ah well, I am sure it will all work out. Your Uncle Walter will be delighted with the inscribed material we have found, Ramses."

"There's no better philologist in the business," Ramses agreed.

"And I mean to ask David to paint a group picture of you and Nefret and the children," his mother continued. "Or perhaps Evelyn; it has been a good many years since she practiced her skills, but I feel sure she will—"

"Now just a bloody minute, Peabody," Emerson exclaimed. "I won't have you assigning extra duties to my staff even before they arrive. I will need them on the dig."

His use of his wife's maiden name indicated that he was in a more agreeable state of mind than the speech might have suggested. The family had learned to interpret those signals: Amelia when he was genuinely annoyed; Peabody when he was in a good humor, in fond recollection of the days of their courtship, when he had paid her the high compliment of addressing her as he would have done a man.

Ramses exchanged glances with his wife. The argument wasn't over; his mother would go right ahead with her plans, and his father would continue to complain. His parents enjoyed those "little differences of opinion," as his mother called them—though "shouting matches" might be a more descriptive term. She was smiling to herself; her cheeks were flushed and her eyes sparkled.

Hers was, her son thought, a rather forbidding countenance, even in repose; when she was annoyed about something, her prominent chin jutted out and her dark-gray eyes took on a steely shine. The years had not changed her appearance much; her carriage was as erect and the new lines in her face were those of laughter. The thick black hair was, according to Nefret, no longer the original shade. Nefret had made him promise he wouldn't say a word, to his mother or father. In fact, he had found that evidence of feminine vanity rather touching.

Catching his eye, she broke off in the middle of a sentence. "What are you smiling at, Ramses? Have I a smudge on my nose?"

"No. I was just thinking how well you look this evening."

. . .

WHEN RAMSES AND EMERSON ARRIVED at the site next morning the sun had just lifted over the eastern cliffs and the little valley of Deir el Medina lay in shadow. High barren hills framed it on the east and west. The main entrance was to the north, where the walls of the Ptolemaic temple enclosed some of the earlier shrines to various gods. The tumbled ruins of other older temples surrounded it. And on the valley floor were the remains of the workman's village that had occupied the site for—at Emerson's latest estimate—at least three hundred years. Evidence of earlier occupation was yet to be found; if it existed, it would lie under the foundations of the later structures.

At first glance there seemed very little to show for over two years of work. When they had first taken over the excavation, the ruins of the village lay under millennia of accumulated debris and blown sand. In the past century it had suffered from random digging, by archaeologists and by local villagers searching for artifacts to sell. On the slopes of the eastern hill were the tombs of the workers, crowned in some cases by small crumbling pyramids. These too had been looted and their contents dispersed. In the recent past a few Egyptologists had conducted relatively scholarly excavations of a few tombs, but the museums of Europe contained masses of papyri and miscellaneous objects that had been bought on the antiquities market during the nineteenth century A.D., many of which had probably come from Deir el Medina, without any record of their origin or location having been made. In short, the site offered a daunting challenge, and Emerson was one of the few men in the field who could do the job right. Ramses drew a deep breath of satisfaction as he gazed out at the unimposing scene. His father preferred temples and tombs, but masses of inscribed material were turning up, ostraca and papyri, awaiting decipherment—the job he enjoyed most. If only his father would let him concentrate on them instead of demanding his presence on the site every day . . .

In fact, considerable progress had been made, under difficult conditions. It had taken a long time to remove the debris down to the top of the remaining walls, and to sift (as his mother had once remarked, in a rare fit of profanity) every bloody square inch of the cursed stuff. The task had been worthwhile; they had come across a lot of material early excavators had missed or discarded. They had also discovered that the village consisted of two sections, divided by a narrow main street and enclosed by a wall. They were working along the north side of this street, clearing each house in turn.

A number of distractions had delayed or interrupted their work. In the late summer of 1917, when it became apparent to Ramses's eagle-eyed mother that Nefret's long-desired pregnancy might have unanticipated complications, she had taken her daughter-in-law off to Cairo and installed them both at Shepheard's, under the close supervision of the two female physicians in charge of the hospital for women Nefret had founded. Despite almost daily bulletins of reassurance, it had proved impossible for Ramses to give his full attention to the job. His father was no more able to concentrate than he, and his temper became so explosive that even their assistant foreman, Daoud, whose placidity very little could disturb, went into hiding. After a week of futile activity Emerson had taken the unprecedented step of shutting down the dig. They had both headed for Cairo, where Emerson proceeded to "carry on like a maniac," to quote his exasperated wife. He spent half his time at the hospital inspecting the facilities and harassing the doctors and the other half staring in alarm at Nefret's increasing bulk.

Only the knowledge that expressing his worry would increase Nefret's kept Ramses from behaving even more erratically. For once his mother's know-it-all manner was a comfort; he felt as helpless as a child who keeps demanding, "Will it be all right?"

"Nefret is a physician, after all," his mother reminded him.

"But she's never had a baby before." He couldn't stop himself. "Will it be all right?"

His mother gave him a tolerant smile. "Of course."

Not until after it was over did it dawn on him that perhaps she had been putting up a brave front too.

When the moment arrived—at night, as his mother had predicted—Nefret didn't give him time to lose his head. He wasn't asleep; he hadn't slept for several nights—and when he felt her stiffen and heard her gasp he shot out of bed and lit the lamp. She looked up at him, her hands spread across the mountainous mound of her stomach.

"Where's your watch?" she asked calmly. "We need to time the contractions."

"I'll go for Mother."

"Not yet. There is such a thing as false labor."

Ramses said something, he couldn't remember what, and bolted out of the room. When he came back after arousing his parents, she was calmly if clumsily getting dressed.

They got to the hospital in good time. Emerson had himself under control, though he had neglected to button his shirt and Ramses couldn't remember ever seeing him so pale. He kept patting Nefret's hand.

"Soon over now," he said.

Nefret, doubled up with another contraction, said distinctly, "Bah."

Everything was in readiness, since his mother had rung ahead. Dr. Sophia took Nefret away and they went to the courtyard. She did not allow smoking in her office and Emerson declared himself incapable of surviving the ordeal without tobacco. He was on his second pipe when the other surgeon, Dr. Ferguson, appeared.

"She wants you," she said to Ramses, adding with her customary bluntness, "God knows why."

He soon found out why.

A remark from his father brought him back from the indelible memory of the most wonderful and terrifying day of his life.

"I beg your pardon, sir?"

"You were miles away," said Emerson curiously. "Where?"

"Months, rather. The night the twins were born."

Emerson shuddered. "I never want to go through anything like that again."

"You didn't go through it," Ramses said. "She did. And she made damned sure I saw and heard everything."

"Did she really swear at you?"

"At your most eloquent you've never surpassed it." He added, with an involuntary shudder, "I've never seen anything so appalling. How women go through that, and then go back and do it *again* . . ."

"They wouldn't let me be with your mother. I'd rather have been, you know, even if she had called me every name in the book. She would have, too," Emerson said pensively.

"I know." He put his hand on his father's shoulder. Emerson, who had been brought up in the Victorian tradition that frowned on demonstrations of affection between men, acknowledged the gesture with an awkward nod and promptly changed the subject.

Their work crew had assembled. All were skilled men who had been with them for years, members of the family of their former reis, Abdullah, who proudly carried on the tradition he had begun. The first to greet them was Selim, who had replaced his father as foreman after the latter's tragic death. Though he was the youngest of Abdullah's sons, no one questioned his right to the post; he had the same air of authority and, thanks to the training he had received from his father and Emerson, even greater competence. Right behind him was his cousin Daoud. Instead of replying to Selim Emerson, hands on hips and head thrown back, stared up at the hill on the east of the village.

"Somebody's up there," he said. "Near our tomb."

Sunlight brightened the high ridge of stone that crowned the hill. Something was moving, but Ramses, whose keen eyesight was proverbial, was unable to make out details at that distance. "Probably one of the indefatigable robbers from Gurneh," he suggested. "Hoping against hope that we overlooked something when we cleared the tomb."

That had been the second major distraction—the cache of mummies and funerary equipment belonging to the late-period princesses and God's Wives. Strictly speaking, it was not Emerson's tomb, but Cyrus Vandergelt's, for that season they had shared the site with their American colleague and old friend, keeping the village for themselves and allocating the tombs on the hillside to Cyrus. Not even Emerson begrudged him the discovery; Cyrus had excavated for years in Thebes without finding anything of importance, and a discovery like this one had fulfilled the dream of a lifetime. Since it was Cyrus's stepson and assistant, Bertie, who had actually located the missing tomb, Cyrus had a double claim. Ramses had been present at a number of exciting discoveries—his father had an uncanny instinct for such things—but he would never forget his first sight of the hidden chamber in the cliff, packed from floor to ceiling with a dazzling collection of coffins, canopic jars, and chests filled with jewels and richly decorated garments. They had all pitched in to help Cyrus clear the tomb and remove the objects, some of which were in fragile condition. The job took precedence over all other projects, since the tomb robbers of Thebes were hovering like vultures, alert for a chance of making off with some of the valuables. It had taken months to record and remove everything, and the process of restoration was still underway.

"Send one of the men up there to run him off," Emerson growled, eyes still fixed on the minute form.

Selim rolled his eyes and grinned, but left it to Ramses to make the obvious objection. "Why waste the effort?" he asked. "There's nothing left. If the fellow is fool enough to risk his neck climbing down that cleft, let him."

"It could be a damned tourist," Emerson muttered.

Ramses wished his mother had come with them instead of lingering to discuss household matters with Fatima. She'd have put an end to the discussion with a few acerbic comments. "We can't run tourists off unless they interfere with our work," he pointed out patiently. "You did that while we were working in the tomb and dozens of them went haring off to Cairo to register complaints."

"We'd never have finished the job if I hadn't," Emerson growled. The memory of those harried days still maddened him. "Morons turning up with letters of introduction from all and sundry demanding to be shown the tomb, trying to climb the scaffolding, perched on every available surface with their cameras clicking, offering bribes to Selim and Daoud. And the bloody journalists were even worse."

During the clearance Emerson had managed to antagonize most of the people who didn't already detest him. Some excavators enjoyed publicity and yielded to demands from prominent persons who wanted to enter the tomb. Emerson loathed publicity and he flatly refused to allow visitors, however many titles or academic degrees they might possess. He had almost caused an international incident when he ran the King of the Belgians and his entourage off. People didn't realize how time-consuming such visits could be for a harassed excavator. Emerson was right, a flat-out interdict was easier to enforce than dealing with the requests case by case—even if it had caused extremely strained relations with the Department of Antiquities.

"It's all over and done with," Ramses said, as Emerson shook his fist at the figure atop the cliff. "If that is a tourist, he's a damned energetic specimen."

"The devil with him," Emerson said. "Why are we wasting time over a fool tourist?"

Scanning the assembled workmen with his all-seeing eye, he demanded of Selim, "Where is Hassan? Has he been taken ill?"

Not until then did Ramses remember the "rather odd thing" he had meant to mention to Nefret. There was no reason why it should have preyed on his mind; it was not worrisome, only . . . rather odd. Selim looked blank, and Ramses said, "I meant to tell you yesterday, Father. Hassan has tendered his resignation."

"Resignation? Quit the job, you mean?"

"Yes, sir."

"What the devil for?"

"I'm not sure," Ramses admitted. "He spoke of making his peace with Allah and devoting his life to the service of a holy man."

Selim let out an exclamation of surprise. "What holy man?"

"I didn't ask."

"Well, I will," Emerson declared. "Good Gad, what is the fellow thinking of? He's one of my most experienced men. I will just have a talk with him and order him—"

"Father, you can't do that," Ramses protested. "It's his right and his decision."

"But Hassan, of all people," Emerson exclaimed, rubbing his chin. "The jolliest, most cheerful old reprobate in the family!"

"He has been acting strangely," Selim said slowly. "Since his wife died, he has kept to himself."

"That accounts for his state of mind then," Ramses said.

Emerson curled his lip in an expression of profound cynicism. "Don't be such a romantic, my boy. Well, well, he must do as he likes.

Your mother would accuse me of breaking some damned command-
ment or other if I attempted to make him see reason."

>=<

WE WERE TO DINE WITH THE Vandergelts that evening. Emerson
always complained about going out to dinner. It was just his way of
making a fuss, since he thoroughly enjoyed the Vandergelts and would
have been sadly disappointed if I had declined the invitation. He
fussed louder than usual on that occasion, since I had insisted he
assume evening dress, which he hates. I was ready long before he, of
course, so I sat glancing through a magazine and listening to the
altercation in the next room, where Gargery was assisting Emerson
with his toilette. Since Emerson never employs a valet, Gargery had
somewhat officiously assumed that role as well.

"Stop complaining and hurry, Emerson," I called.

"I do not see why the devil I must . . . curse it, Gargery!" said
Emerson.

We had been over this several times, but Emerson always pretends
not to hear things he does not want to hear, so I said it again. "M.
Lacau has come all the way from Cairo to inspect the objects from the
princesses' tomb. Cyrus is counting on us to put him in a good mood
so he will be generous in his division and leave a share to Cyrus. By all
reports he is much stricter than dear Maspero, so—"

"You repeat yourself, Peabody," Emerson growled.

He appeared in the doorway.

"You look very handsome," I said. "Thank you, Gargery."

"Thank you, madam," said Gargery, looking as pleased as if I had
complimented *him* on his looks. I could not honestly have done so,
since he was losing his hair and his waistline. Even in his now distant
youth he could not have been called handsome. But handsome is as
handsome does, as the saying has it, and Gargery's loyalty and his willingness to use a cudgel when the occasion demanded more than com-
pensated for his looks.

I bade him an affectionate good night. Emerson inserted his forefinger under his collar and gave Gargery a hateful look.

Our little party assembled in the drawing room, where I inspected each person carefully. Emerson might and did sneer, but looks are important and I knew that though the proper French director of the Service des Antiquités might not notice our efforts, he would certainly take note of their absence. I could not in any way fault Nefret's sea-blue satin frock and ornaments of Persian turquoise; she had excellent taste and a great deal of money—and the additional advantages of youth and beauty. Ramses hated evening dress almost as much as did his father, but it became him well; despite his efforts to flatten it, his hair was already springing back into the waves and curls he so disliked. As for myself, I believe I may say I looked respectable. I have little interest in my personal appearance, and no excuse for vanity. I had just touched up my hair a little and selected a frock of Emerson's favorite crimson.

Cyrus was known for the elegance of his entertainments. That night the Castle, his large and handsome residence near the entrance to the Valley of the Kings, blazed with light. Cyrus met us at the door, as was his hospitable habit, showered us with compliments, and escorted us into the drawing room, where his wife and stepson were waiting.

To see Katherine as she was now, the very picture of a happy wife and mother and well-bred English lady, one would never have suspected that she had such a turbulent history—a miserable first marriage and a successful career as a fraudulent spiritualist medium. Bertie, her son by that marriage, was now Cyrus's right-hand man and devoted assistant. British by birth, as was his mother, he had served his country faithfully during the Great War until severe injuries released him from duty. It was while he was recuperating at the hospitable Luxor home of his stepfather that he had become interested in Egyptology. His discovery of the princesses' tomb ensured him a permanent place in the annals of the profession, but it had not changed his modest, unassuming character. I had become very fond of the lad, and I was sorry to see that he had taken to wearing loose scarves about his neck and letting his hair grow over his collar. Such fashions did not suit his plain but amiable and quintessentially English features, but I knew what had prompted them. Bertie was a lover, and the object of his affections was not with us that season. He had taken a fancy to Jumana, the daughter of Abdullah's brother Yusuf. She was an admirable young woman, fiercely ambitious and intelligent, and we were all supporting her in her hope of becoming the first qualified Egyptian female to practice archaeology. Things had changed since our early days in Egypt; the self-taught excavator was becoming a thing of the past, and with the handicaps of her sex and nationality, Jumana needed the best formal training available. She was studying at University College in London this year, under the wing of Emerson's nephew Willy and his wife.

Bertie had never spoken of his attachment to the girl, but it was clear to a student of human nature like myself. I doubted it would come to anything; Jumana was intent on her career, and shy, amiable Bertie was not the man, in my opinion, to sweep any girl off her feet. If only she weren't so confounded attractive! Men may claim they look for intelligence and moral worth in a wife, but I have observed that when they must choose between a brainless beauty and a woman of admirable character and plain face, the beauty wins most of the time.

"M. Lacau has not yet arrived?" I inquired, taking the chair Cyrus held for me.

"No." Cyrus tugged at his goatee. "I wish he'd come so we could get this over with. I'm so consarned nervous—"

"He may not make his final decision this evening, Cyrus."

"He cannot make a fair judgment, for I have not yet begun restoring the second robe. It will be magnifico, I promise."

The speaker came forward, bowing and smiling a tight-lipped smile. He smiled a great deal, but without showing his teeth, which were, I had once observed, chipped and stained. He claimed to be Italian, though his graying fair hair and hazel eyes were atypical of that nation, and considered himself something of a ladies' man, though his short stature and lumpish features were not prepossessing. He was, however, one of the most talented restorers I had ever encountered, and putting up with his gallantries was a small price to pay for his services (not the only price, either, for Cyrus paid him extravagantly).

I permitted him to kiss my hand (and then wiped it unobtrusively on my skirt).

"Good evening, Signor Martinelli," I said. "So it will be your fault if M. Lacau takes everything for the museum?"

"Ah, Mrs. Emerson, you make a joke!" He laughed, turning his head aside, and reached for another of the cigarettes he smoked incessantly. "You permit?"

I could hardly object, since Emerson had taken out his pipe and Cyrus had lit a cheroot. Martinelli went on without waiting for a reply. "I may claim, I believe, to have done a job of work no one else could have accomplished. It would make my reputation had it not already been made. But if Lacau had had the patience to wait another week, he would have seen the finish."

"So soon as that?" I inquired.

"Yes, yes, I must finish soon. I have other engagements, you know."

He winked and smirked at me through the cloud of smoke. Another of his vexatious habits was to refer frequently if obliquely to a subject we never discussed, even among ourselves—namely, the fact that Martinelli had been for years in the employment of the world's most formidable thief of antiquities, who also happened to be Emerson's half-brother. It was Sethos, to use only one of his many aliases, who had recommended Martinelli. I had every reason to believe my brother-in-law was now a reformed character, but I didn't count on it, and I certainly did not want to discuss his criminal past in the presence of persons who were only slightly acquainted with it. So I did not ask Signor Martinelli about the nature of those other "engagements," though I would have given a great deal to find out.

Before Martinelli could go on teasing me, the servant announced M. Lacau. The enthusiasm with which he was greeted obviously pleased him, though a twinkle in his eye indicated he was not entirely unaware of ulterior motives.

Lacau was at that time in his late forties, but his beard was already white. Although he had been appointed in 1914 to the post which was traditionally the perquisite of a native of France, he had spent a good part of the past five years in war work. No one questioned his fitness for the position, but his patriarchal appearance was not the only reason why he had acquired the nickname of "God the Father." He had already dropped a few ominous hints that he was considering toughening the laws about the disposal of antiquities. Generally speaking, the rule was that they should be shared equally between the excavator and the Egyptian collections. The former director of the Service, M.

Maspero, had been generous—excessively generous, some might say—in his divisions of artifacts. The entire contents of the tomb of the architect Kha, consisting of hundreds of objects, had been handed over to the Turin Museum. But this was a royal cache, and Lacau could legitimately claim that the objects were unique. On the other hand, there were four sets of them—coffins, canopic jars, Books of the Dead. I smiled very sweetly at M. Lacau and told him how well he was looking.

With Katherine's assistance I managed to keep the conversation general throughout dinner. Cyrus made sure the wineglasses were kept filled and Emerson refrained from criticizing the Museum, his fellow archaeologists, and the Service. That left him with very little to say, which was all to the good. After dinner we ladies retired, a custom of which I normally disapprove but which I felt would be approved by Lacau. By the time the gentlemen joined us, even I was unable to control my impatience.

Under ordinary circumstances the artifacts would have been sent to the Museum as soon as they were stable enough to be moved. Circumstances were abnormal, however. The war had left the Museum and the Service shorthanded; Lacau had been away from Egypt a good deal of the time, and political unrest the previous winter made the transport of such valuables risky. Cyrus's home provided the security of stout walls and well-paid guards, as well as ample space for storage and laboratory facilities. The same could not be said of the Museum, which was already overcrowded and understaffed (and I only hoped Emerson had not said so to Lacau—one may know that something is true without wishing to hear it from others).

We went at once to the storage rooms. I had seen the display before, but it never ceased to take my breath away. As it looked now, it was a far cry from the jumbled, faded, broken contents of the small chamber we (Bertie, in fact) had discovered. It was not the original tomb, or, to be more precise, tombs; not one but four of the God's Wives had found their final resting place there. When danger threatened their burials, the essential items had been removed and hidden away—the mummies in their inner coffins, the canopic jars containing the viscera, and other small, portable objects of value. One of the coffins was of solid silver, the face delicately shaped and serene, framed by a heavy wig and crown. The other coffins were of wood heavily inlaid with tiny hieroglyphs and figures of deities shaped of semi-precious stone. Delicately sculptured masks of silver and gold had covered the mummies' heads. The canopic jars, four for each princess, were of painted calcite with the sculptured heads of the four sons of Horus, each of whom guarded a particular organ of the body. Ranged along the tables like a miniature army were hundreds of ushebtis, the small servant statues which would be animated in the afterworld to work for the deceased—some of faience, some of wood, and a few of precious metal. An amazing amount of material had been crammed into that little chamber: vessels of alabaster and hard stone, silver and gold, a dozen carved and painted chests, and the contents of the latter—sandals, linen, and jewelry. Glittering gold and burnished silver, deep-blue lapis, turquoise and carnelian shone in the glow of the electric lights.

"Astonishing," Lacau murmured. "Formidable. I commend you—all of you—on a remarkable work of restoration."

"It did take all of us," I said, remembering one exhausting afternoon I had spent crouched in a corner of the chamber stringing hundreds of tiny beads. They lay in the order in which they had fallen after the original cords had rotted, and by restringing them on the spot I had been able to preserve the original design. "However," I went on, "much of the credit belongs to Signor Martinelli. And we are very grateful for the assistance with the photography given us by Mr. Burton of the Metropolitan Museum. How he inserted his cameras into that narrow space was little short of miraculous. You know, monsieur, that the entire chamber was packed full, yet he managed to get a series of overhead views before we removed anything."

"Yes, I have spoken with him," Lacau said, nodding. "A complex arrangement of long poles and cords and le bon Dieu only knows what else! We are deeply indebted to him and the Metropolitan Museum."

How indebted? I wondered. Enough to allow a certain number of artifacts to go to America, through Cyrus, whose collection would eventually be left to a museum in that country?

Martinelli, who had not yet received the praise he considered his due, drew Lacau's attention to a piece of fabric stretched out across a long table. The entire surface was covered with beads and gold sequins that sparkled in the light. A long sheet of glass, raised a foot over it by steel supports, protected it from dust and air currents.

"This is unquestionably my masterpiece," he said without undue modesty. "It was folded several times over and the fabric was so fragile, a breath would blow it away. I stabilized each layer with a chemical of my own invention before turning it back and exposing the next. No, monsieur!" as Lacau extended his hand. "Do not touch it. I am still debating as to the best method of preserving it permanently. I am not sure that even I can render it sturdy enough to be transported."

Lacau's eyes rested greedily upon the garment, for that is what it was—a robe of sheer, almost transparent, linen, bordered at hem and neck with four-inch strips of elaborate beading. He would certainly claim it, for the Museum had nothing remotely like it—nor had any other museum anywhere in the world.

"Perhaps Mr. Lucas could suggest a solution," Lacau said, adding, presumably for Martinelli's benefit, "he is the government chemist."

"I know who he is," said the Italian. His disgust was so great as to cause him to bare his stained teeth. "He can teach Martinelli nothing, monsieur."

God the Father shot him a look before which most people would have quailed, and I hastened to spread the soothing oil of tact upon the troubled waters.

"There are several similar garments, Monsieur Lacau, still folded in the chests. It took Signor Martinelli almost a month to deal with this robe. If the worst should happen, the garment can be reconstructed. We have numerous photographs, and in a few weeks we hope to have a precise colored scale drawing, of this and several other objects."

"Made by whom?" the director inquired. "Mr. Carter?"

"David Todros. He and the rest of our family will be joining us next week, and I know he is itching to get at the job. You remember him, of course?"

"Ah, yes. The Egyptian boy who once worked for a notorious forger here in Luxor, making fake antiquities?"

"Now a trained Egyptologist and skilled artist," said Emerson, who had controlled himself quite well up to that time, but who resented the condescension in Lacau's voice. "He is married to my brother's daughter, monsieur, in case that had escaped your attention."

"You are fortunate indeed to have so many experts on your staff," Lacau said somewhat stiffly. He turned to Ramses. "How are you getting on with the written material?"

"As you know, sir, there wasn't much," Ramses replied. "Only the inscriptions on the coffins and miscellaneous notations on some chests and boxes. The copies of the Book of the Dead require careful handling. I have not had the time to give them the attention they deserve."

"The arrival of your uncle will no doubt be welcome," Lacau said.

He was referring to Walter, but I could tell by Ramses's involuntary start that he had been reminded of his other uncle. I only hoped to goodness that Sethos would not decide to pay us a visit. He liked to drop in without advance notice. I had not heard from him for several months, at which time he had been in Germany. I assumed he was there on behalf of the Secret Service; he had been one of Britain's top intelligence agents since the beginning of the war and was, to the best of my knowledge, still involved in the business.

In one corner of the room, lying in simple wooden cases lined with unbleached cotton, were the owners of all that splendor. Only an individual insensitive to the mystery of death could fail to pay those shrouded forms the tribute of silent reverence. M. Lacau was unmoved.

"You removed them from the coffins," he said, frowning.

I took it upon myself to reply to the implicit and undeserved criticism. "It was necessary, monsieur. The wood of which three of the coffins were made was dry and brittle and many of the inlays were loose. Before they could be moved they were stabilized, inside and out, with a compound of Signor Martinelli's invention. You see the results, which are, in my opinion, quite excellent."

"Yes, of course," Lacau said. "I see you have resisted the temptation to unwrap the ladies," he went on, with a nod at Nefret. "You have had, I believe, some experience."

"She is a trained surgeon and anatomist," I said indignantly. "No one could do a better—"

"Naturally I wouldn't dream of touching them without your permission, Monsieur Lacau," Nefret said quickly. "Nor in fact would I like to see it done. The wrappings are in perfect condition, and the mummies have been undisturbed since they were placed in their coffins—unlike all the other royal mummies we have. It would be a sin to rip them apart."

"You feel strongly about this, madame," Lacau said, stroking his beard. "But what of the ornaments, the amulets, the jewels, that are unquestionably to be found on the bodies?"

"We have many beautiful pieces of jewelry," Nefret explained. "We don't know what condition the mummies themselves are in, or what lies under those bandages. In the present state of our knowledge we may not be able to learn all that can be learned from those poor remains, or preserve them undamaged for future scholars whose knowledge will certainly be greater than ours."

"A moving plea, madame," said Lacau with a patronizing smile.

Nefret flushed but kept her temper. "What I would like to do is subject them to X-ray examination."

"The Museum does not have the equipment."

"But I do—that is to say, my hospital in Cairo does. Mr. Grafton Elliot Smith carried the mummy of Thutmose the Fourth to a private clinic to have it X-rayed, if you recall."

"By cab, yes. Somewhat undignified and inconvenient."

"We could do better than that," Nefret said eagerly. "A proper ambulance—"

"Well, it is an interesting suggestion. I will think about it."

Nefret had the good sense to thank him and pretend to be grateful for even that degree of consideration. She was accustomed to being patronized by men of a certain kind—most men, I would say, if that were not an unfair generalization. (Whether or not it is unfair I will leave to the judgment of the Reader.)

Lacau inspected the laboratory, but not for long; a medley of pungent odors suggested that Martinelli was trying several chemicals on various pieces of linen and wood. Cyrus then proudly displayed "his" records and generously admitted that they were the result of our joint labors. They were, if I may say so, a model of their kind—photographs, plans, sketches, detailed written descriptions—all cross-indexed and filed. We then returned to the display rooms for a final look.

"I can see that I must give the matter some thought," Lacau said, sweeping the assemblage with a possessive eye. "I would like to place the objects on display at once, and we must consider how we are to find the space. I had not realized there would be so much."

Cyrus's face fell. Lacau appeared not to notice; he went on, "Now I must bid you good evening, my friends. Thank you for your splendid hospitality and for a most astonishing experience."

After we had seen him off we lingered to cheer Cyrus, who had put the most depressing interpretation possible on Lacau's words.

"He can't take everything," Emerson insisted. "Don't borrow trouble, Vandergelt, as my wife would say. Curse it, he owes you for your time and effort and expenditure, not to mention Bertie's claim as the finder."

"I thought you supported the idea that all major objects should remain in Egypt," Cyrus said in surprise. "You handed over the whole contents of Tetisheri's tomb to the Museum."

"It isn't a simple issue," Emerson said, taking out his pipe. "Archaeologists and collectors have been looting the country of its antiquities for decades, and the Egyptians haven't had any voice in the matter. With nationalist sentiment on the rise—"

"Yes, but what about preserving the objects?" Cyrus cried in genuine anguish. "The Museum hasn't the facilities or the staff."

"Well, whose fault is that?" demanded Emerson, who was quite happy to argue on any side of any issue—and change sides whenever he felt like it. "It's a question of money, pure and simple, and who determined how it was disbursed? Politicians like Cromer and Cecil. They never gave a curse about maintaining the Museum, or hiring and training Egyptians to staff it, or paying them enough to—"

"Excuse me, Emerson, but we have all heard that speech before," I said politely but firmly. "We must hope that M. Lacau will be reasonable."

"I just wish he'd make up his consarned mind," Cyrus grumbled. "It's the suspense that's killing me."

When we took our leave I looked round for Signor Martinelli, to no avail. "He might at least have said good night before retiring," I remarked.

"He hasn't gone to bed," Cyrus said. "He's off to Luxor again."

"At this hour?"

"What he does in Luxor can be best accomplished at this hour," said Emerson. He and Cyrus exchanged meaningful glances.

I had heard the stories too, since I have many friends in Luxor, and gossip is a favorite sport. Realizing that Emerson was about to enlarge on the subject of Luxor's disreputable places of entertainment, I took my family away.

We had lingered long over the inspection and it was very late before we reached home; but so overpowering had been the impressions of the evening that we were unable to stop discussing them. The four of us settled on the veranda for a final whiskey and soda. I was a trifle surprised when Nefret accepted a glass; she seldom indulged in spirits. I realized she must have been nervous too, probably about her precious mummies. She had taken more wine at dinner than was her custom.

"His failure to drop even a hint was quite mean-spirited, in my opinion," I said.

"I suspect he was somewhat overcome," Ramses said thoughtfully. "What the devil is he going to do with it all? They will have to rearrange or store a good many of the current exhibits to make room for it—construct display cases—pack everything properly—"

"They? It will be we who pack the objects," I said. "We cannot trust anyone else to do it. Oh dear. I do not look forward to that task. I used bales of cotton wool and every scrap of cotton and linen stuff I could find when we wrapped the artifacts to be moved from the tomb to the Castle. And I have the direst forebodings about that lovely robe. No matter what packing materials we use, I doubt it will survive the journey."

"We'll have a replica made," Nefret said. She finished her whiskey and then chuckled. "I've had a vicious idea. Next time we're in that room I will lose my balance and fall heavily against the table. If the linen shatters into scraps, as I suspect it will, perhaps M. Lacau will let us keep the ornamentation."

"My dear, you are becoming silly," I said with a fond smile. "Fatigue, I expect. Trot off to bed."

"I'd settle for some of the jewelry," Nefret said, giving Ramses her hand and letting him lift her to her feet. "The gold-and-garnet snake bracelet, and the one with strips of lapis lazuli and gold, and the head of Hathor . . . Mother, don't you think a man who truly loved his wife would make an effort to get those trinkets for her? They say they would bring the moon and stars down from the sky and fling them in our laps, but when we ask for a simple little gold bracelet—"

"She's not tired, she's had too much to drink," Ramses said with a grin. He put his arm round his wife's gently swaying form. "Come along, you shameless hussy."

"Carry me." She looked up at him. Her face was flushed and her lips were parted.

I heard his breath catch. He picked her up and carried her out. For once neither of them bothered to bid us good night.

Emerson gave me a long considering look. "I can't recall ever seeing you tipsy, Peabody."

"And you," I retorted, for I knew quite well what was on his mind, "have never offered to fling the moon and the stars into my lap."

Emerson's reply was a rather clever but fairly vulgar play on words, which I will not record. Sometime later he said drowsily, "I could manage a gold bracelet or two, if you like."

It was rather odd, really—that we should have mentioned the bracelets, I mean. For it was those pieces that vanished between night and morning, together with Signor Martinelli.

CHAPTER TWO

We were apprised of the distressing development by one of Cyrus's servants bearing a message from that gentleman. It implored our presence, in a handwriting made almost undecipherable by agitation. Since it was Friday, the day of rest and prayer for our men, we had breakfasted later than was our habit, en famille, including the children. The dear little things insisted on feeding themselves, to the merriment of their grandfather and the resigned acceptance of their grandmother. It was one occasion on which the cats willingly joined us, since there was usually quite a lot of food on the floor—and on the table, and on us. For the same reason Sennia did not join us. Fond as she was of the darling children, she was extremely fastidious in her dress and did not appreciate the generosity that flung orange sections and buttered bread onto her impeccable lap.

When Fatima opened the door I took the note from her, since Emerson was rather sticky with jam, Davy having unexpectedly pressed a bit of lavishly spread toast into his hand.

A vehement cry of "Good Gad!" burst from my lips.

"Don't swear in front of the children," Emerson said, trying surreptitiously to hide the squashed offering in his napkin. "What is the matter?"

"The jewelry of the God's Wives. It has disappeared, and so has Signor Martinelli."

"What?" Emerson bounded up from his chair. "Impossible!"

29

"Only too true, however. Cyrus always goes up to the display room first thing in the morning—to gloat, I suppose, and who can blame him? Not all of it is missing, I gather, only two or three of the bracelets and a pendant, but—"

"That's bad enough," Ramses said. His eyebrows, as heavy and dark as those of his father, tilted up at the corners as they did when he was extremely surprised or concerned. "M. Lacau will hold Cyrus responsible for every item. Has Martinelli left the house?"

"So Cyrus says. He asks us to come at once."

"We must certainly do so," Ramses said. "No, thank you, Davy, you eat the rest of your egg, I've already had mine."

"I'll come too, of course," Nefret said.

We were *not* soon under way, since removing the children and settling them in the nursery with their attendants took some time, and Emerson had to change his trousers, and the horses had to be saddled. Sennia wanted to come along, but I fended her off. This occasioned protest from Sennia, who was inclined to forget when thwarted that she was ten years of age and "almost grown up." In my opinion, the fewer people who knew, the better, at least in our present state of uncertainty.

For once Cyrus did not meet us at the door. He and Katherine and Bertie were in the display room, engaged in a frantic, and I did not doubt repetitive, search. It was also a futile search. There was no way in which the missing objects could have been accidentally misplaced. The emptiness of the spaces where they had reposed was only too conspicuous.

This was apparent to me at a glance, and I immediately set about restoring my agitated friends to a sensible appraisal of the situation.

"We must discuss this calmly," I declared. "Cyrus, stop rushing around, it won't get you anywhere and you may damage something. What precisely is missing?"

Bertie replied, since his stepfather could only stare blankly at me. "Three bracelets—the best of the lot—and the pendant with the two crowned cobras."

"Nothing else?"

"No. That was my first concern, and I assure you, I have been through the entire inventory."

I gave him an approving smile. "Well done, Bertie. I have always admired your cool head. Then let us retire and have a little council of war."

Naturally all agreed. We settled down in Katherine's charmingly appointed sitting room. At my suggestion she ordered tea and coffee to be brought, for, as I pointed out, it was necessary to preserve an appearance of normalcy. The servants were then dismissed and I began my questioning.

I fancy I conducted the investigation as competently as any police officer could have done. My surmise, that Cyrus had discovered the theft early that morning in the course of his customary inspection of the treasure, was correct. Thinking that Martinelli might have removed the jewelry for further consolidation, he had searched the laboratory without result and then, his distress growing, he had rushed to the Italian's room, only to find that his bed had not been slept in and that he was not in the house.

"Let us not jump to conclusions," I said. "He may have spent the night in Luxor on—er—business of his own. Are his clothes and other personal belongings still in his room?"

"What the devil difference does that make?" Cyrus cried wildly. "Wherever he is, he has the jewelry. He is the only other person who has a key to that room. I locked it last night—you saw me do it—and it was locked this morning."

"It is a good thing I sent the servants away," I said severely. "Cyrus, I hope and trust that in your agitation you did not let slip the fact that some of the jewelry is missing."

"I'm not that big a fool," Cyrus snapped. "They know I was looking for Martinelli, though."

"His disappearance, if it is that and not simply delay, cannot be concealed from them," I said. "I take it he has never spent the entire night out before this? No? Some degree of concern for him is understandable, then, and if he does not turn up we will have to conduct inquiries which cannot be kept secret. First, let us ascertain what, if anything, he took with him."

"I'll have a look," Bertie offered.

"Yes, that would be sensible," I agreed. "You are probably more familiar with his wardrobe than I."

Bertie slipped out in his inconspicuous way and Katherine persuaded her agitated spouse to take a chair and a restorative cup of coffee. "I beg your pardon, folks," Cyrus muttered. "Shouldn't have lost my head like that. But, consarn it! This puts me in an awful position."

He was too generous to point out the corollary—that we were in an even more invidious position. Martinelli had been one of the restorers and forgers employed by Sethos in the days when he ran the illegal antiquities business in Egypt. Sethos had recommended him to us, and Cyrus had unquestioningly accepted our word that he was worthy of trust.

The dire implications were not lost on any of us. Emerson, his noble brow furrowed, was the first to acknowledge them aloud. Squaring his broad shoulders, he announced, "The ultimate responsibility is ours, Vandergelt. I regret with all my heart that you have suffered this disaster, but rest assured you will not bear the brunt of it alone."

"That is very noble, Emerson," I said, as Cyrus turned to him with moist eyes and an outstretched hand. "But, if you will excuse me for saying so, not particularly helpful. At the moment we don't know the extent of the disaster, nor have we considered means of lessening it. I have a few ideas."

"I don't doubt it," Emerson muttered. "See here, Amelia—"

Bertie slipped back into the room. "Well?" Emerson demanded.

"If he has gone for good, he abandoned his personal property" was the answer. "Clothing, luggage, even his shaving tackle. His coat and hat and that gold-headed walking stick he always carried are gone, and I think there was a smallish portmanteau which was not there."

"How strange!" I exclaimed. "He did mean to return, then."

"Not necessarily," said Ramses. Ramses's countenance was less phlegmatic than it had been in his younger days, when Nefret had described it as his "stone-pharaoh face." He allowed himself to display emotion now, especially the touching affection he felt for his wife and children; but on this occasion the stony look was back as he pronounced the words that dealt the death blow to my optimistic assessment. "He could hardly pack his bags and carry them out of the house unobserved. As for secreting objects in his luggage when he takes his official departure, he must know Cyrus would have sense enough to check the inventory before allowing him to leave."

I nodded reluctant agreement. "That assumption would certainly be made by an experienced criminal, as he has been, trained by one of the finest criminal minds in—"

"Damnation, Amelia!" Emerson sprang to his feet and fixed me with a terrible glare. "How can you use the words 'finest' and 'criminal' in conjunction?"

Cyrus's stare was hardly less forbidding. "Are you suggesting that Sethos is behind this, Amelia? I thought he had reformed."

"She isn't suggesting anything of the sort." Nefret's musical voice quelled the complainants. "Aren't we getting off the track? We are all in this together, and our first priority is to take what action can be taken before any more time is lost."

"Hmph," said Emerson. His keen blue eyes softened. "Er. I beg your pardon, Peabody."

His use of my maiden name, which he employs as a term of professional approbation, told me I was in favor again. "Granted," I said graciously. "Nefret is correct. We must get on Martinelli's trail at once. If the search is unsuccessful we will consider what steps to take next. After all," I added, attempting as is my custom to look on the bright side, "no one else knows of the theft, and M. Lacau will not be back for several weeks. That gives us time to think of a way out of this. I have several—"

Nefret burst out laughing and the lines in Cyrus's face folded into a grin. "If you can't think of a way out of it, Amelia, nobody can. All right, you're in charge. What do we do first?"

The answer was obvious to me, as it must be to my intelligent Readers. Questioning of the gateman elicited the information that Martinelli had left the house late the previous night—"as he often did," the fellow added with a grin and a leer. He had set off on foot along the road leading out of the Valley toward the river, "walking like a man who looks forward to a happy—" I cut the fellow short and asked another question. Yes, he had carried a small bag, just large enough to contain a change of clothing or a pair of pajamas.

"Or three bracelets and a pectoral, carefully packed," Emerson muttered after we had dismissed the witness.

It took a while to locate the boatman who had taken the Italian across the river. He was nursing a grievance; at the Effendi's request, he had waited for hours to bring him back, but his customer had not come. He had lost money, much money, refusing others . . . and so on, at length.

I doubted there had been many others at that time of night, but we won his goodwill by hiring him to take us over to Luxor.

Tourism was almost back to normal, and the little town was bustling and as busy as it had been before the war. The facade of the Winter Palace Hotel shone pink with fresh paint, and the dusty street was filled with carriages and donkeys and camels. Tourist steamers and dahabeeyahs lined the bank. From the decks of some, indolent travelers who had not chosen to go ashore leaned on the rails, looking out over the limpid waters. Some of them waved at us. I do not believe they knew who we were, since I failed to recognize any of the countenances, but I waved back at them. Emerson cursed them.

"Too damned many people. We won't find it easy to trace him in this mob."

His prediction proved to be correct. Katherine had remained at the Castle, but there were six of us to pursue inquiries, so we divided forces. We agreed to meet on the terrace at the Winter Palace, after making inquiries at the hotels and other, less respectable, places of entertainment. (My offer to question the female persons at certain of these latter establishments was unanimously voted down.)

The results were disappointing if not unexpected. Martinelli was well known at the hotels and cafés, but no one admitted to having seen him the previous night. The female persons whom Emerson had taken it upon himself to question denied he had ever visited them. I was inclined to believe this, since they had no reason to lie. Apparently he had had sense enough (or success enough elsewhere) to avoid such dens.

The last to join our party was Ramses, whose assignment had been the railroad station. "No luck?" he inquired.

"No. And you?" Emerson asked.

"A man of his general description took the morning express to Cairo. It isn't conclusive," Ramses added quickly. "You know how obliging Egyptians are about supplying the information they think you want to hear. None of them remembered the portmanteau or that gaudy stickpin he usually wears."

A dismal silence fell. "It looks bad," Cyrus muttered. "Now what do we do?"

Everyone looked at me. It was most gratifying. "Have luncheon," I said, and led the party into the dining salon.

We were well known to the management of that excellent hostelry and had no difficulty in getting a table. Over a bottle of wine and a meal Cyrus hardly touched, we put our heads together. Cyrus's first idea, that we should wire the Cairo police immediately, seemed the obvious course; but I felt bound to point out its weakness.

"If Martinelli has learned anything from his former master, who was, as we all know, a master of disguise—"

"Yes, we do know," grunted Emerson. "Pray do not go off on a long-winded and wholly unnecessary lecture, Peabody. The bastard may have altered his appearance, but we must at least make the attempt." He bit savagely into a roll.

I took advantage of his tirade to finish my soup. I always say there is no sense in allowing worry to affect one's appetite.

"I agree," said Ramses. "We are fortunate in being well acquainted with the assistant commandant of the police. Russell will act on our request without the necessity for explanations."

"What if he finds the jewelry?" Cyrus demanded.

"Then we will have it back," I replied. "No, Emerson, do not *you* go off on a long-winded and wholly unnecessary lecture. Russell owes us a great deal—at least he owes Ramses a great deal, for his services to the police and the military during the war—and we may be able to get out of this without Sethos's name being mentioned. That is supposing Russell is able to apprehend Martinelli, which I consider to be unlikely."

Emerson had wolfed his food down at a great rate. Now he pushed his plate away and rose. "I will go to the telegraph office."

"How many telegrams do you mean to send?" I inquired.

He stood looking down at me. "Two. Perhaps three."

I sighed. "I suppose we must. Do you have the addresses?"

Emerson nodded brusquely and turned away.

"Hmm." Cyrus stroked his goatee. "Who're the other telegrams going to?"

"You can probably guess," Nefret said.

"Reckon I can. Shall we retire to the terrace for coffee and some confidential conversation?"

It was a bright, warm day. The twin terraces of the Winter Palace, reached by a pair of handsome curved stairs, were high enough above the road so that the clouds of dust kicked up by feet and hooves did not reach us, and the noonday sun sparkled on the river. Tourists were returning from their morning trips. Cyrus took out his cheroot case, and after asking our permission, lighted one. Wine and tobacco had calmed him, and his habitual keen intelligence was once again in the fore. In a way I was sorry for that. For years we had put Cyrus off about certain matters, some personal, some professional. Our responsibility for his present dilemma made it impossible, in my opinion, to keep the truth from him. Anyhow, we would have enough trouble keeping track of the lies we would have to invent for Russell and/or Lacau.

"So you've kept in touch with your old pal the Master Criminal?" Cyrus inquired. "You even know his current address. Where the devil is he?"

"I'm not sure where he is at this moment," I admitted. "He has a house in Cornwall and a flat in London, but he travels a great deal."

"I'll just bet he does," Cyrus said. "All right so far, Amelia. Now—who the devil is he?"

I looked at my children, who were seated side by side, their fingers entwined. Ramses's eyebrows tilted up in amused inquiry. "Are you asking for our advice, Mother? A penny for our thoughts?"

"I'll give you mine for nothing," Nefret declared. "We can trust

Cyrus completely, and I for one am tired of secrets. I move we tell him everything."

"Quickly, before Father comes back," Ramses added.

Since I was of the same mind, I did so. Cyrus was only too familiar with Sethos's former criminal activities, since he had been involved in several of our encounters with our old adversary. He had not heard of Sethos's courageous and dangerous exploits as a British secret agent, but—he claimed—it came as no surprise to him. I explained that I could not go into detail, since Sethos's activities, and those of Ramses, were covered by the Official Secrets Act.

"That's all right," Cyrus said. "I don't need to know the details, I saw some of the results. Back in 1915, when Ramses ended up in bed for a week, just after the first Turkish attack on the Canal had failed, I began to wonder how he got those particular injuries. Not from falling off a cliff, not him! David was hurt even worse; he was in on it too, wasn't he? I kept my mouth shut, since it wasn't any of my business. Then there was that interesting episode the following year, when Sethos suddenly turned up out of nowhere and helped catch a German spy. But even if he and Ramses were in cahoots in that job, it doesn't explain why you are so intimate with the fellow now."

"No," I admitted.

"There's Father," said Ramses, who had been watching for him. "Get it out, Mother."

I didn't want Emerson sputtering and arguing either, so I said in a rush, "Sethos is Emerson's half-brother. Illegitimate, I regret to say, but no less kin and in recent years no less kind. Hmmm. That doesn't sound quite right . . ."

"I get the idea," Cyrus said in a strangled voice. "Holy Jehoshaphat, Amelia! I won't say I didn't suspect there was some relationship, but—"

"I will of course inform Emerson that you have been made aware of the situation," I said hastily, for Emerson was mounting the stairs two at a time. "But he is easier to deal with if he is presented with a fait accompli. Otherwise he wastes time arguing and going into long-winded—"

"Mother!" Ramses said loudly.

"Quite. Not a word to anyone else, Cyrus. Except to Katherine, of course. I trust her discretion as I trust yours."

"Never," Cyrus assured me.

Bertie had said very little. He seldom got a chance to say anything, for he was too well-bred to interrupt and too modest to differ with the admittedly dogmatic statements to which the rest of us are somewhat prone. His ingenuous countenance was a study in astonishment, but he found voice enough to express his sentiments.

"I cannot tell you how much I appreciate your confidence, ma'am."

"You have earned it, Bertie," I said warmly. "And I know I can depend on you to keep the information strictly to yourself."

"Of course. You have my word."

"Word about what?" Emerson demanded, looming over me.

"Never mind, my dear," I replied. "Do you want coffee?"

"No. We had better be getting back. There is nothing more we can do until we receive answers to our messages. I have work to do."

"Your article? Quite right, Emerson."

Emerson rubbed the attractive dimple (or cleft, as he prefers to call it) in his chin. "Oh. That article. There's no hurry, Peabody. I thought I might go to the site this afternoon for a few minutes. Nefret, the light will be perfect for photographs."

"I'm sorry, Father." Nefret's smile was warm, but she spoke firmly. "I promised the twins I would take them to visit Selim this afternoon, to play with his children. I can't disappoint them."

"Oh. No, you mustn't disappoint them. Ramses—"

"Emerson, you know their visit to Selim is a Friday-afternoon custom," I said. "Ramses looks forward to his time with Selim and with the children. In any case, you must finish that article before we leave for Cairo to meet the family. You don't want it hanging over your head once they are here."

"When are you leaving?" Cyrus asked.

"We are taking the train Sunday evening." I gathered my belongings—handbag, gloves, parasol—and rose. "By that time we ought to have heard from Mr. Russell, and possibly from . . . someone else. One way or another, whatever the results of our initial inquiries, we will continue to pursue them in Cairo."

I took Emerson's arm and we started down the curving staircase. "Quite a crowd in Luxor this season," I remarked. "It is nice to see things getting back to normal. Oh—there is Marjorie. Stop a minute, Emerson, she is waving at us."

"Wave back and keep walking," said Emerson. "You may indulge in gossip to your heart's content, Peabody, but on your own time. I have no patience with such stuff."

He put his hand over mine and pulled me with him. We had almost reached the foot of the stairs when I saw a little eddy, so to speak, in the crowd. Raised voices and a flurry of rapid movement betokened a disturbance of some kind. Owing to my lack of inches, I could not make out the cause, but Ramses, who had gone ahead with Nefret, obviously beheld something that provoked him into action. He dropped his wife's arm and ran forward.

Needless to say, the rest of us were not far behind him. Emerson thrust through the ring of gaping spectators. They had prudently backed away from the two principal performers, who were grappling with each other. The struggle was brief; with an abrupt movement Ramses (for as the Reader must have surmised, one of the combatants was my son) caught the other man in a hard grip and twisted his arm behind him. His opponent was a burly, dark-haired fellow whose teeth were bared in a grimace of pain or rage. The third participant lay on the ground, apparently unconscious.

He was no more than a boy, slender and frail, dressed in a suit that could only have been cut by a British tailor. His cap had fallen off. Golden lashes fanned his smooth cheeks, and golden curls crowned his bare head. His gentle countenance and slight form suggested a fallen angel, struck down by some diabolical adversary. The other man looked devilish enough, his face dark with choler and his muscles bulging as he continued to writhe in Ramses's grasp.

"Let me go, you fool," he cried. "Let me go to him."

"Hold on to him, Ramses," I ordered.

"I have every intention of doing so, Mother. They were struggling when I first saw them, and then this fellow struck the boy. Is he badly hurt?"

"I can't see any wounds or bruises," Nefret said. She bent over the youth and was about to loosen his collar when his golden lashes fluttered and lifted, framing eyes of a soft, celestial blue. A dreamy smile curved the delicate lips. "You are very beautiful," he said, catching hold of Nefret's hand. "Are you an angel or a goddess? The Egyptian goddesses had dark hair . . ."

"A friend," Nefret said gently. "I will take care of you."

"François will take care of me." His eyes moved in innocent curiosity around the circle of staring faces. "Where is he? Where is my good François?"

"Here, young master, here." François, for so the boy's smile of recognition proved him to be, had accepted the futility of struggle. His body relaxed and his features lost their ferocity. They were no more pleasant in repose; his nose was crooked and a seamed scar twisted his mouth. He had the shallow, retreating brow that some authorities consider evidence of a criminal nature, and the lower portion of his face was out of proportion, with a long jaw and large cheekbones. "Let me go to him," he begged. "Monsieur, s'il vous plaît—je vous en prie—"

"It appears," I remarked, "that we may have misjudged the situation. Release him, Ramses."

The man knelt beside the boy and lifted him gently to his feet, the tenderness of his manner in striking contrast to his former ferocity. "We will go home now," he murmured. "Come, young master. Come with François."

"Yes." The boy nodded. "But first I must know the names of these new friends, and I must tell them mine. I am Justin Fitzroyce. And you, beautiful lady?"

The sad truth had dawned on Nefret, as it had on me. She spoke to him as she would have spoken to a child, and like a well-trained child he gave each of us his hand as Nefret pronounced our names. "I will see you again, I hope," he said sweetly. "You will come to visit me?"

"Thank you," I said. "Where do you live?"

François, his arm supporting the slim frame of his "young master," nodded toward the river. "The dahabeeyah *Isis*. You may speak to my mistress if you still doubt me." The face that had been so benevolent when he spoke to the boy darkened again, and he turned blazing eyes on Ramses.

"There is no need," I said.

"No! You must come. My honor has been questioned. She will tell you."

"I am sorry," my son began.

"There is no need to apologize," I said firmly. "François surely understands that a stranger might have misinterpreted his behavior and acted in what he believed to be the boy's defense."

A curt nod was the only response from François, but the boy continued to smile and wave as his servant led him away.

"What a sad state of affairs," said my dear, soft-hearted Emerson. "The lad must be subject to fits. It was necessary for his manservant to subdue him lest he harm himself."

"Possibly," Nefret said. "Persons in a state of mania can have extraordinary strength. Frenzy is not typical of epilepsy, however."

"No," I agreed. "And one would have supposed that if François was aware of his master's condition he would have learned how to deal with it less forcibly. Goodness gracious, he is twice the boy's size."

"And built like a prizefighter," Ramses said, absently rubbing his wrist. "He knows a few dirty moves too."

"It is not our affair," Emerson declared. "You heard me, Peabody; you are not to call on his family and pry into their affairs and lecture them about medical treatment. You always—"

"No, Emerson, I do not 'always,' and I have no intention of interfering in this case. We have other matters to attend to."

"Too true," said Cyrus, sighing.

FROM MANUSCRIPT H

They stopped by the Castle in the forlorn hope that the missing Italian had turned up after all. He had not. Emerson persuaded Cyrus and Bertie to go to Deir el Medina with him, and Katherine emphatically seconded the suggestion. They could not expect to hear from Russell until late that night and, as Katherine candidly admitted, "To be honest, my dear, if you search that room one more time, I shall scream."

Ramses helped Nefret collect his vociferous offspring and their paraphernalia. His mother marched off to Emerson's study, with a glint in her eyes that made Ramses wonder what she was up to now. He decided it was more than likely that Emerson would stroll in that evening to find she had finished the article for him. Then there would be a row. About time, he thought. They hadn't had a first-class argument in days.

They rode the horses, since the distance was too great for short legs. Ramses took his daughter up with him on Risha and Nefret held Davy, who was a fraction less wriggly than his sister. They loved riding with their parents and Charla told Ramses so at length. He assumed from her chuckles and gestures that was what she was talking about; he didn't understand a word.

They were eagerly awaited, especially by Selim's four youngest children, who ranged in age from a staggering one-year-old to the big sister of six. Daoud and his wife Kadija had stopped by, too. Ramses knew he wouldn't see much of Nefret for the rest of the afternoon; she and Kadija were close friends, and Kadija, a woman of majestic proportions and the owner of a famous green ointment whose recipe she had inherited from her Nubian foremothers, was still shy of him and his father. She and Nefret went off with Selim's wives and the children, leaving the men to smoke and drink coffee under the shady arcade of the courtyard.

Daoud planted his huge hands on his large knees and beamed at Ramses. His beard was grizzled now, but his strength was unimpaired. It was equaled only by his large heart. "Is there news?" he asked hopefully.

There was plenty of news. Ordinarily Ramses would have taken Selim into his confidence, but although he was extremely fond of Daoud, he was well aware of the latter's weakness for gossip. "Nothing you don't know," he said. "We go to Cairo on the Sunday, and will bring the family back with us a few days later."

"Sooner than later," said Daoud firmly. "It has been too long since they have been here, and to think I have never set eyes on the namesake and great-grandson of my honored uncle Abdullah!"

"They call him Dolly," Ramses said. "They plan to stay the entire season, so you will see a great deal of him."

Selim's fine dark eyes had moved from speaker to speaker. Now he cleared his throat. "This time it is Daoud who has news to tell. He has found out why Hassan left the Father of Curses."

Daoud looked reproachful. He enjoyed his reputation as the family's official storyteller, and he would have worked up to the disclosure with proper rhetoric. However, he rallied promptly. "It is surprising news, Ramses. You would never have imagined it. Even I, when he told me, was struck dumb with amazement. My eyes opened wide and my voice failed me."

"But not for long," said Selim, grinning. He sobered almost at once; Ramses had the impression that something was troubling him. "So, Daoud, do not draw the tale out. Tell Ramses what Hassan said."

"I will show him," Daoud declared, rising ponderously to his feet. "Come, Ramses. It is not far."

Ramses waved Selim's protest aside. Daoud had been deprived of his great announcement; he was entitled to prolong the suspense. "Where?" he asked, rising in his turn.

"Follow me." Selim went to the door of the house and called out, raising his voice to be heard over the bedlam within. "We are going out. We will come back soon."

"So you have to report to the ladies, do you?" Ramses asked as they followed Daoud along the street, if it could be called that. The village had grown like Topsy, without any coherent plan, and the paths wound around and sometimes through modern houses and ancient tombs. "And I hear from Daoud that you are contemplating taking a third wife. Remember the advice I passed on to you last year. Three women are six times as much trouble as two."

Selim smiled and stroked his beard. "I tell them what I choose and I do as I like."

"Of course. And the third wife?"

"They cannot agree whether I should do it."

He glanced at Ramses's carefully controlled face and burst into a hearty laugh. "So. Am I—what is the word?—henpecked?"

"Only wise," Ramses said, joining in his laughter. "Your English gets better all the time, Selim. I say, is Daoud offended by our levity? Even his back looks hurt. What's this all about?"

"Perhaps it is better that you see," Selim admitted.

Their destination was the modern cemetery near the village. Like the ancient burial grounds, it was located in the desert, not in the green strip of irrigation bordering the river. It was the hottest time of the day; the barren ground baked in the sun's rays. For the most part the graves were small and humble, marked only by simple pillars or low benchlike tombstones. The most impressive monument was the tomb they had had built for Abdullah. Designed by David, it was of conventional form—a domed, four-sided structure—but unusually graceful and attractive. Even from a distance Ramses saw that it looked different. His amazement mounted as they drew nearer. A rope slung across the lovely arched entrance held a bizarre variety of what must be offerings—strings of beads and glass, handkerchiefs, a bunch of hair. Under the cupola, next to the low monument over the tomb itself, sat a motionless form, turbaned head bent, hands folded.

"Good Lord," Ramses exclaimed. "It's Hassan. What the devil is he doing?"

"He is the servant of the sheikh," Daoud said.

"What sheikh? Not Abdullah!"

Hassan got up and came to meet them, ducking his head under the rope with its motley attachments. Ramses observed that the white marble floor was strewn with flowers and palm branches, some fresh and colorful, some withered. Hassan did not appear to be practicing asceticism. He had been smoking a narghile and there were plates of bread and other food around him.

"What is this, Hassan?" Ramses demanded. "No one loved and admired Abdullah more than I, but he was no holy man."

"It is good that you have come, Brother of Demons," said Hassan, employing Ramses's Egyptian nickname. His smile was beatific. Ramses wondered if there had been something in the pipe besides tobacco.

"He is a sheikh, without doubt," Hassan went on. "Did he not save the life of the Sitt Hakim at the sacrifice of his own? Did he not come to her in a dream, as holy men do, and tell her to build him a proper tomb?"

Ramses looked at Daoud, who met his critical gaze with an unembarrassed smile. How their large friend had heard of his mother's dreams of Abdullah he could not imagine; she had not confided even in the immediate family until recently. Her belief in the validity of those dreams was one of her few streaks of superstition; but believe she did. The skepticism of the rest of them did not affect her in the slightest, and Ramses had to admit, if only to himself, that the consistency and vividness of the visions were oddly impressive. One of the household staff must have overheard her talking about them, and passed the word on. Once it reached Daoud, the whole West Bank would know.

"But a holy man must perform miracles," he argued.

"He has done that," Hassan said. "When that wretched boy, who had sinned against the laws of the Prophet, would have killed again in the very shadow of Sheikh Abdullah's tomb, did he not destroy the sinner? He performed other miracles for me. My heart was guilty and afraid. As soon as I came here and promised to be his servant I was glad again, and the pains in my body went away, and now you see that others have come to ask for his favor." He gestured at the sad little offerings. "Already he has stopped the cough that kept Mohammed Ibrahim from drawing breath and cured Ali's goat. Come, and pray with me. Ask him for his blessing."

It wasn't hashish that brought the light to his eyes. It was religious fervor—and who the hell am I, Ramses thought, to tell him he's wrong, or deny such a harmless request?

He knew the prayers. He had known them since childhood. Removing his shoes, he followed the prescribed path round the catafalque. Daoud's sincere, deep bass voice blended with his. "Peace be on the Apostles, and praise be to God, the Lord of the beings of the entire earth."

They started back to Selim's house, leaving Hassan cross-legged

45

under the cupola. Daoud was enormously pleased with his surprise. "My uncle Abdullah will be happy to be a sheikh," he remarked. "When next he speaks to the Sitt Hakim he will no doubt tell her so."

"I will be sure to let you know if he does," Ramses said wryly. He couldn't imagine how his mother was going to react to this news.

Selim had joined in the prayers but not in the discussion. He strode along in silence. Ramses was not certain how devout he was; he followed the Five Pillars of Islam, observing the fast of Ramadan and giving generously to the poor, but some of his habits had been affected by his unabashed Anglophilia. He was more indulgent to his young wives than most local men, and he had adopted a number of English customs.

Including afternoon tea, which was ready when they reached the house, and the mingling of the sexes for that meal. Ramses had hoped for a private conversation with Selim; but there was no chance of that, with the children dashing around and shrieking, and the women all talking at once. Accepting a cup of tea from Selim's younger wife, he smiled at Nefret, who had Selim's baby on her lap. Did she want another child? he wondered. They hadn't talked about it. As far as he was concerned, two were quite enough. He never wanted to see Nefret go through that ordeal of blood and pain again. Being a father was such a gigantic responsibility. A dozen times a day he asked himself if he was doing it right.

The dregs of his tea spattered the floor but he managed to hold on to the cup as Davy clambered onto his lap. He held the warm little body close. Maybe he was doing something right.

Kadija was watching them from over her veil. She was the only one of the women who would not unveil in his presence. His mother had often reminded her that since David's marriage to Lia they were all one family now, but Kadija came from a Nubian tribe where the old traditions were strong. She had finally consented to use his first name, however.

"How did you hurt your hand, Ramses?" she asked. "They are like the marks left by the claws of an animal."

He glanced at his wrist, where the cuff of his shirt had been pulled up. The scratches were deeper than he had realized, ragged and ugly.

"A little souvenir from a man named François," he said. "Though he does have some beastly habits, including sharp nails and a willingness to use them. It's nothing."

He tried to pull his cuff down but was prevented by Davy, who clutched his hand and pressed damp kisses on the scratches, murmuring distressfully (or perhaps chanting incantations).

"Why didn't you tell me?" Nefret demanded, putting the baby down.

"It's nothing," Ramses repeated.

Kadija rose and went into the house.

"Not the famous green ointment," Ramses protested. "It leaves indelible stains on one's clothes. Thank you, Davy, that's done the job. All better now."

"I've never been able to isolate the effective ingredient, but the ointment certainly has antiseptic and anti-inflammatory qualities," Nefret said. "Human fingernails are filthy, and I doubt if our François visits a manicurist. Those scratches should have been disinfected immediately."

"What is this?" Selim demanded. "Who is this man like a wild animal? A new enemy?"

"Nothing of the sort," Ramses replied. Kadija came back, carrying a small pot, and Ramses submitted to having the stuff smeared over his wrist while he told Selim about the encounter. Selim's handsome face fell. He had been with them on several of their wilder adventures, and he thoroughly enjoyed a good fight.

"Sorry to disappoint you, Selim," Ramses said. "They are tourists, and it is most unlikely that we will encounter them again. Anyhow, the whole business was a misunderstanding. The fellow bears me no ill will."

"Huh," said Selim.

Before long the children had reached a stage experienced parents know well; tears and howls of juvenile rage became more frequent, and Labiba slapped Davy for pushing the baby. He slapped her back.

"Time we were going home," Nefret said, holding the combatants apart by main force. "They're getting tired."

"Right." Ramses collared his daughter, who began an indignant explanation—or perhaps it was a protest. He recognized two words. One sounded like Swahili and the other like Swedish. Neither could be said to have any particular bearing on the situation.

Daoud enveloped both squirming, grubby children in a loving embrace and handed them up to Ramses and Nefret after they had mounted their horses. "You're disgusting," Ramses informed his daughter. "What is that purple stuff on your face?"

She gave him a wide grin and rubbed her face against his shirt.

As usual, the women took forever to say good-bye. While they were exchanging final farewells and last-minute gossip, Selim came and stood by him.

"Will you tell the Sitt Hakim about Hassan and my father's tomb?"

"She'll find out sooner or later. What's the trouble, Selim? I could see something was worrying you."

"It is not important." Selim tugged at his beard. "Only . . . what did Hassan do, that he should feel guilt and the need for forgiveness?"

>=<

EMERSON STORMED WHEN HE DISCOVERED I had finished his article for him. We had a refreshing little discussion, and then he set about revising my text, muttering under his breath and throwing pens at the wall. I congratulated myself on this idea, which served two useful purposes: it forced Emerson to finish the article, which he would never have done without my intervention, and it stopped him from brooding about the theft and his inability to do anything about it. Emerson is always greatly relieved by his explosions, which in my opinion are an excellent method of reducing an excess of spleen.

As I had expected, our telegrams produced no new information. Thomas Russell's reply arrived on the Saturday. Like Emerson's, his epistolary style was terse. No one of that description or name had been on the train. He had not wasted extra words demanding an explanation; he knew Emerson well enough to know none would be forthcoming.

Emerson crumpled the flimsy paper into a ball and tossed it to the Great Cat of Re, who sniffed it, decided it was inedible, and ignored it.

By the time we prepared to take the Sunday-evening train, there had been no response from Sethos. Emerson had telegraphed him at both his residences. At my request he showed me the telegram, and I must say he had communicated the necessary information without giving away the truth. That would have been disastrous, since the clerks at the telegraph office would have spread the news all over Luxor.

Cyrus's initial frenzy had been replaced by a state of profound gloom. He had been torn between rushing off to Cairo in pursuit of the thief and mounting guard over the remaining artifacts. The latter consideration won out, after I explained to him that although Martinelli might well have eluded the police, we had no certain proof that he was in Cairo. The very idea that the evildoer might be lurking, waiting for an opportunity to make another raid on the treasure, made Cyrus break out into a cold sweat. He did not even come to the railroad station to see us off.

Other friends and family members were there. Daoud considered it his duty to send us away with the proper blessings; he had dressed in his most elegant silken robes, as he always did on such occasions, though he was sulking a bit because he had wanted to come along. The twins were not coming either. If I understood the tenor of their remarks, they were extremely indignant at being left without parents and grandparents for several days. Emerson, who is a perfect coward with children and women, had wanted to creep away without telling them, but Nefret had insisted that we could not suddenly disappear without explanation and reassurance of return. I agreed with her, and began quoting from various authorities on child-rearing until Emerson cut me off with his usual shout of "Don't talk psychology at me, Peabody!"

After bidding the others an affectionate farewell, I turned last of all to Selim. A little pang, half pleasure, half pain, ran through me, for he looked so like his father—more slightly built and not as tall, but with the same aristocratic bearing and finely cut features. He was the only other person we had taken into our confidence.

"Remember, Selim," I said softly, "you are to open all telegrams and send the information on to us at Shepheard's if it is from . . . him. Keep on the alert for any rumors that may—"

Emerson shouted for me to board the train, and Selim showed his white teeth in a smile. "Yes, Sitt, you have told me. Do I not always obey your slightest command? A good journey. Maassalameh."

The train chugged away into the night—it was, as usual, late—and we went at once to the dining car, where I prescribed a glass of wine for Nefret.

"I know you hate to leave the children," I said sympathetically. "But take my word for it, dear girl, you will find that a little holiday from the adorable creatures will do you good. In time you will come to look forward to it."

Nefret's pensive face broke into a smile, and Ramses said, "Good advice, Nefret, from one who knows whereof she speaks. Did you look forward to your holidays from me, Mother?"

"Enormously," I assured him. Ramses laughed, and so did the others; but I thought there was a shade of reproach in Nefret's look. I prescribed another glass of wine.

The lamps on the table flickered and the crockery rattled, and it was advisable to hold on to one's glass. We lingered over our wine, since there are no companions as compatible as we four. However, the car was full and we could not talk confidentially there. Before we settled down for the night we had a little council of war in Emerson's and my compartment.

"Mark my words," I declared. "Mr. . . . What did you say, Emerson?"

"I said, we always do." Emerson muttered round the stem of his pipe.

"Oh. Thank you, my dear Emerson. As I was saying, if Mr. Russell learns we are in Cairo he will be chasing after us, demanding to know why we asked him to detain a harmless traveler and what we are up to now. We must decide how much, if anything, to tell him."

Emerson opened his mouth. I went on, raising my voice slightly, for I believe in an orderly exposition. "Even more important is what

50

to tell Walter and Evelyn. They know nothing of our relationship—their relationship, that is—with Sethos, yet he is also Walter's brother, and in my opinion—"

"It is also my opinion," said Emerson, taking advantage of my pausing to draw breath.

"I beg your pardon?" I exclaimed in surprise.

"Did you suppose I would dare to differ with you?" Emerson grinned at me. "I agree that the time for secrecy has passed. We may get ourselves in trouble with the War Office by exposing Sethos's role as an agent of British intelligence, but I can't see that we have any choice. The rest of it makes little sense unless that is admitted—and, as you might say, my dear Peabody, half-truths are more confusing than out-and-out lies. If I know Walter, the poor innocent chap will be delighted to find he has another brother."

"Aunt Evelyn may not be so delighted," Ramses said. Like his father, he had loosened his tie and unbuttoned his shirt as soon as we were in private. "The poor innocent woman has hoped for years that we would stick to archaeology and stop messing about with criminals."

Curled up on the seat next to Ramses, with her head on his shoulder, Nefret said sleepily, "Then she should be relieved to learn that the greatest criminal of them all is no longer an enemy but a friend and kinsman."

"That is the approach we must take," I agreed. "Very good, my dear. David already knows of Sethos's involvement with intelligence and I expect he has told Lia—he tells her everything."

"No doubt," Nefret said. "Neither of them has referred to it in their letters, but then they wouldn't take the risk, would they?" She raised her hand to her face to hide a yawn. "Sorry."

"Not at all," I said. "Ramses, take your wife off to—er—your compartment, she is half asleep."

After they had gone, Emerson indicated that he was ready to follow suit, so I rang for the porter to make up our berths. We stood in the corridor while this was being done. Emerson chuckled.

"I rather look forward to informing Walter he has an unknown brother who was not only born outside the blanket—"

"A vulgar phrase, Emerson."

"Not as vulgar as certain others that come to mind. As I was saying: but who has broken at least five of the Ten Commandments."

"It will be a shock," I agreed.

"It will do him good," said Emerson heartlessly. "He has led a very sheltered life and is in danger of becoming narrow and intolerant."

That thought, and another that he acted upon immediately following the departure of the porter, distracted him from further discussion, and soon after he returned to his own berth I heard the deep respirations that betokened slumber. It did not come so easily to me.

Our failure to hear from Sethos was frustrating but not fatal. He might be away—temporarily, one could only hope. I considered it possible that the dastardly Italian had sought refuge with his former acquaintances in Sethos's criminal network—supposing any of them were still in Cairo. Curse it, I thought, turning over with difficulty in the narrow bunk, how can we take action when we are ignorant of so many things? I ought to have cornered Sethos years ago and demanded a full accounting of the present status of the organization and the whereabouts of his confederates. Well, but his visits had been brief and infrequent, and there had been too many other things to talk about—his stormy relationship with the journalist Margaret Minton, the tomb and its amazing contents, the twins, the house in Cornwall—which was legally Ramses's property but which he had willingly lent to his uncle—and Sethos's daughter Molly.

Despite—or perhaps because!—of the fact that women found Sethos attractive, his relationships with the female sex had been far from satisfactory. For years he had professed an attachment to my humble self—a lost cause if ever there was one, since Emerson would never have allowed it even if I had faltered in my devotion to my spouse. In recent years he had transferred his affections to Margaret, who returned them with (at least) equal intensity. But Margaret had her own hard-won career, as a writer and newspaper correspondent specializing in Middle Eastern affairs, and she was unwilling to commit herself to a man who put his hazardous occupation ahead of her. Patriotism is all very well, but a woman likes to know where a man is and what he is up to, particularly when there is a possibility he may walk out of the house one day and never come back.

Then there was Bertha, Sethos's mistress and accomplice during his criminal years. Passionately devoted to him at the beginning of their relationship, her tigerish affections had turned to rage when she learned of his purported love for me. She had met a violent death at the hands of my friends after several attempts to kill me, but not before giving birth to Sethos's daughter.

We had encountered Molly—or Maryam, to use her proper name—only once, when she was fourteen years of age, before we were aware of Sethos's real identity and hers. Soon after that she had learned certain disturbing facts about her mother's death and had fled from her father's house. Despite his habitual insouciance I knew Sethos felt guilt and deep concern on her behalf, but his efforts to trace her had failed. We hadn't seen her or heard of her for years.

The waning moon slid long silver fingers through the gaps in the curtains. It was late. I cleared my mind of distractions. Finally Emerson's rhythmic breathing and the swaying of the carriage lulled me to sleep.

A YEAR AFTER THE ARMISTICE Cairo still had the look of an armed camp. Below the very terrace of Shepheard's, a crowd surrounded a young orator who held forth in eloquent Arabic on British injustice and the inalienable right of Egypt to independence. The attempts of the doormen to silence him were frustrated by the pushing and shoving of his followers, and the more timid of the foreign residents of the famed hostelry hung back, fearing to pass the mob. We stopped to listen.

"Anybody you know?" Emerson inquired of Ramses, who had once been involved in a somewhat unorthodox manner with one of the nationalist groups.

"Good God, it's Rashad," Ramses exclaimed. "The last I heard he was in prison."

The speaker caught sight of him at the same moment and broke off in mid-sentence. His blazing eyes moved from Ramses to Emerson, both of whom were conspicuous because of their height. I took a firmer grip on my parasol.

Rashad bared his teeth and pointed a quivering forefinger at Ramses, but before he could speak, one of the bystanders cried, "It is the Father of Curses and his son, and the Sitt Hakim his wife, and the Light of Egypt. Welcome! Have you come to speak for us and for our cause?"

"Certainly," Emerson shouted over the chorus of greeting.

"Not now, Emerson!" I took a firm grip of his arm.

"Well, perhaps not," Emerson conceded. He raised his voice to the pitch that has, together with his command of bad language, given him his Egyptian nickname. "Disperse, my friends, and take Rashad with you. The police are coming."

A troop of mounted men clattered toward the scene, led, as was customary, by a British officer. As Rashad ran off, he twisted his head round to look at us over his shoulder. His lips moved. It was as well we could not hear the words, for his scowling face suggested he did not share the friendly attitude of his followers. By the time the squad of police arrived, they were all gone.

Perhaps it would be in order for me to remind my less well-informed Readers (a small minority, but nonetheless worthy of consideration) of the historical background in order to explain why a British officer was in command of Egyptian troops, and why Cairo seethed with the spirit of revolt. Though it was formally a province of the Ottoman Empire, Egypt had effectively been under British control since the middle of the nineteenth century. In 1914 it was declared a British protectorate, under military occupation, when the Turks were threatening the Suez Canal and it was feared that Egyptians would support their fellow Muslims against an occupying power they had always resented. These fears had not materialized, except for a single abortive attempt at an insurrection in Cairo. Maternal pride compels me to add that it was aborted by Ramses, who had taken on the role of a radical nationalist leader named Wardani in order to intercept the weapons sent by Turkey to Wardani's group. Had it not been for his efforts, and the equally perilous part played by David, the Canal might well have fallen to the enemy.

But as I was saying . . . What Egypt wanted was independence, from Britain, Turkey, or any other nation. Once the war ended, the demands of Egyptian Nationalists intensified.

Britain's response had not been well-thought-out. One bad mistake had been the exiling of Nationalist leader Zaghlul Pasha. A tall, impressive-looking man, he was a splendid orator and much beloved by the Egyptian people. When the news of his summary deportation became known, rioting and demonstrations broke out all over Egypt. Though we were of course deeply distressed by the violence, the uprising in Upper Egypt earlier that year had not affected us personally. Our Egyptian friends were too sensible to engage in such a futile, uncivilized procedure, and naturally no one would have dared inconvenience the Father of Curses and his family.

The rebellion was put down by force. Zaghlul Pasha was released and went off to Paris, where the Peace Conference of the Allies was meeting to decide the fate of conquered and occupied territories. Zaghlul's demands were ignored. The British government insisted that the protectorate must be maintained. As a result, disaffection continued to smolder, isolated acts of violence against foreigners still occurred, and orators like Rashad stirred the populace up. Britain had agreed to send out a high-level commission of inquiry under Lord Milner, the colonial secretary, but few people believed that its report would bring about the changes Egypt demanded.

"There's another complication," Ramses said, as we mounted the stairs to the terrace.

"No, why should there be?" demanded Emerson. "Kamil el Wardani may hold a grudge against you and David, but he is out of the picture, Zaghlul Pasha is the accepted leader of the independence movement. Has Rashad changed allegiance?"

"It doesn't matter," I declared. "We have enough to worry about without becoming revolutionaries, and we must at all costs prevent David from becoming involved with that lot again. Emerson, I strictly forbid you to climb on soapboxes and orate."

"They don't use soapboxes," Emerson said mildly.

I looked from his smiling, self-satisfied countenance to the hooded eyes of my son, and a strong foreboding—of a sort to which I am only

too accustomed—came over me. Sympathy for the rights of the
Egyptian people was one thing, and we had always been of that mind.
Rioting and instigating riots was something else again.

Our rooms on the third floor of Shepheard's were a home away
from home; for more years than I care to admit we had dwelled there
at least once each season. The suite had two bedrooms, one on either
side of a well-appointed sitting room, and two baths. Before she and
Ramses were wed, Nefret had occupied the second bedchamber, with
Ramses in an adjoining (but I assure you, Reader, not connected)
room.

Emerson went at once to the balcony of the sitting room, and
stood gazing sentimentally out across the roofs and minarets of Cairo.
He invited me to join him. I was itching to unpack but I could not
refuse; how many times had we stood on that same balcony, on that
precise spot, in fact, reveling in our return to the land we loved, and
anticipating a busy season of excavation. How long ago it seemed, and
yet how recent!

Having allowed Emerson (and myself) a few moments of nostalgia, I brought his mind back to the present.

"If the boat is on time, our loved ones will be here tomorrow evening, Emerson. That gives us only a little over twenty-four hours in
which to complete our investigations."

"What investigations?" Emerson demanded. "If you are thinking
of pursuing your favorite sport of badgering the antiquities dealers,
dismiss the idea. It would be a waste of time. Martinelli will not dispose of his loot through the usual channels."

"So you can read his mind, can you?"

"Curse it, Peabody—"

"What is the harm of a visit to the suk? I must do a bit of shopping, in the course of which a few innocent inquiries may produce
useful information."

"Hmph," said Emerson.

When the children joined us for luncheon, Nefret readily agreed
to my suggestion, though, like Emerson, she was of the opinion that
we were not likely to learn anything about the stolen jewelry. "I need

to buy things for the twins," she said. "They are growing like weeds and they are very hard on their clothes."

Ramses and his father exchanged conspiratorial glances. They were trying to come up with excuses for not accompanying us. I didn't want them along anyhow; Emerson always stood by shuffling his feet and grumbling under his breath, and Ramses always wore an expression of exaggerated patience which was even more trying.

"You needn't come," I said. "Nefret and I will shop for the twins and for other boring necessities such as sheets and pillowcases, which you seem to believe appear out of thin air. Shall we go, Nefret? Emerson, I expect you and Ramses to behave yourselves. No hobnobbing with thieves and spies, no orating."

"The same to you," Emerson grunted.

"Take your parasol," Ramses added.

I did, of course. My parasols have become the stuff of legend in Egypt. They were no longer fashionable but I always carried one since I had found them to be invaluable, serving as sunshade or walking stick, and sometimes as a defensive weapon. A good hard whack over the head or across the shins will bring down most assailants, and mine were specially made, with a heavy steel shaft and—in one case—a concealed sword. Thanks to Daoud's preposterous stories, superstitious persons had become convinced that the parasols had additional magical powers. In some quarters the mere sight of that deadly object was enough to bring a miscreant to his knees. Since I had no reason to fear danger, the one I carried that day was not one of the heavy black instruments, but a delicate saffron in color to match my frock.

Nefret and I had a successful shopping trip. I do not enjoy buying bed linens any more than certain other people do, but when a task is necessary I complete it efficiently and thoroughly. Purchasing little garments for the twins provided greater pleasure, though Nefret firmly vetoed most of the frilly frocks and miniature coats and trousers I would have selected. She was undoubtedly correct; even Fatima had balked at ironing the dozens of frocks Charla got through in the course of a week.

After taking tea at Groppi's, we returned to the hotel to find that the merchandise we had ordered had been sent on. The suffragi had placed all the parcels in the sitting room, and we were going through them to make certain all was in order when Ramses returned.

"Did you get everything you wanted?" he asked, taking a chair.

"Yes, my dear, thank you for your interest," I replied. "Where is your father?"

"Isn't he back yet?"

"No, he is not. I thought you two were going somewhere together."

"Were we supposed to?"

"Stop that," I ordered. Shopping does leave one weary (which is one of the reasons why men make women do it) and Ramses's habit of answering questions with additional questions was, I did not doubt, designed to tease.

"Yes, Mother. Father went off on some errand of his own; he declined my offer to accompany him, nor did he mention what it was."

"Hmmm," I said. "And what did you do?"

Ramses's amused smile faded. There was no way he could avoid a direct answer this time. "I called on Rashad."

Nefret dropped the little shoe she was inspecting. "Not alone!" she exclaimed.

"Except for several hundred tourists, vendors, merchants, and miscellaneous citizens of Cairo," said Ramses. "I thought he might have the same rooms he occupied several years ago, when I crawled through his window from the back of a camel. Such proved to be the case. He wasn't at home, though."

"Why did you want to see him?" I asked.

Ramses leaned back and lit a cigarette. "I wanted to know why he has come back to Cairo and where his former leader has got to. If Wardani is planning some new stunt, he may try to recruit David again."

"But surely he knows that David betrayed him once before," I said uneasily. "He wouldn't be likely to trust him again, would he?"

"One never knows," Ramses replied. "Wardani is a pragmatist. If he believed David could be useful, he might be willing to overlook past indiscretions."

"We cannot permit that," I said. "However, I see no point in anticipating trouble. Have you had tea, my dear? Nefret and I took tea at Groppi's, but I will send the suffragi to bring it if you would like."

"Thank you, I'll wait for Father."

We had to wait some time. Emerson finally turned up, in an unusual state of dishevelment even for him. He had not had a hat to begin with—he lost them so often that I no longer insisted on his wearing one—and his hair was standing on end. His tie was undone, his coat open, and his shirt streaked with some dark oily substance.

"Good heavens, what have you been up to?" I inquired. "That looks like oil. Did you fall?"

"What?" Emerson glanced down at his chest. "Oil? Fall? No. Yes. Another shirt ruined, eh, my dear?"

He laughed, loudly and unconvincingly.

"Would you like tea, Emerson?" I asked.

"No, no, let's go and dine in the suk, eh?"

I had planned to dine at Shepheard's in the expectation of encountering acquaintances and catching up on the news, but I did not mind making this small concession to marital accord. Emerson dislikes elegant hotels, formal attire, and most of my acquaintances. So we assumed garments suitable for the littered alleyways and grimy buildings of the Khan el Khalili, and I changed parasols.

"Not your sword parasol!" Emerson protested. "Don't tell me you are having one of your premonitions, Peabody, for I won't stand for it."

"Nothing of the sort, my dear. Just a general precaution."

A return to the Khan el Khalili was a trip into the past. The few small changes had not altered the general character of the place—an Aladdin's cave of shining brass lamps and mother-of-pearl inlaid tables, carpets like woven gardens of flowers, fine leather sandals and silver bangles. Greetings showered us and Emerson's countenance brightened, even when Nefret or I delayed to examine a jewel or a length of gold-woven brocade from Damascus. He even went so far as to permit me to call on several of the antiquities dealers, including our old acquaintance Aslimi. Aslimi was not glad to see us, but then he never was. Emerson made him extremely nervous. I beheld no unusual degree of nervousness or sign of guilt, however. Nor was there any response from him or the other dealers to the only question we dared ask: "Anything of interest?"

"I hope you are satisfied, Peabody," said Emerson, as we strolled on.

"I am not at all satisfied, Emerson. If Martinelli did not dispose of his loot in Luxor or with any of the Cairo dealers, what did he do with it?"

"Sold it to a private buyer, of course," Emerson said impatiently. "Now may we dine? Where?"

"It had better be Bassam's," Nefret said. "If we go elsewhere and he learns of it—which he will—he will be cut to the quick."

Emerson snorted at her tender consideration for Bassam's feelings, but since it was his favorite restaurant he made no objection. Bassam came running to greet us, his bare forearms shining with perspiration, for he was cook as well as proprietor. He was not at all surprised to see us. He had heard of our arrival, and of our presence in the Khan; where else would we dine but with him?

"So," said Emerson, studying Bassam's apron—the closest thing to a menu the establishment provided. "Since you expected us, you have no doubt prepared one of those delicacies you keep promising— ostrich, or antelope."

He hadn't. The offers were only generalized and extravagant gestures of goodwill, which he knew would never be accepted.

Bassam liked to advertise our presence, so our table was, as usual, near the open doorway. This was mildly annoying, since passersby paused to greet us and an occasional beggar summoned up courage enough to risk Bassam's wrath by asking for baksheesh. He ran most of them off that evening, but after the meal, while we were enjoying Bassam's excellent coffee, a ragged man took advantage of his temporary absence to sidle up to Ramses, his hands moving eloquently in appeal. Ramses handed over a few coins—and got in return a folded paper. After performing this maneuver, which had been done with deft, sleight-of-hand skill, the beggar retreated out the door.

"How curious," I exclaimed. "What does it say, Ramses?"

Ramses's expressive brows tilted as he read. "It is from Rashad. He wants me to meet him."

"No," Nefret exclaimed.

"Under no circumstances," I said.

"My dears," said Emerson. "Please."

It was a mild-enough remonstrance, coming from Emerson, but his tone silenced me and Nefret. Emerson went on, "Well, Ramses?"

"He says . . ." Ramses looked again at the curving Arabic script. "He says there is danger awaiting David in Cairo. He wants to warn him."

"What danger?" I asked.

"He'll tell me when I see him. I must go, this may be a false alarm, but if it is true—"

"Not alone," Nefret said.

"Yes, alone, he is very clear about that. Do you suppose you—any of you—can follow me without his knowing? We are obviously under surveillance. This cannot be a trap," he added impatiently. "He's signed his name and given explicit directions. The place isn't far from here. Do you know it, Father?"

Emerson read the message. "I can find it."

"Wait for me here." Ramses rose. "I'll be back in an hour or less."

He vanished into the darkness outside.

"It could be a trap," I said.

"Oh, yes," said Emerson. "Bassam, more coffee, if you please."

Nefret did not speak. Her wide eyes were fixed on Emerson's face. He smiled at her, and patted her hand.

"You couldn't have held him back, my dear, nor wanted to—not when there was a threat to David."

"I can't sit here waiting for an hour," Nefret said tightly.

"You won't have to. We will give Ramses and anyone who may be following him time enough to get well away from here. Ten minutes, then we'll go there ourselves."

It was an admirable scheme; there should have been no flaw in it. Rashad had not given a street address. Cairo does not boast such conveniences, except in the modern European quarters. The description had been explicit, however, and Emerson was certain we had found the right place. No one was there except a half dozen impoverished and extensive families, who denied any knowledge of Rashad or of Ramses. Cowering before the thunder of Emerson's voice and the sight of the terrible parasol, they protested their innocence in terms impossible to doubt; but we searched the wretched place from top to bottom. We found no sign of Ramses.

CHAPTER THREE

He wondered where he was, but he couldn't bring himself to care much. Dimly lit by hanging lamps, the room was small and luxuriously furnished, the walls draped with fabric. A brazier on a stand nearby glowed, giving off a pale cloud of cloying, strange-smelling smoke. He lay on a soft, yielding surface, and not until he tried to move did he realize his hands and feet were immobilized. Vaguely curious, he flexed his wrists; the bonds were soft as silk, tight enough to hold without hurting.

Considerate of them, he thought sleepily. Whoever they are. I wonder what they want. He was quite comfortable, but he hoped someone would come soon and tell him. Nefret would worry . . .

He saw his wife's face, as clearly as if she stood beside him. Like a crack opening in a prison wall, it pierced the clouds of darkened memory. Bassam's, the beggar, the message . . . How much time had passed—an hour, a day? Nefret didn't know where he was. She always worried . . . Fighting the pleasant lethargy that weakened his limbs, he hung on to the thought of her, turning his head away from the smoke of the brazier, twisting his hands, trying to loosen the bonds. A stab of pain ran from his wrist up his forearm. An injury of some kind? He couldn't remember, but he twisted harder, deliberately inducing renewed pain and the temporary clarity of will it brought.

"Do not struggle. You will hurt yourself."

It was a whisper, barely audible, but in the silence it rang like a shout. Ramses turned his head toward the sound.

How she had entered he did not know. If there was a door, it had closed behind her. Light surrounded her as if her flesh shone through the thin linen that covered her body. Even with the fumes of the drug clouding his mind—or perhaps because of them—he took note of the fact that it was a young woman's body, slim and firm. Her face was veiled and on her head rested the horns and sun disk of an Egyptian goddess.

"Who are you?" He forced the words past lips that felt rubbery and unresponsive.

"Don't you know me? You have seen me before, many times, though not in the flesh."

Still a whisper. The words were English, but the accent was odd. Not German, not French, not . . . He found it increasingly difficult to think clearly. How much was real, how much illusion? The sheer linen veiled but did not conceal the lines of her body, the rounded hips and breasts. "Put that damned brazier out," he gasped.

She let out a breath of soft amusement and clapped her hands. A dark form materialized behind the couch where he lay. Featureless as she, androgynous in outline, it moved the brazier away and then vanished. He drew a long, uneven breath and tried to focus his eyes. She took a step toward him.

"Look closely. Do you know me now?"

She was jeweled like a queen, gold enclosing her slim wrists and arms. The robe of fine linen, the beaded sash and collar, the crown—and protruding from the black hair coiling over her shoulders, the ears of an animal. A cow's ears. A rapidly shrinking core of sanity told him he must be imagining some of it, seeing what she wanted him to see.

"You've gone to a great deal of trouble assembling that costume," he muttered. "But no. I don't know you. Why am I here? What do you want?"

"Only to see you and cause you to remember me. Stay with me for a day . . . or two. I promise, you will find it pleasurable."

He didn't doubt that he would. There were a number of euphoric drugs available, and she seemed to know how to use them. With an effort he pulled himself to a sitting position. She stepped back and raised her hand.

"You waste your strength," she murmured. "I mean you no harm. You are under my protection. Remember that, and do not fear for yourself, whatever befalls. You will know me when next you see me."

A beam of white light shot from her hand, striking him full in the eyes. Blinded and dizzy, he fell back against the cushions. When he was able to see again, she was gone and the brazier had been replaced.

Ramses knew he had only a few minutes in which to act before the drugged smoke overcame him. He rolled as far away from it as he could get, and pulled his knees up.

He had practiced the maneuver many times, but his movements were clumsy now and it took an interminable time for his stretched fingers to find the heel of his boot. After he had twisted it off he lay motionless, forcing his shaking hands to steadiness, breathing through the fabric of the cushions. Then he extracted the thin strip of steel coiled in the heel. It was serrated and very sharp; before he got it wedged against his wrists his fingers were slippery with blood. Afraid of losing his hold, he slashed hard and fast, risking additional cuts, and getting several. The steel slipped out of his grasp, but not before the job was done; a final tug freed his hands, and without daring to pause for rest he picked it up and cut through the cloth around his ankles. It was silk, twisted into a cord. He sat for a moment staring bemusedly at it, and then flung it aside and started to stand.

His knees gave way, so he crawled, to the farthest corner of the room, and fumbled along the wall, behind the draperies, trying to find a window. His fingers finally slipped into the carved apertures of a mashrabiya screen, used in harem quarters to allow the ladies to look out without being seen. With the last of his strength he forced it open and fell across the high sill, drawing in the sweet night air in long gasps.

Sweet by comparison to the atmosphere of the room, at any rate. He'd have known those variegated smells anywhere—animal dung and rotting vegetation, burning charcoal, the scent of night-blooming flowers—the ineffable perfume of Cairo, as his mother was fond of saying. He was still in Cairo. But where in Cairo? The fresh air cleared some of the cobwebs out of his brain and he raised his head, searching for landmarks. He was high above the street, on the first or second floor of the house; across the narrow way the tall shape of another of the old houses of Cairo faced him, its latticed balcony almost within arm's reach. No lights showed in the windows. It must be late. Late the same night? How much time had passed?

The thought of his wife and parents frantically searching for him spurred him to haste. Holding his breath, he stumbled back to the divan and found the discarded boot heel and the strip of steel; it had been specially made and replacing it would be difficult. He didn't bother searching for the door to the room. It would be locked. There was enough silken stuff in the room to make a rope, but he was afraid to take the time. The lunatic lady might decide to pay him another visit. He went back to the window, lowered himself to the full length of his arms, and let go. He landed, ankle deep, in a pile of rotting garbage, slipped, and fell to hands and knees.

The stench was vile, but he preferred it to the scented smoke of the brazier. Picking himself up, he leaned against the wall and inspected his surroundings, trying to orient himself. He knew the old city fairly well, but the streets were all similar, narrow and winding, walled in by high buildings, ending in unexpected cul-de-sacs. He rubbed his eyes. Then a sound from above made him look up. Against the faint light from the window was the black outline of a man's head and shoulders. He moved away, as quickly as he dared in the darkness, turning at random into one tunnel-like passage after another.

Luck was with him; the soft sounds of pursuit faded, and finally he emerged into a plaza so small it didn't even have a name. He'd been there before. The time-stained sabil in the center spouted a dribble of water. On one side was a disreputable coffeeshop that he and David had occasionally frequented. The coffeeshop was shuttered and dark. The place was deserted except for the motionless shape of a beggar huddled in a doorway.

Movement and the passage of time had brushed most of the cob-webs out of his head. He knew where he was: not far from the Rue Neuve, less than a mile from the hotel. He paused long enough to wash the blood and odoriferous muck off his hands and arms in the fountain. Before he started off toward the hotel, he dropped a few coins onto the ground by the sleeping man. An offering to some god or other seemed appropriate. Some god—or goddess. The woman's costume had been that of Hathor, Lady of Turquoise, Golden One.

THE WINDOWS OF THE SITTING room began to pale with the approach of dawn. Nefret and I had been waiting for hours. We had expected Emerson back long before this; he had promised to let us know the results of his search before morning. Nefret bore the delay better than I. Since childhood she and Ramses had shared an odd rapport; she claimed—and a number of events confirmed it—that she could always tell when he was in imminent danger. No such terror afflicted her now, she assured me. Logic informed me that Ramses got into scrapes like this all the time, and that he usually got himself out of them. But logic is poor comfort when the fate of a loved one is unknown.

Despite Nefret's composure, she was the first one on her feet when a knock sounded at the door. A sleepy-eyed suffragi handed her a note and stood waiting hopefully for baksheesh. I supplied it, while Nefret opened the paper and read it. A tremulous expletive burst from her lips.

"Language, my dear," I said, taking the paper from her.

"No harm done," it read, in Ramses's unmistakable scrawl. "I'll be with you shortly."

"Thank God," I breathed. "Sit down, Nefret."

Nefret snatched the note back. "He might at least have said 'Love.' Damn him! Where is he?"

She pulled away from my affectionate grasp and started for the door. Before she reached it, Ramses opened it and stepped into the room.

Ramses's tentative smile faded as Nefret flew at him, her hands gripping his arms. "Where have you been? What happened? How dare you send that stupid message instead of coming here straightaway?"

"The last time I appeared without advance warning, you collapsed in a dead faint," said Ramses. "Good evening, Mother. Or rather, good morning. Where is Father?"

"Looking for you, of course." My voice was a trifle husky. I cleared my throat. "Nefret, stop trying to shake him."

"And don't come any closer," Ramses said, holding her off. "I'm absolutely filthy and I smell like a rubbish heap."

She pushed his hands aside and clung tightly to him. "It must be love," he remarked. "Darling, let me bathe and change. Then I'll tell you the whole preposterous story. Is there any way you can reach Father and tell him to call off the hunt?"

"We expect him momentarily," I said. "He should have been here before this. Proceed with your plan, my dear boy; you really do not smell very nice. I will order breakfast. If your father has not returned by that time, I will try and find him."

"Thank you, Mother. Nefret, let go, will you? I won't be long."

"I'm coming with you." She took his hands and turned them over. "You've torn those scratches open again, and cut yourself rather badly. What the devil—"

"Let him change first," I cut in. "And—er—freshen yourself as well. He seems to have rubbed off on you."

After calling the suffragi and ordering a very large breakfast I splashed water on face and limbs and changed my dusty, crumpled garments for a comfortable tea gown. Invigorated and by now very curious, I returned to the sitting room to find Emerson there, shouting orders at the suffragi.

"Don't bully the poor man, Emerson," I said. "I have already ordered breakfast, and Ramses has come back."

"I know."

"How?"

"You were singing, Peabody. The door was closed, but your voice is particularly penetrating when you are in a cheerful frame of mind."

"Sit down and rest. You look very tired."

Emerson passed his hand over his bristly chin and sank with a sigh into a chair. "I did not feel fatigued until just now. When I heard your voice raised in song, and saw that Nefret was not in the sitting room, I hoped—but I was afraid to believe. I stood outside their door for several minutes, listening, until finally I heard his voice."

"Oh, my dear Emerson," I began.

"Bah," said Emerson, after a great clearing of his throat. "All's well that ends well, as you are fond of remarking. I do wish you could come up with more original aphorisms. Has he told you what happened?"

"Not yet."

A procession of waiters filed through the door, carrying trays; while they were arranging the food on the table, Ramses and Nefret joined us. Emerson greeted his son as coolly as if he had not been frantic about him for hours, and Ramses replied with an equally nonchalant "Good morning, sir."

Emerson stared at his bandaged hands. "I suppose it would be unreasonable to expect you to come back without some injury or other," he grumbled. "Er—can you hold knife and fork, my boy? If you like, I will just cut—"

"That won't be necessary, sir, thank you. I hope you weren't put to too much trouble on my account."

"It was Russell who was put to the trouble," said Emerson with satisfaction. He held a grudge against the gentleman because of a trick he had once played on us. "I suppose I had better tell him to call off the search before he comes round annoying us." He went to the escritoire and scribbled a few words on a piece of the hotel stationery. "Take this to the concierge and have it sent at once," he ordered, handing the paper to one of the waiters. "The rest of you chaps clear out of here. Now, Ramses, let's have your story."

I have heard a number of bizarre stories in my time. A number of the events that have befallen me personally might be described as bizarre, even preposterous, by those of limited imagination (for in my opinion life itself is often more extraordinary than any invention of fiction). Ramses's tale unquestionably ranked high on the list. He told it without being interrupted by us and without pausing to eat. He had said he wasn't hungry.

Nefret was the first to break the silence. "No wonder you aren't hungry. What was in the brazier—opium?"

"Opium and somthing else I couldn't identify."

"Another hallucinatory drug?"

"No doubt." Ramses had picked up his fork. Now he put it gently down. The effect was the same as if he had slammed it onto the table. "You don't believe me, do you? Any of you? You think the whole thing was a hallucination."

"What other explanation is there?" Nefret demanded. Her color had risen. "A room furnished like a bordello and the immortal Hathor, in all her youthful beauty, promising you—"

"Now, now," I said. Ramses's face was as flushed as hers, and he was on the verge of an angry protest. "We are all tired and excited. Obviously Ramses did not see the goddess, he saw a woman costumed like Hathor. As for rooms furnished in that fashion, there are many of them in Cairo. Curse it," I added, in sudden vexation. "I ought to have thought of it before. Could you find the house again, Ramses?"

"I doubt it. I've no recollection whatever of how I got there. The last thing I remember is a pair of hands closing round my neck."

"There are no bruises on your throat," Nefret said. Her tone was studiously neutral.

"Need I remind you," said Ramses, in the same tone, "that it doesn't take much pressure or much time to put someone out, if you know how to do it. On the other hand, I might have imagined that, too."

"Still, perhaps we ought to make an attempt to find the place," I said quickly. "When you left the house—"

"I was in too much of a hurry to pay attention to where I was going, and still in something of a fog. Anyhow, they've had time to clear out. Whoever they were."

"There were at least two of them," I mused. "Assuming that the beggar and your assailant—and perhaps the shadowy acolyte—were one and the same. Which need not be the case."

Nefret was watching Ramses, who was concentrating on his breakfast. "I did not mean to give the impression that I doubted Ramses's word," she said stubbornly. "I'm only trying to understand what happened, and why."

I am not in the habit of disparaging my own gender, but there are times when even the best of us "behaves like a woman," as men put it. "Goodness gracious," I said in exasperation. "That is what we are all trying to ascertain, is it not? Let us face facts, no matter how unpalatable they may be to you, Nefret. Your husband, like mine, is irresistibly attractive to women. I must say, though, that this one has gone to extraordinary lengths to capture his attention. The costume, you say, was authentic?" Ramses nodded. He was now annoyed with *me,* for pointing out a fact he also found unpalatable. Unperturbed, for I am accustomed to the vagaries of the masculine mind, I went on. "The seemingly supernatural touches would have been easy to arrange. Electricity has been a great boon to charlatans. An electric torch fastened to her person, a quick press of the switch, and voilà! She appears, out of nothingness. She must have used the torch again to blind you before she left the room, hoping you would take it for a bolt of divine lightning. Rather childish, that."

"Not to a man whose senses are befuddled with opium," Emerson said. He pushed his plate away and took out his pipe. "It is remarkable that Ramses managed to keep his wits about him as well as he did."

Ramses's tight lips relaxed. He glanced at his hands. "Pain helps. So do . . . other things. Unfortunately, I observed nothing that would enable me to recognize her, not even her height, which is, as you know, difficult to determine without something with which to compare it. She was young and slim, but not an immature girl. A woman. She disguised her voice by whispering and by using an artificial accent. That's all I know, and without wishing to be rude, Mother, your theory as to the woman's motives is pure imaginative fiction! I don't want to talk about it. What were you about all night, Father? I suppose you went after poor old Rashad?"

"It was the only clue we had," Emerson replied. He grinned round the stem of his pipe. "I persuaded your mother and Nefret to stay here, in case you came back, and went off to see Thomas Russell. I had the satisfaction of rousting him out of bed, at any rate. I was somewhat surprised to learn that all the revolutionaries have been freed, even your friend Wardani, though nobody knows his present whereabouts. Russell already had a few of his lads looking for Rashad, who had sensibly refrained from returning to his rooms after trying to foment a riot earlier. We located one of his associates—Bashir—sleeping the sleep of the just and weary; he denied any knowledge of a plot against you or David. I was forced to believe him, since I couldn't prove he was lying."

"I don't believe he was lying," Ramses said. "Rashad had nothing to do with tonight's event. He hasn't the imagination to invent such a scenario. This could be connected in some fashion with our missing thief."

"Do you suppose he has that sort of imagination?" I inquired.

"He or one of Sethos's other associates," Ramses replied. "Admit it, Mother, this has Sethos's trademark. I don't believe he was personally involved, but his influence was widespread and pervasive."

"Still no reply from him?" Emerson asked me.

"No, curse the man. Did Russell have anything more to say about Martinelli?"

"That was one good thing resulting from the events of the evening," Emerson replied. "Russell is now under the impression that we asked him to detain Martinelli because we suspected him of being involved with a Nationalist plot—the same plot that resulted in Ramses's disappearance. It is inherently unlikely, but not as unlikely as—er—"

"The veiled Hathor," Nefret murmured. Ramses gave her a long, unsmiling look, and I said hastily, "Speculation can take us no further at this time. It was a most peculiar incident, but no harm was done—except what Ramses did to himself—and apparently none was intended. She actually said so, didn't she? Ramses?"

"What?" Ramses looked up. "Sorry, Mother. If my memory can be trusted, she said something of the sort."

I decided it would be advisable to change the subject. "We had better get some rest. Do you realize the family will be arriving this evening?"

"Yes, Mother," said Ramses.

They took their leave. "And you, Emerson," I said.

"I don't need to rest," said Emerson. "What's wrong with those two, Peabody? They seem to be out of temper with each other."

"I will be happy to explain, Emerson, if you will allow me to do so without forbidding me to talk psychology."

"Try to avoid the word if possible," muttered Emerson.

"Nefret's reaction is unreasonable, but quite understandable to a student of . . . that is, to me. It would be difficult to say which would bother her more—the suspicion that her husband has fantasies about beautiful desirable women pleading for his favors, or the possibility that a beautiful, desirable woman really *is* pleading for his favors."

"Hmmm," said Emerson, rubbing the cleft in his chin. "So if a similar sort of thing should happen to me, you would . . ."

"Be mad with jealousy," I assured him, and saw his lips curve into a smile that was not without a touch of smugness. I went on, "We cannot help being jealous, my dear; we care too much for you to remain indifferent to the fear that you care less for us."

Of course it was not as simple as that. Contrary to the opinions of sentimentalists, children put a strain on a marriage. It takes a while to sort out new feelings and new responsibilities. I know whereof I speak, Reader; it had taken me over twenty years! The large fortune Nefret had inherited from her grandfather had enabled her to found a hospital for fallen (as well as upright but impoverished) women in Cairo, and she had fought a hard battle against masculine prejudice to acquire surgical training so that she could better assist these unfortunates. She had given up her medical career in favor of matrimony, motherhood, and archaeology. Although she had never expressed regret, I wondered if she missed it. However, it would only have confused my dear Emerson if I had entered into a serious analysis. His is a very straightforward mind.

There are other psychological difficulties connected with the birth of children, but they were not the sort of thing one can discuss with a male person.

"Hmmm," said Emerson again. "Well, my dear, in this case I must bow to your expertise. They will settle their differences, won't they?"

"In their own way, Emerson, in their own way. I would be sorry to see them settle into the bland tedium of most marriages. I consider that unlikely. We never did, and in my opinion—"

"We are all the better for it," Emerson declared, his broad brow clearing. "I prescribe a rest for you too, my love."

"I haven't time. I want—"

"There is plenty of time," said Emerson.

SINCE SCHEDULES OF BOATS AND trains were uncertain, we had agreed to await our family at the hotel instead of hanging about the railroad station. It wasn't as if they were strangers to Egypt. Walter and Evelyn had not been out for many years, but David knew his way about.

Having made certain their suite was in perfect order, with fresh flowers in every room, there was nothing left for me to do but fidget, which I confess I did. Anticipation mounts as the longed-for event draws nearer. I was leaning perilously over the rail of the balcony for the third or fourth time when Emerson took hold of me and led me to a chair.

"It would be a poor welcome for the family to find you spattered on the front steps," he remarked. "They cannot possibly be here for several more hours, even if all the connections are on time, which they seldom if ever are. Sit down, my dear, and have a whiskey and soda. I will ask Ramses and Nefret to join us."

Upon his return he announced in a pleased voice, "They have made it up. It took Ramses quite a long time to answer the door."

"Don't be vulgar, Emerson."

"Drink your whiskey, Peabody."

The bright faces of my children assured me that they had indeed settled their little difference. Except for his bandaged hands, Ramses appeared none the worse for his adventure. Despite his dismissal of my theory, I remained convinced that the woman's motive could only be personal attraction. It was not Ramses's fault, or Emerson's, that their handsome features and athletic frames and gallant manners attracted shameless females. Who on earth could this one be? I had already gone over in my mind—as I was sure Nefret had also done—the rather extensive list of women with whom Ramses had been involved— before his marriage, I hardly need add. None of the names that came to mind seemed to fit. However, there had probably been others. I wondered if I could persuade him to give me a list.

It did not seem likely.

Feeling my speculative eye upon him, Ramses tugged nervously at his tie and burst into speech. "When are you going to tell Uncle Walter?" he asked.

"About Sethos? Certainly not tonight" was Emerson's reply.

"Certainly not," I agreed. "Let them enjoy their return to Egypt and their reunion with us before we drop the bombshell."

"More than one bombshell," said Nefret. "Martinelli and the missing jewelry, the Nationalists rioting, and now the mysterious lady. Is it only a coincidence that all those things have happened within the last few days?"

They were not the only things that had happened. Other events, which had seemed of little import, were to bear bitter fruit in the coming days. I am a truthful woman; I do not claim I sensed this. Yet a quiver of uneasiness passed through me, that vague sense of something forgotten or overlooked with which, I daresay, my Readers are also familiar.

The hours of waiting went by. Nefret was dozing in the circle of Ramses's arm, with her head on his shoulder, when at last they came. It would be vain to attempt to describe the joyful hubbub that ensued—embraces, laughter, questions, and tears. A querulous wail from the youngest member of the group brought me back to practicality. Evvie, David and Lia's youngest, was an angelic little creature, blue-eyed and fair like her mother. At the moment she did not look angelic; her mouth was open so wide it seemed to fill her small face, and her whimper rose to a penetrating howl.

Having greeted the adult members of the family, Emerson was advancing on Dolly, with his arms held out and a fond smile curving his lips. The sturdy little chap, who had been named for his great-grandfather Abdullah, was only four, with David's black hair and eyes and his mother's delicate features. He squared his shoulders and stood his ground, but he looked a trifle uneasy—as what three-foot-tall person would not, with that imposing form looming over him!

"Don't pounce on the child, Emerson," I ordered. "He doesn't remember you. Give him time to get used to all these new faces."

"Oh," said Emerson. He came to a stop. "Er—sorry."

Then the little boy lived up to his proud name. "He is my uncle Radcliffe," he said and held out his hand. "How do you do, sir?"

Emerson did not even flinch at the name, which he thoroughly dislikes and with which few people venture to address him. His features wreathed in smiles, he took the small hand carefully in his. "How do you do, my dear boy? Welcome to Egypt."

"Very nice," I said, for it was clear to me that Emerson, overcome by sentiment, was about to pounce again. "Let us get the children tucked away, shall we?"

It did not take long; both of them were too tired to make a fuss. I had caused a nice little cold supper to be supplied for the nursemaid.

"Sound asleep," I reported, returning to the others. "Perhaps the rest of you would also like to retire? You have had a long tiring trip."

"Impossible," Evelyn exclaimed, holding out her hands. "I at least am too happy and excited to be weary. Come and sit with me, Amelia, and let me look at you. Have you won the favor of some god, that you never change?"

The little bottle of hair coloring on my dressing table was owed some of the credit. I saw no reason to mention it. To her loving eyes, perhaps, I could never change; but I had, and so had she. The fair hair shone pure silver now, and she was painfully thin; but the blue eyes were as fond and clear as ever. She was right after all. Neither of us had changed in any way that mattered.

No doubt the same could be said of Walter, but his physical appearance was something of a shock. We had paired off, as we used to do; the contrast between Emerson's sturdy, vigorous frame and Walter's stooped shoulders and myopic squint made the latter look years older than his elder brother. He had Emerson's dark hair and blue eyes, and he had once been a sturdy young fellow, not as quick to anger as his excitable brother but ready to defend himself and his loved ones when danger threatened. I did not doubt his willingness to do so now, but years spent in sedentary scholarship poring over faded papyri had taken their toll. Emerson, though he is not especially observant, had noticed it too. He broke off in the middle of an animated description of Deir el Medina, and squeezed Walter's arm.

"High time you came out," he declared. "We'll put some muscle in that arm and some color in your face."

Walter only laughed. He knew this was Emerson's uncouth way of expressing affection and concern.

Lia and Nefret sat side by side, talking of . . . of babies, of course! What else would two young mothers talk about? Lia had been named for me, but preferred the shorter version of the name—to avoid confusion and because Emerson's bellow of "Amelia!" when he was put out with me had always made the poor girl very nervous. Blue-eyed and fair-haired like her mother, she brought back fond memories of the young Evelyn, who had been my companion on that first memorable voyage to Egypt. Little did I dream that our lives would become so intertwined, and that the passage of time would bring such a bountiful harvest of happiness, with a second generation following in our archaeological footsteps.

It was good to see Ramses and David together again, close as brothers and almost as alike, their black heads close together as they began catching up on the news.

They were not given much time to chat, for Emerson, assuming that everyone else would be as eager as he to talk Egyptology, drew the rest of us into his conversation with Walter and began outlining the plans he had for them. He was telling Evelyn about Cyrus's hope of having all the tomb paintings at Deir el Medina copied and published, when there came a peremptory knock at the door.

"Who can it be, at this hour?" I wondered aloud.

Then I remembered we had told the concierge to send up any telegrams as soon as they arrived, no matter how late the time.

Emerson's eyes met mine. "I'll see," he said, and went to the door. In his customary fashion he flung it wide . . . and stood transfixed.

Emerson is a very large person, but his bulk was not sufficient to conceal completely the man who faced him. I saw a head of black hair and the shape of a shoulder covered in brown tweed. It was enough. I sprang to my feet. Emerson shifted position; he was trying, I think, to block the doorway, but the visitor pretended to take it for an invitation to enter, and slipped neatly past him.

I recognized the tweed suit as one he had borrowed from Ramses on a previous occasion, and never returned. A black beard and mustache hid the lower part of his face; the upper part was transformed by the waving locks that fell across his high brow, and by a pair of tinted eyeglasses that darkened his ambiguously colored eyes to brown. They swept the room in a quick, comprehensive survey; and the bearded lips parted in a smile.

"How good to see you, brother," he exclaimed, clasping Emerson's palsied hand. "And the rest of the family, too—never did I dare hope for such a pleasure. This must be—it can only be—my dear sister Evelyn. Allow me the privilege of a kinsman . . ." He lifted her hand and kissed it respectfully while she gaped in bewilderment. He greeted Lia in the same fashion, embraced me and Nefret, shook David's hand and that of Ramses. Our surprise was so paralyzing, and his movements were so quick, that he got through the entire rigmarole without interruption. When he turned last of all to Walter, his face working with simulated emotion, I knew I had to intervene. Unfortunately, in my confusion and vexation, I said the wrong thing.

"Sethos, please! Walter doesn't know . . . Oh, curse it!"

I did not know his real name; this alias, of all the others he had used, came easiest to me. It was the final straw for Walter. He had been more stupefied than any of us, but not so stupefied that he could not put the pieces together. He looked in silent appeal at Emerson—got no response, no denial, no protest—clapped his hand to his breast—turned white—and fell over, unconscious.

"IT WAS ONLY A FAINT," Sethos said. "Nothing serious."

"No thanks to you," I said angrily. "If his heart had been weak, that might have been the end of him. You put on that performance deliberately and with malice aforethought. Shame!"

Never let it be said of me that I take the offensive in order to distract listeners from my own misdemeanors. It wouldn't have done me a particle of good, anyhow. Emerson, whose feelings for his reprobate half-brother vacillated between grudging affection and violent annoyance, froze me with an icy blue stare.

"You were the one who administered the coup de grâce, Amelia. Walter might have been able to assimilate the existence of an unknown brother; to have that same brother identified as the criminal of whom he has heard us speak so—er—critically, finished him off."

"Well, curse it, I don't know his real name," I retorted. "Since we are on that subject—"

"In retrospect, my little joke was ill-advised," Sethos said smoothly. "I am sorry, Amelia. You know my unfortunate sense of humor. But look on the bright side, my dear, as you are so fond of doing. You were planning to tell them, weren't you? Now it's over and done with, and you won't have to fret about how to break the joyous news."

He gave me an insolent smile. To do him justice, he had not been so cool when he helped Emerson carry the unconscious man to his room. He had hovered anxiously over Walter until Nefret finished her examination and announced there was no damage to the heart. When Walter opened his eyes and muttered, "Where am I?" he stepped back, folded his arms, and tried to look unconcerned. On my advice, Nefret gave Walter a sedative, and we left him with Evelyn, who had accepted Sethos's muttered apology with a dignified nod.

The rest of us had returned to the sitting room. Emerson served whiskey all-round. Sethos was himself again, unrepentant and unmoved. I thought he looked tired, though. Leaning back against the cushions, he sipped appreciatively at his whiskey.

"Do they know about the robbery?" he asked.

David started. "What robbery?"

"I suppose they will have to know," I admitted. "But I certainly don't intend to wake Walter up and drop that on him too."

"It can wait," Sethos said coolly. "But you might tell me a little more about it. Emerson's telegram was of necessity cryptic." He fished in his pocket and took out a crumpled piece of paper. He handed it to me and I read it aloud.

" 'M. gone missing with ladies' property. Where would he take it? Advice urgently needed.' "

"How did you get here so quickly?" I asked.

"I was in Constantinople. Margaret sent the message on, since it sounded urgent. I came as soon as I could. Now tell me the rest of it. What precisely is missing?"

"Three bracelets—the most valuable of the lot—and a magnificent pectoral." In my usual efficient fashion I summarized the facts that were known to us. David exclaimed, "Poor Cyrus! What a blow."

"It is as great a blow to me," Sethos said. "I had nothing to do with it, Amelia. Do you believe me?"

"Yes. You would have taken the lot."

Sethos threw his head back and laughed heartily. "You flatter me, my dear. I thank you for your confidence. To be honest, I am surprised at Martinelli. If he has reverted to his old habits I would have expected him to be more thorough. Unless he had found a particular buyer who wanted particular items, for reasons unknown . . . I will of course pursue inquiries here in Cairo, but don't get your hopes up. My old organization is dispersed and its members scattered."

"You can't do anything until tomorrow," Emerson said. "I—er—you—er—Amelia is tired." I had not been the only one to observe the lines of weariness in Sethos's face. He must have traveled day and night to respond to our plea.

"Quite," I said. "Have you booked a room here?"

"I have quarters elsewhere."

Emerson's eyes narrowed. Affection had been replaced by suspicion. Sethos went on, "Before I leave you in peace, we must confide fully in one another."

"You mean you expect us to confide fully in you," snapped Emerson.

"I assure you, brother, I will reciprocate as soon as I have something to confide. Is there anything you haven't told me that might have bearing on this business?"

The indeterminate color of his eyes had been very useful to a master of disguise, since they could appear gray, green, or brown with the skillful application of makeup. Sunk in shadowed sockets, they looked darker now, as they came to rest on Ramses's bandaged hands.

"That has nothing to do with—" Ramses began.

"We cannot be certain," I interrupted. "Sethos may see a connection that eludes us. You young people needn't stay, if you are tired, as you must be."

"Wild horses couldn't drag me away," David declared. "Have you ever had an entire season without some kind of mischief? Don't think for a moment that you can keep me out of it."

"Or me," said Lia firmly.

Sethos's hard face softened. "The family blood runs true," he said, in a tone that made Lia's face turn pink. "All right, Ramses, let's have it."

"Hell," said Ramses, running his fingers through his hair. "Must I?"

"Allow me," I said, for I knew Ramses would not mention the most interesting details. He was inclined to be self-conscious about his encounters with amorous females. "You can correct me if my narrative goes astray."

I made the narrative as matter-of-fact as I could, but I had not got far along before Sethos's mouth began to twitch. His amusement was so evident, I frowned severely at him.

"The story appeals to your notorious sense of humor?"

His smile faded into sobriety. "Good God, Amelia, you don't suppose I had a hand in it, do you? In my bygone and exceedingly ill-spent youth I was guilty of a number of extravagances, but never anything so wild as this."

"Hmph," said Emerson, glaring.

"Well, there was one that came close," Sethos conceded, with a sentimental look at me.

"Stop that," I said sharply. Emerson had never forgotten or entirely forgiven that occasion when I had been held prisoner by my amorous (had I but known) brother-in-law, in surroundings as voluptuous as those Ramses had described.

"I beg your pardon. And yours, Rad . . . Emerson. But really, if one cannot laugh at folly, what hope is there for the human race?" He shook his head. "I am at a loss to explain the affair. Perhaps we must attribute it to—er—personal interest on the part of the lady. It would not be the first time, would it?"

Ramses was almost as red in the face as his father. Sethos could not refrain from stirring people up. I recognized the symptoms of fatigue; it always put him in a quizzical mood.

"It is almost morning," I said. "We would all be more sensible, I think, after some sleep. How can we reach you?"

"You can't." He rose. "I will come round tomorrow evening. Perhaps you will all dine with me? A celebratory—"

"Oh, go away," I snapped.

FROM MANUSCRIPT H

Somehow Ramses had not been surprised to see his reprobate uncle. To give him his due, Sethos had a gift for turning up without warning when his assistance was needed, but this time he appeared to be intent on stirring up trouble. He had shocked his unsuspecting half brother into a faint, provoked Emerson into a rage, offered no useful information and no prospect of any—and (most infuriating of all) he had refused to take Ramses's story seriously. One of these days, Ramses thought savagely, he'll drive me into smacking that supercilious grin off his face.

"What did you say?" Nefret asked

"Nothing." He finished undressing and got into bed. "Let's get some sleep."

She was sitting at the dressing table brushing her hair. "I'm too keyed up to sleep. Don't you want to discuss the amazing appearance of Uncle Sethos?"

The long locks of unbound hair rippled with light and movement, but for once the sight failed to arouse him. "No," he said curtly, and rolled over, his back to her. When she finally joined him he pretended to be asleep.

The only person he wanted to talk to was David. There hadn't been time the night before; his mother had bustled them off to their rooms as soon as Sethos left. But they knew each other pretty well, he and David. An exchange of glances and a few words had arranged a meeting for the following morning.

He had been waiting on the terrace for a quarter of an hour before David came, with a smiling apology. "Couldn't get away from the affectionate arms of the family," he explained.

"How is Uncle Walter?"

"Fully recovered and bursting with curiosity. He and the Professor are taking the children to the Museum. I wish them luck. I suggested leads, but was shouted down."

"And the others?"

"The hospital with Nefret, except for Aunt Amelia. I believe she has decided to accompany the Museum party. She asked where I was going."

"She would. What did you tell her?"

David's black eyes widened in affected surprise. "The truth, of course. That you and I wanted some time to ourselves." His contemptuous gaze swept the terrace, with its crowd of well-dressed tourists and Anglo-Egyptian officials and dark-faced waiters. "But not here, if you don't mind. The place hasn't changed a bit, has it?"

"No. Will it ever?"

"Oh, yes," David said softly. "It will."

Ramses turned to him, brows furrowed; he shook his head and smiled a little. "Let's not talk politics. Where shall we go?"

They found a favorite coffeeshop, and David settled onto a bench with a sigh of contentment. "Just like old times. D'you remember the night we were here, you as Ali the Rat and me as your faithful henchman, and your father walked in? He looked straight at you, and you shouted, 'Curse the unbeliever'?"

"'Whimpered' is more like it." Ramses laughed, yielding to the mood of sentimental nostalgia. "I was so scared he'd recognize us, I almost fell off my chair."

A waiter brought the coffee they had ordered, and a narghile for David. "We had some good times," David said wistfully.

"In retrospect, perhaps. Some of them weren't much fun at the time."

David looked older, Ramses thought. He did too, he supposed. But some of the lines on his friend's face were those of pain, deeply carved into the skin. He would never be entirely free of it, according to Nefret; the injury he had suffered in 1915 had damaged some of the nerves in his leg, though you'd never have known it from the way he moved. How much it cost him to maintain that even stride Ramses could only guess. He knew better than to ask or commiserate, but his awareness lent greater emphasis to his next statement.

"We're old married men now, and fathers. It's time we gave up the follies of our youth."

David drew the smoke deep into his lungs and let it trickle out. "Not bloody likely we'll be allowed to, with valuable antiquities disappearing from under Cyrus's very nose and a lady who is obviously not what she seems. That's the damnedest story I've ever heard—and I've heard quite a few."

"And lived quite a few. You do believe it really happened, then?"

"Of course it happened."

"Nefret thinks some, if not all, was a hallucination."

"Would you recognize the woman if you saw her again?"

Ramses laughed wryly. "Nefret asked me the same thing. D'you know what I was fool enough to say? I didn't stop to think, I just blurted it out: 'Not her face.'"

David grinned sympathetically. "Her face was veiled."

"That was what I meant. I saw a good deal of the rest of her, but a shapely figure isn't useful for purposes of identification. I was fool enough to say that too. Nefret made a number of blistering remarks."

"She's worried, that's all. So am I. Tell me about Rashad."

"It wasn't he who sent the message."

"How do you know? Do you still have the note?"

It was like old times—too much so. David had always been able to back him into a corner, and he wasn't going to be put off now.

"No, I don't have it," Ramses admitted. "I must have dropped it somewhere along the way. What does it matter? The modus operandi was not typical of Rashad and his lot. He doesn't care much for me, but I can't believe he harbors enough animosity to go to all that trouble. And for what? To get his hands on you?"

"He doesn't like me either," David said. "But taking you hostage would be a damned roundabout way of getting at me. I had no idea he was in Cairo."

"Is that the truth?"

David simply looked at him, his finely arched brows elevated. Ramses's eyes fell. "I'm sorry, David. I know you wouldn't lie to me. But there have been riots and strikes and bloody murder here, and that sort of violence irresistibly reminds me of our old friend Wardani. He's still wanted by the police for collaborating with the enemy during the war, and God knows what he's been up to since."

"Not much," David said calmly.

"Was he behind the rioting this past spring? They killed eight unarmed people in one incident alone, and—"

"That was a spontaneous demonstration protesting Zaghlul Pasha's arrest and deportation."

Ramses made a rude noise, and David said, "Yes, all right. It was murder, bloody and inexcusable, but there was no organized plot, just a lot of poor frustrated fools who were stirred up by a troublemaker. Wardani wasn't involved, and neither were the Turks or the Germans, despite the hysterical accusations of certain officials. Stop lecturing me and listen, will you? Wardani did communicate with me a few months ago. And no, I don't know where he is. Possibly Paris, lurking around the Peace Conference, in the hope that he can worm his way into the proceedings. It's a forlorn hope; Zaghlul Pasha is the accepted leader of the independence movement and Wardani has no influence except with a few isolated radicals."

"Like Rashad."

"Rashad is no revolutionary," David said contemptuously. "All he does is make speeches and then scuttle into hiding. Wardani is intelligent enough to know he has to play politics now, not foment riots. Oh, he lets people like Rashad spout sedition, but I would be very surprised to learn that Rashad is still part of Wardani's organization."

"Then you don't intend to become involved?"

David threw out his hands. His forehead was furrowed. "Damnation, Ramses, I'm an artist—of sorts—not a fighter. I gave Lia my word I would stay away from Wardani. I told him the same thing. I haven't heard from him since. Now can we forget about politics and concentrate on more imminent matters?"

He placed a few coins on the table and rose. "Come on. We're going to look for your exotic prison."

"It will be a waste of time," Ramses warned. David hadn't really answered his question. David wouldn't lie, not to his friend, but he was holding something back, and until he was ready to talk freely, it would be pointless and disloyal to press him.

"One never knows. Let's start with the—what was it?—the Sabil Khalaoun and try to retrace your steps."

The coffeeshop was open and the tiny plaza was filled with people. Three streets, or alleyways, led into it. "Which one?" David asked, acknowledging the salutation of an old acquaintance sitting by the sabil.

They covered the area as methodically as the crooked streets and byways allowed. The tall old houses of Cairo turned the alleys into man-made canyons, dim with shadows, roofed by screened balconies. Women leaned out of windows, calling to passing sellers of food; donkeys jostled them and people brushed past on various errands. The bustling, busy streets were so different from the dark silence of his stumbling flight that they might have been in another city.

Finally David said in exasperation, "Can't you remember a single landmark—a mosque, a shop?"

"I saw plenty of landmarks, including a pyramid and the sails of a felucca," Ramses snapped. "Opium does that. I had just enough wits left to know I was imagining them, but I was too damned busy trying to keep ahead of the fellow who was chasing me to distinguish between reality and hallucination. And no, I didn't mention them to the family. That would have confirmed their belief that the rest of it was also the product of my lurid imagination."

"It wasn't."

"No . . . Hell, David, I'm no longer certain how much of it was real."

"One thing is certain," David said practically. "You were missing for hours and you weren't at the place to which the note directed you. That spells abduction to me." He ducked his head under a tray of bread, carried at shoulder height by a strolling vendor. "Well, it was worth a try. Let's pay a visit to the suk."

"If you plan to question the antika dealers about Cyrus's jewelry, the parents have already done that, without result. They're a good deal better at intimidation than either of us."

"But we are much more charming." David grinned and slapped him on the shoulder.

They went on in single file, under balconies draped with laundry, until they reached the square before the mosque of Hosein.

"What's become of el-Gharbi?" David asked, without preamble.

"Who?" Ramses asked in surprise.

"That perfumed Nubian pimp who controlled the Red Blind district until the British stuck him in the prison camp at—"

"I know who he is," Ramses interrupted. "Who could forget el-Gharbi? What made you think of him?"

"He had a hand in everything illegal that went on in Cairo, and he shared information with you on several occasions."

El-Gharbi was indeed unforgettable: perfumed and jeweled and dressed in a woman's white robes. One couldn't like or admire a man who ran his kind of business, but he had been a kinder master than some. "Yes, he was useful, in his own fashion," Ramses said. "Unfortunately he's no longer in control here. Father got him out of the prison camp, in return for certain favors—it was always tit for tat with el-Gharbi—and he was exiled to his village in Upper Egypt. I suppose he's still there, if he is alive."

"Too bad."

They made the rounds of the more prominent dealers. David explained that he wanted a bracelet for his wife, and ended up with several silver bangles, all of recent Bedouin workmanship. They were shown strings of faded faience "mummy beads," any of which, the merchant explained, could be made into bracelets. He had recognized them and didn't really suppose they would buy the wretched things, but it was worth a try. The Inglizi, even these, were unpredictable.

"I could have told you they wouldn't offer us Cyrus's bracelets," Ramses said. "They know who we are."

"I suppose we haven't time to try our jolly old tourist disguises," David said. He sounded regretful. Ramses laughed, but shook his head. "Put it out of your mind, David."

"Ah, well. Let's have lunch at Bassam's."

"He won't be able to tell us anything."

"But we will have an excellent meal. It will put me in a better frame of mind to spend the evening with Uncle Sethos."

⋙⋘

I EXPECT THE ONLY ONE who looked forward to that celebratory dinner was Sethos himself. I had prepared Walter as best I could, finding him fully recovered physically, if thoroughly bewildered. He took the news of his father's infidelity better than I would have expected—possibly because he, too, had suffered from the coldness of his mother—but despite my assurances that Sethos had redeemed himself by his heroic services to his country and was now reformed, I could see Walter had reservations. (So did I, which may have weakened the effect of my assurances.)

It had been a rather tiring day, especially for those of us who took the children to the Museum. I had determined to accompany them, since I knew Emerson and Walter were likely to become absorbed in some antiquity or other and let the little ones wander off. I lost Davy twice, retrieving him on the second occasion from the interior of a huge granite sarcophagus. (I was tempted to leave him there for a while, since he could not get out of it, but Emerson would not let me.)

At my insistence, we all assumed our most elegant attire and tried to behave as if this were a conventional meeting of long-parted friends and relations. Faultlessly attired in white tie and tails, Sethos was waiting for us when we stepped out of the lift, and swept us into the private dining room he had booked. The table positively glittered with crystal and silver, and there were flowers along its length and at every lady's place. Florid compliments bubbled from his lips; he insisted Emerson take the head of the table, and as soon as we were all seated, corks popped and champagne filled our glasses. Since it was obvious to the dullest wits that Emerson was not about to propose a toast, Sethos did so. "To the King and the loyal hearts who serve him; to love and friendship!" Even Emerson could not refuse to honor that.

As the meal progressed, through course after course, I found it increasingly difficult to stifle my laughter. It may have been the champagne. However, to see the effect of Sethos's performance on various persons entertained me a great deal. He had set himself to win them over, and no one could do it better. Dear Evelyn, who would have forgiven Genghis Khan had he expressed repentance, succumbed at once to his charm, and Lia was visibly fascinated. He praised Walter's philological work, citing examples to prove he was thoroughly conversant with it; he spoke admiringly of Emerson's accomplishments—and mine—and paid tribute to the heroism of the younger generation.

"They are the children of the storm," he declared. "The storm has passed, thanks to their sacrifice—not only the young men who risked, and gave, their lives, but the gallant women who suffered the even greater pain of waiting and of loss."

Evelyn's eyes filled with tears. Nothing could have been more graceful than the acknowledgment of the death of her son in battle. Even Emerson appeared moved. The only face that did not soften was that of Ramses, though the tribute had obviously been meant for him and David as well. He glanced at me, his eyebrows tilted skeptically.

Before long, Emerson began to fidget. It was impossible to carry on what he would have called a sensible discussion—that is, a discussion about Egyptology—at a dinner party, and I could see he was itching to interrogate Sethos about quite a number of things. However—thanks to my frowns and winks and piercing looks—he contained himself until the last course had been removed before remarking in a loud voice, "This has been very pleasant, no doubt, but let us get down to business. I want to know . . . Oh. Er. Amelia, did you happen to mention to Walter—"

"If you are referring to the theft of Cyrus's artifacts, she did," Walter said cheerfully. "A pity. But I daresay Amelia will solve the case soon." He finished the last of his wine and gestured to the waiter.

"Hmph," said Emerson. "Walter, you have had quite enough to drink. Either go to bed or pay attention."

"Then I will go to bed." Flushed and smiling, he rose, and of course Evelyn rose too. "Good night, all. And thank you for a most enjoyable evening, uh—er—brother."

After they had left the room I suggested that perhaps we ought not discuss the matters Emerson was determined to discuss in the presence of the waiters. Resuming his chair, Sethos shrugged.

"I have nothing of importance to report."

Emerson's scowl indicated he was not willing to accept this, so Sethos elaborated. "I went the rounds this afternoon. As I already knew, my chief lieutenants were gone."

"Gone," I exclaimed. "Do you mean—"

"Several of them died in France. Do you remember René? He was killed in the first week of the war."

I did not conceal my distress. I had liked the young Frenchman. He had been a criminal and a thief, but he had been a gentleman.

"Your admirer Sir Edward is alive and well," Sethos assured me. "Never mind the others; suffice it to say they are out of the picture. The rank and file also suffered attrition. Without my guidance they grew careless and paid the penalty. A few of the antiquities dealers with whom I was acquainted are still in business, but they were never permanent members of the organization. To sum it up—and I hope I may be allowed to do so, since Nefret has been swallowing her yawns for several minutes—I can think of no one in Cairo to whom Martinelli might have taken the objects."

"Can we believe that?" Emerson asked bluntly.

"You will have to" was the equally brusque reply. "There are certain persons with whom I had private dealings, but they are scattered, some in Europe, some in America, some elsewhere in the Middle East. I will continue my inquiries, but not just now. I must return to Constantinople tomorrow. My business there was unfinished."

"I don't suppose you would care to tell us what it is," I said.

"You are, as always, correct, Amelia," said Sethos, his smile broadening.

"Then we will say good night," I said, cutting off Emerson's incipient protest.

I had no intention of letting Sethos get away so easily. Thinking that he might speak more openly if the others were not present, I sent them off to their rooms—getting an extremely fishy look from Ramses—and turned to my brother-in-law.

He anticipated me, as he so often did. "Yes, Amelia, we have a few things to say to each other."

"And to me," said Emerson, who, as I hardly need mention, had stood motionless as a rock when I dismissed the children.

"Quite," Sethos agreed. "Let us find a cozy corner."

We found one, in the Moorish Hall. The surroundings were seductive, shadowy nooks and dim lamps, but Sethos did not waste time in idle conversation. "If you will take my advice, you will get out of Cairo as soon as possible."

"I had come to the same conclusion," I informed him.

"Curse it," exclaimed Emerson, who was, in the vernacular, spoiling for a fight, it didn't much matter with whom. Being around Sethos for any length of time has that effect on him. "When did you conclude that, Peabody? Don't tell me you've been talking to Abdullah again."

Sethos's well-shaped eyebrows shot up. "I beg your pardon?"

"She dreams about him," Emerson said. "I am a reasonable individual; I have no objection to my wife having long intimate conversations with a man she—er—greatly admired. What the devil, I was fond of the old fellow too. I do object to her passing off her own opinions as those of a dead man."

"I am surprised to find you so dogmatic, Radcliffe," said Sethos. " 'There are more things in heaven and earth—' "

"Bah," said Emerson. "And don't call me Radcliffe."

Sethos's lips twitched. "I will endeavor not to do so. But I expect Amelia, like myself, came to her decision after rational consideration. I've been thinking about that strange adventure of Ramses. It worries me."

"You gave the impression of being amused and incredulous, not worried," Emerson said, scowling.

"I couldn't resist teasing the boy a little. He does take life so seriously! It is conceivable that some—shall we say 'lady'?—has developed a tendresse for him and has taken a somewhat unorthodox method of getting his attention. Like certain other members of the family—modesty and consideration for the feelings of my dear brother prevent me from naming them—he appears to have a considerable attraction for women."

"Balderdash!" Emerson exclaimed.

Sethos shrugged and became serious. "The alternative isn't so harmless. Your son hasn't been idle these past few years; he has annoyed almost as many people as I have—the Turks, the Senussi, the Nationalists, even a few people in our own service. David isn't in the clear either; he is known to the police as a member of one of the nationalist groups. Civil unrest could break out again at any time, and if it does, he'll be one of the first to be suspected."

"Surely not!" I exclaimed. "His services to England during the war—"

"Put him at additional risk. Though his activities are not known to the rank and file, they are known to high-ranking members of the service, and it wouldn't surprise me to learn they hope to make use of him. Some of the members of his former organization are at large, and they regard him as a traitor to the cause. Is it only a coincidence, do you suppose, that Ramses was abducted the day before David was due back in Egypt?"

"It cannot have been a case of mistaken identity," Emerson protested.

"I said I couldn't explain it. There may be no connection. In any case, the boys will be safer in Luxor."

Emerson fingered the cleft in his chin, and looked enviously at his brother's beard. He still resented my refusal to allow him to have one. "I sincerely hope so," he grunted. "But—"

"I will follow you in a few days," Sethos said.

"Your word on it?" I asked.

"My word on it. Barring unforeseen accidents."

"What are you—"

"Good night, Amelia. Good night, brother."

I HAD INDEED ARRIVED AT my conclusion by strictly rational means—for I include in that category the deductions of the unconscious mind, which some persons (I name no names) dismiss as intuition. My occasional dreams about Abdullah, who had sacrificed his life for mine, might have been regarded as products of the unconscious; but they were strange dreams, as vivid and consistent as encounters with a living friend. I had not dreamed of him for some time, but I did so that night.

We met always at the same place—the heights above Deir el Bahri, on the path that leads to the Valley of the Kings—and at the same time—daybreak, as the rising sun drives away the darkness and fills the valley with light.

He had not changed since I began dreaming of him (which I suppose is not surprising). Tall and stalwart, his beard black as that of a man in the prime of life, he greeted me as if we had met only recently, and in the flesh.

"You must go to Luxor at once."

"I intend to," I said somewhat irritably. "I would waste my breath, I suppose, by asking you to explain. You enjoy your enigmatic hints too much."

"Because," said Abdullah, "there is trouble there."

"I am well aware of it."

Abdullah waved this away with an impatient gesture. "Not the theft of Vandergelt Effendi's treasure. That is part of it, but only the least part. Watch over the children."

I reached for him, gripping his arms tightly. "Good God, Abdullah, don't be enigmatic about that, of all things. If the children are in danger, I must know how they are threatened and why."

He smiled, his teeth white against the blackness of his beard. "If I knew I would tell you, even if it meant breaking the commandments that control me here. I see danger to all of you—there is nothing new in that!—and they are unable to protect themselves. Guard them closely and they will be safe."

"You may be certain I will. And you—you will watch over them too?"

"Over all of you. You have not visited my tomb recently."

"Why, no," I said, surprised at the change of subject. "When we get back to Luxor—"

"Yes, you will go there and bring the others. Take my grandson's son, my namesake, to pay his respects. I think you will be surprised at what you find, Sitt."

Gently he removed my clinging hands and turned away. His final words were not addressed to me; they were the old querulous grumble, as if he were thinking aloud. "She is not careful. She takes foolish chances. I will do my best, but she would tax even the powers of a sheikh."

I stood where he had left me, watching him stride along the path toward the Valley. "What do you mean?" I called, knowing I would receive no answer. Nor did I. Abdullah looked back at me and smiled. Raising one arm, he beckoned me to follow—not then, along that well-known path, but back to Thebes.

THE REST OF THE FAMILY readily accepted my decision, which, of course, I framed as a suggestion. Before we left, we made arrangements to send the youthful nurserymaid back to England. Even on the voyage out she had admitted she was homesick, and she did not like Egypt at all. It must have been the hurly-burly and shouting at the railroad station that frightened her, since she had seen almost nothing else of the country. So I found a respectable family who were returning to England and who were happy to have her care for their children. The last thing we needed was another helpless innocent on our hands, and as soon as we reached Luxor, Lia would have all the enthusiastic help she wanted. Every woman in the family—I speak of our Egyptian family—was itching to get her hands on David's little ones.

We took the evening train. All those who travel with small children prefer this schedule, since there is a chance they will sleep through part of the journey. From the haggard looks of her parents next morning, I deduced that Evvie had not. It hadn't taken me long to realize she was something of a handful, with an explosive temper that belied her dainty looks. No doubt she had been badly spoiled; her parents and her grandparents on the maternal side were gentle souls. I looked forward to seeing how she would get on with the twins. Neither of them could be called a gentle soul. I was a trifle concerned about Dolly, who had taken on the role of protector of his little sister and whose equable temper would no doubt be sorely tried in the days to come. Such is life, however. I would do all I could to defend him.

I had not reported Abdullah's warning to the others. They would not have taken it seriously, and indeed some might consider it only the expression of the natural concern felt by an adult who is responsible for the weak and irresponsible. It was infinitely reassuring to see the entire family waiting for us at the station in Luxor. Daoud and Selim were there, Kadija's loving impatience had overcome her timidity, Basima hovered in the background. Sennia and Gargery waved and shouted greetings. With those stalwart aides and the others who awaited us at the house, the children's every movement would be watched.

"Where are the twins?" was Evelyn's first question.

"We don't take them anywhere unless we have to, madam," said Gargery gloomily.

Evelyn looked a little shocked. "Certainly not into a mob like this," I added. "Goodness, what a crush. I have never seen so many people here."

My first impulse was to put an end to the demonstration for fear of its upsetting the children. I reminded myself that I was not in charge of them. They were being passed round from eager hand to eager hand, but they seemed none the worse for it. Evvie was giggling at an obviously infatuated Daoud, and Dolly, solemn and wide-eyed, shyly returned Kadija's embrace. So I stood a little aside and found myself next to Bertie, who had come to represent his family.

"Mother and Cyrus decided not to add to the confusion," he said with a smile. "They hope you will dine with us this evening—a simple gathering of old friends, nothing formal."

"I believe I can speak for all when I accept with pleasure, Bertie." I lowered my voice and then had to repeat the question in louder tones, the noise was so great. "Has there been any news of—er—"

"No. You learned nothing?"

"We would have telegraphed Cyrus at once had we found the jewelry. One or two little matters of interest did occur, but . . . My dear boy, why the wild-eyed stare?"

"I beg your pardon, ma'am. It's just that your little matters of interest are often what others might call narrow escapes or close calls. What has happened? Is Ramses—"

"It usually is Ramses, isn't it? As you see, he is perfectly fit. We will tell you all about it this evening, Bertie. May I take the liberty of bringing Selim? He and the others have been fully briefed on the situation. I don't suppose poor Cyrus is capable of discussing anything else."

"Selim is always welcome, of course," Bertie said. "And you are right about Cyrus. He prides himself on his spotless reputation, and he feels it is in jeopardy."

"Nothing of the sort," I said firmly. "We'll get him out of this with his reputation not only intact but enhanced. Tell him I said so, and that we will see you all this evening."

CHAPTER FOUR

By the time we had the luggage sorted out and got it and ourselves across the river, the sun had passed the zenith. I decreed a light repast and a rest for our visitors, particularly the oldest and youngest of them. Evvie was borne off, howling, by her mother and Kadija, with Dolly trotting anxiously after them. The others dispersed, until only Emerson and I were left with the three younger men, who had settled down on the veranda and were engaged in animated conversation. What fine-looking young fellows they were, all three! The family resemblance between David and his uncle Selim was strong, and Ramses might have been kin to both, with his bronzed complexion and black curls.

As I watched them with a fond smile I realized that Emerson was watching them too, but with calculation predominating over fondness. Rubbing his hands, he declared, "It is still early. What do you say we go to the site?"

"Leave them alone, Emerson," I said firmly.

"But, Peabody, I want—"

"I know what you want. For pity's sake, give them this afternoon to enjoy one another's company before you put them to work. Is it not delightful to see them so friendly together?"

"Hmph," said Emerson. "Well . . ."

"Run along, Emerson."

"Where?"

"Anywhere you like, so long as you do not disturb their privacy."

Emerson thought it over. "Where has Sennia got to? I might give her an archaeology lesson."

"I am sure she will play with you, Emerson, if you ask nicely."

Grinning, Emerson went into the house, and I approached the boys. Their heads were close together, and solemnity had replaced their laughter. "Is there anything I can get you?" I asked, as they rose to greet me. "Coffee? Tea?"

"No, thank you, Mother," Ramses said.

After a moment, David said, "Won't you sit down, Aunt Amelia?"

"I would not want to disturb you, my dear."

"Not at all," said Ramses. The corners of his mouth turned up a trifle. "Take this chair, Mother. Would you like a cigarette?"

David had taken out his pipe and Selim a cigarette; so, in order to put them at ease, I accepted. "What is this I hear about Abdullah becoming a holy man?" I asked, attempting to blow out a smoke ring. The attempt was not successful. I had not yet got the trick of it, probably because I did not indulge often in tobacco. Every art requires practice.

"How did you find out about that?" David asked. "Ramses said he hadn't mentioned it to you or the Professor."

I turned a mildly reproachful look upon my son, who immediately began to invent excuses. "So much else has happened . . . it didn't seem important . . . at the time."

"At the time," I repeated slowly.

Selim remarked, rolling his black eyes, "It was my father who told you? In a dream?"

Fearing skepticism (which I got, especially from Emerson), I had told only a few about my strange dreams of Abdullah, but I was not surprised that the story had spread. Fatima and Gargery were both accomplished eavesdroppers, and either would have passed on the information as a matter of general interest. Once Daoud got hold of the tale, all Luxor would know.

"As a matter of fact, I heard the news from Daoud," I said. "Was that what you were discussing? You looked very serious. And what did you mean, Ramses, by 'at the time'? Has something happened to alter your view?"

Ramses blew out a perfect smoke ring, eyeing me thoughtfully. David laughed. "There's no use trying to hide anything from her, Ramses. Why should we, anyhow? It's only an odd coincidence. A pity about Hassan, but I expect he died happy."

"Died!" I exclaimed. "Hassan, Munifa's husband? When? How?"

"Didn't Abdullah tell you about him?" Ramses inquired. "Hassan was the one responsible for Abdullah's new status; he proclaimed himself servant of the sheikh, and took charge of Abdullah's tomb. The idea was quick to catch on. People began going there to bring offerings and pray for favors. Hassan was happy, or so he seemed, when I saw him last. He was found dead two days ago, by an early-rising pilgrim."

"We buried him that night," Selim said. "It was his heart, Sitt."

"How do you know? Did a doctor examine him?"

"What need? There was no mark upon him and his face was peaceful. He was not a young man, Sitt Hakim."

"I am sorry." I spoke the truth. Hassan had been with us for years, a loyal workman and a merry companion. "I expect you will want to visit Abdullah's tomb one day soon, David. You will be pleased, I am sure, at how well your plans were carried out. I will go with you, if you don't mind."

"Yes, Aunt Amelia. Lia and I have spoken of it."

"You might take Dolly, too."

David's fine dark eyes widened. "D'you really think we ought? A bit morbid for a little chap like him, isn't it?"

"Not at all. To hear of his great-grandfather's courage and noble character will be an inspiration. I promised—"

I stopped myself, somewhat abruptly, and rose. "I must be about my duties. Don't get up, boys."

They did anyhow. I had of course trained all of them in proper manners, but I suspected Ramses was looming on purpose and looking down his nose at me. I smiled, and patted him on the shoulder. "You will always be boys to me," I informed him.

As I went about my varied tasks, my mind kept returning to Hassan's death. One could not even call it a coincidence; when he died, as he was bound to do one day, the odds were that the event would occur at Abdullah's tomb, since that was where Hassan spent most of his time. What puzzled me was why he should have chosen to spend his declining years in holy works. Until the death of his wife he had practiced hedonism insofar as the bounds of his religion allowed—and occasionally beyond them.

Ah well, I thought, religious fervor is inexplicable except to the one who feels it, and a good many individuals seek the comfort of religion in old age. Hassan would probably have agreed wholeheartedly with Saint Augustine, who asked God to forgive him for his sins—but not until after he was finished committing them.

One might have supposed that Abdullah would have mentioned Hassan's death. He had made rather a point of our visiting the tomb, but he had not said why. That was just like Abdullah, though—he delighted in hints and provocative statements. He always claimed he was restricted by the undefined rules of whatever afterlife he presently enjoyed, but I couldn't help suspecting some of his reticence was designed to tease me.

We were to have tea at four, since Fatima was determined to provide such a lavish repast as had never been seen in that house. She had half a dozen haggard young women helping her in the kitchen; when I put my nose in, she told me to go away. One does not argue with Fatima when she is in one of her rare bullying moods, so I went.

FROM MANUSCRIPT H

Seated on the settee with his wife on one side and his mother on the other, Ramses felt like Ulysses trying to steer a course midway between Scylla and Charybdis. Not that either of the ladies he loved resembled those mythical monsters, but they both had decided opinions on the subject of child-raising, and those opinions did not always agree. When they disagreed, they appealed to him.

The spacious veranda was crowded with so many of them there— the adults lined up along the walls and on the ledge, the children playing in the center. He supposed it could be called playing. They had stood staring at one another until Davy, nudged by Nefret, offered Evvie a carved wooden giraffe and a long, incomprehensible greeting.

"He can't talk," said Evvie, who could, and did incessantly. "Can the other one?"

"She is your cousin Charlotte," Lia said, with an embarrassed glance at Nefret. "It isn't polite to call her 'the other one.'"

"Then who is this one?" Evvie inquired.

"He is named after your papa," said Nefret. "You may call him Davy."

Little gentleman that he was, Dolly introduced himself and his sister, and offered to shake hands. Charla's emphatic dark eyebrows had drawn together in a scowl that was comically like that of her grandfather. It cleared temporarily as she responded to Dolly's friendly gesture; then Evvie held out a hand to Davy and showed several small pearly teeth in a smile. "I like this one," she announced.

Struck dumb, and bedazzled by fat honey-colored curls, dimples, and dainty features, Davy pressed the giraffe into her hand and invited her, with an expansive gesture, to join him on the floor, where the rest of the menagerie had been arranged. This did not sit well with Charla. The wooden animals—which included a lion, a hippopotamus, and an improbable elephant—had been carved by a Sudanese living in Luxor, and for the moment at least they were the twins' favorite toys.

Luckily no one understood what Charla said. "Wouldn't you and Evvie like a biscuit?" Ramses asked quickly.

All in all, it didn't go too badly. The only actual casualty was Dolly, who, in the way of all peacemakers, got a sharp blow on the face when he tried to settle an argument between the two little girls over a doll. It had no hair, since Charla always stripped her dolls of clothing and wigs as soon as she got them; in the struggle it lost an arm and both legs and Evvie hit her brother with one of the legs. She may not have meant to.

His big eyes bright with tears, Dolly was swept up by Emerson, who had watched the whole business with a fatuous grin. He gave the little boy a hug and then handed him over to his wife and got down on the floor, where he helped the other three finish dismembering the doll, talking all the while about the process of mummification.

"The Egyptians didn't take the heads off," he explained to his rapt audience. "They shoved a hook here." He demonstrated, with a long forefinger. "Here, deep into—"

"Father," Nefret murmured. "Please."

"Children love mummies," said her mother-in-law—who probably would have objected if Nefret had not done so first. She was cuddling Dolly in a way that aroused Ramses's direst forebodings. He was a dear little fellow, and she had been utterly devoted to his namesake, so it was not surprising that she should take him under her wing. He hoped Nefret would see it that way. Up to this time the twins had had no rivals for the attention of their paternal grandparents. With four children, and one of them Evvie, he saw trouble ahead.

The only ones who did justice to Fatima's superb tea were his uncle Walter and David, both of whom had apparently decided to leave the discipline to their wives, and, of course, the children, whom Emerson stuffed with cakes and biscuits. Feeling somewhat stifled by motherhood, Ramses got up and went to sit on the ledge next to David.

"How do you do it?" he asked.

David never had to ask what he meant. He glanced at the juvenile maelstrom, which had expanded to include Horus. The cat was fascinated by small children, but his attempt to creep under the settee, whence he could observe them unmolested, had been a failure; only Emerson's brisk intervention saved him from the fate of the doll.

"They'll settle down," David said lazily. His artist's eyes dwelled lovingly on the long stretch of golden pale desert, fringed by the green of the cultivation and canopied by the blue-gray of twilight. He threw his arm round Ramses's shoulders and sighed deeply. "God, it's good to be back!"

"I hope you feel the same tomorrow morning when Father rousts you out at daybreak and drags you off to Deir el Medina."

David laughed and flexed his hands. "I've been looking forward to it for years. What's this project of Cyrus's?"

"He's got several in mind. He wants to produce a series of volumes on the tomb paintings of Deir el Medina. Some of them are quite marvelous, you know, and they've never been copied properly. First, though, I expect he'll want you to paint some of the artifacts from the princesses' tomb. Black-and-white photographs can't begin to do them justice. There's a beaded robe that will make your eyes bulge."

"I can hardly wait to see the collection." David sobered. "Is there anything more we can do to trace the missing jewelry?"

"You know what Luxor is like," Ramses said with a shrug. "News of unusual objects spreads, and Selim knows everyone in Luxor. He hasn't heard a thing. We have to take Sethos's word for it that he learned nothing in Cairo. If he failed, we can't hope to succeed. We've done all we can."

"Perhaps if I talked to some of the dealers here—"

"We've done all we can," Ramses repeated vehemently. "Damn it, David, I hate to sound selfish, but I wish we could forget distractions and concentrate on our work."

"What about the veiled lady?"

"I thought we had agreed to forget that business."

"I've had a new idea," David said. "I can't think how to put this . . ."

"I believe I can." Ramses had known this was coming, but that didn't mean he liked it. He ran his fingers through his hair. "Is there a woman in my past, seduced and callously abandoned, who wants revenge? That's what you're thinking, isn't it?"

"You had better lower your voice," David said coolly. "Nefret is looking at us. I did not and do not think that."

"She does."

"Has she said so?"

"No." Ramses got his temper under control. "In a way, I wish she would. There's a quality in Nefret's silences that is worse than a direct accusation."

"I know exactly what you mean," David said feelingly. "It's a woman's most effective weapon. If you deny guilt before you've been accused, they regard it as tantamount to a confession. Look here, Ramses, I know you never behaved dishonorably with any woman, but not all women are as reasonable as we men. Are you sure you can't think of someone who might harbor *unreasonable* resentment?"

"No. And don't ask me to go through the list name by name."

"All right, I won't." David's eyes were bright with amusement. "Just give the theory some thought."

His daughter, denied another biscuit (she had already eaten six) let out an ear-splitting roar. David winced. "We'll talk about it another time. I'd better help Lia cage the lion for the night."

The children were carried off, in various stages of protest, and the rest of them dispersed to change.

"What were you and David talking about?" Nefret asked casually.

If there was one thing marriage had taught him, it was that he had better have a quick, sensible answer to a loaded question. "He was concerned about the missing jewelry. Wondered if there were anything he could do."

"Is there?" Nefret sat down and removed her shoes and stockings.

"I can't think what. Selim has already covered the rumor mills."

"Was that all?"

Ramses finished undressing, with more haste than neatness. "We discussed future plans. I'll bathe first, if that's all right with you."

"Go ahead."

Once in the bath, he cursed himself for turning tail when he might have brought the subject into the open and fought it out. David's theory had occurred to him, but he had been reluctant to consider it seriously. The confounded woman hadn't injured him or indicated any intention of doing so. What she had done was embarrass him and get him in trouble with his wife. That was the sort of thing—wasn't it?—that some women might consider an appropriate revenge for a fancied injury.

Dolly Bellingham, for example? He had only been sixteen and perhaps he hadn't been awfully tactful in his efforts to elude her determined pursuit. She was selfish and vain, and she might blame him for her father's death. With good reason, he thought wryly. But was she clever enough to plan such a complex, malicious scheme and had she the resources to carry it out? He had no idea what had become of her.

Christabel? The idea of that dedicated suffragette undulating about in the robes of Hathor, murmuring sweet nothings, was so ludicrous he laughed aloud. They had not parted on the friendliest of terms, but she wasn't the sort to abandon her cause for a petty revenge. What about . . .

The door opened to admit Nefret. He started guiltily, snatched a towel and fled, mumbling apologies for being so long. Had he really been lolling in the bath running over the list of his . . . conquests, some might call them? In his own defense he could truthfully claim that a good many of them had been one-sided and unconsummated. Except for Enid and Layla and one or two others . . . three or four others . . . No. It was a ridiculous theory, and he wouldn't think about it again.

THE SUNSET CALLS OF THE muezzins died into silence and the skies darkened as they drove along the path to the Castle. Selim arrived a few moments later, while they were getting out of the carriages. He made a dashing figure in his flowing robes, astride his favorite stallion; in the crimson glow of the torches that lit the courtyard he was a picture of pure romance, and he obviously knew it. Evelyn exclaimed in admiration, and Lia applauded. Selim grinned complacently.

"Well-timed, Selim," Ramses said.

Selim swung himself out of the saddle and handed the reins to one of Cyrus's stablemen. "I should have come earlier or later. Someone shot at me."

Exclamations of alarm and concern arose, especially from the newcomers. Having got the sensation he desired, Selim put on an air of manly indifference. "I am not hurt. It did not touch me."

"Those damned-fool hunters, I presume," said Emerson, unimpressed. "They go out at twilight to shoot jackals. There are more of them than there were in the old days, Walter, and some of them shouldn't be trusted with a weapon."

"Dear me," said his brother in alarm. "Isn't that dangerous?"

"Dangerous, no. Annoying, yes. Just don't go for a quiet stroll at twilight near the Valley or the Ramesseum."

"Come on in, folks," Cyrus called from the doorway of the house. "Welcome! It's great to have you back."

While Cyrus was shaking hands all round, Selim beckoned Ramses aside.

"One does not wish to frighten the women," he began in a low voice.

"Frighten my mother?"

"The Sitt Hakim fears neither man nor beast nor demon of the night," said Selim, adapting one of Daoud's sayings about Emerson. "But someone should speak to the police about the hunters, Ramses. They are becoming careless."

He held out his arms, stretching the fabric of his outer garment. The light was poor, but Ramses knew what to look for. There were several holes. When Selim lowered his arms, the fabric fell into graceful folds, and the rents overlapped. One bullet. But it had passed dangerously close to Selim's side.

"I'll have a word with Father," Ramses promised. "And you be more careful."

The gathering was informal; in deference to Emerson's well-known dislike of evening kit, Cyrus wore one of his elegant white linen suits. Bertie was looking more and more like one of the minor poets, with a scarf draped round his neck and, on this occasion, a blue velvet coat and a pensive expression.

The pleasure with which Cyrus had greeted them soon passed, however, and his long face relapsed into lines like those of a mournful hound. As Ramses had expected, his mother didn't allow that state of affairs to continue.

"Now, Cyrus, it is high time you got a proper perspective on this business," she said, briskly buttering a roll. "It is not really that important."

"Not important!" Cyrus cried in anguished tones. "But I—"

"There are literally hundreds of objects in the collection, Cyrus, including other bracelets and several pectorals. After a single visit M.

Lacau cannot claim to remember every one of them. It would be his word against ours."

Her tone was so matter-of-fact that for a moment the preposterous suggestion almost made sense. Emerson stared at his wife. "Good Gad, Peabody, you can't be serious. That would be . . . Hmmm."

"It would be extremely difficult as well as thoroughly unethical," Ramses said, alarmed by the look of dawning speculation on his father's face. "We would have to alter all the records—there are dozens of references to those pieces, all methodically cross-indexed. Your reputation would be seriously damaged, Cyrus, if we were caught trying to play a trick like that. As it is, you have preserved for Egypt and the world a spectacular find, giving unstintingly of your energy and your wealth. Not even Lacau can hold you accountable for the venality of an employee. That sort of thing happens all the time." He added, "Mother was making one of her little jokes. Weren't you, Mother?"

She met his accusatory look with a bland smile. "A little joke is never out of place. You have put the case very nicely, my dear."

"Do you think Lacau will see it that way?" Cyrus asked, looking a little less tragic.

"If he does not," said Emerson, "I will point out a few embarrassing incidents involving the Service des Antiquités. Good Gad, their own storage magazines have been robbed, and as for the Museum—"

"Yes, Father, we know what you think of the Museum," Nefret said.

Emerson was not to be repressed. "Our mummy," he growled. "The one we found in Tetisheri's tomb. They lost it, you know. Lost it!"

"We do know, Emerson," said his wife. "You have presented an excellent argument, and I feel sure it will make an impression upon M. Lacau. Anyhow . . ." She paused to nibble daintily on a slice of tomato. "Anyhow, he won't be back for several weeks. Something may yet turn up!"

After dinner they went upstairs to view the collection. It took Cyrus several minutes to open the door; there were two new locks, one of them a padlock heavy enough to have anchored a small boat. Meeting Ramses's quizzical eye, Cyrus smiled sheepishly.

"Locking the barn door after the horse has been stolen, I reckon."

"Not at all, sir. Martinelli had the key to the other lock. One must presume he still has it."

"Wherever the son of a . . . gun is."

"How many other people have been let in?"

"Not as many as wanted in," Cyrus replied, tugging at his goatee. "You know what it's like when you've found something unusual. For a while I was getting requests from every tourist who arrived in Luxor, all claiming to be old friends of mine or friends of my old friends, or of some important person. I turned most of 'em down. There were a few I couldn't refuse, though—those that had letters of introduction from Lacau, and colleagues like Howard Carter . . . Say. You aren't suggesting that one of them had a hand in the theft?"

"I don't see how," Ramses admitted.

A question from Lia called Cyrus away, leaving Ramses to wonder what had prompted him to ask about visitors. Even if one of them had yielded to temptation, he (or she) wouldn't have found it easy to pocket an object under Cyrus's very nose, and the timing made Martinelli's guilt certain. Yet the limited extent of the theft was more in line with an attack of kleptomania than the work of a professional thief who had had access to the entire collection and plenty of time in which to operate. A good many of the smaller items could be safely transported, including the rest of the jewelry, and they wouldn't take up much space if properly packed.

But if a lucky amateur had been responsible, then what had become of the Italian?

Cyrus expanded with pride as the newcomers exclaimed over the dazzling exhibition. Perhaps David was the only one who fully appreciated the effort that had gone into preserving the pieces. He had helped with the clearance of Tetisheri's tomb and been actively involved in restoring many of the artifacts. Walter inspected the other objects appreciatively but casually before gravitating to the inlaid coffins.

"The standard inscriptions," he said to Ramses. "No papyri except the Books of the Dead?"

"No, sir, but there's plenty of inscribed material from the village itself—ostraca and scraps of papyrus. A few weeks ago we came across an astonishing cache of papyri—it might almost have been someone's private library, thrown into a pit and covered over by a descendant who wasn't a reader. There appear to be parts of a medical book and several literary texts, among other things. I've been trying to find the time to work on them, but . . ."

His uncle's thin face broke into a smile. "I understand. Well, my boy, perhaps I can lend a hand. A medical text, you say?"

Emerson, whose hearing was annoyingly acute when one hoped he wasn't listening, strode up to them. "Never mind the cursed texts, they will keep. I need you both on the dig. Unless you have forgotten everything I taught you about excavation technique, Walter."

"It's been a long time" was the mild response.

"You'll soon pick it up again," Emerson declared.

Before they left, Emerson had settled everything to his own satisfaction. "Everybody at Deir el Medina tomorrow morning, eh?" He didn't wait for answers.

I TRY TO AVOID CONTRADICTING Emerson's dogmatic pronouncements in public. It is ill-mannered, and although a good brisk argument never bothers me—or, to do him justice, Emerson—it upsets some members of the family. However, I had no intention of allowing him to brush aside the needs and interests of his staff so dictatorially. I had not realized, until I overheard the conversation between Walter and Ramses about the masses of ostraca we had found, how badly Ramses wanted to get at those texts. Like his uncle, he was primarily interested in the ancient language and its literature. The eager note in his voice, the brightness of his eyes were those of an excited boy. Those eyes were somewhat sunken, however; he must have been sitting up half the night, every night, over the ostraca, after putting in a long day at the site. That could not be good for his health—or, come to think of it, his marriage. The instincts of a mother informed me that I had failed him. I ought to have stood up to his father. Emerson takes a good deal of standing up to.

I would have to stand up for Walter, too. And for Cyrus. In a few weeks the majority of the objects from the tomb would be removed to the Museum. Heaven alone knew how they would survive the transport and the handling they would receive in Cairo. Now was the time to make copies, and the opportunity to avail ourselves of the skills of two trained artists was not to be missed.

I did not doubt that Emerson had also decided to ignore other, more serious, matters. M. Lacau had not questioned Martinelli's antecedents when Cyrus hired the latter, but now that he had turned out to be a cunning thief, Lacau might well inquire why we had employed a restorer who was unknown to the Department of Antiquities. Sethos might turn up at any minute, in some guise or other, to make a nuisance of himself. Then there was that strange encounter of Ramses's. I had formulated a little theory about it, which I meant to investigate when I found the time.

I raised several of these issues with Emerson after we had retired to our room that night. One after the other he pooh-poohed them. One after the other I demolished his arguments. We ended up nose to nose, shouting at each other. Emerson shouted because he had lost his temper, whereas I raised my voice only because I had to do so in order to be heard.

"So how do you explain the veiled lady?" I demanded.

"I don't see why the devil I should have to!"

"Are you indifferent to a threat to your son's life?"

I had known that would fetch him. The angry color faded from his face. "Peabody," he said in plaintive tones, "from what I have been able to gather about that encounter, she did not threaten Ramses with anything except—er—um. It may have been meant as a joke."

"Joke? Really, Emerson!"

"The word was ill-chosen," Emerson admitted, fingering the cleft in his chin. "Damnation, Peabody, you know what I mean. Sethos suggested it the other evening. Some lunatic female has taken a fancy to the boy. Egypt is full of people like that," Emerson went on sweepingly. "Believers in mystical religions, reincarnation, the wisdom of the ancients, and that sort of rot. We've run into a number of them over the years."

There *had* been a number of them, including Madame Berengeria, who claimed to have been wedded to Emerson in not one but several past lives, and poor confused Miss Murgatroyd, a theosophist and believer in reincarnation. (I should add, in justice to my sex, that the delusion was not limited to females.) If Emerson was correct, the woman need not have been anyone with whom we were previously acquainted.

"Admit it, Peabody, that is the most logical explanation," Emerson went on. "It is unlikely that she would follow us to Luxor, and Ramses is even more unlikely to fall into a similar trap. I will watch over the boy, as I always do. Why the devil won't you let me get on with my work?"

"But you do agree that the others are entitled to get on with the work that interests them? Walter is a philologist, not an excavator; Ramses is itching to get at those ostraca. Evelyn and David—"

"Can draw every bloody artifact in Cyrus's collection, if that is what you want. I don't know why I bother arguing with you," Emerson muttered. He began removing his garments and tossing them round the room. "You always win."

"My dear, with us it is not a question of winning or losing." I sat down at my dressing table, took the pins from my hair and shook it out. "We are always of one mind, are we not? I am, as you have so often told me, the other half of yourself—the voice of your own conscience and sense of fair play."

Emerson came up behind me and gathered my loosened hair into his hands. "The better half of myself is what you mean. Well, my love, you may be right. You have not yet won me over completely, but if you care to try another sort of persuasion . . ."

I was more than happy to do so. Emerson's fits of temper are particularly becoming to him.

I had it all worked out, so when we met for breakfast I explained their duties to the persons concerned. The presence of all four of the children and both of the cats was somewhat distracting, but I persevered. "Cyrus awaits you at the Castle, Evelyn," I said, returning to Davy the boiled egg he had handed me. "He would like you to begin, I believe, with the ornamentation on the robe. I trust that is agreeable to you? Good. I—that is, we—Emerson and I—offered him David's services for several hours each afternoon, subject, of course, to David's approval . . . ? Good. Walter, you will want to have a look at the site, but it would be inadvisable for you to put in a full day until after you have become reacclimated. Is that not so? Yes. If you feel up to it, you may work on the inscribed material after luncheon. Ramses will show you how far he has got, won't you, my boy? Yes. Lia, dear, the Great Cat of Re only scratches when he is cornered. Evvie appears to have cornered him. Perhaps you had better . . . Thank you.

"I believe," I continued, as the children's parents and Fatima pulled them out from under various pieces of furniture and attempted to scrape them off, "that except on special occasions the children might take breakfast by themselves from now on. We are going to be late."

This was a little hard on Dolly, whose manners were impeccable. However, I felt sure he would prefer to be with the others.

If I may say so, we made a handsome party as we set out on horseback. The animals, progeny of a pair of fine Arabians given to Ramses and David some years back, were splendid beasts. Ramses bestrode his great stallion with easy grace, and Nefret was no less at home in the saddle. Walter kept up better than I had expected; when I commended him he informed me that he had been in the habit of riding each day to prepare himself for the trip.

"But," he added somewhat wistfully, "the years have taken their toll, Amelia dear. It has been a long time since I had the skill of those two lads."

I did not contradict him, though, in fact, he had never been up to the standards of the boys. They rode like Arabs, a much more graceful method in my opinion than our stiff English style.

As we went through the narrow opening that led into the valley from the north, past the walls of the Ptolemaic temple, the sun lifted over the heights of the eastern hill. Even in the clear light of morning the narrow valley had a gloomy air about it, or so it had always seemed to me. Isolated and remote, walled in by rocky slopes and steeps, it was a monotony of grayish buff, with no ripple of water or verdant plant anywhere. It was also a silent place. The voices of visitors echoed like an intrusion.

I reminded myself that it would not have seemed that way to the ancient inhabitants, when the houses were intact and the streets were crowded with people bustling about on various errands, their voices raised in cheery greetings—and, people being what they are, acrimonious arguments. Though crowded close together, the dwellings were comfortable enough for their time; the basic plan consisted of several rooms, including reception room and kitchen, with sometimes a cellar for storage. Windows were limited, but the flat roof served as an airy retreat. There are few village sites in Egypt, and we were fortunate to have the firman for this one. To Emerson's everlasting credit, he had tackled the job with his usual energy and dedication; but I knew that in his heart he yearned for temples and tombs. Candidly, so did I. If his explosive temper had not led to a falling-out with M. Maspero . . .

But no, I told myself, again giving Emerson his due; it was not entirely his fault. Most of the interesting sites in Thebes had been allocated to other expeditions, and Lord Carnarvon was unlikely to give up his firman for the Valley of the Kings. He was a gracious gentleman, but my hints had had not the slightest effect on him.

It immediately became apparent that Emerson had paid no attention whatever to my little lecture the previous evening. Instead of allowing the others time for their own activities, he had determined to set a second crew to work in another area outside the village itself. I bit my lip with vexation as he outlined his intentions and issued his orders. Walter, looking a trifle bewildered, went off with Selim to continue excavating along the village street. Emerson led the rest of us toward the temple, lecturing all the while.

The Ptolemaic temple was surrounded by an enclosure wall of mud brick. This common, convenient building material is remarkably resistant to the destructive forces of time and nature; in some places the walls had survived to a height of almost twenty feet. They enclosed not only the later temple, which was fairly well-preserved, but the tumbled ruins of earlier shrines that had been built by the villagers for their devotions. The remains of other such structures lay outside the walls, to the north and west. Some of our incompetent predecessors had dug pits in that area, finding nice little votive stelae and other objects. It was Emerson's intention to clear the entire area methodically and completely. It presented a challenge even to Emerson's powers.

"What a mess," Lia murmured, her eyes moving over the ground.

"Precisely," said Emerson. He rolled up his sleeves. "We'll take it in meter-square sections, starting . . . here. Ramses and David, help me get the markers placed."

During the weeks when we had been removing the artifacts from the tomb we had been swamped with visitors hoping for a glimpse of the treasure. The effrontery of certain people never ceases to amaze me; some had offered bribes to our men, while others had actually forced their way past our guards and tried to snatch off the coverings that protected the more fragile objects. Emerson had dealt with them in his usual forthright manner. Now that there was nothing to see except a group of grubby people digging, the flood had slowed. However, some tourists came that way, since the temple was mentioned in Baedeker. I did not suppose they would cause us much trouble; the tumble of stones held little attraction and the dragomen who led the parties knew better than to get in Emerson's way.

Nevertheless, I deemed it advisable to keep an eye on them, so I was the first to see a somewhat unusual group. There were four of them, in addition to several donkey boys and a dragoman. One of the women leaned heavily on the latter individual. Her shoulders were stooped, and the wisps of hair that had escaped from the mantilla-like veil over her head were pure white. Supporting her on the other side was another female, who appeared to be some years younger, though not in her first youth. Her dark hair was streaked with gray and her face was lined. She helped the older lady to a seat on a fallen stone and began fanning her.

But it was the other two members of the party who caught my attention. They were not a pair one easily forgot. Emerson had seen them too. He straightened and stared.

The boy who had introduced himself as Justin Fitzroyce caught sight of us. Crying out in recognition, he came toward me, scrambling nimbly over the uneven ground and followed closely by his black-a-vised protector.

"It is my friends the Emersons," the lad exclaimed. "Are you archaeologists? What are you doing? Where is the pretty lady?"

Emerson had opened his mouth. Now he closed it and looked helplessly at me. It was impossible to be curt with the young chap, whose bright face shone with ingenuous goodwill.

"Good morning, Mr. Justin," I said. "So you are still in Luxor."

"Yes, we like it here. I have seen all the tombs in the Valley of the Kings and several of the temples. But there is still a great deal to see." Seeing Nefret coming toward us, he exclaimed, "There she is. I remember her name—another Mrs. Emerson. There are two Mrs. Emersons."

"Three, in fact," Nefret said pleasantly. "You haven't met the other one. Did you and François come here alone?"

His attendant's scowling face was like a thundercloud hovering over the boy's sunny countenance. "I can take care of the young master," he growled.

"But we did not come alone." Justin turned and gestured at the two women. "That is my grandmother. Her health has improved greatly since we came. But this is her first excursion and she must be careful not to tire herself."

"Who is the other lady?" I asked.

"She is not a lady," Justin said carelessly. "She is Miss Underhill."

"Your grandmother's companion?"

Justin nodded, dismissing the non-lady. "I will tell them to go back to the hotel. I will stay with you."

"Let me speak to your grandmother," I said, anticipating Emerson's protest. Surely the old lady would forbid such a scheme.

She remained seated, her shoulders bowed and her head bent as I introduced myself and Nefret. At first there was no response. Then she said, in a voice cracked with age, "My name is Fitzroyce. You will forgive me, I hope, if I say good-bye instead of good morning. It has been most interesting, but at my age even the smallest exertion leaves one exhausted."

"Of course," I said. "Can we assist you in any way?"

"Thank you, no." She pressed a handkerchief to her lips.

"I help the lady," the dragoman volunteered.

I knew the fellow; he was one of the more dependable of the Luxor guides. Mrs. Fitzroyce seemed to have all the attendants she needed, though her companion had retreated a few steps into the shadow of a column, and had adopted the humble pose of a dependent. She wore the garments suitable for that role, drab and shabby and ill-fitting. Cast-offs of her mistress? I wondered. No self-respecting woman would have purchased a hat like hers; it was an aged straw with faded ribbons that tied under her chin. The spotted veil had several rents in it.

"I am staying here," Justin announced. "I want to see the temple of Hathor and help my friends dig."

I began, "I am afraid—"

An unexpected cackle of laughter from the old lady interrupted me. "You don't want him getting in your way, Mrs. Emerson? You heard the lady, Justin. Come with me."

There was authority in that aged voice, despite its tremulous pitch. Justin pouted, like the child he was mentally if not physically. His actual age I would have judged to be approximately fourteen. His mental age was not so easy to determine. His vocabulary and ease of speech were sometimes fairly advanced. It was his social and emotional adjustment that seemed not quite normal. His manners were quite engaging, and I was sorry to have to disappoint him; but aside from the inconvenience, I did not wish to be responsible for the boy.

"Oh, very well," Justin said. "I will come and visit you another day. Where do you live?"

"That would be nice," Nefret said, tactfully avoiding an answer. "But now we must get back to work. Good-bye."

It took them some time to get themselves away; looking up from my work periodically, I caught glimpses of Justin's bright head as he darted to and fro, and heard his attendant's voice pleading with him to come. Then I saw them no more. It was getting on toward midday by then, and I reminded Emerson he had promised to send Walter back to the house for the afternoon. One look at Walter halted any objections my spouse might have made; he had not complained nor faltered in his tasks, but he was red with sunburn and staggering with fatigue. Emerson did not even complain when I sent Ramses with him. The rest of us settled down in the little shelter I had erected in the shadow of the temple walls and opened our picnic baskets.

Most of the tourists had also sought repose and refreshment, at Cook's Rest House or at their hotels. A welcome quiet descended upon the valley—quiet, that is, except for Emerson's voice, lecturing. I let him talk, since it would have been difficult to stop him. I had been a little concerned about Lia, but she had kept up well. David was the same as he had always been, lean and lithe and enthusiastic. As soon as he had wolfed down a few sandwiches he jumped up and declared he wanted to have a closer look at some of the reliefs of the Ptolemaic temple.

"Look all you like, but don't get too interested," said Emerson. "Vandergelt has some scheme of copying the tomb paintings. The tomb of Sennedjem . . ."

His voice trailed off. He was looking at the hill, where the crumbling remains of small brick pyramids and little chapels marked the site of the village cemetery. Slowly and deliberately he put down his half-eaten chicken leg and got to his feet.

"What is it?" I asked. "What do you—"

Emerson was on his way, running and leaping over the broken ground toward the hill. A very loud "Hell and damnation" was the only response to my question. Then I looked up and saw what had prompted his action. High above were two figures, moving slowly along one of the paths that crossed the slope. I recognized, as Emerson must have done, the brown tweeds and slender form of the boy Justin, followed by his bulkier shadow.

"Good heavens," Nefret exclaimed. "Is that Justin? He shouldn't be up there."

"Emerson reached the same conclusion and, as you see, he is acting upon it with his customary promptitude," I replied. "I had better go along too, in case a woman's soothing presence proves necessary. The rest of you stay here."

Nefret had half risen. She nodded in agreement, though her brow was furrowed. "Be careful, Mother."

I felt sure a soothing presence would be necessary—not, in this case, because of a premonition or foreboding, but because I was only too familiar with my husband's character and habits. I knew I could never catch Emerson up, but I went as fast as I dared, and I uttered a few low-voiced expletives of my own as I hurried along. Had the boy eluded his grandmother, or had he persuaded her to go on without him? Ordinarily I would not have been concerned, for the path, though steep in some places, was not beyond the skill of an ordinary healthy young lad. A slip and a tumble could result in serious injury, however, and I doubted that François could act promptly and effectively enough if Justin had another of his seizures. Neither of them was accustomed to terrain like this.

I was on the lower slope when Emerson reached the pair. His voice rolled like thunder. "What the devil do you mean, letting the boy attempt this? Come with me, Justin."

As I could have told Emerson, and would have, had I been closer, it was precisely the wrong approach. Emerson compounded it by taking peremptory hold of the lad. His grasp, affected by anxiety, was heavy, but not so painful as to explain Justin's reaction. He let out a thin high-pitched scream, and began to writhe and twist, trying to pull away.

I doubt that any admonitions of mine could have prevented the accident; in any case, I was too out of breath to shout. I was still ten feet away when François grabbed Justin by the shoulders and tugged at him. Emerson held on. The boy's head flopped back and forth and his hat fell off. He was still writhing and screaming. François let him go and caught Emerson by the throat. The three became a Laocoön-like group of intertwined bodies and flailing limbs. Emerson broke away, realizing, as he later explained, that the combat was likely to injure the boy; but as he stepped back he fell headlong and rolled down the slope in an avalanche of broken stones.

Crying out in alarm, the others of our party ran toward the foot of the hill, with Selim in the lead. A quick look showed me that Emerson was standing up, despite the attempts of the others to restrain him. A string of expletives and complaints, loudly uttered, assured me that his vocal powers at least were unimpaired. Anxious as I was to lend my assistance, I did not feel I could leave the boy. However, he had come out of his fit and was calmly brushing himself off. He gave me a puzzled smile.

"What has happened to Mr. Emerson?" he inquired innocently.

"He fell," I replied. "I think your attendant tripped him."

"Shame on you, François," Justin exclaimed. "You should not have done that. It was wrong."

"He was hurting you," the fellow muttered.

"Was he? I don't think so; he seems to be a very kind man. I hope he is not injured."

"So do I," I said, giving François a long hard look.

It would have been impossible for François to look harmless, but he did appear somewhat subdued. "It was an accident," he mumbled. "I did not mean to harm him. But no one touches the young master."

"I am going to touch him now," I said firmly. "Take my hand, Justin, and we will go down together. Stay well back, François, we don't want another accident, do we?"

The boy slipped his hand confidingly into mine and let me lead him back down the path. He was a few inches taller than I, but slimmer. The brief violent interlude had been forgotten; his countenance was, if anything, complacent.

"You should not have gone up there, Justin," I said.

"I wanted to see the tombs."

"That could be even more dangerous than the path. Some of the shafts are open; a tumble into one of them would hurt you badly. Promise me you will not go there again."

"Can I see the temple, then? It is a temple to Hathor. She is a beautiful goddess, like the other Mrs. Emerson. Does she ever come there?"

With a slight shock I realized he was not speaking of Nefret.

"No, I don't think she does, Justin."

"The dragoman said she does. On the night of the full moon. He has seen her and so have some of his friends."

I promised myself a word with that gentleman. He had no business putting such notions into the boy's head. It might be advisable to have a word with Mrs. Fitzroyce as well. How could she entrust her young grandson to a villainous character like François? Devoted he undoubtedly was, but his judgment left something to be desired. In some ways he was as deficient in sense as Justin.

Emerson came stalking to meet us. Fearing that he might renew the combat, I interposed my person between him and François.

"Well, you are a sight," I said, inspecting him. "Another shirt . . . not only your shirt this time, you have torn the knees out of your trousers."

"Better my trousers than my head," said Emerson. "As you see, my dear, I am relatively unscathed. Is the boy all right?"

Justin shrank back. "He is bleeding. I don't like blood."

Fearing, from the boy's alarmed expression, that he was in danger of falling into another fit, I forced a laugh.

"He is not badly hurt, Justin."

"Not a bit of it," said Emerson heartily. "In a tumble of that sort, the trick is to shield one's head, and roll, rather than—"

"We don't need a lecture on tumbling, Emerson," I interrupted. "Come to the shelter and let Nefret disinfect those cuts. Justin, go home at once. Do you have transportation?"

I directed the question at François, but it was Justin who answered. "Our horses are waiting. I ride very well. But I don't want to go yet. I want to stay with the pretty Mrs. Emerson."

"You must do as you are told. François—"

"Yes, madame. We will go now. I regret . . ."

"Hmmm," said Emerson, fixing him with a steady stare. "It is lucky for you that you didn't try your tricks on a less—er—athletic individual."

"It is my duty to protect the young master," François muttered sullenly.

"If you injure someone in the course of your duty, you will be dismissed and possibly imprisoned," said Emerson. "I promise you that. Control your temper, as I am controlling mine. Only the boy's presence prevents me from teaching you a lesson you would not soon forget."

Emerson really was controlling himself quite well, but in my opinion he ought to have omitted the last sentence. It was meant as a challenge and it was understood as such. François's scarred face twisted and he gave Emerson a hostile look.

"Go now," I said sharply.

I sent David with them to locate their horses. When he returned, he reported that they had departed, and that Justin's naive boast was not greatly exaggerated. "He handles a horse well. And he has excellent manners. He thanked me nicely. How did you become acquainted with an odd pair like that?"

Emerson, twitching impatiently under Nefret's attempts to bandage a few of the deeper scratches on his arms and knees, said, "She's always getting involved with lame ducks and hapless lovers."

"It was Ramses who got involved this time," I retorted. "The poor lad had one of his fits on the corniche in Luxor, and Ramses—quite understandably—misunderstood François's efforts to restrain him. He is too young to be a lover, hapless or otherwise."

"I don't know about that," Lia said with a knowing smile. "He could hardly take his eyes off Nefret. Boys of that age sometimes develop violent attachments."

"There isn't a scrap of violence in the lad," I said. "And he thinks of Nefret as a goddess—Hathor, perhaps. He seems to have got it into his poor confused head that she manifests herself here in her temple."

Selim, who was waiting for instructions, looked up. "He is not the only one to think so, Sitt Hakim. Two of the men of Gurneh say they have seen a white lady, veiled and crowned with gold, standing before the temple."

The description struck a chord of unpleasant familiarity. "Why didn't you tell me about this, Selim?" I demanded.

Selim shrugged. "Such tales are common, they spread quickly among superstitious persons. The men prowled here after nightfall, looking for something to steal; they saw a moonbeam or a shadow and wished to make themselves important by telling lies . . ."

His eyes moved from my frowning face to that of Emerson, and widened in sudden comprehension. "Are you thinking of the woman in Cairo? Surely it is only a coincidence. This was a vision, a dream, a lie."

"My grandfather might have said that the old gods still linger in their holy places, for those who have eyes to see," David said. "It would make a good subject for one of my popular romantic paintings: the temple ruins by night, dim shapes in the darkness, and between the pylons, shining in her own light, the veiled and crowned goddess . . ."

"Well, it is cursed unlikely that one of the old gods would pop up in a Cairo tenement," I said. "You are right, Selim, it is only a coincidence."

"Are you going to tell Ramses about Hathor?" Nefret asked.

I said in surprise, "If the subject arises. Why not?"

"Because he will want to see for himself. What if—"

"Nonsense," I said firmly. "You are too sensible to talk of 'what ifs.' Has everyone finished eating?"

"Back to work," Emerson exclaimed, jumping up. "That little episode cost us over an hour."

"Goodness, yes," I said, looking at my watch. "You had better run along, David."

"Run along where?" Emerson demanded indignantly. "I need him to—"

"I promised Cyrus he could have David during the afternoons. We will see you at the house at teatime, David."

Emerson's jaw set. "And you, Emerson, ought to change your clothing," I went on. "You are even more unkempt than usual."

"I am not modeling proper archaeological attire for the admiration of the cursed tourists," Emerson declared.

David left, and Nefret very kindly offered to give me a hand with my sifting, for the rubbish heap had piled up. She seemed somewhat pensive. After a long silence she spoke.

"That fellow François does not seem a suitable attendant for a boy like Justin. Should we speak to his grandmother?"

"Emerson would call both of us interfering busybodies."

"That has never deterred you from interfering."

"Certainly not. I am the judge of my own conscience and my own behavior. That idea had occurred to me," I admitted, picking a small piece of broken pottery out of the sieve and setting it aside. "But interference might do more harm than good. Old people are set in their ways and dislike criticism. And, to be fair, we don't know what is wrong with the boy. He is a strange mixture of innocence and savoir faire, of reasoned discourse followed by unexpected non sequiturs."

Nefret sat back on her heels and wiped her perspiring forehead with her sleeve. "Some of his symptoms are characteristic of grand mal seizures. Most epileptics are of normal, even superior, intelligence, however. He seems childish for his age. Of course I am no authority on mental disorders. I've always wanted to study the subject."

"In addition to surgery and gynecology? My dear girl, you have enough to do—your husband and children, the hospital—to say nothing of Emerson dragging you out to the dig every day."

I had meant it as sympathetic commendation, but she did not return my smile. "I've done almost nothing at the hospital for two years, Mother. It's in good hands, but sometimes I miss it. As for the clinic I meant to open here in Luxor . . . Well, you know what's happened to that."

"You have your instruments and ample space for consulting and operating rooms," I said. "Now that the children are older, there is no reason why you cannot proceed with your plan for a clinic."

"I've become very rusty, Mother. Like some of my instruments! All I've done is assist at a few difficult births and set a bone or two."

"All the more reason to hone your skills again. I had no idea you felt that way, Nefret. You ought to have confided in me. I will take steps immediately to have the rooms made ready."

Her brow cleared and she let out one of her musical chuckles. "Mother, you are incomparable. I didn't mean to complain. Please don't trouble yourself. You have enough to do managing the rest of the family!"

"Compared with managing Emerson, it will be a pleasure," I assured her.

I CANNOT IMAGINE HOW I missed the signs. Excuses do not become me, so I will not mention that I had been extremely busy making the arrangements for Nefret's clinic. I had had such a scheme in mind when I had the house built, so the space had been provided—three smallish but adequate rooms, set off from the rest of the house, with a separate entrance. They had lain dusty and unoccupied for two years, so every surface had to be scrubbed, whitewashed, and disinfected before the necessary furnishings could be installed. We were able to obtain basic supplies from the chemists in Luxor, and I suggested the names of several girls whom I considered possible candidates for the position of nursing assistant.

Nefret had already settled on someone. "Kadija's granddaughter Nisrin came round as soon as she heard about the clinic. She has always been interested in nursing and Kadija has taught her a great deal."

"Ah, yes, I remember her. A pleasant but rather—er—plain young woman."

"She's only fourteen, and already betrothed," Nefret said, with the bite in her voice that marked her disapproval of the Egyptian custom of early marriages.

"You mean to 'rescue' another one, do you?"

"If she does as well as I expect and wants to continue—yes. It's her father who is set on the marriage, but if Daoud and Kadija back me up, he'll have to give in."

Since Daoud was putty in Nefret's hands and Kadija was one of her greatest friends and admirers, I did not doubt they would back her up. I interviewed the girl myself. Nisrin had, for some reason, always been rather shy of me, but I managed to overcome her diffidence and concluded that she would do.

What with one thing and another . . . Suffice it to say that I did miss the ominous signs, so that the disaster came upon me with the violence of a bolt of lightning out of a clear sky.

Later, I realized that Emerson had been behaving oddly for several days. I attributed his fits of preoccupation to concern about his confounded stratigraphy, which was proving to be more complicated than he had expected. His unusual interest in the post could have been explained by his concern for his half-brother; there had been as yet no reply to our telegrams. Selim, who, as I later discovered, had been in on the plot all along, was wise enough to keep out of my way. Not until I went looking for him one afternoon did I realize I had not set eyes on him all day. I went immediately to Emerson.

"Where is Selim? I want to ask him about—"

"Yes, yes," said Emerson, in a strange, high-pitched voice. "I know where he is."

"Emerson, what is the matter with you?"

Emerson's bronzed countenance widened into a broad, terrifying grin. "I have a surprise for you, Peabody."

"Tell me," I implored in a voice that resisted my attempts to keep it steady. "Do not leave me in suspense. What—"

"No, no, I will show you. I will show everyone!" He took out his watch, glanced at it, and then raised his voice to the shout that could be heard throughout the West Bank. "We are closing down for the day! Everybody come with me!"

And not another word would he say. It was early afternoon; the cessation of work at such an hour was unheard of. Bewildered, and, in my case, exceedingly apprehensive, we mounted our steeds and set out for the house. I asked Ramses, I asked Nefret, I asked Lia; one and all claimed to be as ignorant as I.

Emerson, who had outstripped the rest of us, was on the veranda, pacing up and down. "Perfect timing," he announced. "Here they come."

Looking out, I beheld an extraordinary caravan heading toward the house. A string of carts drawn by donkeys and mules, two camels carrying heavy loads, and several dozen men, chanting and cavorting, were led by Selim, mounted on horseback.

The carts drew up in front of the house. They contained several huge packing cases. The men set about unloading them and the donkeys. Emerson rushed out. "Is it all here, Selim?"

"We will soon see, Emerson." Selim brandished a crowbar. Emerson snatched it from him and began prying at the largest of the wooden cases.

The hideous truth began to dawn. "Oh, good Gad," I said in a hollow voice. "It cannot be."

Under Emerson's vigorous assault the top of the case lifted and the sides fell, disclosing a metal framework. At first glance it bore little resemblance to the object I had expected and feared to see, for many of the parts were missing. I knew what they were, and where they were—in the other packing cases, which the men, under Selim's direction, were prying apart. One by one they appeared—the metallic shapes of the bonnet and fenders, four large wheels, and a number of other objects I could not identify.

We had owned several motorcars. My primary objection to the cursed things was that Emerson insisted on driving them himself. When we were at our English home, in Kent, the local population soon learned to clear off the roads when Emerson was on them; in the crowded streets of Cairo, motoring with Emerson took a good deal of getting used to. They were fairly common in the city by now, and during the war the military had built roads in other areas, but when we moved to Luxor for an indefinite stay I had managed to persuade my husband to sell the vehicle, pointing out that its utility in the Luxor area was limited.

Emerson had quite an audience by then—ourselves, including Walter, our workmen, the porters, and half the population of Gurneh. Some squatted on the ground to watch, others pushed and shoved to get a better view; there was a positive whirlpool of fluttering robes.

When I finally found my voice I had to raise it to a scream in order to be heard over the hubbub. Emerson, kneeling beside the mechanism, pretended not to hear, but on the third emphatic repetition of his name he decided he might as well face the music. Rising, he approached me, extending a hand stained black with grease.

"Come and have a look, my dear," he said. "Everything seems to be in working order, but of course we cannot be certain until we get it back together. Ramses, would you care to lend a hand? You and I and Selim—and David . . . Where is he? I sent someone to the Castle to fetch him."

"He'll be along shortly, I expect," Ramses said, with an apprehensive glance at me. "Father, wouldn't it be advisable to clear away the remains of the packing materials first? Someone is going to step on a nail or run a splinter into his foot."

"Excellent idea," exclaimed Emerson.

"You are going to put it back together here—on the spot?" I cried in poignant accents. "Smack in front of the house? Why did you take it apart in the first place? That's what you were doing that day in Cairo! Why, Emerson? Why?"

"It seemed the quickest way of getting it here undamaged," Emerson explained disingenuously. He wiped his sweating forehead with the back of his hand, leaving a long black streak. "It was supposed to be on yesterday's train, but apparently they could not find the space. Selim most efficiently supervised the unloading and got the cases onto the ferry, and found these obliging fellows—"

"That isn't what I meant, and you know it! What possible use can you have for a motorcar here? There are no proper roads!"

"Good Gad, Peabody, we motored clear across the Sinai and through the wadis in a vehicle like this one. The roads are much improved since the war." He then proceeded to contradict himself by adding, "The Light Car Patrols, which did such a splendid job against the Senussi, are being disbanded, and nobody in the military gives a curse about maintaining the desert roads. That is how I was able to get my hands on this vehicle. It is an improved model of the Ford Light Car—"

"I don't want to hear about it."

Emerson can only be intimidated up to a point. He drew himself up, glared at me, and rubbed the cleft in his chin, leaving additional black streaks. "I suppose a fellow can purchase a motorcar if he likes."

I knew I had lost the argument. It had been lost, in fact, the moment the confounded thing arrived. Moreover, every male person in the vicinity was clearly on Emerson's side; Ramses had abandoned me and was helping Selim sort bolts and nuts and other undefined bits, and Walter had removed his coat and was rolling up his sleeves. Additional reinforcements were about to arrive. One of the approaching horses was David's mare Asfur. There were two other riders—Cyrus and Bertie, I presumed. Evelyn and Katherine had resisted the lure of the motorcar.

Nefret put her arm round me. "Come in and have a cup of tea, Mother."

"We may as well," Lia said. "They'll be playing with the car for the rest of the day."

Fatima had not ventured to come out; clutching the bars, she stared at the vehicle as if it were a large, dangerous animal. At my request she rushed off to brew tea and we three females sat down to watch the proceedings.

"Thank goodness Gargery isn't here," I said. "He'd want to pitch in too. I hope they can get the confounded thing together and drive it into the stable before the children join us for tea."

"It doesn't seem likely," remarked Lia. David had not even greeted her. Except for Cyrus, who was watching from a safe distance, the men had stripped to the waist and were waving their arms and arguing. The porters dashed about gathering up the debris; every scrap of wood, every nail would be of use to them.

"They will waste a good deal of time arguing about what to do and who is to do it," I remarked. "A woman's clear head is what is needed, but we may as well leave them to go about it in their own disorganized way. Ah, thank you, Fatima. Join us, if you like; it should be amusing."

FROM MANUSCRIPT H

For once, Emerson's consuming passion for excavation yielded to an even greater passion. A man of iron discipline, he went out to the dig every morning—dragging most of them with him—but he could hardly wait to get back to his new toy. Emerson's reasons for dismembering it made a certain amount of sense—manhandling an entire motorcar onto and off of a flatcar had certain built-in risks, given the makeshift methods the Egyptians employed—but Ramses suspected his father had done it partly because he wanted the fun of taking it apart and putting it back together. He didn't even object to the audience that collected every afternoon. Few Luxor men had ever seen a motorcar. They sat round in a circle, round-eyed and breathless, watching every move Emerson and Selim made. After the first afternoon Ramses and David became part of the audience, since they weren't allowed to do anything. Naturally, a number of essential bolts and nuts had gone missing. Selim managed to find replacements. You could find almost anything in Egypt, or, if necessary, find someone to make it. Selim was an expert mechanic, but the process took a lot longer than it ought to have done, with Emerson "helping."

His mother bore the circus with surprising equanimity. Once or twice Ramses thought he saw a suppressed grin, as she stood at the barred door watching. They were besieged with visitors, not only local people but foreign residents and tourists offering advice and assistance. Emerson ignored the advice and refused the assistance, but he was perfectly willing to stop and talk, answer questions, and generally show off. The children did their best to get out and join in the fun; the only one who managed to elude the watchers was Davy, who was snatched up by Emerson as he was reaching for a spanner. He tucked the child under one arm, a procedure Davy found immensely entertaining, and carried him back to the house.

"Good Gad, Peabody, why did you let him out?" he demanded. "He could hurt himself with those heavy tools, you know."

His wife raised her eyes heavenward. "Yes, Emerson, I do know. If you had had the elementary good sense to move the motorcar to the stableyard, out of sight of the children—"

"Bah," said Emerson. "One would suppose that four women could keep track of a few little children."

Her lips tightened into invisibility, but she said only, "I will take steps, Emerson."

What she did was pen the children into an area at the far end of the veranda. The barricade consisted of furniture and boxes; any one of them could climb over or squirm under them, but not without alerting an adult. Inside the enclosure she placed their toys, cushions and rugs, and a child-sized table and chairs borrowed from the twins' room. Their initial indignation faded when she explained that this was their own special place, into which no grown-up could enter without an invitation, and handed over a box of crayons and a pile of blank paper.

"Now we will see who can draw the best picture," she said.

Ramses thought it would take more than a few boxes to keep Davy penned in, so he volunteered for watch duty and took a chair next to the barricade. After approximately fifteen minutes he wished his mother hadn't added a challenge to what was otherwise an excellent scheme. Paper after paper was thrust at him, and admiration demanded. Except for Dolly's, which were very good for a boy that age, he couldn't even tell what the scribbles were supposed to be. Evvie's were as unidentifiable as those of his children. He tried not to be glad of that. He hadn't been much concerned about the twins' inability to communicate, but having Evvie around chattering like a magpie invited invidious comparisons. Women—mothers—couldn't help making such comparisons, he supposed. They even counted teeth. He had been informed by Nefret that Charla had two more than Evvie.

Late Thursday afternoon the final bolt was tightened and the entire family was summoned to watch as Emerson, sweating, oil-stained, and blissfully happy, gave the starting handle a vigorous turn. The engine caught with a roar that was echoed by a resounding cheer from the audience and Emerson jumped into the driver's seat. Ramses saw a spasm cross his mother's face. She hadn't the heart to forbid him to try the vehicle out; nothing short of a earthquake could have stopped him anyhow.

"Slowly, Emerson, I beg," she shouted. "Slowly and carefully, my dear!"

Emerson refused to come in to tea. Grudgingly he allowed Selim his turns behind the wheel; for the next hour they drove back and forth in front of the house. Their offers of rides were enthusiastically received by the children but firmly declined by both mothers and grandmothers. Only the bursting of a tire put an end to the performance; apparently not all the nails had been picked up.

After Emerson had gone off to bathe and change, his wife said wryly, "Let us hope the worst is over. We really ought to get back to our duties. Tomorrow is Friday. I presume, Nefret, that you and Ramses will be paying your weekly visit to Selim? What about you, David?"

"Not this week, though Selim was good enough to ask me. I want to see Grandfather's tomb."

"Are you taking the children?"

"Dolly wants to go. He has made something of a hero of his great-grandfather. I suppose we'll have to take Evvie as well, she always insists on going where Dolly goes."

Nefret's raised eyebrows indicated disapproval of some part of the scheme, but she said nothing at the time. The following afternoon, after they had returned from Deir el Medina, Ramses, delayed by a lecture from his father, went to their room to change. Nefret was standing in front of the mirror, so absorbed in what she was doing she didn't hear him. Her head and shoulders were thrown back and her hands stretched the fabric of her thin undergarment tight across her body, so that it outlined every rounded curve.

"Can I help you with that?" he asked, studying the effect appreciatively.

Nefret let out her breath in a little scream and whirled round. "I wish you wouldn't creep up on me like that!"

"I wasn't . . . Sorry. What were you doing?"

"Nothing." She let the fabric fall into its normal folds and went to her dressing table. "I was surprised to hear David say they are taking the children to the cemetery. We've never taken the twins."

"Do you want to?"

"I was attempting," said his wife, with uncharacteristic sarcasm, "to induce your opinion, not a question about mine."

"Oh. I don't think I really have one. It's entirely up to you." Her expression told him this wasn't what she wanted to hear, so he tried again. "They never knew Abdullah; he is as remote to them, at their age, as—well, as one of the heroes in the books you read to them. It can't hurt, surely, to tell children about the brave deeds of their friends and ancestors."

"That's one way of looking at it."

"Do you want to go with them?"

"Some other time, perhaps. Selim is expecting us, and Kadija would be disappointed if we didn't go. Do you mind?"

"Of course not." He added with a smile, "Fond as I am of our family, it will be good to be with you and the twins."

"Ramses . . ."

"What is it, dear?"

She had been playing with the objects on her dressing table, shifting them back and forth. Turning, she put her hands on his shoulders. "Did Mother tell you . . ."

"Tell me what?"

Her hands cradled the back of his head and bent it down to meet her upturned face. Her mouth was soft and yet urgent, and as he held her close he began to think of other things he'd rather do than pay social calls.

"I love you very much," she whispered.

"I love you too. What brought this on? Not that I really care," he added. "Let's do that again."

He tried to hold her, but she slipped away, laughing. Her face was unclouded. "Darling, you know the children will be pounding on the door if we don't come."

She was right, of course. Children were a blessing, no doubt of that, but there were times . . . With nostalgia not unmixed with guilt he remembered the days when their embraces hadn't had to be calculated, and the only interruptions came from criminals—and, occasionally, his father.

He kept thinking about it all afternoon, abnormally conscious of his wife's presence. She'd started to ask him something and then changed her mind. Did she know something he didn't—something his mother had told her—that caused her to fear for him? Was that what had prompted that spontaneous, passionate kiss? It would be just like the two of them to decide they needed to protect him . . .

Selim had to speak to him twice before he responded. "Sorry, I was thinking of something else."

Selim hadn't missed his fixed stare at Nefret. He murmured, "And a happy thing it is to think of. But when will you all come to us? Daoud wants to have a fantasia, here at Gurneh."

"Talk to Mother," Ramses said. "Where is Daoud? He usually joins us."

"A scorpion stung him."

Scorpion stings were seldom fatal, but they were extremely painful and often debilitating, even for a man of Daoud's strength. "When did this happen?" Ramses asked. "Why didn't he come to Nefret?"

"This morning. There was a meeting of the creatures in his sleeping room, it seems," Selim said with a grin. "The sting is on his foot and he cannot walk. But Kadija has taken care of it. He will be ready for work tomorrow."

"The famous green ointment," Ramses murmured. It probably would have the desired effect; Daoud was a firm believer in its efficacy, and the stuff did seem to work. "Tell him to stay at home if it is not better."

Selim nodded and went on to speak of something else. Scorpions were only too common in Egypt, but it was unusual for them to be found indoors.

When they took their departure Ramses promised to speak to his mother about a date for the fantasia. The children had spent the entire time playing some incomprehensible game that involved running, hopping or rolling back and forth across the courtyard, and the twins were characteristically filthy and uncharacteristically limp with fatigue. Ramses looked down at the curly black head that rested against his chest.

"They should drop off to sleep right away," he said hopefully.

Nefret chuckled. "Don't count on it. The Vandergelts are dining, you know."

"All the more reason to hurry."

There was no hurrying the horses on the hillside, among the clustered houses of the village. They reached the level floor of the desert and he was about to let Risha run when he heard something.

"Listen," he said, reining the horse in.

"I don't—" It came again, and now Nefret heard it too—a high-pitched, wavering scream.

Ramses plucked his drowsy daughter off his shirtfront and held her out. "Take her. Quick."

Nefret obeyed instantly and instinctively, cradling both small bodies tight in her arms. He thanked God she was a superb horsewoman and that Moonlight was responsive to her slightest word or gesture. The scream came again; this time it was followed by a cry for help. The words were English, the voice was a woman's. Nefret's eyes opened wide.

"Ramses, what—"

"Get the children home. Right now."

He didn't wait for a response. Glancing back as he headed Risha toward the hills, he saw that Moonlight had broken into her long, smooth gallop. If they had been alone, Nefret would have insisted on accompanying him, but the children's safety came first, even though it was unlikely that the agitated female was in serious trouble.

The woman continued to call out; her voice was weakening and broken by long gasping sobs. He found her at last, backed up against a rock outcropping. The man who confronted her was laughing as she struck at him with what appeared to be a fly whisk. It wasn't much of a weapon compared with his knife. He was deliberately playing with her, easily avoiding her feeble blows and cutting at her arms and face. He was enjoying the game so much he failed to hear the hoofbeats until Ramses was almost on top of them. He had to pull Risha up to avoid running both down. The man let out a bleat of alarm and ran. Ramses was about to go after him when the woman sank to the ground.

Not knowing how badly she was hurt, he abandoned the idea of pursuit. He'd recognized her immediately, from her clothing. It was the same she had worn the day Justin and his grandmother had been at Deir el Medina—a drab, dark gown and a hat that even he recognized as a hand-me-down. Mrs. Fitzroyce's companion. What the hell was she doing here, alone and under attack? The Gurnawis didn't attack tourists.

There was blood on the ground—not much, but it was still flowing. He turned her carefully onto her back. The blood came from a cut on her arm. He couldn't see any other wounds on her body. Gently he untied the ribbons of her atrocious hat and removed it.

Her eyes were open. They were hazel, fringed with long lashes. Tears and a peculiar grayish film smeared her cheeks. Under it her skin was smooth, her cheeks dotted with freckles.

He remembered those hazel eyes.

"My God," he whispered. "It can't be . . . Molly?"

CHAPTER FIVE

Our little expedition to the cemetery did not get off until later in the afternoon. Emerson had decided to accompany us, and it always takes him a while to turn his mind from his work to more mundane activities (if one can call a visit to a saint's tomb mundane). His suggestion that we all drive in the motorcar was doomed from the start; he only did it to stir me up. In my opinion it was not really a useful method of transportation. Like the one we had used in Palestine, it had seats for only two people, with a sort of platform behind on which goods or persons could ride. Someone, most probably Selim, had fitted that other car with a canopy and relatively comfortable seats; crammed into this "tonneau," as it might loosely be called, Nefret and I had suffered the long tiring journey across the Sinai. What final modifications Emerson and Selim meant to make to this one I did not know, and I rather doubted that they did themselves. They were always taking parts off and putting them back on.

With the natural ingratitude of the young, all the children preferred Emerson to everyone else, including the mothers who had nurtured them and the devoted souls who kept them safe, clean, and healthy. His unorthodox notions of entertainment and his uncritical admiration no doubt explain this. Children are not noted for rational discrimination. After Evvie had made her desires plain, he took her up with him. I had hired several donkeys for the season, since Evelyn candidly admitted she preferred their plodding pace. To his great delight I assigned one of them to Dolly.

We did not take the animals into the cemetery. I don't know that there was any particular prohibition against it, but it seemed disrespectful. When Emerson put her down, Evvie tried to squirm away from him, but he held her firmly.

"This is like a church," he explained. "You must be quiet and not run over the graves."

"Are there dead people down under the ground?" Evvie asked curiously.

"Yes. And there—" I pointed. "There is your great-grandfather's tomb."

David had not seen the completed monument. While the others attempted to restrain Evvie (and tried to get her off the subject of dead people), he and I went on ahead. "It is odd, you know, to think of my grandfather as a saint," he said. "He was the bravest, truest man I ever knew, but . . ."

"He had his little failings," I agreed with a reminiscent chuckle. "Most people who become saints have them, David. Sanctity is attained by overcoming one's baser instincts."

Emerson came up in time to hear my comment. He let out a loud "hmph" but did not speak. We stood in silence outside the arched doorway of the monument. Dolly said proudly, "I have his name."

I put my arm round him. "Yes, you do. And he is—that is, he would be—very glad and proud that you have it."

"Tell me again about what he did," Dolly said, standing very straight.

So I told him, in the simplest language, of how Abdullah had died, giving his life to save mine, and of the many other occasions on which he had risked himself for me and Emerson. "He was a good man and a brave man," I concluded. "We all loved him and we miss him."

"But he is happy in Heaven," said Dolly.

"He certainly seems to be," I agreed, without thinking.

There was a general shuffling of feet and clearing of throats, and Evelyn, whose religious views are more conventional than mine, hastily changed the subject.

"The design is really lovely, David. Simple and traditional, yet it has an extraordinary grace."

"Yes, indeed," Walter agreed. "What a pity it has been disfigured by this unseemly rubbish."

The cord strung across the opening supported what was admittedly an unsightly collection of objects. They were not unseemly, however, and I felt obliged to mention this.

"It is not up to us, Walter, to decide what is proper to believers in any faith. For instance, our custom of entering our churches without removing our shoes would be considered quite unseemly by Muslims. These humble tokens are thanks to the holy man for favorable answers to prayers."

Emerson had, with great effort, refrained from making any of the sarcastic comments that express his views on organized religion of all denominations, though he did roll his eyes rather a lot. It was my insistence that he refrain from heretical comments when the children were present. Religion is difficult enough without people like Emerson confusing the issue.

Now he cleared his throat and remarked, with a slight curl of his lip and a provocative glance at me, "Abdullah seems to have answered a good many prayers in a rather short period of time."

"So he has," I agreed. I had no intention of allowing Emerson to provoke me into a theological discussion.

"I find it touching," Evelyn said gently. "What is it they ask for, I wonder?"

"The same things all human beings want," I said with a sigh. "Health, children, a peaceful life, and forgiveness of sin."

Evvie sat down quite suddenly and began to unlace her shoes. I fear it was not propriety that moved her so much as an excuse to remove these objects of attire, to which, like most children, she strongly objected. Her mother remonstrated, for she was of course concerned about scorpions, snakes, and sharp stones. As we debated the matter, a form emerged from the darkness of the interior and greeted us in Arabic.

His appearance gave me something of a start; I had not realized anyone was there. He wore the usual turban and galabeeyah and the usual beard covered the lower part of his face. It was vaguely familiar to me, but I could not place it immediately. However, I returned the greeting, as did David, while the others murmured politely. A closer examination of the fellow's face finally gave me my clue. He was obviously a member of Abdullah's far-flung family.

"You are Abu's son Abdulrassah, are you not?" I inquired.

"I am the servant of the sheikh," was the reply, accompanied by a pleased smile.

"I see. You have taken Hassan's place?"

The boy—he was hardly more than that—nodded. "Have you come to pray? It is good."

"I don't believe I will," Walter murmured in English. "Do you mind, Amelia? I mean no disrespect, it's just that—"

"Quite all right," I replied. "What about the rest of you?"

Evelyn decided to stay with Walter, and after receiving a somewhat dubious look from Abdulrassah, Lia said she would stay outside with her daughter. "I don't remember the prayers," she explained. "And I don't think it would be 'seemly' for Evvie to be running around inside."

Emerson's excuse was audible only to me, at whom it was intentionally directed. "I don't mind praying when prayer is expedient, but Abdullah would laugh himself sick to see me capering around his tomb."

I saw no reason why my old friend should not enjoy a hearty laugh at Emerson's expense, and I felt sure he would be more amused than offended to have an innocent descendant playing nearby. However, Dolly was taking the business very seriously. His small face grave and his eyes wide, he had already removed his shoes. So only three of us went inside—David and I and Dolly—and it was fitting, since we were the ones who cared most. David took his son by the hand and led him through the prescribed ritual. Though his father had been a Copt—an Egyptian Christian—he had been raised among Muslims, and by us. Narrowness of belief is not one of our failings, and both Emerson and Ramses are thoroughly familiar with the beautiful prayers of Islam. David remembered them quite well. Dolly's wide eyes and quick breathing showed that he was mightily impressed, though I don't believe he understood much of what was said.

When we came out into the daylight, Abdulrassah came with us. "The saint is happy that his family came," he announced. "Now will you make an offering?" He indicated a bowl that sat on the floor just inside the entrance. There were a few coins in it.

"Certainly," Walter exclaimed. Good-hearted man that he was, he wanted to compensate for what might have been viewed as a lack of respect, so I made no objection when he emptied his pockets of most of the coins they contained. Abdulrassah's face took on a positively seraphic smile.

"What is the money used for?" I inquired.

The ingenuous youth did not dissemble. "For me, Sitt Hakim. Am I not the servant? I say the prayers, I sweep the pavement."

In evidence thereof he picked up the broom that was used only for that purpose, and began energetically sweeping our footprints away. It was one of those fascinating survivals one finds in Egypt; so the ancient priests had swept the corridors of the tomb after the mummy had found its last resting place and the mourners had gone, removing all traces of the outer world.

We left him to his prayers, or a facsimile thereof. I said thoughtfully, "He was a very lazy little boy."

David burst out laughing. "Aunt Amelia, you are a hopeless cynic. Are you suggesting that he took on the job to avoid manual labor?"

"Far be it from me to impugn anyone's motives, David. Someone would have succeeded Hassan."

"His death might be considered a bad omen, though," David murmured.

"That is not how religious persons think," I explained. "To a true believer, in our faith as well as that of Hassan, death is not an end but a beginning; and what greater guarantee of immortality could there be than service to a holy man?"

Emerson opened his mouth. Then he looked down at the little boy who was holding his hand, and closed it.

"Shall we go by Selim's house and collect the others?" I asked.

"We had better get young Sekhmet home," David said. He was carrying his daughter, and I was forced to admit that the nickname suited her, with her lion-colored mane of hair and her explosive temper. At that moment she was like the goddess in one of her more benevolent moods, limp and yawning in her father's arms.

"We must arrange for a proper visit," Lia added. "Not just a quick call and quicker departure. We are all tired."

Evvie roused long enough to insist on riding with Emerson, and promptly fell asleep in his strong embrace. We went slowly, to spare the donkeys and their riders. Shadows lengthened across the sand as the sun sank westward.

"The others must have returned," I said, as we drew near the house. "Is that Nefret on the veranda?"

"Go on in," David said, quickly dismounting and assisting Evelyn to do so. "I'll take the animals round to the stable."

I had seen a glimmer of golden hair, but I had been mistaken as to the identity of the individual in question. Seated, perfectly at ease, he greeted us as coolly as if he had been an invited guest. "There you are at last! I have been waiting quite some time."

"Justin," I exclaimed. "What are you doing here?"

FROM MANUSCRIPT H

There could be no doubt of her identity, despite the smeared lines of makeup and the unattractive garments. Her hazel eyes overflowed. "I didn't mean you—any of you—to see me. Let me go. I'm all right."

"You can't just walk off into the sunset," Ramses said. He had never seen anyone cry so much; the tears were not a trickle but a flood. Fearing she would go into hysterics if he said the wrong thing, he ventured, "How did you get here? Not on foot, surely."

She gave him a blank, wet stare. He drew his knife and she shrank back with a little cry. "I'm just going to cut your sleeve away," he said. "It's too tight to roll up, and I need to see how deep that cut is. For God's sake, Molly, you aren't afraid of me, are you?"

"I had a donkey," she whispered. "It ran away when that man . . ."

"It's all right, he's gone." He slit the tight sleeve and pushed it up. The cut was long and shallow, across the back of her forearm. "Not bad," he said, with a reassuring smile. "You had better come with me to the house and let Mother bandage it properly."

"No, I can't! Don't make me go there. If you could take me back—to the dock—I can get a boat . . ."

She was trembling violently. "Don't argue, you're not in fit condition to think straight," he said. "Small wonder, after an experience like that. Mother loves tending to people. She will be happy to see you."

He picked her up and put her onto Risha's back. She looked very small and frightened, perched there with her feet dangling. He mounted behind her and supported her with one arm. She sat stiff as a statue, her face turned away, and took a handkerchief from a pocket in her skirt.

"I didn't want any of you to see me," she repeated in a small quavering voice.

Made up like a middle-aged woman, a paid dependent? She had certainly come down in the world since they'd last heard of her. She had been only fourteen at the time of that hideously embarrassing encounter in his room, when she told him she loved him and wanted to stay with him. The memory still made him cringe; she had been so passionate and so pathetic, and so young! That had been four years ago—or was it five? She didn't look much older now, but they had heard from mutual acquaintances that she was married. What had happened to the rich doting American husband? What was she doing alone on the West Bank, and who was the man who had attacked her? Ramses decided to leave the questions to his mother. He didn't want to interrogate the child when she was in such a nervous state. One more question might be risked, though.

"What were you doing on the West Bank?" he asked casually.

"Justin." Carefully she wiped her face, removing the last traces of makeup and tears. "He got away from François this afternoon. I thought he might have come across the river. He kept talking about watching you excavate, and about the other temple ruins. I went to the Ramesseum and I was going to Deir el Bahri when—"

"It's over now," Ramses said quickly. "I'm sorry about the boy. We'll get you straightened out and then I'll take you across the river. If he hasn't turned up we'll help you look for him."

"She'll be angry." The words were muffled; she had relaxed and turned her face against his breast.

"Mrs. Fitzroyce? It wasn't your fault. We'll find him, I promise." He went on talking, since his matter-of-fact manner seemed to have put her more at ease. "Do you suppose he went to our house? He said something the other day about visiting us."

There was no answer. He wondered uneasily if she had fainted. She was as limp as a rag doll, her face hidden against his breast. He tightened his grasp.

THEY WERE ALL ON THE veranda, adults, children, cats—and a slim figure in brown tweeds whose fair head glowed like a nimbus. "There, what did I tell you?" Ramses said cheerfully. "He's here. Unhurt and perfectly happy."

Accustomed as the family was to unexpected appearances, the sight of him with an unconscious female in his arms was startling enough to capture everyone's attention. Nefret had been watching for him. She was the first to reach the door, but his parents weren't far behind her.

"What happened?" Nefret demanded. "Who is she?"

His mother, of course, had the answer. "Mrs. Fitzroyce's companion, I believe. I remember that—er—garment quite well. Is she hurt?"

"Not seriously, Mother. Can someone take her? I think she's fainted."

"No." The slender figure stiffened. She turned her head to look up at him. Except for the piebald hair, she looked no older than the girl of fourteen he remembered so well. Her eyes were dry and her expression was wary but resigned. "You can put me down, please."

His father held up his arms. "Let me help you, Miss—er."

"You're in for a surprise, Father," Ramses warned.

"Good Gad," Emerson exclaimed. He lowered the girl gently to the ground and stared at her. "That isn't Miss—er. She looks familiar, though. Now where . . ."

"Molly," said his wife. Only a slight catch of breath betrayed her surprise. Imperturbably she went on, "And, I believe, Miss—er—as

well. Might one ask . . . But perhaps not now. You appear to have suffered a slight accident. Come with me, if you please."

Head bowed, Molly allowed herself to be led into the house.
Ramses looked at his wife. "What the hell—" she began.

"Language," Ramses said. "Come in and close that door. Davy, no!"

He captured the little boy before he had got far, and carried him
back.

"Well, well," said Emerson. "This is a surprise. What's she doing
here?"

"She is Mrs. Fitzroyce's companion," Ramses replied. "She came
to the West Bank looking for Justin."

The boy's smile was sunny and untroubled. "She didn't find me,
though. I'm glad. I have had a nice time with my friends and the
pretty Mrs. Emerson."

Ramses began, "You shouldn't have . . ." Then he stopped himself.
It wasn't his job to scold the boy.

"I would like another cup of tea, please," Justin said politely. "And
Evvie would like another biscuit."

He directed his charming smile at Evvie, who was standing next to
him, with obvious designs on the platter of cakes. Justin patted her
cheek. "I like her," he announced. "I like all the children."

⬟

I HAD QUITE A LONG conversation with Molly—or Maryam, as she
said she preferred to be called—while I cleaned and bandaged the cut
on her arm. The conversation was, however, somewhat one-sided. Her
answers to my questions were brief and uninformative, her manner
withdrawn. If I had not known better, I would have thought she was
afraid of me. Only once did she respond with her old energy, when I
told her that her father had been searching for her and would be
extremely relieved to know she was safe and well.

"You mustn't tell him!" she cried. "Promise you won't."

"I cannot promise that. He certainly would not like to hear that
you have been reduced to working as a paid companion. You must tell
Mrs. Fitzroyce that you are leaving her employ."

"I can't," Maryam said in a low voice. "You've seen what Justin is like. He trusts me. He has difficulty getting used to new people, and François, though utterly devoted, has his failings."

"He certainly does," I said. "Well, Maryam, your sense of duty does you credit. However, your father—"

"I will not be dependent on him or anyone else." Her chin lifted. "He doesn't care about me. He used me when he needed me for his own purposes."

"You are mistaken about that," I assured her.

"Perhaps. May I go now? Mrs. Fitzroyce will be worried about Justin."

"I cannot detain you if you choose to leave. Please think about what I have said. There is no shame in honest labor of any kind, but your position is onerous, and as a member of our family you are entitled to our assistance."

"Thank you." Her remote expression did not change. She got to her feet, pulling her torn sleeve down.

Despite the artificially grayed locks she looked little older than she had when I last saw her, though she must now be eighteen or nineteen. Her long-lashed hazel eyes were shaped like those of her father. The dreadful frock did not entirely hide a trim little figure.

I said, "May I give you a hat?"

It was quite a nice hat, of natural straw with quantities of veiling and several artificial flowers. Justin, who was nothing if not candid, remarked that she looked almost pretty. He added, "She would like a cup of tea, I expect."

"No," Maryam said quickly. "We must be getting back, Justin. Your grandmother will be worried."

"We can't go yet," Justin said comfortably. "My donkey has run away."

"I will get the motorcar," Emerson announced, and went out after shooting a defiant glance at me. He was a trifle sensitive still about the car, which he had not been allowed to use as often as he would have liked. I was as anxious to be rid of the pair as he, and I didn't suppose he could kill them between here and the landing, so I raised no objection.

I had persuaded Emerson to put the machine in the stableyard, though I did not suppose for a moment that it would remain there. Its admirers were numerous, and some had got into the habit of paying it a daily visit—from a distance, since Emerson and Selim had made it clear that anyone who ventured close enough to touch it would be subject to dire punishment, and possibly a curse or two. When the vehicle appeared I was not surprised to see Selim seated beside Emerson. He spent a good deal of his spare time tinkering with the confounded thing.

The appearance of the motorcar distracted Justin and altered the tenor of his demands. "A motorcar! Am I to ride in it? May I operate it?"

"Do you know how?" I asked.

"No, but I expect it is quite easy to learn. I would like it very much."

"No one drives the motorcar except me and Selim," said Emerson forcibly if somewhat inaccurately.

"Let Selim drive them, Emerson," I ordered. "There isn't room for all of you, and anyhow, I need you here."

Emerson grumbled a bit, but I knew that he too was anxious to discuss the latest developments. Selim moved over to the driver's side, and Emerson caught Justin by the collar as he was climbing up into the seat.

"Let Miss—er—get in first," he ordered.

The boy's slim frame stiffened. "Let go of him at once, Emerson," I said, remembering how he had reacted to being grasped.

"I'm not going to hurt him," Emerson shouted furiously, but he complied. "Do as I say, Justin. Do not attempt to touch the controls. You are to obey Selim as you would me. If you give him any trouble you will never be allowed to visit us again. Selim, go across with them and deliver the boy to the dahabeeyah."

"That won't be necessary," Maryam said. "He won't run away from me, will you, Justin?"

"Of course not." He smiled sweetly. "Good afternoon, everyone. I will see you again soon."

I watched somewhat apprehensively as the motorcar went off in a cloud of dust. It seemed to be operating correctly. I then asked Fatima to fetch the children's nursery maids and get them off to bed. For once, the children's parents did not offer to assist; everyone sat unmoving and silent, waiting for me to speak first. I dropped rather heavily into a chair. "It is somewhat early, but I do believe that if I were offered a whiskey and soda I might be inclined to accept."

Emerson at once obliged, and poured a rather stiff one for himself. Observing Walter's bemused expression, he poured an even stiffer one and pressed it into his brother's hand.

"Cheer up, Walter. That is the last hitherto unknown relation you are likely to encounter."

"I certainly hope so." Walter took a long drink of whiskey. "Don't we have any respectable missing relations?"

"To the best of my knowledge, Maryam is perfectly respectable," I replied. I spoke, as I always endeavor to do, the literal truth. I might harbor suspicions, but I did not know for certain.

"But she is—"

I cut him off with an imperative gesture, for I thought I knew what word had been on the tip of his tongue. Sennia did not consider herself "one of the children"; she had remained, and was paying close attention. Illegitimacy was not a topic I intended to discuss in her presence. She had heard the word—and worse—from horrid children at her Cairo school—who had got it from their parents; when she first came to me, tearful and bewildered, to ask what it meant, I had done my best to convince her that only ignorant, vulgar people cared about such things.

"What did you think of her, Sennia?" I asked.

Sennia primped up her mouth and rearranged the bracelets that encircled her slim brown wrists. "I don't like her. I didn't like her before."

"We must not be unkind, Sennia. She has had a hard time, and after all, she is kin."

"What is she to me?"

"No more than Hecuba to Hamlet," Ramses murmured. "In actual fact . . . a cousin of some degree, I suppose, Sennia. Is that right, Mother?"

"Let me see. Sennia's father was my nephew, and Maryam is . . ."

In some confusion, I finished my whiskey. "Oh, good Gad, what does it matter?"

Sennia was not to be put off. "What is she to Ramses?"

"Time for bed, Sennia," I said, giving it up.

"You are going to talk about things you don't want me to hear." Miss Sennia rose with great dignity, arranging her skirts. "I understand. Good night, everyone. But I still don't like her."

"It is somewhat overwhelming," Evelyn said, shaking her head. "Emerson told us of her background, Amelia, while you were with her. Did she explain what has brought her to this pass?"

"Briefly." I sipped my whiskey. "Her husband died suddenly—he was not a young man—and left her with nothing. He had speculated unwisely, it seems. She had to sell her engagement ring to bury him."

"From the description we got of the diamond, it must have been an extravagant funeral," Nefret murmured.

"Be that as it may, Nefret, she had to seek a situation. Lady's companion was the only occupation for which she was fitted, and she soon discovered that her youthful appearance was against her. Hence the gray hairs and the artificially aged countenance. She had, I expect, learned something of the art of disguise from her father. Still, she was unable to find work until she answered an advertisement from a lady who wanted someone familiar with Egypt, where she intended to spend the winter. No doubt," I added, "Mrs. Fitzroyce's age and poor eyesight made it easier for Maryam to carry out her masquerade."

"All this is very interesting," Ramses said in a tone that implied he did not find it so. "What I want to know is why she was attacked today. I thought when I heard her scream that some nervous female tourist was being harassed by an importunate beggar, but the fellow was actually slashing at her with his knife. That sort of thing is unheard of."

"I asked her that, of course," I replied.

"What did she say?"

"That she had no idea why anyone would want to injure her. There must be a reason, though," I declared. "Not a good reason— there is never an excuse for violence—but something she has done, or is believed to have done, that inspired a desire for revenge."

"What nonsense!" Emerson burst out. "That is just your melodramatic imagination, Peabody, always constructing mysteries. What could she have done, a child like that?"

"And that is just your masculine naïveté, Emerson, always assuming that youth and a pretty face guarantee innocence. Oh, I grant you that irrational persons may react violently to relatively harmless offenses, but mark my words, there is something behind all this, and for her own sake we must discover what it is. I allowed her to go today because I could hardly detain her by force, but I hope eventually to persuade her to come to us."

"Here?" Nefret exclaimed.

"At least until her father can take charge of her. He said he would see us soon, but I will send a message anyhow. She still harbors a grudge against him, but I believe I can set her straight on that. Emerson, were you about to speak?"

"No," said Emerson.

"You were rolling your eyes and moving your lips."

"I may be allowed, I hope, to alter my expression without asking your permission."

"Hmmm. As I was about to say, she will be more receptive to his explanations now. There is nothing so destructive to pride as poverty. It is our moral obligation to bring about the reconciliation of father and child, and assist a member of our family who is in need."

"Curse it," said Emerson hotly. "When you start quoting pious axioms there is no use trying to change your mind."

"What objection do you have to her being here?"

"None. None, damn—er—confound it. I feel sorry for the girl, but—"

"A premonition!" I exclaimed. "Are you having a premonition?"

"I never have premonitions! They are pure superstition. You are the only one who—"

"There is one thing that worries me," Nefret said, cutting Emerson off on the brink of an explosion. "Justin. If she is here, he will come again. You saw how he was with the children."

"He was charming," Lia said. "And they obviously like him."

"Oh, he's charming," Nefret said. "And utterly irresponsible. If he enticed them to go with him, for a walk or a game, he might have one of his attacks, or wander off and leave them."

Ramses spoke with unusual heat. "Nefret, that couldn't possibly happen. Even if he visits us again—which he is as likely to do whether she is here or not—no one would be fool enough to leave him alone with any of the children, or let him take them from the house."

"Quite right," I declared.

In fact, Maryam's reappearance had disturbed me more than I wanted to admit. Yet—I assured myself—what reason had I to mistrust the girl? During our brief acquaintance with her she had been a nuisance, headstrong and undisciplined, but never a danger. Her father believed that after she fled from him she had found a masculine protector, but even if it was true, she was more to be pitied than censured.

"Never a dull moment," I declared cheerfully. "Now I suggest we all get ready for our guests."

By the time the Vandergelts arrived I had bathed and changed, and written out a telegram. Emerson had insisted on seeing it before I sent it off.

"I did not want to be explicit," I explained, handing it over. "Sethos's colleague Smith, who promised to pass on messages, is not the sort of individual to be trusted with such painfully personal information."

"He has used it against us before," Emerson muttered. "Hmmm. Well, this should be all right. 'Missing person found. Come at once if possible.' I will send Ali across to the telegraph office."

With that matter taken care of I was able to greet our guests with a mind at ease and a smiling countenance. The evening had turned chilly, so we gathered in the sitting room instead of on the veranda.

"Hope we're not too early," Cyrus said, for Evelyn and I were the only members of the family present.

"No, the others are late," I said in mild vexation. "I do apologize. I try my best to inculcate proper manners, but sometimes I think it is a hopeless chore, especially with Emerson."

"And Walter," his wife said with a smile. "I expect he decided to steal a few minutes with his texts. When he is involved with a tricky translation I sometimes have to shake him to get his attention."

Lia and David entered, closely followed by Nefret. Ramses was conspicuous by his absence, and I observed that Nefret's brow bore faint lines of worry or annoyance. "I am so sorry," she began.

"Not at all," Katherine said graciously. "Were the children restless tonight?"

"Ours were," David replied. "We took them to Abdullah's tomb this afternoon. They couldn't stop talking about it. Dolly wanted to hear every story I could remember about my grandfather, and Evvie asked the most outrageous questions—"

"She is only two," Lia expostulated. "I don't see what was so outrageous about them."

"'Do all dead people look like the ones in Uncle Radcliffe's books?'" David was obviously quoting.

"Good heavens," Katherine exclaimed. "Has he been showing those poor children photographs of mummies?"

"I strictly forbade him to do that," I said indignantly.

"It doesn't seem to have bothered them," David said.

"What did you tell Evvie?" I asked.

"I said no, they didn't. And changed the subject before she could inquire further," David added with a laugh.

I decided I would do the same, for I did not want to fall into the error of some doting females, who assume that others enjoy an entire evening of stories about their grandchildren.

"We had an interesting visitor this afternoon," I said. "Katherine, do you remember a young person called Molly Hamilton?"

Katherine nodded. "That spoiled child who raised such a fuss when her uncle wanted to—" She broke off, her green eyes narrowing. "Major Hamilton's niece . . . but he wasn't . . . He was . . ."

"Not Major Hamilton," I said. "And she was not his niece. She was his daughter. And still is."

They listened to my brief summary in fascinated silence. "The plot thickens," said Cyrus, shaking his head. "What are you going to do about her?"

"Take her into the bosom of the family, of course," said Emerson from the doorway. "As my—er—other brother once remarked, it is

Amelia's habit to adopt every unfortunate innocent she comes across, by force if necessary."

"You are very late, Emerson," I said reproachfully. "Really, it is a shame! And have you been showing those children pictures of disgusting mummies, after I strictly forbade . . . after I requested that you refrain from doing so?"

Not at all discomposed by this double-barreled attack, Emerson addressed a general smile and mumble of greeting at our guests and went at once to the sideboard, where he began pouring from various decanters. He had not abandoned the argument, however. Over his shoulder he remarked, "I am not the latest, my dear. Ramses and Walter are still to come."

"That only makes it worse, Emerson. Why don't you go and find them?"

"Such a fuss about nothing," said Emerson, handing me a glass. "There you are, Peabody; drink your whiskey and behave yourself. I hear them coming now."

They came in together, so absorbed in conversation that I verily believe Walter was unaware of his surroundings until Ramses, who had him firmly by the arm, brought him to a stop and directed his attention to the others.

"I say, I am sorry," Walter exclaimed, blinking. "Have we kept you waiting? It is entirely my fault. I came across a particularly fascinating text, and wanted to consult Ramses about one or two obscure words. It seems to be—"

"Sit down, Walter, and be quiet," said Emerson amiably. "No one wants to hear about your obscure philological interests. Vandergelt, I was surprised not to see you at Deir el Medina in recent days. Are you abandoning your part of the concession?"

"Don't get your hopes up," said Cyrus, stroking his goatee. "Those tombs are mine, and I'll be back at work pretty soon. We've been busy."

"Doing what?" Emerson demanded in honest surprise.

Fatima announced dinner and we withdrew to the dining room. Cyrus began explaining to Emerson in a somewhat indignant voice that the preservation and recording of the treasures of the God's Wives took precedence over other activities at this time—facts Emerson knew perfectly well, but preferred to ignore because he had his own plans.

The only thing I have against large parties is that it is impossible to keep track of everything that is being said. We are—I say it without apology—a wordy lot, and since we are also an intelligent lot, our conversations are worth listening to. Even Bertie had perked up and was talking animatedly to Lia. (I had seated him next to her, since she was less likely to interrupt him than some of the others.) Then I heard an isolated phrase and realized he was extolling the virtues of his absent beloved, Jumana.

Not until the end of the meal did the discussion become general. It was a comment of Emerson's, delivered in his usual ringing tones, that caught everyone's attention.

"I see no reason why we should do anything about it."

"About what?" I inquired.

Emerson had addressed Ramses, who took it upon himself to answer me. "About the attack on Molly—Maryam—this afternoon. I suggested to Father that we must make an attempt to locate her assailant."

"Right," Cyrus agreed. "We can't have that sort of thing going on. With all respect to your theories, Amelia, the most likely explanation is that the fellow is demented. He may attack other tourists. How do you propose to go about it?"

"For one thing, the police must be notified," Ramses said, over Emerson's grumbles. "And Father is the one to do it. They'll listen to him. I also suggest offering a reward, starting with our fellows tomorrow morning. They know everyone on the West Bank and they will spread the word."

"That makes sense," I agreed. "Emerson?"

"Oh, curse it, I suppose I must," Emerson muttered.

"Tomorrow morning," I said.

"Tomorrow afternoon," said Emerson.

I agreed with a show of reluctance that persuaded Emerson he had won the argument. In fact, the timing suited me very well. There were several other matters I meant to attend to while we were in Luxor.

WE PUT PART OF RAMSES'S scheme into operation as soon as we arrived at Deir el Medina the following morning, gathering our men and telling them of what had happened. Shock and surprise and expressions of their readiness to cooperate were the only results, however. Selim summed it up by declaring that no resident of the West Bank villages could have been responsible. Moral considerations aside, they knew only too well that attacks on tourists would be severely punished. There were always a few harmless madmen wandering about; they were well known and watched over with the respect Muslims show to the mentally afflicted, and none of them was given to violence.

"We will pass the word," Selim promised. "And ask about strangers."

So that was that. David and Evelyn had gone to the Castle, but Bertie was with us and so was Sennia. Letting her come was a reward and a distinction to which I felt she was entitled. Unfortunately, bringing Sennia along meant that we also had to bring Gargery and Horus. They were both frightful nuisances. Horus growled and snapped at everyone who came near Sennia, and Gargery refused to admit that he was no longer quick enough and strong enough to guard her from danger. Watching Sennia dash around the site with Gargery hobbling after her, cursing at Horus, who swore back at him, would have been amusing if it had not been so inconvenient. I hadn't the heart to deny Gargery, though—or the courage to deny Horus.

Sennia's self-appointed task was to collect inscribed ostraca for Ramses, so I persuaded her to help me sift the debris the men had removed from the house we were clearing. She had keen eyes and had been trained to recognize the cursive hieratic writing. The shards of broken pottery, some small, some quite large, sometimes had sketches instead of inscriptions. Fortunately I was able to snatch one particular scrap away before she got a good look at it. Later, I handed it to Ramses.

"Thank you, Mother," he said. "Is this . . . Oh. Good Lord. Did Sennia see it?"

"No, I sent her off to help Emerson. You have been allowing her to fit broken pieces together, I believe; I hope and trust she has not come across others of this nature."

"So do I," Ramses muttered, holding the fragment by the edges. "I don't think so, Mother. Knowing Sennia, she would have shown them to me and asked me to explain them. I will go over the others again before I let her work on them."

"This is part of a larger piece. You see where this lower limb—"

"Yes," Ramses said quickly. He was visibly embarrassed, not by the subject matter of the drawing itself but by my discussion of it. Young persons never quite accept the fact that their parents—particularly their mothers—are familiar with the mechanisms of the human body.

"It reminds me," I went on, "of the drawings on that papyrus in the Turin Museum."

"How the hell—" Ramses almost dropped the scrap. "I beg your pardon, Mother. How did you get a look at that papyrus? Women aren't supposed to—"

"Have you ever known me to be deterred from my research by a foolish convention? It is quite possible that though its origins are unknown, that papyrus was found here at Deir el Medina, early in the last century. The villagers seem to have been a—er—merry lot."

"Quite," said Ramses, flushed and perspiring. "If you will excuse me, Mother—"

"Not just yet. I want to discuss another matter with you."

Resignedly, Ramses subsided into a sitting position. I did not doubt he would find this subject even more embarrassing, but if it had not already occurred to him he was no son of mine. I plunged straight in medias res.

"The reappearance of Maryam casts a new light on the Affair of the Veiled Hathor and lends greater credence to one of our theories. She was not on my list—"

"List?" His jaw tightened and his black eyes narrowed to slits as comprehension was succeeded by outrage. "What list? Mother, you didn't!"

"It was a legitimate, indeed, necessary, part of my criminal investigation."

Ramses pushed his hat back and covered his flushed face with his hands. "I suppose you consulted Nefret," he muttered between clenched fingers.

"My dearest boy, how could you suppose I would do such a thing? I waited until I could get you alone before raising the subject. And," I went on, "I beg that you won't waste time with false modesty. Emerson will be shouting for you soon. Maryam, as Molly, fancied herself in love with you—"

"For God's sake, Mother, she was only fourteen. It was a youthful fancy, nothing more."

I did not need to remind him of what she had done; the picture was probably as clear in his mind as it was in mine: Alone with him in his room, her dress pulled down to bare a youthful but unquestionably mature shape. What had preceded that moment I had no need to ask. She had been the aggressor, and he had immediately summoned me.

"All the same, she may have considered herself a woman scorned," I said. "Fourteen is a difficult age, given to melodrama and long-held resentment."

"Not for four years!" Ramses wiped perspiration off his forehead with his sleeve.

"Was there anyone else who might hold a grudge?"

Instead of protesting, he shrugged helplessly. "How the devil should I know what a woman considers . . . Oh, all right, Mother, since you insist. There was Dolly Bellingham. The fact that I murdered her father might reasonably prejudice her against me."

"You acted in defense of yourself and of me," I said. "I considered her, of course—"

"Of course," Ramses muttered.

"But she was a thoroughly selfish little creature who cared nothing for her father. And easily distracted, would you not say?"

"Definitely." An unwilling smile curled Ramses's mouth. "She has probably been through a dozen men since."

"I wouldn't have put it quite that way, but I agree. Anyone else?"

"No. There's Father, looking for me. May I be excused?"

I let him go, since I didn't suppose I would get any more out of him—at that time. No doubt he was right about Maryam's passing infatuation; but she had another, more compelling, reason for hating the entire lot of us. I wondered if Ramses had forgotten that her mother had met a violent end at the hands of one of our men—we had never ascertained which. Bertha had been in the process of attempting to kill me at the time, but Maryam might not see it that way. I remembered Sethos's words: "If she blames me for her mother's death, how do you suppose she feels about you?"

I gave myself a little shake and told myself to be sensible. I did not know how the girl felt about a number of things, and neither did her father.

I meant to add her to my list, though.

I managed to get Emerson away from the site and forced into a proper suit by mid-afternoon. Everyone had decided to come along. We were to dine at the Winter Palace after completing our various errands. Daoud had offered to take us across in his new boat. He had bought it for one of his sons and set him up in business, ferrying tourists back and forth from Luxor to the tombs and temples of the West Bank. Sabir was, his proud father informed us, one of the most successful of such entrepreneurs, which was not surprising, since his boat was the most attractive—brightly painted, immaculately clean, and fitted out with rugs on the floor and colorful cushions on the seats along both sides.

We pulled up to the dock amid a group of similar vessels, and Daoud announced he intended to visit relatives and would wait to take us back. I attempted to dissuade him, explaining that we might be late, but he was determined, and as the other boatmen gathered round I realized that he was looking forward to a good gossip with his friends. After disembarking we separated. David and Walter went off to look for antiquities and renew their acquaintances with various dealers; Evelyn and Lia decided to stroll about and perhaps visit a few shops. I declined their invitation to join them.

"I suppose you want to go to the police with me," said Emerson resignedly.

"Why, no, my dear, I will leave that to you. Ramses, are you going with your father?"

Ramses nodded. "I believe we also ought to inform the police about the carelessness of the hunters. We will meet you at the hotel later."

They started off down the dusty road side by side. "That's got them out of the way," I said to Nefret, who had remained with me.

"Yes. I presume you mean to call on Mrs. Fitzroyce. Father wouldn't approve."

"That is why I wanted him out of the way. You see the necessity of such a visit."

"I see why you believe it to be necessary."

"You don't agree?"

"I don't know," Nefret said, frowning slightly. "I have nothing against the girl, and I would like to see her reconciled with her father, for his sake as much as hers."

"But?"

"But . . ." Nefret's brow smoothed out and she smiled affectionately at me. "No buts. You offered to assist her, and if I were in your place I would wait for her to make the next move. It's your decision, though."

The *Isis* was one of the few private dahabeeyahs moored alongside the tourist steamers. Nefret let out a low whistle (an unladylike habit she had got from Ramses) when she saw it. It was a steam-dahabeeyah, one of the largest and most ostentatious boats I had ever seen. Brass railings shone and gilt tassels adorned the gold-and-crimson awning that shaded the upper deck. Large gold lettering spelled out the name, and the British flag flew at the stern. A wide carpeted gangplank extended from the boat to the bank. There was no one in sight on deck or on the shaded upper deck, but as soon as I set foot on the gangplank, a man dressed in Egyptian style appeared and hailed me in English, asking what I wanted. I replied in Arabic that I had come to call on the Sitt. "Take this to her," I went on, handing the fellow one of my cards. "And ask if she will see me."

He bowed very politely, but instead of going on his errand he handed the card to another servant who had come up, soft-footed in felt slippers. "You will wait here, please," he said.

He was a sturdy, muscular fellow, who was obviously prepared to stop us if we disregarded his request. I did not blame Mrs. Fitzroyce for taking such steps to prevent intrusion. As I knew from personal experience, some idle visitors had no scruples about forcing themselves on persons they believed to be important.

We did not have to wait long. When the second servant returned he was accompanied by a portly person wearing a fez on his large head. His hair was very black and very thick, and his face was practically spherical. It was a young face, fair-skinned and good-natured, and set off by a set of curling mustaches. He was formally attired in frock coat and striped trousers and an extraordinary waistcoat embroidered with pink roses.

"It is an honor to meet you, Sitt Hakim," he said, nodding vigorously and smiling broadly. "I am Dr. Mohammed Abdul Khattab, Mrs. Fitzroyce's personal physician."

I presented him to Nefret, which brought on another round of nods and grins. "I trust Mrs. Fitzroyce is not ill?" I inquired.

"She is only old," said the doctor nonchalantly. "She will receive you, but may I remind you that she tires easily."

"You may," I said. "We won't stay long."

The curtains of the windows of the saloon had been drawn to shut out the direct rays of the declining sun. There was enough light for me to see reasonably well, however. The room was elegantly furnished—over-furnished, in fact—with a pianoforte, rows of bookshelves, tables and chairs and sofas. It was reminiscent of the style of decoration popular before the turn of the century, and the lady who awaited us was also reminiscent of that era. She sat bolt upright in an armchair with her hands resting on the head of her stick, and her widow's weeds were as black and enveloping as those of the late Queen, who had mourned her deceased husband for—in my opinion—far too long. Instead of gloves she wore black lace mitts, of a style I hadn't seen for years. Dr. Khattab went at once to her and took her hand, his fingers pressed against the pulse in her wrist. She shook him off.

"I trust Mrs. Emerson will not be offended," she said in a creaking voice, "if I say that welcome as her visit is, it is not likely to overexcite me."

"Not at all," I said, acknowledging her little jest with a genteel chuckle.

"Please take a chair," she went on. "May I offer you tea?"

"No, thank you. We will only take a few minutes of your time. We called to—"

"Complain of my grandson," she broke in.

She appeared to like plain speaking, so I decided to oblige her. "No, we came to complain about Justin's manservant. He was responsible for my husband's fall off a cliff yesterday."

"I trust he was not seriously injured."

It was not the words but the tone that I found somewhat irritating. Old age has its privileges, but in my opinion rudeness is not one of them.

"No thanks to François," I retorted. "Do you consider him a suitable person to look after a gentle boy like Justin?"

"That is, I presume, a criticism couched as a question. Obviously I do, or I would not continue to employ him." She went on in a less autocratic tone. "I regret the injury to your husband, and I have spoken to François. It won't happen again. Why did you give my companion that hat?"

The abrupt change of subject left me speechless for a moment. I rallied instantly, of course. "She had lost hers and it was improper for her to appear in public without one."

"It is a pretty hat," said Mrs. Fitzroyce. "I had an even prettier one when I was a girl. It had on it a stuffed cockatoo with rubies for eyes."

Her head bobbed up and down and she spoke in a soft, crooning voice quite unlike her earlier peremptory tones. I looked questioningly at the doctor. He smiled and shrugged. Evidently the old lady had "spells" too, sinking into senile reminiscence without warning.

"Is she here?" I asked.

"No, she has been dead for twenty years," murmured Mrs. Fitzroyce. "She was a beautiful girl, but not so beautiful as I . . ."

"Miss Underhill has gone with Justin and François to Karnak," said the doctor smoothly.

"Quite right," said Mrs. Fitzroyce, snapping back into coherence. "Why do you take it upon yourself to answer questions addressed to me, Khattab?"

"Your pardon, madame." The doctor's grin appeared to be glued in place.

Not knowing how long the old lady would keep her wits, I said, "We discovered, Miss Underhill and I, that we had acquaintances in common. I wonder if she might be allowed to come to us, for dinner, or for the day, at some time."

"She is a good girl," Mrs. Fitzroyce murmured. I was not sure whether she was referring to the long-dead beauty or to Maryam, until she went on, "Very faithful. She has not missed a single day since she came to me."

She raised a limp hand, which was promptly grasped by Dr. Khattab. "Faint," he announced portentously. "Too faint, dear lady."

"We are tiring you," I said, rising. "Good day."

"Has not the pretty Mrs. Emerson something to say?" the old lady inquired.

"Only good day," said Nefret, on her feet.

"You are very pretty," said Mrs. Fitzroyce judiciously. "But not as pretty as she was."

The doctor remained with his patient, and one of the crewmen escorted us to the gangplank.

"You didn't tell her about Maryam," Nefret said in a low voice.

"There is a limit to the degree of interference even I consider appropriate," I replied. "I do not have the right to expose Maryam's secret to her employer. Mrs. Fitzroyce is an interesting individual, isn't she?"

"She must have been quite a commanding character before her mind began to go. No wonder they need such a large staff, with Mrs. Fitzroyce increasingly feeble in mind and body, and Justin utterly unpredictable."

Since it was still early, we strolled back along the corniche toward the suk. Luxor is not a large town; it was not long before we ran into Lia and Evelyn. At my suggestion we joined forces and went looking for Walter and David, who were likely to lose track of the time in their search for antiquities. We located them in the shop of Omar, drinking tea and inspecting the old rascal's collection of dubious papyri and questionable ushebtis. Omar's shop was always worth a look, since he occasionally mixed a few genuine articles in with his spurious artifacts. I believe he enjoyed testing the knowledge of his buyers, for he always gave in with good grace and no shame at all when his duplicity was exposed. David was particularly skilled at recognizing fakes, since he had made a number of them in his youth.

"What, is it time for tea already?" he asked when we entered the shop. "I am at your disposal, ladies; Omar has nothing of interest except this amulet of Isis, for which he is asking too much."

His eyes twinkling, Omar let out a heartrending groan. "Too much? I let you have it for nothing, for less than I paid!"

"I presume you have been asking about jewelry in general and bracelets in particular," I said, after we had bade Omar farewell— without purchasing the amulet.

"I put out a few feelers," David admitted, offering me his arm. "Cyrus seems to be resigned to his loss, but I am mystified at how Martinelli and his loot could have disappeared without a trace."

"It is not difficult to lose oneself in the teeming tenements of Cairo, my dear, as you ought to know. I do not doubt that he went there. If he had remained in Luxor we would have located him by now."

The Winter Palace enjoyed an unparalleled view from its raised terraces, straight across the river to the cliffs of the West Bank. They shone pink in the rays of the declining sun, and the river blazed all shades of crimson and scarlet with reflected sunset. Ramses was waiting for us.

"Where is your father?" I asked.

"He stopped off at Cook's." He resumed his chair and beckoned a waiter. "They handle most of the tours, so perhaps they can be more effective than the police at controlling the hunters in their parties."

Nefret chuckled. "Lia, what do you say we run down and listen at the door? I do love hearing Father read someone the riot act."

Lia laughed, and Ramses said, "You are in a cheerful mood this evening, Nefret. What have you and Mother been doing?"

Nefret began regaling them with a vivacious description of our visit to Mrs. Fitzroyce. She was interrupted after a few sentences by the arrival of Emerson, and, at his request, began again at the beginning.

"I knew you went there," said Emerson to me.

"No, you didn't."

"I ordered you a whiskey and soda, Father," Ramses said, in what he must have known was a vain attempt to prevent Emerson from continuing the argument. "I trust that is satisfactory."

"Thank you, my boy. Yes, I did. And," said Emerson triumphantly, "I will tell you how I knew. We met Daoud outside the zabtiyeh, on his way to his cousin's house, and—"

"He saw us go to the *Isis* or someone who had seen us reported to him," I finished. "Daoud is better than a newspaper at disseminating information. By now all of Luxor knows where we have been, and where we mean to be for every minute of the remainder of the evening!"

"What's the harm in that?" David asked.

We were soon to find out.

Enjoying one another's companionship and exchanging greetings with friends, we passed a carefree evening; but shortly before ten I reminded the others that we had agreed to meet Daoud at that hour. He did not own a watch, but he could tell time quite accurately by the sun and the stars (and by asking other people), and he was punctilious about keeping appointments. Sure enough, he came hurrying to meet us as soon as we reached the dock. Several other boats bobbed at their moorings, but there was no one in sight except for our party. The night air was cool, and there was a rather stiff breeze. After we had crossed into the boat and taken our places, Daoud pulled in the gangplank, which was nothing more or less than a plank, approximately eight inches wide and as many feet long.

It was a lovely night for a sail. The moon, near the full, cast silvery ripples across the water, and the stars were very bright. We were several hundred yards from shore when I became aware of an uncomfortable coolness on the soles of my feet. Before I could comment, the coldness rose over instep and ankle.

"Dear me," I remarked, "I do believe we have sprung a leak."

"I do believe you are correct," said Emerson calmly, as water enveloped our ankles. The others drew their feet up with exclamations of alarm, and Daoud, who had been preoccupied with sail and tiller, let out a loud cry.

"It is not possible! The boat is sound!"

Since this was clearly no longer the case, no one bothered with a verbal contradiction. Ramses bent over and began pulling back the soaked rugs. He found the trouble almost at once, and announced his discovery aloud.

"There are three holes drilled through the bottom. Daoud, turn back at once, we'll never make it to the other side. Nefret, give me your scarf."

"No use," said Emerson curtly. He was kneeling, feeling about with his hands under the rapidly rising water. "They are each over an inch in diameter. Must have been plugged with some substance that would slowly dissolve or be knocked out by the motion of the waves."

David had joined Daoud in the bow and was helping him with the sail and the tiller, but the boat moved slowly and sluggishly. It was clear that we were going to sink before we could make it back to shore. Emerson pulled off his coat and waistcoat. Ramses had already done so. Raising the long heavy plank, he pitched it over the side and then lowered himself into the water. "Nefret!" he called.

She followed him without an instant's hesitation. Water had reached the seats and was still rising. "Give it up, David," Emerson shouted. "Help me with the others."

He turned to me. I knew I had to get out of the long skirts that would encumber my limbs, but I was having a hard time with my buttons, for my hands were not as steady as I would have liked. I am not skilled at aquatic exercise. I was not the least worried about myself, however, since my dear Emerson was at my side. He was completely at home in the water, and so were Ramses and David. It was the others, especially Evelyn and Walter, who were the objects of my concern. It was somewhat reassuring to see Walter carefully removing his eyeglasses and tucking them into his inside pocket, Evelyn slipping out of her velvet evening wrap, Lia crawling along the bench toward her mother. I could only thank God this had not happened when the children were with us.

As I continued to fumble with my buttons Emerson caught hold of the neckline of my frock and ripped it down and off, picked me up, and tossed me over the side. I came sputtering back to the surface, supported by my son's firm hands, and saw that the others had abandoned ship as well. Emerson had seized his brother and sister-in-law, one in each arm, and was guiding them toward the plank to which Nefret clung. David had Lia in tow. I pushed the wet hair out of my eyes and rapidly took stock of the situation. Yes; everyone was present and accounted for, safe for the moment at least. Everyone except . . .

A thrill of horror ran through me. A dark shape against the silvery ripples, the boat went down, and with it went Daoud, sitting bolt upright in the bow. The last I saw of him was his large, calm face, eyes wide open and mouth tightly closed, as the water rose up and over it. Only then did I remember he could not swim a stroke.

CHAPTER SIX

D aoud!" I shrieked. "Save him! Hurry!"

That is what I meant to shriek. Unfortunately, a wave washed over my head and only a prolonged gurgle expressed my sentiments. Clinging one-handed to the plank, I blinked the water out of my eyes in time to see Ramses's feet disappear under the water. My admonition had been unnecessary; he had gone to Daoud's rescue as soon as he was certain I was safe.

"Hang on, Peabody!" Emerson bellowed directly into my left ear. "And for God's sake close your mouth!"

His hands hoisted me up till my arms rested across the splintery surface of the plank. Then they were gone, and I knew that Emerson too was gone, down into the dark depths after Daoud.

So there we were, bobbing up and down in the eddies, lined up along the gangplank like diners at a table. With a thrill of patriotic pride I observed that all the faces, though streaming with water and plastered with wet hair, were as unperturbed as those of well-bred persons at an evening party.

Then a more remarkable sight drew my attention. It was the head of Daoud, his eyes still open, his mouth still closed, erupting from the water. Next to appear were his arms, spread out wide. Emerson had him on one side and Ramses on the other.

Daoud blinked, looked round, and cautiously opened his mouth. "Now what must I do?" he inquired.

There is not much traffic on the river after dark, except for an occasional tourist wanting a moonlight sail. Evidently none of them had been romantically inclined that evening; and so, after a brief discussion, Ramses struck out for shore. At my suggestion we all kicked vigorously in order to ward off chills and cramp, and David kept our spirits up by giving Daoud his first swimming lesson. Daoud's trust in us was unlimited; he followed David's instructions and discovered, to his delight, that his very large frame floated as lightly as a leaf. (I do not understand why this should be so; it has something to do with buoyancy, I believe.) To see him lying on his back, with only his toes and smiling face above water and his robe wafting around him like the wings of a bird in flight was a sight I will long remember.

Entertaining though this was, I was relieved to behold at last a light approaching, and to hear the shouts of several men who (as Ramses later described it) he had found sleeping in their boat and had aroused in a somewhat peremptory fashion. They took us aboard and we were soon on the West Bank, where our carriages awaited us. Daoud declined our offer of a ride—and indeed, it would have been an extremely tight squeeze, since he took up the space of two people. He went off, still smiling, with his wet skirts flapping and his turban, which had remained miraculously in place, looking rather like a squashed cauliflower. Immediately upon our arrival at the house Fatima and I put Evelyn into a hot bath and then popped her into bed.

"Will she be all right?" Walter asked anxiously. He bent over her. She smiled drowsily at him, but her eyelids were drooping.

"She is chilled and exhausted, but has taken no lasting harm, I believe," I replied. "Bed for you too, Walter."

"While the rest of you gather for a council of war?" He was still quite damp, but he had dried and replaced his eyeglasses and his eyes were bright. "Good heavens, Amelia, who could sleep after an adventure like that? I want to talk. I want to listen. I want—yes, by Gad, I want a whiskey and soda!"

"And food," Fatima said firmly. "There is cold chicken in the larder, and kunafeh, and bread, and lettuce—"

"Very well, Fatima, come and join us. Just don't wake Gargery, I am in no mood to be scolded by him tonight."

It was Fatima's inveterate habit to feed us at any hour of the day or night, but in this case, as I well knew, her primary motive was to be the first to hear the news of our most recent escapade, so she could lord it over Gargery next morning. The two of them were in amiable but uncompromising competition on such matters.

Though we had not agreed upon a conference, it was obvious that all shared Walter's opinion about its necessity; the others came in, clad informally in dressing gowns and robes, and we all tucked into Fatima's spread. Strenuous physical exercise does give one an appetite.

Handing his brother the requested whiskey and soda, Emerson remarked, "You are looking very pleased with yourself, Walter. Why, I wonder?"

"I may not have been of much use," said Walter, "but at least no one had to rescue me."

How clearly I comprehended the emotion behind that simple statement! He had feared that his sedentary life had rendered him unfit for adventure—that in a crisis he would not measure up. I smiled affectionately at him, but Emerson, who has a more literal mind than I, said, "I trust you are not blaming Daoud for requiring to be rescued."

"Good heavens, no!" Walter exclaimed. "You mistake my meaning, Radcliffe. He was splendid. And never a word of complaint about his boat. It is a considerable financial loss to him."

"We will replace or repair the boat, naturally," said Ramses.

After a brief silence, Lia said, "Because you believe we were somehow responsible for its loss? Why couldn't it have been an accident, or a private vendetta?"

Emerson's heavy brows lifted in surprise. "I took it for granted that the—er—gesture was aimed at us. Such demonstrations usually are. It certainly cannot have been an accident. Someone drilled holes through the bottom of the boat and plugged them with clay or some other substance that would gradually dissolve."

Fatima clapped her hands over her mouth and stared in horror. "Who would do such a thing?"

"That is indeed the question," Ramses replied. He leaned back and lit a cigarette. "The job must have been done shortly before we got to the dock."

"Half the population of Luxor knew our schedule," I mused. "The miscreant was taking a chance, though. If we had been half an hour later, the boat would have been filling with water by the time we came. Half an hour earlier, and we would have caught him in the act. Didn't anyone see or hear him?"

"There was no one nearby," Ramses said. "Most of the boatmen had gone home. He wasn't taking much of a chance, you know. If he hadn't finished the job before we got there he'd have heard us in time to make himself scarce."

"We are none of us children or cowards," I said. "We must face the facts. I cannot imagine any boatman in Luxor being so vindictive, or so stupid as to risk Daoud's wrath. No; it was aimed at us, but I must say it seems a very haphazard method of committing murder."

"And somewhat wholesale," said Emerson round the stem of his pipe. "Was he hoping to drown the lot of us, or was he after some one individual?"

"We can all swim," I said thoughtfully. "That is generally known, I believe."

"All except one," said Ramses. "And that, too, is generally known."

"Daoud," Emerson muttered. "Impossible! He hasn't an enemy in the world."

NATURALLY NONE OF US ALLOWED our little misadventure to disturb our work schedule. The younger children were breakfasting in their own quarters, under the benevolent eyes of Fatima and Basima, so our own morning repast was soon concluded. However, we were subjected to a scathing lecture from Gargery, who had graciously ceded attendance on the children to Fatima. He pretended he was doing her a favor, but I fancy he had found four little ones a bit too much for him.

"Something is going on," he declared, dribbling coffee into Emerson's cup. "You've no right to keep it from me, sir and madam."

It was one of Gargery's more annoying habits (he had several) to dole out food and drink in minuscule quantities when he was annoyed with us. Emerson wrested the coffeepot from him.

"I don't know what the devil is going on, Gargery," he snarled. "And I do not intend to discuss it with you, especially in the presence of . . ." He nodded and winked in an exaggerated fashion, indicating Sennia.

For once she was tucking into her porridge without argument. She looked very neat and pretty that morning, with her hair tied back in a bow—and, I observed with a slight pang, very grown up. Emerson's reference was not lost on her. With a slightly patronizing smile, she remarked, "I know all about it, Professor. Fatima told Gargery and me this morning."

Gargery growled deep in his throat. He did hate hearing things secondhand from Fatima.

"It is very strange," Sennia continued. "Who would want to hurt Daoud?"

"We don't know that it was meant to hurt anyone," Ramses replied. "The most the fellow could reasonably expect was that we would all get a ducking. The boat can be replaced, and will be, Sennia."

His attempt at reassurance did not convince her. "Daoud can't swim."

"But we can," Ramses insisted. "Father and I had him up within half a minute." He laughed a little, and went on in a sprightly manner, "You should have seen him, Sennia. He never lost his calm, or his head—or even his turban!"

"It was a mean trick, though," Sennia said, frowning. "What shall we do?"

"Go about our business as usual," I replied. "That is our tradition, Sennia."

"With a stiff upper lip?" Sennia inquired seriously.

"Quite right," David agreed. "I hope you aren't worried, Little Bird. It was a mean trick, as you said, but no one can possibly do something like that to you."

"I am not at all worried. Aunt Nefret is teaching me to shoot with the bow."

"Good Gad," I exclaimed. "You haven't taken up archery again, have you, Nefret? You were once expert at the sport, I know, but with the children around—"

"I've been very careful, Mother." Nefret avoided her husband's critical look; I could see that this was news to him too, and that he did not much like it.

"Hmmm," I said. "Evelyn, are you sure you feel up to working today?"

"Of course." She looked up with a smile. "I am enjoying it more than I can say. Sennia, dear, get your books and we will go."

Sennia no longer objected to her lessons with Katherine, since she was allowed to learn drawing from Evelyn afterward. She trotted off and I accompanied Evelyn onto the veranda. Drawing on her gloves, she said gravely, "Do you think I should be armed, Amelia?"

I wanted to laugh and embrace her; but the solemnity of her sweet face in its frame of silvery hair warned me not to hurt her feelings. With equal gravity I inquired, "What sort of weapon did you have in mind, Evelyn? A pistol?"

"Dear me, no, Amelia, I am terrified of firearms and would probably shoot the wrong person. A knife, perhaps?"

The idea of gentle Evelyn plunging a knife into a human body would have struck most people as impossible. I had seen her do something almost as unbelievable, though, when she pumped four bullets into the chest of a thug while under the (happily erroneous) belief that he had murdered her husband. Gentle persons can be extremely dangerous when they are roused to maniacal fury by danger to those they love.

She saw my expression. Vehemently she exclaimed, "Do you suppose I could not act, if Sennia were threatened?"

"I believe you could and would," I said, and meant it. "But, Evelyn, Gargery will be with you, and Abdul, the coachman, is a strong, devoted young fellow. There is absolutely no reason to suppose Sennia is in any danger."

"We don't know who is endangered," Evelyn replied. "Do we?"

"Well—er—no. I have it! Take one of my parasols. You have, upon occasion, wielded one effectively."

"The sword parasol?"

It was not really a request. She meant to have it. I heard Sennia's voice, and said hurriedly, "All right, I'll get it. Just don't tell Emerson!"

I didn't have to warn her not to tell Walter. He would raise a great fuss. Good gracious, I thought, as the carriage drove off, what a bellicose lot we have become! Evelyn with a sword, Sennia and Nefret with bow and arrow . . .

I might ask Nefret to give me a few lessons too.

And not tell Emerson.

FROM MANUSCRIPT H

"Damnation!" said Emerson. "Look at that! It will take hours to get them settled down to work."

Ramses brought Risha to a stop beside his father's mount. A crowd had gathered next to the blocked-off area of excavation behind the temple. In the center, his head rising over those of the shorter spectators, was Daoud. From his sweeping gestures it was evident that he was relating the dramatic events of the previous night.

"He's entitled to his moment in the spotlight," Ramses said tolerantly. "Not only did he lose his boat, but he almost drowned."

Daoud proceeded to drown, sinking slowly down out of sight. A chorus of awed exclamations greeted the performance, erupting into cheers when his head popped up again and he began waving his arms.

The others, who had been following at a more leisurely pace, drew up beside them. "What's going on?" Walter asked.

Lia giggled. "Daoud is dramatizing his rescue. I think those arm motions are meant to indicate swimming. Bless his heart, don't stop him, he's putting on a splendid performance."

"Bah," said Emerson.

Selim, standing on the outskirts of the crowd, was the first of the absorbed audience to notice them. He called out, "He is here, the Father of Curses. It is time—"

"Yes!" Daoud shouted. "They are here, my saviors! The Father of Curses and the Brother of Demons, who lifted me out of the water, and the others, the brave ones who faced death with smiling faces. They are heroes!"

A great cheer broke out. Hiding his smile behind his hand, Emerson muttered, "What a showman the old fellow is! He picked up his cue as neatly as any actor."

"I wonder how accurate his story was," said Ramses, acknowledging the plaudits of the crowd with a wave of his hand. "Hullo, Selim. Sorry to have interrupted."

"It was time," said Selim, frowning. "My respected uncle is a great liar, but . . . Is it true that the sinking of the boat was deliberate?"

Emerson had dismounted. Politely fending off two admirers—Daoud's sons—who were trying to embrace him, he said, "It is true. Ramses, will you address the crowd, since Daoud has got them in the proper frame of mind?"

"Yes, sir," Ramses said. He raised his hand for silence, and the faces turned expectantly toward him. "My friends! Daoud has told you what happened. It was no accident. We will replace the boat, but we must find out who was guilty of such an evil act. We ask for your help, knowing you will give it as you have always done." He would have stopped there, but the sight of Daoud's hopeful face made him add, "Though he was too modest to say so, Daoud is also a hero. Honor him for his courage."

"Well done, my boy," Nefret murmured.

She hadn't called him that for a long time. He turned quickly to her, but she had already started to dismount. The rest of them followed suit and one of the men led the horses away, to the shelter his mother had rigged up with poles and pieces of canvas.

"Get the men started, Selim," Emerson ordered.

"Not yet," said Selim, looking severely at Emerson. "This is a bad business, Father of Curses. We must discuss our strategy."

"I don't have a strategy," Emerson retorted. "What the devil, Selim—"

His wife poked him with her parasol. "Perhaps Selim has one, Emerson. You might at least pay him the courtesy of listening."

Before Selim could reply, they were joined by Bertie Vandergelt.

Ramses hadn't seen him until then, but he had obviously been one of the audience, for his face bore a frown instead of its usual affable smile. Removing his pith helmet, in acknowledgment of the ladies, he exclaimed, "This is frightful, Professor. You might all have been killed! How can you dismiss the incident so casually?"

"If you or Selim has any practical advice, I would be pleased to hear it," said Emerson, folding his arms and scowling.

They didn't. Neither did Daoud, though he informed them that his son, the nominal captain of the sunken craft, had gone across to Luxor early that morning to see if the boat could be raised, and to question the other boatmen.

"We have done all we can for the present," said Emerson firmly. "If anyone knows anything, Selim will hear of it. Now may I be allowed to carry on with my work? Bertie, I want a plan of the house we finished excavating yesterday. David, get the cameras. Walter, there are several graffiti on the facade to be copied."

Selim dared to linger for a moment. "Is it true that Daoud can now swim? He was boasting that David had taught him."

"He may need a few more lessons," David said. His amused smile faded. "Perhaps he'd better have them. You too, Selim."

"I do not think so," said Selim, backing away. "I swim well enough. Now, Father of Curses, I will start the men who are working at the temple."

Emerson was already striding away. "Ramses!" he shouted.

The ruins of the structures north of the Ptolemaic temple presented a few nice little problems in excavation. Not a wall had been left standing, and it wasn't easy to determine precisely where the fallen blocks had fit in. Many were missing, carried off by later builders. Fellahin and archaeologists searching for artifacts had dug holes more or less at random, leaving piles of debris and further confusing the stratigraphy. Emerson let out a particularly ripe string of swear words when one of the men found a page from a German newspaper, dated January 4, 1843, two feet below the surface. They made good progress, though, and later that morning Emerson cheered up when they located a piece of column with the cartouche of Seti I. When they stopped for luncheon he surveyed the collection of objects that had been found with visible satisfaction. They included fragments of statues and stelae.

"Nineteenth Dynasty," he declared. "Dedicated to Hathor."

"She does keep turning up, doesn't she?" David murmured.

For once they had divided into groups by age, the parents sitting off to one side and the younger foursome together. Ramses glanced at his friend and clamped his jaws together to prevent a rude response. He was becoming sensitive to references to that particular goddess.

David went on, with seeming irrelevance, "Tomorrow is full moon, isn't it?"

"What about it?" Lia asked.

David finished his sandwich and leaned back, supporting himself on his elbows. "It's been a long time since we had a moonlight ramble. Luxor and Karnak temples are magical under a full moon."

Lia shook her head. "The tourists all turn out for that."

"Then how about Medinet Habu or Deir el Bahri? Or the temple here? I've been thinking of painting it."

"Fine with me," Ramses said lazily.

Nefret uncrossed her legs and rose to her knees, fixing David with a hard stare. "You told him, didn't you?"

"Told me what?" Ramses asked.

"Told him what?" David demanded. Then his face cleared, and he laughed. "That's right, he wasn't here the other morning when the boy was babbling about people seeing Hathor manifest herself in her temple on the night of the full moon. Come now, Nefret, you don't believe those wild tales, do you?"

"Nobody told me," Ramses said. He tried to keep his voice neutral, but apparently he didn't succeed; Nefret's cheeks darkened and she refused to meet his eyes. The other two remained silent, aware of a certain tension in the air. Finally Nefret muttered,

"I'm sorry. It's silly and superstitious of me to see a connection between the wild tales and what happened to you in Cairo. But there haven't been such stories about Deir el Medina before, have there?"

"Not so far as I know," Ramses said. "We've all heard of the giant cat who haunts Karnak and turns into a scantily clad female who seduces men and then smothers them. Legends like that are common, so perhaps it isn't surprising that Deir el Medina should acquire one. I don't understand, Nefret. Why didn't you want David to tell me? Did you suppose I'd come here, secretly and alone, to investigate, and . . . And what? Allow myself to be lured away by a feeble-witted female in fancy dress?"

She had tried several times to interrupt him. The last sentence brought her to her feet, flushed and sputtering. "I . . . You . . . That's outrageous, Ramses. I didn't suppose any of that! Why are you so quick to take offense? I was only trying—"

"Calm down, both of you," David said placidly. "You'll have Aunt Amelia over here in a minute, wanting to know what you're yelling about. Maybe you ought to listen to each other instead of firing off accusations. Unless, that is, you are enjoying the argument for its own sake."

Nefret sat down. "I'm not enjoying it."

"Well, there's a switch," Ramses snapped. "You're always accusing me of avoiding confrontations. I was only trying—"

A burst of laughter from David stopped him. "Shake hands," David suggested, "and say you're sorry."

Somewhat sheepishly Ramses took the hand Nefret had offered. "I'm sorry," he said. "Is that how you deal with your obstreperous children, David?"

"It doesn't work with Evvie," David said.

"She's never sorry," Lia added.

"I am," Nefret murmured, bowing her head. "The truth is I can't explain, even to myself, why I've got so worked up about this."

"I think I understand," Lia said. Nefret looked up. Her eyes met those of Lia, who gave her a nod and a confidential smile before continuing. "The inexplicable is always unsettling. And if either of you gentlemen breathe the words 'feminine intuition' . . ."

"Heaven forbid," David said in a shocked voice, and with an irrepressible twinkle in his eyes. "I have a few forebodings of my own. But the situation is inexplicable only because we haven't figured out the motive yet. We will. And I believe it would be a serious error to dismiss the purported epiphanies of Hathor as unrelated. Nefret is right; there've been no such stories before this year. It's worth investigating, at any rate."

It was agreed that they would limit the expedition to their four selves. David had expressed an interest in painting the temple by moonlight; that would be their ostensible motive.

"Though why the devil we are obliged to have a reason for going off by ourselves I don't know," Ramses muttered. "They cling a bit, don't they? Especially—"

"For all you know they may be anxious to be rid of us for a time," David said with perfect good humor.

After luncheon he and Walter left, David to the Castle and Walter back to the house, to work on his translations. Ramses watched them go with unconcealed envy. They had turned up a lot of inscribed material, most of it fragmentary but all of interest and, so far as he was concerned, at least as important as the bloody temple ruins. His father didn't really need him on the dig. After years of being shouted at by Emerson, the men knew the techniques of excavation; many of them, including Selim, could read and write and keep accurate records. With Bertie and Lia and Nefret, and his wife, Emerson had a staff more than adequate for his requirements. Ramses decided he would raise the subject again that evening. He had already discussed with his uncle the prospect of jointly publishing some of the more interesting texts. Walter wasn't awfully good at standing up to Emerson—neither was he!—but perhaps if the two of them joined forces they could present a convincing case.

After they returned to the house that afternoon he hastily changed, left Nefret with the children, and went looking for his uncle. One of the rooms in the new wing had been fitted up as storage and work space. Shelves along one wall contained boxes of potsherds, sorted and labeled. Numbers in India ink on the edge or back of each piece referred to the index that had been kept as they were found. A long table served as desk. Ramses found his uncle bent over it, his nose a scant inch away from the surface of the brown, brittle papyrus in front of him, his eyes shifting back and forth from it to the sheet of paper on which he was copying the hieratic signs.

"Ah, Ramses," he said. "I'm glad you're here. What do you make of this group of signs? It resembles the word for 'mooring post,' but that doesn't make sense in this context."

Ramses had hoped to work on the inscription he had begun translating, but he couldn't refuse his uncle. He took the sheet of paper. In contrast to the faded, sometimes broken, signs on the papyrus, Walter's copy was neat and clear, except where gaps indicated signs he had been unable to make out.

"You've made good progress," Ramses murmured, scanning the lines. " 'It is the day when the dead go about in the necropolis in order to . . . something . . . the enemy . . . of the mooring post'? That's a metaphor for dying, driving in the mooring post. Safely reaching the land of the West?"

"The enemy of the mooring post?" Walter repeated doubtfully. "It's a bit esoteric, even for the Egyptians, isn't it?"

They were still at it, arguing with perfect amiability and happily oblivious to the passage of time, when the door opened. Nefret had come looking for them. Ramses was about to apologize for their tardiness when she spoke, in a strained voice.

"Mother wants you to come right away. We have a visitor."

≽≼

I WAS SITTING ON THE veranda all by myself. Such moments of privacy were rare of late, and I found myself wishing selfishly that I could enjoy them more often. I love every member of my family, but there are times when an individual of reflective temperament wishes, even needs, to be alone. Why didn't they go off and do things by themselves? Not all the time; just now and then.

I particularly enjoy that hour of the evening, when the light lies like a wash of gold across the desert and sparkles on the distant river. My view that evening was spoiled by the confounded motorcar, which Emerson continued to leave standing outside the house instead of putting it in the stable. I did not see the approaching carriage until it stopped and a man got out. I knew him. A hideous foreboding robbed me of breath. Instead of replying to my telegram he had come in person to tell me . . . what?

The honorable Algernon Bracegirdle-Boisdragon, more commonly known as Mr. Smith, advanced toward the barred door, his thin lips stretching into a smile.

"Do forgive my intrusion, Mrs. Emerson. I came by earlier, but your butler informed me you were not at home and refused to allow me to wait for you."

Here was a man whom even Gargery could not stare down. His own eyes were sharp as gimlets; they did not change expression when he smiled, nor did his narrow face broaden.

"What has happened?" I cried. "Is Sethos . . . Is he . . ."

"My dear Mrs. Emerson! Forgive me for alarming you. I assure you, our friend is alive and in no immediate danger. However, his—er—present situation is somewhat complex, and I thought it better to explain in person. Ah, Professor. How good it is to see you again."

Emerson came to my side. "What are you doing here?" he demanded. "Is Sethos . . . Is he . . ."

"He is alive, Emerson," I said.

"Oh. Well then, what the devil do you mean by worrying Mrs. Emerson? She is pale and trembling. You had better have a whiskey, my dear."

"I assure you, Emerson, my nerves are in perfect order. But perhaps you—"

"No, why? There is nothing wrong with my nerves," said Emerson, passing his hand over his brow, where the perspiration had popped out in little beads.

"May I come in and explain?" asked Mr. Smith, peering through the bars.

"You may as well," Emerson said. He unfastened the door.

"Dear me," said Mr. Smith pensively. "I seem to have put my foot in it. And I had hoped to spare you! The truth is—" He broke off with a twist of his thin lips as the door to the house opened. Nefret was in the lead, followed by Evelyn and Lia. She stopped dead when she saw Smith.

"You know my daughter-in-law," I said. "This is Mrs. Walter Emerson, and her daughter, Mrs. Todros. Evelyn and Lia, may I present

Mr.—er—Smith. He has come to bring us news of our kinsman. Never mind the courtesies, Mr. Smith, tell us. I would not like to accuse you of deliberately prolonging our suspense."

"I assure you, that was not my intention," said Mr. Smith. "In a nutshell, then, your kinsman is in hospital. His injuries are not life-threatening—"

"Injuries!" I exclaimed. "What's he been up to?"

"I don't know. I didn't know," said Smith, through his teeth, "that he was in Jerusalem. He was not supposed to have been in Jerusalem. I received a written message from him a few days ago, hand-delivered by a turbaned ruffian, informing me that he had run into a spot of difficulty, as he termed it, but would be out of hospital and on his way here before long. That is all the information I have; but knowing you, Mrs. Emerson, I felt certain you would be in Cairo invading my office if you didn't get an immediate reply to your telegram."

"Thank you," I said, pleased by the compliment, even if it had not been intended as such.

"But how dreadful," said Evelyn, her eyes soft with sympathy. "What sort of hospital can there be in Jerusalem?"

"It is run by a French sisterhood," Smith replied. "He is receiving excellent care, I assure you."

Not at all discomposed at being the focus of several inimical stares, he settled himself comfortably in a chair, prepared, as it seemed, to remain. Aha, I thought. Delivering the news had not been his sole motive for coming.

"Will you stay for tea, Mr. Smith?" I inquired.

"Thank you, Mrs. Emerson, I would enjoy that."

We exchanged equally false smiles. "I will see what is keeping the others," I said, going to the door.

Emerson followed me. "Peabody!" His attempt at a whisper made my ears ring. "Have you lost your mind? The bastard wouldn't be so agreeable if he did not want something from us. If he thinks he can recruit Ramses for another job—"

"Sssh." I drew him farther into the house. "The war is over, Emerson."

"But Sethos is still meddling, God knows with what. If my brother," said Emerson, rolling his *r*'s fiercely, "has got himself into another mess from which he expects Ramses to extricate him—"

"He wouldn't do that."

"You always defend the . . . the man!" Emerson shouted. Even in an extremity of temper, he avoided using his favorite epithet to describe his illegitimate brother.

"Mother." Nefret tugged at my sleeve. "Send him away."

"I have my own reasons for wanting Smith to remain," I said. "I will explain them later. Oh, there you are, Fatima. Thank you for waiting; you may bring tea now, if you will be so good. Nefret, will you find Walter and Ramses and David and tell them to come here? And bring the children too. All the children."

Smith's expression, when the rest of the family erupted onto the veranda, gave me a great deal of malicious satisfaction. The three youngest children whizzed round like projectiles, bouncing off one adult after the other, delivering embraces and greetings in their sweet, high, *extremely* penetrating voices. They ended up standing in a row in front of Smith, who had the wild-eyed look of a man cornered by pariah dogs.

"Who are you?" Evvie asked.

"This is Mr. Smith," I said. "Say hello nicely."

They continued to stare unblinkingly.

"Hello there," said Smith. He reached out to pat Evvie on the head.

"I hate people to do that," she announced, pushing his hand away. "So does Davy. And Charla bites."

"All right, children, that's enough." Ramses took hold of his two. "Go to Mama. Leave the gentleman alone."

"What charming children," said Smith, with a forced smile. "Yours?"

"Two of them. Including the one that bites."

"That doesn't surprise me," Smith murmured. "And this must be Mr. Todros. A pleasure to meet you at last."

David nodded without speaking, his dark eyes cool. Nefret must have told him the identity of the visitor.

"This is my uncle, Mr. Walter Emerson. I would introduce you formally if I knew what name you are currently using," said Ramses.

A fleeting, tight-lipped smile acknowledged the gibe. "Smith will do. Good afternoon, Mr. Emerson."

"And I am Sennia Emerson," said that young person, holding her skirts and curtsying. "You have heard of me, I expect."

"Yes—quite—er—how do you do?"

"Very well, thank you. And you?"

"Sit down, Sennia," Ramses said somewhat sharply. "A gentleman remains standing until all the ladies present have seated themselves."

This was actually directed at Nefret, who stood clutching the twins like Niobe trying to protect her children from the deadly arrows of Apollo and Diana. She flushed and sank onto the settee next to Lia.

"Tea, everyone?" I asked.

Ramses came to take the cups as I filled them. "I presume you have a reason for this?" he inquired sotto voce.

"I always have at least one reason. Now that he has been thrown off-balance by the dear children, I may be able to get a few sensible answers out of him."

Having dispensed the genial beverage and asked Sennia to pass the biscuits round, I cleared my throat. "Mr. Smith came to bring us news of our kinsman. He has been ill, but is recovering."

"Malaria again?" Nefret asked, professional interest overcoming maternal protectiveness.

"No. He suffered certain injuries. Nothing serious."

Walter had been thinking it over. In describing Sethos's wartime activities to him we had not mentioned Smith, but Walter's analytical mind was quick to make the connection. "What is his name?"

"I beg your pardon?" Smith turned those gimlet eyes on him.

"I gather that he works for you, or with you, or under your direction, in a certain governmental agency," said Walter, unintimidated by the stare. "I cannot believe the British bureaucracy would employ a man without investigating every detail of his past life—including his name."

The question seemed to arouse Smith's usually dormant sense of humor. His eyes narrowed, wrinkles fanning out at the corners.

"None of you know? Well, well. If he has not seen fit to tell you, it would not be right for me to betray his confidence."

"Where is he?" Ramses asked.

"Just a moment, please," I said, with a warning frown at my son. "Sennia, dear, would you take the children to their little corner and give them their paper and crayons? Thank you. Very well, Mr. Smith, you may answer Ramses's question."

"I fear I am unable to do so."

"Because you cannot or because you will not?" Nefret leaned forward, hands tightly clasped. "Frankly, I don't care what he has done. The war is over and if Sethos is back into the antiquities business, he's on his own. You can't expect Ramses—"

"I beg your pardon for interrupting, Nefret," Ramses said.

"I beg *your* pardon." She sat back, clasping her hands.

The exchange had amused Smith. He would find differences of opinion amusing—and potentially useful. "I don't expect your husband to do anything," he said smoothly. "There's no denying that his talents could be useful; intelligence gathering does not end with an armistice, and the Middle East and Egypt are potential powder kegs."

"Thanks to our incoherent and devious policies," said Emerson. "There is a flagrant contradiction between the principle of self-determination, which we support in theory, and the politics we practice. France won't give up Syria, and we won't give up Egypt, and we've promised Palestine to both the Zionists and the Arabs."

"Some would claim that the natives of those areas are not capable of self-government," Smith said.

He was trying to egg Emerson on. It is not difficult. "Ha," exclaimed my spouse. "Oh, I admit we've done better by Egypt than some occupying powers might have done, but it's time we got the hell out and let the Egyptians work out their own destiny. Who are we to look down on them? Our great Western, Christian civilization has burned people alive, forced them into ghettos, seized their territory by guile or by force—and we've just fought the bloodiest war in history."

"Our guest is not interested in your views, Emerson," I said, watching Smith.

"Oh, I am, Mrs. Emerson. Very much interested. I trust that the

Professor's sympathy with various Nationalist aspirations would not prevent him from notifying Cairo should he learn of plans for rioting in Upper Egypt."

"None of us believe in violence," said Ramses, whose eyes, like mine, were fixed on the bland countenance of Mr. Smith. "As you ought to be well aware. What are you driving at, Smith?"

"Charla is eating her crayon," said Evvie.

The evidence certainly seemed to point that way. Charla's crayon was now a stump and her pursed mouth strongly suggested that the pretty red object hadn't tasted as good as she had expected. Ramses rushed over and snatched his daughter up. "Spit it out," he ordered. "This minute!"

"I told her not to do it," said Evvie self-righteously.

Ramses inserted a finger into Charla's mouth. "What's in the damned things? Are they poisonous? Ouch! Mother, can you make her—"

"That is not the way to go about it," I said. "Give her to me."

I turned Charla over my arm and smacked her hard between the shoulderblades. A shower of repellent fragments flew out. Most of them landed on Mr. Smith's neatly pressed flannels. Inspecting the pieces, I remarked, "I don't believe she swallowed any of it. We'll just make sure, shall we, Nefret?"

"I can manage," Nefret said, snatching the squirming child from me. "Ramses, will you give me a hand?"

"What are you going to do?" Emerson demanded in alarm.

"Believe me, my dear, you don't want to know," I assured him.

They went off with Charla, who was protesting volubly if unintelligibly.

"Good Gad!" Emerson exclaimed. "You don't mean . . . Poor little creature!"

"It isn't the first time," I said. "She is one of those children—endlessly inquisitive and too young to understand the consequences—who employs all her senses to investigate the world. One day she may be a distinguished scientist, if we can prevent her from poisoning herself before she reaches the age of reason. Mr. Smith, I am so sorry about your nice trousers. I suggest you allow the bits to dry before you brush them off."

He had already tried. The result was very nasty and the stains, I felt sure, were indelible.

"A small price to pay for this delightful glimpse into family life," said Smith, with a conspicuous absence of sincerity. "However, I must go. I am taking the night train to Cairo. Good-bye to you all, and thank you for your—er—charming hospitality."

"Emerson and I will escort you to your carriage," I said.

Smith watched me undo the bolts and hooks. "I trust," he said in a low voice, "that these precautions have not been taken in expectation of danger? You know you have only to ask us for assistance."

"The bars and bolts are not to keep enemies out, but to keep the children in." I captured Davy, who tried to look as if getting out the door had been the last thing on his mind. The wide blue eyes and golden curls and angelic smile would have deceived anyone but an experienced grandmother. I handed him over to Evelyn.

"I heard about the motorcar in Luxor," said Smith, stopping to inspect it. "It is the talk of the town. As is your little accident last night. It was an accident, wasn't it?"

"Stop fishing, Mr. Smith," I said, with perfect good humor. "I suggest you send Sethos to us as soon as he can travel. He will recuperate more quickly in our care than in any hospital. You did forward our original message, I presume."

"Yes, certainly. Who is the missing person?"

"If he has not chosen to confide in you, it would not be proper for me to do so."

"Damn right," said Emerson. "One more thing, Smith, and then you can go to Luxor or to the devil. What were you driving at with those hints about rioting in this area? Have you received intelligence pointing to such a possibility?"

"Lord Milner's Commission is due to arrive in a few weeks," Smith said. "It will not offer the terms Egypt wants. There will be trouble."

"There certainly will be if Britain refused to abandon the protectorate," Emerson muttered, rubbing his chin. "You didn't answer my question, Smith."

The driver stood by the door of the carriage, waiting for Smith to get in. "He isn't going to answer it, Emerson," I said. "Good-bye, Mr. Smith."

He paused with his foot on the step and looked ruefully at his ruined trousers. "Did you enjoy that, Mrs. Emerson?"

"You are, I believe, a bachelor, Mr. Smith?"

He ducked his head and climbed nimbly into the vehicle. I heard a stifled sound that might have been a laugh.

"SO THAT IS THE MYSTERIOUS Mr. Smith," said Walter. "It was good of him to come all this way in order to reassure us."

"His real name is Bracegirdle-Boisdragon," said Emerson. "And his real reason for coming had nothing to do with goodness."

"What did he want, then?" Ramses asked. "You and Mother spoke with him for several minutes; you must have been able to get something out of him."

"He spent most of the time trying to get something out of *us*," I replied. "He did not succeed, but he gave away nothing of interest— except that they anticipate disaffection when Lord Milner's Commission arrives, which anyone might have deduced."

"Was that what he meant by his hints about riots here in Luxor?" Walter asked. "If there is a chance of violence, the women and children must be sent to safety."

"Nonsense," Evelyn said calmly.

"Utter nonsense," Emerson agreed. "Selim would know of such rumors well in advance, and none of the men of Luxor would bother us. We had not the slightest trouble last spring."

"What about you, David?" Walter demanded. "The fellow kept looking at you. You promised me that you had severed your connections with the Nationalists. Your responsibilities to your wife and children—"

"I am well aware of them, sir," David said. He had always treated his father-in-law deferentially; the interruption and the tightening of his jaw were the only signs of controlled anger. "I gave you my word, and I have never broken it."

"Then why did that—that Smith person introduce the subject?" Walter demanded. "It sounded like an accusation."

"Or a warning," I murmured. Several of us spoke at once, Lia indignantly defending her husband, Evelyn trying to soothe her husband, and Emerson drowning out the softer voices with a bull-like bellow. "You are the one who is making unfounded accusations, Walter. Do not allow that bas—um—that rascal Smith to sow dissension among us."

"What about a nice whiskey and soda?" I suggested. Muttering irritably, Emerson went to the table, and I turned with a smile to the little boy who had shyly approached me. "Have you a new picture to show me, Dolly? Well! That is very good, very good indeed. Show it to Grandfather Walter."

"He has quite a talent," said Evelyn proudly.

"It is a donkey," Dolly explained. "I am riding it."

"Yes, I see." Walter's dour face softened. "And a very good donkey, too. Er—why does it have six legs?"

"Because it is running." Dolly took the paper from him and examined it critically. "I think I will give it more legs. It is running very fast."

The dear child's innocent intervention had reduced the tension. I wondered if he had been aware of the discord between his father and grandfather; he was a very sensitive little chap. Walter looked self-consciously at David. "I apologize. It is only that I—"

"You worry about your hostages to fortune." David was not the man to bear a grudge. His brown eyes were warm with affection and understanding. "So do I, sir."

"What are those papers you have, Walter?" I asked, accepting a glass of whiskey from Emerson.

"What papers?" Walter asked blankly.

Evelyn picked them up from the floor and handed them to him. "He has been working on a very important manuscript," she explained. "I expect you wanted to read us your translation, Walter?"

"Oh, yes, to be sure." Walter smoothed the papers out. Someone had drawn an object that may have been meant to be a pyramid on the back of one.

"He isn't supposed to bring his work to a social occasion," Emerson grunted. "Ramses, have a look at these."

He extracted a roll of paper from a portfolio beside his chair and handed it over. "David's work?" Ramses inquired, examining the meticulously tinted sketch of a section of coffin lid.

"Evelyn's," Emerson corrected. "This is David's. He's finished drawing the decoration on the robe."

"They're both marvelous," Ramses said in sincere admiration.

"Put them away before someone spills tea on them," I said. "You ought not have brought them to a social occasion, Emerson."

Emerson ignored this dig with the skill of long experience. "How much longer are you going to work on Vandergelt's collection? How many more objects to copy?"

"We could spend years at the job," David answered, taking a cup of tea from me. "Obviously that's not practical. We'll have to settle for the most important and fragile objects. That decision is up to you and Cyrus."

Emerson opened his mouth but before he could voice his opinion I cut in. "We will have a little committee meeting, Emerson, and solicit the advice of all those concerned—including Cyrus. Tomorrow afternoon, perhaps? Excellent. I will inform Cyrus. Now let us listen to Walter's translation."

"Oh, very well," said Emerson. "What is this text you find so important, Walter?"

"I told you about it a few days ago, Radcliffe. The horoscope."

"Ah, yes," said Emerson, who obviously had no recollection of any such conversation.

"The word isn't entirely accurate," Walter explained eagerly. "It doesn't seem to be based on astrology, or any other system familiar to us. It lists the days of the year, classifies them as good or bad, and predicts what is likely to happen. For example: 'First month of Akhet, day twenty-four. Very good. The god sails with a favorable wind. Anyone born on this day will die honored in old age.'"

"Akhet is the first season of the year, isn't it?" Lia asked.

Her father nodded. "The season of inundation, when the Nile rose and overflowed its banks. The first day of the year was marked by the reappearance of the star Sirius."

"Well, well," Emerson said, making a valiant effort. "Most interesting."

"Isn't it?" Walter beamed at him. "But that's not the most interesting section. I came across this bit yesterday. 'The day of the children of the storm. Very dangerous. Do not go on the water this day.' "

He had succeeded in capturing Emerson's attention—and mine, and that of several others. Ramses's eyebrows lifted.

"You remember what our—er—what—er—Sethos said the other evening, about the children of the storm?" Walter went on with innocent enthusiasm. "It gave me quite a strange feeling to see the same phrase in an ancient Egyptian text. Of course the reference is not at all the same. Er—Sethos—was speaking poetically and figuratively, whereas this has a specific religious meaning."

Somewhat belatedly he became aware of the unblinking stares of his companions. "Quite a coincidence, isn't it?" he asked uncertainly.

David was the first to speak. "Yes. Quite a coincidence."

"And that is all it is," Emerson declared with considerable vehemence. "Coincidence is the foundation of all the occult sciences—coincidence, and the desire to believe. One fortuitously accurate guess is remembered by the gullible, while a thousand inaccurate predictions are forgotten. Even if the date proved to be . . ." His voice trailed off.

"What is the date, Uncle Walter?" Nefret asked.

Walter looked at the paper. "Third month of Akhet, day nineteen. In modern terms . . . Impossible to say offhand. As you are all aware, the Egyptian calendar consisted of three hundred and sixty-five days, but since the solar year is actually longer than that, the Egyptians were one day off every four years or so. It would be difficult to calculate the correspondence. One might try, of course . . ."

"One won't," declared Emerson. "It would be a complete waste of time. Gargery, what do you want? Don't bother removing the tea things now."

"It's no trouble, sir," said Gargery, collecting cups.

"Good of you to say so," said Emerson sarcastically. "I assure you,

Gargery, you won't be missing a thing. We are discussing an ancient Egyptian text."

"Yes, sir. However, sir, I couldn't help overhearing—"

"Damnation!" Emerson shouted. "Eavesdropping again?"

"I happened to be passing by the door, sir." Gargery's face took on an expression of hurt reproach. "That there calendar Mr. Walter was reading from—"

"Is a pack of nonsense," Emerson broke in.

"Well, sir, those Egyptians may have been heathens, but they knew things. It seems to me that you ought to read more of it and find out what else is going to happen."

Ramses cleared his throat. "Speaking of the papyrus, Father, I've been wondering if I might—"

"Curse it!" Emerson shouted. "Damn you, Gargery, how many times have I told you—"

"Father," Ramses said loudly. Emerson's bulging eyes followed the wave of his hand toward the corner where Sennia sat, rigid with shocked surprise.

"Oh," said Emerson. "Er. I didn't see you, Sennia. I apologize for my language. I—"

"You should apologize to Gargery," Sennia said severely. "He was only trying to help."

"That is quite all right, sir," said Gargery, with an infuriating smile. "I have said my say, as was my duty. Come along, Miss Sennia, it is time for your supper."

They went out together, holding each other's hands, and Emerson, still boiling with repressed fury, looked round for a victim. "See what you've done, Walter," he exclaimed. "Filling that child's head with nonsense!"

"It's Gargery's head that's the problem," Ramses murmured. "Father, I've been meaning to ask you—"

His father paid no attention. "And another thing, Walter. Will you kindly refrain, in future, from referring to our brother as—'er—Sethos'? Can't you pronounce the word without stuttering?"

The injustice of this brought a flush to Walter's face, and he spoke up with unusual vehemence. "No, I cannot, Radcliffe. What sort of name is that for an Englishman and a Christian?"

"I don't know that he is a Christian," Emerson said, diverted. "Never asked."

"Didn't you ever ask his real name? Don't tell me he was christened Sethos."

"Thus far he has avoided our attempts to discover it," Emerson said grumpily. "Why the devil don't you ask him, if it is so important to you?" As far as he was concerned, that ended the discussion. He turned to me. "Isn't it time for these children to go to bed?"

"Past time," I said. "Nefret . . . Oh, she is still with Charla."

"Superstitious idiot," his father muttered. He meant Gargery, as his next words made plain. "He'll tell Fatima and the rest of them about the cursed papyrus, and they'll wring their hands and find ominous omens all over the place. Probably want me to exorcise the evil spirits. Damnation! Oh—what was it you wanted to ask me, my boy?"

"It can wait." Ramses slung Davy over one shoulder. Davy, who favored unorthodox methods of transport, chuckled appreciatively. "I want to see how Charla is."

"Oh, good Gad," said Emerson in consternation. "I completely forgot the poor little creature. I will come too. Perhaps a few biscuits would cheer her up."

He emptied the remaining biscuits into his pocket. I did not object. Children have cast-iron stomachs. I had seen Charla devour a huge supper an hour after the latest such episode. (A handful of scarlet poinsettia leaves. The color red obviously attracted her.)

In my opinion, Emerson had been extremely rude to Walter, and deserved to be put in his place. Instead of scolding him, I determined upon a more subtle form of punishment, which would have the additional advantage of arranging matters as I thought best. I waited until the following afternoon to put my scheme into effect. The first step was not accomplished without some little difficulty, for Emerson resisted my "suggestion" that we stop work early. It was not really a suggestion, though, and once he had got that into his head he did as he was told. We went straight to the Castle, where Cyrus awaited us.

I had not seen my old friend for several days, and was distressed to observe that his goatee showed signs of wear. He continued to tug at it as he showed us to his office, where he had made the arrangements along the lines I had tactfully proposed in my note. The mahogany table had been cleared and chairs arranged around it, with paper and pen set out neatly at each place. Cyrus offered me the chair at the head of the table, but I insisted he take it, adding, "I will just sit here at your right, Cyrus, and act as secretary. You have prepared an agenda, I presume?"

"Not exactly," said Cyrus, eyeing the papers I removed from my bag. "I sort of figured you would."

"A few notes," I said modestly.

"Hah," said Emerson, seated opposite me. "What I want to know—"

I rapped sharply on the table with my pen. "You are out of order, Emerson. We must have the committee reports first."

"Committees?" Emerson burst out. "What committees?"

"But before that, a few preliminary remarks from the chairman." I nodded at Cyrus.

"You better make them, Amelia," said Cyrus, trying not to smile as he glanced at Emerson's darkening countenance. "This was your idea."

I had expected he would say that, so I was able to begin speaking immediately, before Emerson could do so. "It has become evident to me, as it must have done to the rest of you, that we must define our aims and goals and decide how to allocate time and personnel most efficiently to the various projects presently underway. We are fortunate indeed to have so many talented persons with us—" I directed a series of smiles and nods at those persons. I got a few nods and smiles in return. From Emerson I got a silent snarl. Nefret, seated next to him, with her hand on his, was trying not to laugh. David had put his elbows on the table and propped his chin in his hands; his fingers covered his mouth, but I could see it twitching.

". . . but the very amplitude of the talent available renders organization imperative," I went on. "Otherwise we run the risk of dissipating our collective energy and wasting valuable time."

Ramses, who had been watching his father, said smoothly, "Well put, Mother. Have you by chance made a list of these projects?"

I took the hint. "Yes, certainly. These are not necessarily in order of importance, mind you, I simply jotted them down as they occurred to me. The princesses' treasure is first. M. Lacau will turn up again at any time and he has not had the courtesy to inform us of what he means to do. For all we know, he may demand we pack and remove everything. Therefore David and Evelyn should concentrate on finishing their copies of the most important objects. We are agreed on that, I expect? Good. I felt certain we would be. I suggest that after this meeting we adjourn to the storage rooms and go over the objects together. I trust that is agreeable to all of you? Good. One other question concerning the treasure requires to be considered, but I will postpone that until Cyrus is ready to make his report.

"The second project is the excavation and copying of the Deir el Medina tombs. The latter will have to be postponed until David and Evelyn are finished here, but in my opinion Cyrus should start making the preparations.

"Project number three is the inscribed material we have found—the ostraca and papyri. They should be collated, translated, and published."

I turned over a page, cleared my throat, and proceeded. "Project number four is, of course, the excavation of the village and its surroundings."

Even Nefret's touch could not control Emerson any longer. "I wondered when you would get round to that, Peabody," he burst out. "I have been under the naive impression that it was our primary purpose."

"There is no reason why you cannot proceed with the excavations, Emerson."

Emerson was so outraged he choked on the words he had been about to utter and began coughing violently. Raising my voice, I went on, "I suggest the following allocation of personnel. Ramses and Walter on the textual material; Evelyn and David on the princesses' treasure. That leaves you, Emerson, with Lia and Nefret, Selim and me—more than adequate, especially since Bertie will be working with us until the princesses' treasure has been sent off to Cairo, and Cyrus is ready to return to the cemetery. If we are agreed, I suggest we retire to the storeroom and evaluate the situation there."

"What about the committee reports?" Ramses asked, in a suspiciously muffled voice.

I was ready for that. "As your father so cogently indicated, until now we have had no committees. We will have those reports at our next meeting."

I gathered my papers into a neat pile and stood up, indicating that this meeting was at an end. The others immediately followed suit—except for Emerson. As I passed him on my way to the door, he said softly but distinctly, "I will have a few words to say to you later, Amelia."

I didn't doubt that he would. It was an exhilarating thought.

FROM MANUSCRIPT H

Contrary to Ramses's expectations, he didn't have to invent excuses to keep his parents from joining them on their moonlight ride to Deir el Medina. His mother gave him a sentimental smile and murmured, "Enjoy yourselves, my dears." His father only grunted. Emerson had been brooding over his defeat, as he would consider it, and could hardly wait to get his wife alone. After dinner he hastily swallowed his coffee, announced that it was time to retire, and invited her to join him. They went out together, Emerson's face set in a lordly frown and his wife's bright with gleeful anticipation.

"Why are they retiring so early?" Walter asked in mild surprise. "I plan to put in a few hours' work."

"We'll say good night too," Ramses said. "Since we probably won't be back until late. Don't let him strain his eyes over that papyrus, Aunt Evelyn, it's difficult enough to read in a good light."

"I won't," his aunt said, smiling.

THEY LET THE HORSES WALK, enjoying the cool night air and the quiet. The dark arch of the sky blazed with stars. "I told you they'd be glad to be rid of us," David said.

"I know why Father was," Ramses muttered. "Does she do that deliberately? Stir him up, I mean."

"Partly." Nefret chuckled. "Haven't you ever noticed how she looks at him when he's in a rage—eyes shining, trying not to smile? It's a game they've played for years; both of them know the rules and thoroughly enjoy the moves."

"I suppose so." Ramses knew how the game was played and how it would end, and although he approved in theory, he was still a trifle embarrassed to think of his parents . . . "At any rate, she was her usual efficient self this afternoon. Laid it all out and got everybody to agree."

A flood of light spilled over the cliffs and spread across the landscape. Stones and sand, trees and houses sprang into existence as if an invisible painter's giant brush had washed them onto the darkness. The moon had risen.

It was impossible to think of it in any other way—impossible to visualize that luminous orb as a ball of cold rock two hundred thousand miles away, or to believe that the surface on which they stood was imperceptibly but steadily turning. No wonder the ancients had viewed the lunar orb as a divinity.

By the time they reached the entrance to the valley of Deir el Medina the temple ruins glimmered with pale shadows. David let out a long breath of satisfaction. "In another half hour the light will be perfect. I won't even need a torch."

They left the horses near the shelter and picked their way over the fallen stones. Both men were loaded down, David with his drawing materials and Ramses with blankets and baskets of food and drink—a real picnic, as Nefret had declared. Either she had got over her nervousness about the place or she was determined to overcome it. Ramses had tentatively suggested they spend the night; she hadn't said yes or no, but the blankets were a hopeful sign. His spirits rose. They hadn't slept out under the stars for a long time—not since the children were born.

After casting back and forth for a while, with the other three trailing him and offering their opinions, David settled on a spot from

which the view satisfied him. It was on the opposite side of the temple from which they had approached, just inside the enclosure wall
and a little to one side. There wasn't a completely smooth surface anywhere, but they cleared away the larger and sharper of the bits of stone
that littered the ground and spread the blankets. Nefret scattered the
cushions she had brought from the shelter and subsided luxuriously
onto them, motioning Lia to join her.

"You and I will loll," she declared. "And be waited upon. Ramses,
will you open this?"

He took the tall slim bottle. "Wine?"

"Yes, why not? We can get a little drunk. All of us except David.
He has to paint."

David had managed to set the easel up, bracing its legs with stones.
"David too," he said with a laugh. "It might be just the inspiration I
need."

"I presume you mean to employ a certain amount of artistic
license," Ramses said, holding the bottle between his knees and
removing the cork. "As temples go, this one is fairly dull."

"I'll add a broken obelisk or two, and perhaps a headless colossus."
David began drawing with quick, sure strokes of his charcoal. He
dashed off several sketches and then joined them.

The wine was pale as moonlight, cool and dry as the night air.
They finished one bottle and David glanced at the dark ruins. "Inspiration, a fickle goddess, continues to elude me," he said. "Is there more
wine?"

Ramses laughed and opened the second bottle. He hadn't felt so
relaxed and happy for weeks. It wasn't only the wine, it was everything—the peace and silence, the stark beauty of the setting, the
company of his best friends—including his wife—and the fact that
his adored children and beloved parents were a long way away.
Nefret was singing softly to herself. He caught a few words and recognized one of the sentimental ballads she favored. In her sweet
voice, with moonlight glowing in her hair, the words didn't sound
as banal as they should have. He had forgotten their ostensible purpose for being there, and David, stretched out on the blanket with

his head on Lia's lap, had obviously lost interest in art, though the moon rode high and the facade of the temple was well lighted. Ramses wondered lazily which of them would be the first to propose that they separate. He reached for Nefret's hand, and then dropped it and jumped to his feet.

"What is it?" Nefret demanded.

"Someone's coming. Listen."

"Hathor?" David sat up.

"If it is, she's making the devil of a racket," Ramses replied.

The voices grew louder. They were coming closer, following the enclosure wall toward the entrance. He couldn't quite make out the words; the crunch of stone under feet or hooves drowned them out. Whoever they were, this was no surreptitious approach by would-be thieves or cautious villagers hoping for a glimpse of the goddess. It could only be a party of tourists, looking for some unusual experience, egged on by one of the enterprising dragomen who had invented the Hathor story. Irritation overcame his initial surprise. He headed for the doorway, meaning to meet the party and run them off. As he left the enclosure he saw them coming toward him—two people on donkeyback, one in galabeeyah and turban, the other . . .

"Good God," he exclaimed, and ran forward to catch hold of the animal's bridle. "Maryam, what are you doing here?"

She was wearing the absurd flowered hat his mother had given her. She pushed it back from her face. "Have you seen him?" she gasped. "Is he here?"

"You mean Justin, I presume," said Nefret's cool voice from behind him. "What made you suppose he would come here?"

"He wanted to see the goddess. He's talked of nothing else all day. Thank goodness you're here! Please help us look for him."

"We've been here for several hours," David said. "We've seen no one."

"He could be hiding somewhere." Her voice rose. "He could have fallen, hit his head, he has no more sense than a child."

Ramses had to admit it was possible. The enclosure wall was climbable in several places, and the tumbled stones provided plenty of cover. He could imagine Justin crouching behind some of them, hugging himself in childish delight as he spied on them and waited for the epiphany of the goddess.

"Oh, very well," he said grudgingly. So much for his moonlight idyll. "Nefret, why don't you call him?"

He turned toward his wife, and bit off an oath when he saw that she was holding a bow. An arrow was nocked and ready. "For God's sake, Nefret! How did you—"

"Never mind," she cut in. "Are you two the only searchers? Where is the devoted François? Who is this man?"

The Egyptian was a stranger to Ramses too. He bowed over the donkey's neck and—of course—replied not to Nefret but to her husband. "I am a crewman on the *Isis*, lord. The others are searching the ruins on the other side of the wall."

"Justin would be inside the enclosure," Nefret said. "If he wanted a proper view."

Maryam shouted, so piercingly and unexpectedly that they all jumped. "Justin! Justin, where are you? Answer me!"

She dismounted, stumbled, and caught hold of Ramses's arm. In the distance Ramses heard others calling the boy, François's gruff, accented voice among them.

"Get the torches, David," Ramses said. "You and Lia go round to the left. We'll have to look behind every bloody boulder, the little devil is playing hide-and-go-seek. Nefret, will you please put that goddamned bow down?"

"Language," said Nefret sweetly.

David started toward the place where they had left their supplies. Before he reached it a quavering cry from Maryam drew all eyes to the temple. "Look! There, between the pylons—a woman—shining—glowing—"

Ramses tried to free himself from her convulsive grip but she hung on, her fingers clenched. The figure stood in the gateway, pale as a shaped column of alabaster—but it was no statue, it moved, raised flowing sleeves. He thought he saw a glitter of gold. Something whistled past him; he flung himself around, breaking Maryam's grip, and snatched the bow from Nefret.

Lia let out a gasp of incongruous laughter. "You killed her."

A crumpled shape lay on the ground where the figure had stood. When they reached it, they found an empty white robe, with Nefret's arrow caught in its folds. It took several more minutes to find Justin, stretched across a broken column base like an ancient sacrifice. His hands were folded on his breast and his upturned face wore an ecstatic smile.

CHAPTER SEVEN

I presume you searched the entire area thoroughly," I said, neatly decapitating my boiled egg. "But perhaps I ought to have a look round myself."

Emerson lowered the piece of toast he had held poised in midair ever since Ramses began his account of the Affair at the Temple of Hathor, as I may term it. Slowly he turned his piercing blue gaze from his son to me.

"Amelia," he said.

"More coffee for the Professor, Gargery, if you will be so good."

"I don't want any damned . . ." He did, however, so he neglected to finish the sentence. Gargery, who had been a fascinated listener, immediately obliged, and Emerson said, in the same ominously mild voice, "Thank you, Gargery. Ramses, why did you wait until breakfast to tell us about this?"

"We agreed—all of us—that there was no need to wake you," Nefret said, emphasizing the phrase in a manner that made me suspect agreement had not been reached without a certain amount of disagreement. "There was nothing you—or Mother—could have done. We did search as thoroughly as was possible. It wasn't easy, with so many people milling about and only torches for light, and—and . . . I'm sorry, Father."

"Sorry," Emerson repeated. He rose, magisterial as Jove, even without the beard. "Is anyone coming with me to the dig, Amelia, or have you made other plans for them? Not for all the world would

I venture to interfere with your arrangements; I ask only out of curiosity."

"Don't you want to discuss the affair, Emerson?"

"No, Amelia, I do not." Fixing me with a horrible scowl, he added, "I am motoring to the site. If anyone cares to join me, he or she must come at once."

With long measured strides he left the room.

"Oh dear, he is angry," Lia murmured.

"He'll have got over it by midday," I replied. At least I hoped he would; the fact that he had addressed me by my given name three times in a row indicated a degree of exasperation beyond his usual norm. "However, it might put him in a better humor if some of you went with him this morning. You will not have to risk your lives in the motorcar; it seems to have slipped his mind that he and Selim had one of the wheels off last night and did not replace it. Not you, Evelyn, or you, Walter."

"Do you want me to go with the Professor, Aunt Amelia?" David asked.

"If you don't mind, my dear. Just for a few hours."

"Not at all." He looked at Ramses, who nodded agreement. "We meant to have another look round in daylight anyhow."

"I am going too," Walter declared, squaring his jaw and settling his eyeglasses firmly on the bridge of his nose. I knew the signs; he was suffering from an attack of detective fever. I didn't suppose he would discover anything useful, but he would enjoy himself puttering around and finding clues the others had already discovered. I got rid of Gargery by asking him to accompany Evelyn and Sennia to the Castle, and that left me alone except for Nefret.

"I'd like to talk to you, Mother," she said.

"We are, as always, in rapport, my dear. I was about to request a chat with you."

We found a secluded spot in the garden between our two houses, where no one could overhear. I was proud of that garden; though Egypt's climate is salubrious, allowing for the cultivation of both tropical and temperate blooms, it had required a great deal of effort to keep the plants irrigated and fed. Once a barren stretch of ground, it was now shaded by young lebakh and tamarisk trees. Rose and hibiscus bushes flaunted their colorful blossoms, and beds of nasturtium and other homely flowers were nostalgic reminders of old England.

"Now," I said, pinching off a dead rose with my nails. "Tell me everything. Ramses's narrative was somewhat terse."

"Of necessity," said Nefret, with a faint smile. "He knew Father wouldn't let him get more than a few sentences out."

"From the beginning," I urged. "Recall, if you please, every sight and sound and your reactions to them. One never knows what seemingly meaningless detail may be seen to be relevant."

Her narrative was complete and detailed, though I felt certain she omitted a few things—such as the effect of moonlight and solitude on four young persons. I doubted that any of them had been in a proper state to respond with alacrity to the astonishing events of the evening. Of course I did not say this, or reproach her for not inviting me to be present.

"Curse it," I remarked. "Just when I had everything under control, including Emerson! This new development is unexpected and unwelcome."

"To say the least," Nefret replied wryly. "But is it really unexpected, Mother?"

"You expected something of the sort? My dear, I wish you would confide more freely in me. I am a firm believer in premonitions. They are the workings of the unconscious mind, which fits together clues—"

"Yes, Mother, I agree. In this case, though, it was my conscious mind at work. Ramses's escape from the woman in Cairo must have disappointed her, considering the effort she made to get her hands on him. Isn't it logical that she would try again?"

"If that was another attempt at abduction it was very poorly organized," I said critically. "She'd have needed a dozen sturdy henchmen to deal with all four of you. Not to mention that hysterical boy and his entourage."

Nefret's lips parted in a reluctant smile. "It was ludicrous, really—pure melodrama, without a competent stage director. Everyone was rushing around, getting in one another's way, tripping over things and shouting. François and his lot—there were three of them, crewmen from the dahabeeyah—tumbled over the wall and joined in the confusion." Her smile faded. "I was too worried about Justin to enjoy the farce, however. When I saw him stretched out across that slab, white-faced and rigid, his eyes wide open, staring up at the moon, I thought he was dead."

"But he wasn't."

"He was alive and fully conscious," Nefret said somewhat sourly. "François wouldn't let me examine him. I didn't insist, since the little wretch was as happy as a schoolboy on holiday, laughing exultantly and crowing about how the goddess had smiled and held out her hands to bless him."

"Did she?"

"Damned if I know. I lost my head," Nefret admitted. "I took my bow because . . . Well, because I felt someone ought to be armed with something, just in case. You know how Ramses feels about guns."

"A firearm would have been excessive."

"One couldn't have shot the woman in cold blood," Nefret conceded. "I'm better with a bow than with a gun anyhow, and I aimed at her feet, or rather, at the ground in front of where I thought her feet must be. Ramses snatched the bow from me—he had to detach Maryam first, she was hanging on to him and screaming. By the time we reached the temple entrance she was gone. Ramses and David searched, but she had plenty of time to get away if she knew the plan of the place, which she obviously does."

I filed this fact away for future consideration. By itself it meant nothing—or rather, it might mean a number of different things. Once all the facts were put together, a picture might emerge. I would have to find the time to make one of my little charts, which had proved useful in earlier investigations.

"I expect we had better get out to the dig," I said. "Emerson's initial reaction to any annoyance is to blame ME, but once he cools off he is the most reasonable of men. Don't worry, my dear, I will get everyone back on track tomorrow, and Ramses will have the chance to work on his texts."

"You think of everything, Mother."

"I have let one or two matters slip of late," I admitted handsomely. "For one thing, I am concerned about Sethos. I hope he is well enough to travel soon; I want to get Maryam away from that unpredictable boy and his grandmother, but I would rather not beard Mrs. Fitzroyce in her lair until Sethos is here. She was most uncooperative when I asked if Maryam could visit us."

"Perhaps you can catch the old lady in one of her senile moods," Nefret suggested.

"That would be convenient. Then there is M. Lacau to be dealt with," I continued, as we strolled slowly along the path. "The missing jewelry is now a dead issue, in my opinion. It, and the thief, are probably out of the country and there is no possibility of recovering it. I will break the news to Lacau myself, when he condescends to turn up, but I see no advantage in inviting him to do so."

Nefret nodded agreement. Her brow was still furrowed, however, so I endeavored to make her look on the bright side. "That leaves only the matter of Maryam to be settled, and we can do nothing until her father comes—which he will, in his own good time. I will, of course, turn my analytical talents to bear on the identity of the imitation Hathor, but in my opinion she is only a red herring—a nuisance, a distraction. What actual harm has she done?"

"Until we know who she is and why she is doing this, we cannot predict what harm she is likely to do." Nefret stopped. Avoiding my eyes, she plucked a bright-yellow zinnia and began pulling off its petals. "Mother, I can't discuss this with Ramses, but you must have thought of the possibility that she is a past . . ."

"Lover? Don't be afraid of shocking me, Nefret, I am quite familiar with the word and tolerably familiar with Ramses's—er—history along those lines."

"How familiar?" She looked up from the poor mutilated flower.

"Perhaps 'suspicious' would be more accurate. Naturally he never admitted anything. All of it took place before you were married. Surely you have no reason to doubt his fidelity. He loves you—"

"Madly, passionately, not at all," Nefret murmured, plucking a petal with each word. "I don't doubt him, Mother. I only wondered if there was one in particular. But I wouldn't ask you to talk about him behind his back."

She tossed the flower away without finishing the little verse.

"That would not be fair or well-bred," I said. "But I will give the matter some thought."

She took my arm and we walked on. On the path behind us the golden petals of the flower shone bright in the sunlight.

AFTER FATIMA HAD PUT THE finishing touches on one of her extravagant picnic lunches, Nefret and I rode to Deir el Medina. Upon our arrival we had to avoid a large group of Cook's tourists and their morose little donkeys. We did not avoid their attention, however; I heard one of the cursed guides proclaim our identities in a loud voice. Cameras began to click, and one very stout lady shouted, "Stop for a moment, Mrs. Emerson, so that I can get a good picture."

Needless to say, I went on without halting or replying.

"You ought to be used to it by now, Mother," Nefret said with a chuckle. "We are among the most popular sights of Luxor."

It was Emerson's fault that we were. As one of our journalistic acquaintances had once observed, he made splendid copy, always shouting and hitting people. He hadn't actually hit anyone lately, but he had made quite a spectacle of himself during our clearance of Cyrus's tomb, waving his fists at tourists and threatening importunate journalists—who delightedly wrote down every bad word.

I was relieved to observe that none of the tourists had dared come near the area which Emerson had roped off. Within its parameters the rudiments of a plan had begun to emerge, though only a trained eye (like my own) could have made sense of the fragmentary walls and occasional column bases. Nefret and I left our horses with the others and approached Emerson, who was standing over Bertie, his hands on his hips, while the boy plotted out the fragments on his drawing paper.

"Coming along nicely, I see," I observed amiably. "This must have been the forecourt of the Seti the First temple."

"As a matter of fact, it is the pillared hall of an even older temple,"

Emerson replied. "Where have you been, Peabody? The debris is piling up."

"I will get to it at once. Well done, Bertie. How neatly you have drawn all those bits and pieces!"

"Thank you, ma'am." Bertie pushed his pith helmet back and wiped his perspiring brow. "Selim and David have been helping with the measurements, but it's a tricky plan."

"Where is Ramses?" Nefret asked.

"Over there." Emerson gestured. "Running a test trench along the north side of the enclosure wall, to see if he can find a place that wasn't disturbed by our bloody predecessors digging for artifacts. I don't know which are worse, local thieves or cursed Egyptologists. How can I make sense out of the stratigraphy when they've jumbled everything together?"

"All the more credit to you, my dear, for making sense out of the chaos they have left."

Emerson gave me a rather self-conscious look, and drew me aside. "I apologize, Peabody," he said, squaring his magnificent shoulders. His black hair shone like a raven's wing. This did not seem the time to ask what he had done with his hat.

"It is forgotten, Emerson."

"Oh, really? Are you sure," inquired Emerson, "that you have not filed it away for future reference, along with my other sins?"

"My dear, I couldn't possibly keep track of them all."

Emerson chuckled, reached for me, glanced at Bertie, and let his arm fall to his side. "We gave the place a thorough search, Peabody. The ground had been trampled by bare and shod feet. The only thing we found was a scrap of fabric caught on the enclosure wall, on a section where it would be fairly easy to scramble over it. There is debris piled on both sides."

He searched his pockets, and after removing pipe, tobacco pouch, scraps of pottery, and a variety of the odd items men carry about with them, produced a strip of white stuff, which he handed to me.

"Hmmm," I said, examining it. "Fine linen, with, I do believe, the remains of pleating. I will keep this, if I may. Put your pipe away, Emerson, before you drop it. Why do you have a pocketful of nails?"

"I was putting up a sign," Emerson explained, pricking his finger on one of the nails. He sucked it, and then went on, "A more emphatic sign, warning the cursed tourists off. One of them actually offered me money to pose for a photograph."

"Kodaking has become another curse of the working archaeologist," I agreed. "But I hope you didn't strike him, Emerson."

"It was a female," said Emerson gloomily. "I couldn't even swear at her. Lia had to do it for me, since you weren't here."

I decided I had better have a look at the sign. It began, "I will kill with my bare hands . . ." and went on in the same vein for several more sentences. While I was inspecting it, Selim, relieved of his surveying duties, joined me.

"I am to make another one, in Arabic," he announced with a grin. "With the exact words."

"We may as well do German and French too. Find more boards, Selim. Is there any news?"

"About last night? It is a great mystery, Sitt Hakim. The other men were as astonished as I."

"Was it known in Gurneh that Ramses and the others were to be here?"

"Oh, yes, Sitt. They made no secret of it." Selim delicately scratched his beard and glanced at me from under his lashes. "It is also widely known that the White Lady has come before, on the night of the full moon."

"How many people have actually seen her?"

Selim thought about it, frowning. "It is a good question, Sitt. I have not spoken with any who saw her; they heard the stories, as did I, from others."

"The women do not come here, seeking her favor? The ancients prayed to Hathor for happiness in love, and for children."

"They would be afraid to come after dark, Sitt. They fear demons and ghosts."

"Interesting," I said thoughtfully.

"Yes, Sitt. But what does it mean?"

Another good question, and one to which I had no answer.

Selim had one piece of relatively good news. The boat had been located a few hundred yards downstream, run up against the bank. The men who had found it had immediately reported the discovery to Daoud; though the damage was extensive, it was not beyond repair, and the boat had already been towed to the landing near Luxor.

"Until the repairs on the boat are completed, Sabir is without a means of income," I said, after we had all gathered round the luncheon basket. "Tell him to purchase another vessel, Daoud. We will pay for it, of course."

"It will be a loan," said Daoud firmly. "He will repay you."

"Bah," said Emerson. "It is our responsibility—unless Sabir had a business rival who resented his success. Can you think of any such man?"

"They are all jealous," said Daoud proudly. "All the boatmen. Because Sabir made more money than they. But none would destroy another man's boat, it would not—it would not be . . ."

"Honorable," I suggested, as Daoud groped for the right word. "A matter of professional ethics."

"Yes," said Daoud, relieved. He looked inquiringly at the last of the sandwiches and I said, "Take it, Daoud, the rest of us have finished. Even if your assessment is not correct—and I feel certain it is—I cannot imagine anyone daring to risk injury to US."

"The wrath of the Father of Curses is more dangerous than a sandstorm in the desert," Daoud agreed.

EMERSON IS ALWAYS IN A better state of mind after he has been fed. After Fatima's excellent luncheon he agreed without demur to the dispersal of his staff. Ramses said he would stay to finish excavating the trench, and I returned to my rubbish heap, with Lia to help. When we returned to the house that afternoon I fully expected Emerson would retreat to his study with Bertie's plan and his own field notes, but he declared he did not want to miss his time with the dear children.

"We don't see enough of them," he complained, returning from the bath chamber and hastily assuming clean garments. "You won't let them take breakfast with us, and they go to bed so early—"

"The amount of time we spend with them is entirely up to you,

Emerson. If you would give up a few hours each day we could take them sightseeing and visiting, arrange little games, teach them to ride, and so on. Evvie and Dolly haven't been to the Castle, or to Selim's house, or even to Luxor."

"You are an absolute genius at putting the blame onto a fellow," Emerson grumbled.

I went to the veranda, where Evelyn was chatting with Fatima as she set out the tea things. Walter was sorting through a pile of letters.

"I hope you don't mind, Amelia," he said. "I was looking to see if there is anything for Evelyn or me."

"Pray continue sorting it, Walter. The post has rather piled up the last few days. I haven't had time to look at it."

After extracting several letters, one of which he handed to Evelyn, he passed the basket with its overflowing contents to me.

"From Raddie," Evelyn said, and began reading with a happy smile.

"A brief note from Willy," said Walter. "And a letter from Griffith. He wants more Meroitic inscriptions."

"Why the devil does he suppose we will find them in Luxor?" Emerson demanded.

"One never knows what the dealers may have," Walter said mildly. "I've given up Meroitic, as you know, so anything I find will go to Frank."

"You and Mr. Griffith have a remarkably cordial relationship," I remarked, handing Emerson a pile of letters. "Most Egyptologists are quarrelsome and possessive."

"If that was meant for me, Peabody, I flatly deny it," said Emerson, hastily looking through his letters and tossing them back into the basket.

"Wasn't that a letter from Mr. Winlock?" I asked.

"I don't care what the bastard has to say."

Shrieks of childish anticipation prevented me from asking what Mr. Winlock had done to incur Emerson's ire. The twins burst in, accompanied by their parents, and I lifted the post basket high in the air, out of reach of Davy, who loved letters and believed everything that came was directed to him. Emerson took the children on his lap. I handed Ramses and Nefret their messages and began opening my own.

"Nothing from . . . ?" Emerson asked.

"No. Most of these are the usual thing."

"The usual thing?" Evelyn inquired.

I read a few aloud, for the amusement of the others. " 'My dear Mrs. Emerson. You don't know me, but my brother is the son-in-law of Lady Worthington, and I would like to make your acquaintance. At what time would it be convenient for me to call on you?' "

"Who is Lady Worthington?" Nefret asked.

"I have no idea. 'My dear Mrs. Emerson. It would be a great privilege to be shown round the sites of Luxor by your husband. We will be at the Winter Palace this week.' "

"More letters from impertinent visitors?" David asked. He and Lia came in with the two children and Sennia. Evvie ran to Davy and embraced him fiercely. He hugged her back, twittering melodiously, while Charla scowled at both of them.

"We get that sort of thing all the time," said Sennia in a worldly manner. "Read some more, Aunt Amelia, they are quite amusing, really."

"This is a particularly charming example," I said. " 'We are two young American ladies who are anxious to meet your son. Mr. Weigall, whom we met in London last month, assures us he is very knowledgeable, and handsome, too.' "

"I owe Weigall one for that," Ramses muttered.

"I doubt he said any such thing," I replied, tossing another half-dozen epistles into the wastepaper basket.

"He was certainly the social butterfly when he was inspector," Nefret remarked. "Always bragging about Prince This and Lady That."

"We mustn't be uncharitable, my dear. In his official capacity Mr. Weigall had to be polite to important visitors. So do some of our colleagues who are dependent upon private contributions. We are under no such constraints, and people like that are only a nuisance if one allows them to take advantage. Gargery has been quite useful in that respect; if strangers turn up asking for us, we send him out in full but-ling mode. When he looks down his nose and intones, 'The Professor and Mrs. Emerson are not at home,' even the most importunate Americans beat a retreat."

"Gargery can't look down his nose at everyone," said Lia with a laugh. "He's only five— Oh, Gargery. I am sorry; I didn't see you."

"That is quite all right, Miss Lia," said Gargery, putting her in her place by calling her miss instead of madam.

"Gargery can look down his nose at anyone," I said. "It is not a matter of height, but of presence."

"Thank you, madam," said Gargery. "Shall I bring the drinks tray, Professor?"

"Yes, why not?" He sat down on the floor and beckoned the chil-dren to gather round. "See what I found today."

It was a small statue of limestone, approximately six inches high. The workmanship was rather crude, but the face had a smiling, naive charm. "This was dedicated to the queen Ahmose Nefertari by a fel-low named Ikhetaper," Emerson explained, tracing the line of hiero-glyphs with his finger. "You may look but don't touch. It is not a dolly."

"I would like to go and dig with you and Mama and Papa," said Evvie. "If I find something, can I keep it?"

Charla shot her an evil look, which Emerson did not miss. He knew better than to accede to that request. "I'll tell you what," he said heartily. "Supposing I teach you all how to ride a donkey. As I said to your grandmother the other day, it is high time you learned."

The offer was received with general acclamation. I am not a petty-minded woman. I did not mention that it had been my idea.

On the whole, the riding lesson was a success. That is to say, it was a success with the children. The donkeys were less than pleased and one of the adult persons present behaved rather badly. I refer of course to Emerson, who kept snatching the children off the little beasts whenever they (the latter) moved faster than a walk. Evvie fell off twice and Davy once—to express his solidarity, I believe, on the second occasion. The happiest of all was Dolly, who trotted round and round the courtyard like someone who had been riding all his life. When Emerson, puffing and dust-covered, declared an end to the lesson, Dolly obediently dismounted. He came to me and took my hand.

"That was very good," I said. "We will keep this particular donkey for you."

"Thank you, Aunt Amelia. When I am older I will ride a great white horse, like my great-great-grandfather."

"Only one 'great,'" I said, wondering what the devil Emerson had been telling him. Abdullah had never been an enthusiastic horseman.

"When will we go and see him again?"

"Soon. Run along now and wash up for supper."

Charla did not want to get off the donkey. She stuck like a cocklebur until Ramses detached her and carried her away.

Since I had remained a safe distance from the circus it did not take me long to tidy myself. I treated myself to a brief stroll through the gardens, checking on my plantings. One of the roses appeared to me to be a trifle wilted; I made a mental note to remind Fatima to remind Ali to water it. What a restful place it was—the sweet scent of blossoms, the melodious songs of birds. A bee-eater flashed overhead, iridescent bronze and steel blue and green, and a dove let out its strange cry, almost like a human laugh. The cry ended in a squawk and I plunged into the shrubbery in time to detach Horus from the dove before he could do much damage. The dove flapped off and Horus swore at me. Such a peaceful place . . .

I had been guilty of a certain degree of hubris when I implied to Nefret that I had everything under control. I had not exactly lied to her—I never lie unless it is absolutely necessary—I had only applied the reassurance I thought she needed. However, things had happened so fast that it was hard to keep track of them. The infuriating Mr. Smith's visit had added additional complications.

It was time to make one of my little lists.

As soon as dinner was over I excused myself, claiming I had work to do—which was the truth. Seating myself at my desk, I began by ruling my paper into neat sections and then headed one column

"Annoying and Mysterious Events," the next, "Theories," and the third, "Steps to Be Taken."

"The Veiled Hathor of Cairo" was the first event to be considered. Three possible explanations occurred to me: first, that she was someone out of Ramses's past; second, that she hoped to be someone in his future; third, that her motive was something other than personal attraction. I could not think what on earth that motive could be. The only course of action open to me was a thoughtful consideration of the women who had been involved with my son at some time or other. Asking Ramses would have been the logical next step, but I knew that wouldn't get me anywhere. I drew another sheet of paper to me and began another list.

After I had finished, I studied it in some surprise. I hadn't realized there had been so many. Nor, I felt sure, was the list complete. However, several of the names merited investigation.

A hairpin dropped onto the desk and a lock of hair fell over my eyes. I brushed it back with a muttered "Confound it," and shoved several other loose pins back into place. When I am deep in thought I have a habit of pressing my hands to my head. This has a deleterious effect upon one's coiffure, but it does seem to assist in ratiocination.

The Affair at the Temple of Hathor came next to mind. Had it been the same woman? It is the duty of a good detective to consider all possibilities, but it seemed hardly likely that there were two resentful females in league. At any rate, Maryam could not have been the second Hathor.

The incident had, at least, supplied two physical clues. Nefret had given me the crumpled white garment found at the temple. I took it and the torn scrap of linen from the drawer and spread the robe out across the desk, determined to subject it to a closer analysis than I had been able to give it before.

It was of plain white cotton and simple pattern—two rectangles sewed up the sides and across the top, leaving spaces for arms and head. It had been sewn by hand, rather clumsily. There were several rents, one of them near the hem, where Nefret's arrow had penetrated the fabric, the others along the seams where the stitches had parted, possibly as the result of a hasty removal of the garment. There was absolutely nothing distinctive about it. I felt certain it had not been purchased in the suk, but had been constructed by the wearer.

The scrap of cloth snagged on the wall had not come from the robe. The fabric was completely different—finely woven linen, pleated and sheer. It must have been torn from the garment she wore under the robe, when she scrambled over the wall—a diaphanous, seductive garment like the one Ramses had seen in Cairo.

Agile though she must be, and familiar with the terrain, luck had played a large part in her successful escape. If Justin and his entourage had not thrown her plans into disarray . . . An unpleasant prickling sensation ran down my spine as a new theory trickled into my mind. She must have known of the children's intention of visiting the temple that night. Yet she had risked capture and exposure, for she had been alone and there had been four of them, all young and quick and just as familiar with the terrain.

Unless she stopped them before they got close enough to seize her . . . Had there been a weapon concealed in the folds of that voluminous garment? A single bullet would have prevented pursuit if it killed or seriously wounded even one of them. She had assured Ramses she meant him no harm, so he could not have been the intended victim. Which of them, then? David? Lia? Nefret? Or was it Ramses after all? He had managed to free himself. Who could tell what her real intentions toward him had been?

So deeply engrossed was I in ugly speculation that I let out a little shriek and bounded up out of my chair when the door opened.

"Expecting a murderer, were you?" Emerson inquired. "I am sorry to disappoint you, Peabody."

"Oh, Emerson, I have just had a horrible idea."

"Nothing new about that," said Emerson. His smile faded and he caught me in a hard embrace. "My darling girl, you are all atremble. Tell me your horrible idea."

Emerson likes me to tremble and cling to him. In his opinion I do not do it often enough. So I dutifully clung and trembled, while I explained my latest theory. I had hoped he would scoff and tell me my rampageous imagination had run away with me; but when I looked up into his face his brow was furrowed and his lips compressed. Slowly he shook his head.

"Damnation, Peabody," he remarked. "I hate to admit it, but it makes a certain amount of sense."

"I had hoped you would scoff and tell me my rampageous imagination had run away with me."

The lines in his forehead smoothed out and he smiled a little. "It has, my darling, it has. The plot would do nicely for a sensational novel, but it is all based on surmise. Here, give me a kiss."

"What does that have to do with—"

"Nothing at all," said Emerson, removing the remaining pins from my hair with a single sweep of his fingers and tilting my head back.

When he had finished kissing me, he drew a long satisfied breath. "That's better. Now then, sit down and tell me what other brilliant deductions you have made. I presume that is one of your famous charts?"

Meekly I handed him the paper. He perused it in a single glance—admittedly there wasn't much to see. "Hmmmm. With all due regard for your abilities, my dear, I can't see that this gets us any farther. What's this?" He picked up the other list and ran his eye down it. It was self-explanatory, particularly to a man of Emerson's intellect. When he looked at me his expression was a mixture of admiration and consternation. "How the devil did you get this? Not from Ramses, surely."

"Of course not. I would not be ill-bred enough to approach him about such a sensitive subject. I don't suppose you—"

"Good Gad, no!" Emerson's handsome countenance changed from bronze to copper.

"Well, then, can you think of anyone I have omitted?"

"I would not be ill-bred enough to speculate," said Emerson primly. But his eyes remained fixed on the paper. "Hmmmm. Yes, I remember the Bellingham girl. Dreadful young woman. Who is Clara?"

"A girl he met in Germany. He mentioned her in his letters."

"How do you know he . . . Never mind, don't tell me. Violet? Oh,

Lord, yes, she was in hot pursuit, wasn't she? But I'm sure he never . . .
Good Gad. Not Mrs. Fraser! Though I did wonder at the time . . ."
His voice rose from a mumble to a shout. "Layla? See here, Peabody,
you cannot possibly be sure they . . ."

"I am not sure of any of them," I retorted. My composure had
returned; it was delightful to engage in detective speculation with my
dear spouse, and even more delightful to see him enjoy the sort of
rude gossip he pretends to deplore. "She saved his life, at some risk to
herself, and I assume she expected something in return. She was a—
er—hot-blooded woman. She had her eye on you at one time, I
believe."

"She had her eye on a good many men," Emerson retorted. "That
was her profession. She couldn't have been the veiled Hathor, Peabody.
Ramses said she was young. Layla was a mature woman ten years ago."

"She does have one of the qualifications the latest apparition must
have possessed, however. She knows every foot of the West Bank."

"And all the men who live there," Emerson agreed, with the sort
of smile I make it a habit to take no notice of. "What's become of
her?"

"I don't know. But Selim will. Emerson, there are a number of
other perplexing issues facing us, but in light of my latest theory we
must consider the unmasking of Hathor of primary importance."

As if drawn by a magnet, Emerson's eyes returned to the list of
names. "Mrs. Pankhurst?!"

I HAD BEEN OF TWO minds as to whether to tell the children about
my unpleasant new theory. A good night's sleep, a bright morning, and
(particularly) the affectionate attentions of my spouse restored my natural optimism and reminded me that they were not children but
responsible adults, and that it was my duty to warn them of a potential
danger. I waited until Sennia had finished breakfast and gone off to
gather her books before I told them.

The only one who took it seriously was Gargery. Like the romantic he was, he had been vastly intrigued by the veiled lady. The others
expressed the same reservations Emerson had hinted at the night

before, namely and to wit, that the whole thing was a figment of my imagination.

"What made you think she might have had a weapon?" Ramses asked, the tilt of his brows expressing his skepticism. "I feel sure one of us would have noticed if she had pointed a pistol at us."

"I am not at all sure you would have," I retorted. "With all respect to you, my dear, nobody seems to have noticed very much."

"There was quite a lot going on," David said. He reached for the marmalade. "I'm beginning to feel rather sorry for the poor woman. It must have been disconcerting in the extreme to have her performance interrupted by that screaming mob—and can you picture her scrambling over the wall, tearing her elegant robe?"

"Nevertheless," said Emerson, who had finished eating and was glancing pointedly at his watch, "we must take every possibility into account. Peabody's wild—er—unorthodox theories have often—er—sometimes proved true. Keep a sharp eye out, all of you."

As soon as we arrived at the site I found Selim and informed him I wanted to talk to him. He had been a bit shy of me since the arrival of the motorcar, but this morning he had a new grievance.

"When may we give a fantasia of welcome, Sitt Hakim? It should have been done before this. Ramses said he would talk to you, and we have been waiting for you to say when it will be."

"I am sorry, Selim," I said, acknowledging the justice of his complaint. "Ramses did speak to me, and the matter slipped my mind. You know how difficult it is to get Emerson to agree to attend a social event."

"This is not a social event," said Selim. Now that he had me on the defensive, he folded his arms and gave me a severe look. "It is an obligation and an honored custom as well as a pleasure. The Father of Curses will obey your slightest wish."

"He ignored my wishes about the motorcar."

"You did not forbid him to get one, Sitt."

His beard twitched, just as his father's had done when he was trying to repress a smile. I could not help laughing.

"You are in the right, Selim. I have been remiss about entertaining the family. Mrs. Vandergelt wants to give a party for them too, and several old friends in Luxor have sent invitations. But your fantasia must come first. Would this coming Friday suit you?"

Selim no longer repressed his smile. "I will tell Daoud and Kadija."

"Now that that most important matter is settled, I want to go over a few things with you." I unfolded a piece of paper. I had found time to make another list. It was headed "Outstanding Questions."

"Ah," said Selim. "A list."

Several of the items were of long standing and Selim had nothing new to add. The purported madman who had attacked Maryam had not been identified, nor had the individual responsible for the sinking of Daoud's boat. There had been no sign of the jewelry stolen from Cyrus, or of Martinelli. Selim's face grew longer and longer as I read on. He prided himself on his connections and he hated admitting he had drawn a blank. The last question took him by surprise.

"Layla? Yes, Sitt, of course I remember her. The third wife of Abd el Hamed. Why do you ask about her?"

"I have been trying to think of people who might bear a grudge against us," I explained.

"Why should she bear a grudge? You treated her more kindly than she deserved." Selim stroked his beard. "She is no longer in Luxor, Sitt. I think someone told me she had gone to live with the sisters in Assiut."

"What?" I exclaimed. "Layla a nun?"

Selim grinned. "I do not believe she would dare turn Christian, not even Layla. But she was a woman of extremes, Sitt."

"That would certainly be going from one extreme to the other."

"People sometimes do," said Selim with a worldly-wise air. "Shall I investigate, Sitt?"

"Never mind. It was a far-fetched idea. Thank you for your help, Selim."

"I have not been able to give enough help, Sitt. Sitt . . . I have a question." He shuffled his feet and looked down, like a shy schoolboy. "Will you ask Emerson if he will allow me to drive the motorcar to the fantasia?"

"All the way up the hill to your house? It can't be done, Selim."

"It can, Sitt!" He raised shining eyes. "Did I not drive the other motorcar through the Wadi el Arish, and up the hills and across the desert? The fantasia will be at the house of Daoud, which, as you know, is on a lower slope, and there is a track, a good track, not so very steep except in a few places, and a good wide space in front of the house to turn the motorcar, where everyone can see. Some of the women and the children have not seen it, nor seen me drive it."

"I will talk to Emerson," I promised, patting him on the shoulder.

"Thank you, Sitt! Thank you!"

I watched with a fond smile as he walked away, with a spring in his step. He wanted to show off in front of his wives and kinfolk. Who were we to deny our loyal friend such a harmless pleasure?

When I put it that way to Emerson he was forced to agree. After observing that the infernal machine appeared to be operating properly, I had allowed him to drive it down to the river and back a few times. He enjoyed himself a great deal, and while he was busy playing with the car I was able to get on with my other duties.

I had promised to take tea with Katherine that afternoon and see how the work on the collection was progressing. After assuming proper attire I went to the room we had designated as Walter's study, where I found him and Ramses sorting through ostraca. They were so happily absorbed I had to cough several times before they became aware of my presence.

"Sorry, Mother," said Ramses, getting to his feet. "Have you been there long?"

"No, my dear." I waved him back into his chair. "An interesting text, is it?"

"Fascinating! Listen to this. 'The house of Amennakhte, son of Bukentef, his mother being Tarekhanu; his wife Tentpaoper, daughter of Khaemhedjet, her mother being Tentkhenuemheb . . . ' It's the same fellow whose house we cleared earlier this year! I'm sure I saw another fragment of this same text somewhere . . ." He saw my glazed expression and laughed. "I know it doesn't sound like much, but it's a kind of census, don't you see? And it gives a genealogy for one family—several generations, if I can find the rest of it."

It warmed my heart to see his sober face light up with laughter. "Splendid!" I exclaimed heartily. "And you, Walter—have you given up on the papyrus?"

"No, not at all," Walter said, adjusting his eyeglasses. "I was just helping Ramses look for more fragments of his genealogy. It requires a certain experience to recognize the same handwriting."

His long thin fingers continued to sort through the fragments, moving as rapidly as a woman's might have done while matching patches for a quilt. It was an impressive demonstration of his expertise, for the pieces were of all sizes and shapes and the writing on them ranged from the neat scribal hieratic script to the scribbles of the later, more cursive, demotic—which had always reminded me of a row of hen tracks.

"That is good of you, Walter," I said. "How far have you got with the horoscope?"

"Here is my copy, if you would like to look at it." Walter indicated the pages.

"My dear Walter, you might as well offer me a manuscript in Chinese. Aren't you going to translate it?"

"Eventually. Ah." He picked up a fragment and examined it. "No. The handwriting is similar, but this is part of a list of supplies."

"I didn't mean to disturb you," I said. "I am off to the Castle for tea. Any messages for Cyrus?"

Walter only grunted. Ramses got up and went with me to the door. "What's on your mind, Mother?" he asked, eyebrows tilting.

"Nothing, my dear. Er—you haven't come across any other interesting predictions in the papyrus, I suppose?"

He took me by the shoulders and gave them an affectionate squeeze. "Honestly, Mother! You don't credit that nonsense, do you?"

"Certainly not," I said, laughing. "À bientôt, then."

As Walter had explained, it would be virtually impossible to match the date on the papyrus with a modern calendar. However, if one took as a point of departure the day on which our accident had occurred, and counted the days from then on . . . It was only a matter of academic curiosity, and one I would not be able to satisfy unless I could persuade one of the absorbed scholars to translate the text for me.

▪ ▪ ▪

EMERSON WAS NOT AT ALL pleased when I informed him I had accepted Katherine's invitation to a reception on Sunday. He had already begun to work himself into a state of aggravation about the fantasia.

"Selim has been so busy making arrangements he isn't worth a piastre," he grumbled. "And Daoud is almost as bad. Now you are proposing I waste another day. I won't do it, Peabody, and that's flat."

"Supposing I let you have Ramses and David tomorrow and the next day to make up for your lost time."

"Let me? Hmph," said Emerson.

Everyone was agreeable, even Walter, who said he wouldn't at all mind a day in the fresh air. All of us, including Sennia and Gargery, were at the dig the following afternoon. Horus went everywhere with Sennia and the Great Cat of Re had decided to accompany us as well. He and Horus got on reasonably well, since the former was attached to Ramses and did not challenge Horus's preemptive claim on Sennia. The Great Cat of Re, who specialized in snakes, flushed an angry cobra out of its hole and was with difficulty prevented from attacking it. Emerson killed the poor snake. It was only behaving as a snake is entitled to behave, but a venomous serpent is a dangerous neighbor. We did not often encounter them, for they avoid human beings.

I was alone with my rubbish, since the others found the task tedious and had found excuses to be elsewhere. I watched them enviously, for I, too, had become bored with rubbish. Evelyn was under the shelter, taking a little rest; her silvery hair glowed even in the shadows. Emerson, bareheaded in the boiling sunlight, was lecturing Walter about something . . . As my eyes wandered, I became aware of a strange insect-like buzzing. As it grew louder I looked about, trying to find the source.

Ramses, whose keen hearing is proverbial in Egypt, popped into sight from behind the ruined wall he was digging out. Like his father, he was without a hat. Shading his eyes with his hand, he looked up.

I sprang to my feet, staggering just a little, and hurried to Emerson. The others had seen it too; frozen in identical postures, heads raised, they stared in astonished silence as the aeroplane circled and headed off across the river.

"What's everybody gaping at?" Emerson demanded, recovering from his initial surprise. "Haven't you ever seen an aeroplane before?"

A good number of them had—during the rioting the previous spring. Planes had dropped leaflets all over the country, warning that anyone committing acts of sabotage would be shot, and bombs had been dropped on any gathering that struck the military observers as suspicious. It is not surprising that as this one turned and came back toward us, a great outcry arose, and some of the men flung themselves flat on the ground. I found the confounded things unnerving myself. When they were airborne they looked unreal—not like a bird or a machine, but like some mythological flying insect, rigid and fragile, gliding on the wind with motionless wings.

This time it passed directly overhead, so low that I could see the concentric circles of red, white, and blue on the wings, and the heads of two persons protruding from the body of the machine. Their faces were concealed by helmets and goggles. One of them raised an arm and gestured.

"Damnation!" Emerson exclaimed. "What does the damned fool think he's doing?"

"He wants to land," Ramses said in disbelief. "On this side of the river."

He ran toward the shelter where we had left the horses, vaulted onto Risha's back, and set the stallion at a gallop toward the road that led around the hill of Kurnet Murai toward the river.

"Where is he going?" Nefret demanded. She tore her eyes from the plane, which was making another circle, and started after Ramses.

Emerson moved with long strides toward the horses. "To guide them to a suitable landing place, I presume. Why they aren't landing on the East Bank, where there are great stretches of empty desert, I cannot imagine."

"Wait for me!" I cried, and ran after him. Nefret and David had already mounted.

Our assistance, I felt sure, would be needed. The stretch of low desert between the cultivation and the cliffs was rock-strewn and hilly, with pits and tombs and ruins all over the place. How much space an aeroplane required to land I did not know, but the main tourist road seemed to offer the best possibility. When we reached it the aeroplane was circling again, while Ramses tried to get donkeys, carts, camels, and people off a relatively level stretch. It was not an easy task, since they were running in all directions, some scampering for cover, the braver and more curious trying to get closer. By dint of shouting, shoving, and, in a few cases, towing balky mules and arrogant camels, we managed to empty a part of the road, though it was lined with spectators.

"That should do it," Ramses panted. Turning, he shouted Arabic curses at a camel driver who was edging closer. "Keep back!"

"What is he waiting for?" Emerson asked.

"Something to do with the wind," Ramses replied. He rose in the stirrups and waved. The import of his gestures eluded me, but they must have meant something to the pilot, for on its next approach the machine came in for a landing. The wheels touched the ground; in a series of alarming bounces and at considerable speed it rushed toward us. The remaining spectators scattered, shrieking and braying, and finally the machine jolted to a stop.

"Nobody hurt, thank God!" Emerson growled. "I will just have a word with the damned fool and ask him what he means by this."

The aeroplane had stopped several hundred feet away. Everyone converged on it except the donkeys, who were unaccustomed to loud noises and were kicking and braying. I followed more slowly. I had just had one of my premonitions.

When I arrived on the scene the pilot had removed his headgear and was shouting cheerfully at the audience. "Get away, you fellows. Imshi! Clear off or I will tell the big bird to bite you."

The second man, in the observer's seat, waited until I came up before unmasking. "Ah, Amelia, there you are. Good afternoon, every-one."

"You!" Emerson croaked.

"Weren't you expecting me?"

"Not in this fashion," I said.

Sethos gave me a provoking smile. Like his brother, whom he

closely resembled, he was a handsome man, but his face was discolored and not so well-shaped as usual. It looked to me as if someone had given him a severe beating. "I was in a hurry," he explained. "Rob was good enough to give me a lift. Flight lieutenant Wickins, may I present you to Mrs. Emerson, her husband, Professor—"

"Not now, for pity's sake!" I exclaimed. "Get out of that cursed machine at once!"

Sethos shifted position, winced theatrically, and reached out to Emerson. "Give me a hand, will you, old chap? I am a trifle stiff."

CHAPTER EIGHT

Lieutenant Wickins politely declined my invitation to join us for tea.

"Can't leave the old bus unguarded, ma'am, these beggars will strip off everything they can carry. Must start back anyhow. Due for a nasty wigging from my C.O. as it is. Absent without leave, stealing one of His Majesty's valuable aeroplanes."

He chortled like a mischievous child. He wasn't much more than nineteen or twenty, with a fresh complexion and merry brown eyes under brows as sun-bleached as his hair.

"I do hope you won't get in trouble for this," I said.

"Couldn't refuse good old Badger, ma'am. Wouldn't have missed it for the world."

The slower members of the party had caught us up. Lia was carrying the Great Cat of Re, and I could hear Horus spitting and swearing in his basket. Walter stared. "Badger?" he echoed.

I gave him a little poke, and the boy went on blithely, "I'll need petrol. Can you help me there?"

He addressed Emerson, who could never be taken for anything but the leader of any group of which he made part. However, Emerson was glowering at his brother, who leaned pathetically on his arm, so Ramses took it upon himself to reply.

"Yes, of course. It will be dark before long, though. Wouldn't you prefer to wait until morning?"

"Piece of cake" was the breezy reply. "Just follow the river. Can't miss Cairo. Sooner the better, though, so if you don't mind . . ."

"Quite," said Ramses. "Selim will . . . Selim?"

Selim was gaping at the aeroplane in open adoration. He had seen them, not only here but in Palestine, during our little hegira to Gaza, but I believe this was the first time he had ever seen one on the ground—not a distant flying thing but an actual machine, with an actual engine. "Yes," he said, starting. "What did you say, Ramses?"

Sethos let out a faint groan. "I had better get—er—good old Badger back to the house," I said, giving him a hard look. "Will you excuse us, Lieutenant? The men will stay—of course—to help you. I hope you will come for a proper visit one day."

"Delighted, ma'am."

"Frightfully good of you, old chap," said Sethos, overdoing the accent a bit.

"I will be along shortly," said Emerson. He heaved his brother unceremoniously onto Selim's stallion and went back to staring at the aeroplane with the same expression of vacant adoration as Selim's. A sense of deep foreboding ran through my limbs.

When we reached the house I sent Sethos to our room to freshen up and asked Fatima to make tea. A few tactful hints dispersed most of the others, though Evelyn had to drag Walter away and I knew Gargery would probably listen at the door.

Sethos was back almost at once. His face and hands were cleaner, but the uniform, that of a major in the Egyptian Army, was a mass of wrinkles. Passing his hand over his bristly chin, he said, "I know I look like the devil, Amelia, but don't lecture me. I haven't been able to shave for a week. I brought a change of clothing with me, but not much else; cargo space in those machines is limited."

"What happened to your face?" I asked.

Sethos settled himself in the most comfortable chair. "I encountered several fellows who considered I had no right to be where I was."

"Doing what?"

"Never mind." He leaned forward, hands clasped. "Where is she?"

"Employed as companion to an elderly lady and her mentally disturbed grandson. They are staying on their dahabeeyah in Luxor."

His expression did not alter. "That doesn't sound like her. What became of the rich husband?"

"Imprudent investments stripped him of his fortune. He died leaving her penniless."

"You are uncharacteristically terse, my dear. What are you keeping from me?"

Gargery came out with a tray, which he placed on the table. I had to speak to him sharply before he sulked away.

"I think it best if you hear the details from Maryam herself," I said, pouring a cup of tea. "But not here."

He drank thirstily and I refilled his cup. "I suppose you have it all worked out," he said.

"Certainly. It would not be advisable for you to go to her. There is no need for her employer to meet you or learn of your relationship at present. I will go across to Luxor and fetch her back."

"Tomorrow will be soon enough."

"Don't tell me you are getting cold feet? The sooner the better, in my opinion. We are somewhat crowded here, and you will want privacy, so you had better stay on the *Amelia*. You will be quite comfortable. Fatima has kept it ready for guests. Gargery, when the Professor comes back, tell him where we have gone."

"Yes, madam," said a voice from just inside the door.

"Yes, madam," said Sethos.

It required only a few minutes to explain the arrangements to Fatima, and we were soon on our way to the dahabeeyah. I left Sethos there, and got one of the crewmen, two of whom were always on duty, to take me across the river. I was not properly dressed for a social call, since I had not taken the time to change from my working costume, but I had put on my second-best hat, which had a nice wreath of pink roses and chiffon streamers that tied under the chin. Parasol in hand, I marched up the gangplank of the *Isis*, announced myself to the guard, and was shown into the saloon.

Tea had just been brought in, and they were all present—Justin and Maryam, Mrs. Fitzroyce, and the doctor. The doctor was the only one who appeared pleased to see me; he bounded to his feet, cheeks rounded in a smile. His waistcoat was a rainbow of bright embroidery. Hands resting on the head of her stick, Mrs. Fitzroyce looked me up and down, from my dusty boots to my rose-trimmed hat, as her late Majesty might have eyed a mongrel dog.

"I apologize for my intrusion," I said. "I will not stay. I came only to ask if I might borrow Miss Underhill for the evening. An old friend has arrived unexpectedly and would like to see her."

A faint gasp from Maryam was the only response. The doctor's fixed smile did not change; Mrs. Fitzroyce did not move an inch. I am not easily disconcerted, but as the silence lengthened I began to feel slightly uncomfortable. There was something uncanny about the shadowy room, the motionless figures, and the eyes of Justin, gleaming like those of a cat.

Finally the old lady stirred and cleared her throat. "I cannot permit Miss Underhill to absent herself. She knew when she accepted the position that I expected her to be on duty all day every day."

"You mean she hasn't had a day or an hour to herself since she joined you?"

My tone was incredulous and critical; it seemed to me, as it must have done to most persons, that the arrangement was cruelly unfair. Mrs. Fitzroyce responded with a brusque "That is correct."

"But surely . . ." I modified my indignation. "Since she has been so faithful in her attendance all this time, can you not spare her for a few hours? I would be extremely grateful. We will bring her back immediately after dinner."

Unexpectedly and unnervingly Mrs. Fitzroyce's face broke into a broad smile, which added a new and interesting collection of wrinkles. I realized she was having another "spell." "Very good," she mumbled. "Go and get your hat, Miss Underhill. The nice hat Mrs. Emerson gave you."

Maryam got slowly to her feet. That she knew the identity of the "friend" I did not doubt. I could not see her features clearly, but her bent head and bowed shoulders suggested that she had resigned herself to face her father.

"You are inviting Miss Underhill to your house?" Justin's clear treble rang with surprise. "Then I will come too."

"I am sorry——" I began.

The old lady cut me off with a rusty chuckle. "No, Justin, you have not been invited."

"But she is only a servant," Justin protested. "Why can't I go? I want to see the pretty Mrs. Emerson and the children and the cats."

The door opened to admit one of the guards, a swarthy fellow in turban and striped robe. He seemed out of breath. "There is a gentle-man——"

"Yes, yes," said the gentleman, pushing him out of the way. "My apologies, madam. I came to fetch my wife."

Ill-mannered and unexpected though it was, his appearance dispelled the uncanny atmosphere as a fresh breeze blows away fog. It would never have occurred to him to change into proper clothing; but Emerson never looks to better advantage than when he is attired in the casual garments he wears on the dig, his shirt open at the throat, his muscular arms bared to the elbow. Mrs. Fitzroyce inspected him with more interest than she had bestowed on me. Emerson has that effect on females, and in my experience a lady is never too old to appreciate a fine-looking man.

"Won't you and Mrs. Emerson stay for tea, Professor?"

"No," said Emerson. I coughed meaningfully, and he amended his reply. "Er—thank you, but we have not the time. Confounded rude of Mrs. Emerson to burst in on you, but the circumstances . . . Hmph. Amelia, shall we go? Where's the girl? That is, I mean Miss——"

I poked him with my parasol before he could shove his foot farther into his mouth.

Maryam had slipped out of the room. I hoped she had only gone to get her hat, but I wasn't taking any chances on her eluding me, so I rushed through my farewells and removed Emerson from the room. Somewhat to my surprise, Justin did not renew his demand to go with us. He had retreated and stood with his back against the wall like a cornered animal.

"He doesn't like me," said Emerson, who had also observed the boy's reaction.

"You keep catching hold of him. It is just as well; he was deter-mined to come along until you turned up. Now where is that girl? We will wait here at the head of the gangplank so she can't get away."

"You think she may bolt?"

"I do not know, Emerson, but I prefer not to take the chance. That is why I came here at once, before she learned of the arrival of a mysterious stranger in an aeroplane. Whatever possessed you to follow me?"

"I wanted to be sure you had gone where you said you were going, Peabody."

"You don't trust me?"

"Not one whit," said Emerson. His curious gaze moved round the deck, taking in the elegant fittings and the crewmen who watched him with equal curiosity. "The old lady must be filthy rich. She's set herself up in style. I don't recognize any of the crewmen. A sturdy lot, aren't they?"

"They are Cairenes, I suppose. She probably hired them with the boat."

When Maryam came she was wearing the flowery hat. She had washed the paint off her face and loosened her hair. She looked very young and frightened. Emerson immediately offered her his arm and told her not to worry.

Emerson left us at the *Amelia;* he dislikes emotional scenes and anticipated that this one would be particularly fraught. I led Maryam to the saloon, where we found young Nasir furiously dusting various articles of furniture. Fatima must have rousted him out of his house in the village and sent him to the boat to resume his former duties as steward. I had known I could leave everything to her; her standards were a good deal higher than mine.

"The beds are made, Sitt," he announced proudly, waving the cloth, so that the dust immediately settled back onto the surfaces he had cleaned. "And the tea is made, and the food is here, and Mahmud is ready to cook, and—"

"Very good," I said. "Where is the gentleman?"

"In his room, Sitt. There is hot water and towels and—"

I told Maryam to sit down and went to fetch Sethos. By accident or design, he had selected the same room he had once occupied when he was ill with malaria. He was standing at the window looking out across the rose and golden ripples of the river.

"She is here," I said, though I knew he must have been aware of our arrival. "I will leave you two alone."

"No." He turned slowly to face me. "Please stay."

"Come now, don't be such a coward. You aren't afraid of her, are you?"

"I am afraid of saying the wrong thing." He passed a hand nervously over his hair. I decided it was not a wig, though the color was a peculiar shade of rust-streaked brown.

"Very well," I agreed. Only courtesy had led me to make the offer. I was immensely curious to know what they would say to each other, and it was likely that a mediator—or referee!—might be wanted.

Nasir had served tea; I told him we would wait on ourselves, and sent him away. After a brief interval, during which time Maryam sat with bowed head and Sethos stood staring, for once bereft of speech, I took a chair and said briskly, "Maryam, will you pour, please? Milk only for me. Your father takes lemon, no sugar."

The social amenities are considered meaningless by some, but in my experience they are useful in helping people over an awkward spot. Mechanically she followed my instructions. I gave Sethos a little nudge and gestured to him to take the cup from her. Not until then did she look up into his face.

"You've changed," she whispered.

"For the worse." He had regained his sangfroid. The practiced charm settled onto him like a garment. "The same cannot be said of you. You have become a beautiful woman."

"Like my mother?"

He flinched, but replied calmly, "Not at all like your mother. I will answer your questions, Maryam, in due time, and make all the amends I can for my past mistakes. For now, can we not talk a little, get to know one another better?"

His humility gave her increased confidence. Her chin lifted, and she smiled faintly. "What shall we talk about?"

"You." Remembering his manners, he brought me my cup and then seated himself next to her on the divan. "Mrs. Emerson has told me of your present situation. It cannot continue."

"Has she told you the boy is dependent on me, and that I have given Mrs. Fitzroyce my word to remain as long as she needs me?"

"We'll find someone to take your place."

"And then what?" She responded as any woman of spirit would, with flashing eyes and heightened color in her cheeks. "Will you take me to live with you and your latest mistress?"

I feared that would arouse the sort of cutting response at which Sethos was so expert. Instead he replied quietly, "The lady to whom you refer is my dear companion, and will be my wife as soon as I can persuade her to accept my proposal of marriage."

"She has refused you? Why?"

It might not have been intended as a compliment, but her tone of surprise made it sound like one.

"She doesn't consider me reliable. I can't imagine why." His rueful smile would have been hard for any woman to resist—and, as I had realized from the start, she did not want to resist. Hardship and suffering had softened her; only stubborn pride had prevented her from yielding at once. Her lips trembled and her wide hazel eyes overflowed. She turned to him; slowly, almost timidly, he held out his arms and gathered her into his embrace.

It was a touching sight. Emerson would have been sniffing and clearing his throat. I put my cup on the table and rose. "I will leave you alone now," I said. "You have everything you need, I believe."

Over the tumbled brown curls that rested against his breast, Sethos looked up at me. "Everything," he said. "Thank you, Amelia."

They were all waiting for me on the veranda. I had to admire six or seven crayon scribbles before the children retired to make more, and I was able to satisfy the curiosity of the adults. I waved aside Evelyn's offer of tea. Emerson immediately handed me a stiff whiskey and soda.

"All's well," I said. "When I left them she was sobbing in his fatherly embrace."

The reactions were somewhat mixed. Evelyn's sweet face glowed, Emerson gave a great sigh, and David and Lia murmured words of approval and congratulation. My son's phlegmatic countenance did not change.

"I find it difficult to picture Sethos as a doting father," he said. "Now what, Mother?"

"I have made all the arrangements," I replied, holding out my empty glass to Emerson. I felt entitled to the indulgence, for really, it had been a tiring day. "They will dine together on the dahabeeyah, where Sethos is staying, and afterward he will escort her back to the *Isis*. She will give in her notice and then . . . Then I suppose she had better come to us until he makes permanent plans for her. I have a number of ideas about that, but I did not want to mar the warmth of their reunion with practical suggestions."

The last of the sunlight vanished as the sun sank below the western mountains; in the dusky twilight the lights of distant Luxor twinkled like fallen stars. The genial beverage—I refer in this case to whiskey and soda—had its usual soothing effect; I was somewhat slow to realize that silence had followed my statement, instead of the eager questions (and commendations) I had expected.

"I trust there was no difficulty getting Lieutenant Wickins and the aeroplane away safely?" I inquired.

"He got off all right," Ramses said. "Whether he makes it to Cairo is another matter. It will be a near thing—the range of that aircraft is between three and four hundred miles—but he seemed to regard it as a fine lark. He was carrying extra petrol. Nefret, shouldn't the children go to bed?"

This process ordinarily took quite some time. It began to dawn on me, as the young parents hurried their offspring through good-night kisses and embraces, that something had happened, something they did not want to discuss in front of the children. My affectionate concern pictured one disaster after another: Selim mangled by the propeller of the aeroplane, Cyrus suffering a heart attack, Bertie pale and dead of poison, a suicide note clutched in his stiffening hand . . . No, that was too absurd. He had better sense, even if I did suspect him of writing poetry on the sly.

Sennia was the last to leave—she considered that her right, since she was the eldest. Horus followed her out, and the Great Cat of Re emerged from under the settee, his tail waving like a plume of dark smoke.

"Well?" I cried. "Do not keep me in suspense, Emerson. Something terrible has happened, I know it. Is it Cyrus, or—"

"Nothing like that, Peabody. Good Gad, you must learn to control your rampageous imagination. There's been a body found. The remains of one, rather."

"Ah," I said, relieved. "No one we know, then."

"That seems to be the question," said Emerson. "The police think the fellow was not an Egyptian. They've asked Nefret to come to the zabtiyeh and examine him. Them. Bones."

"Where were they found?"

"In the desert east of Luxor."

"In that case," I said, rising, "I will tell Fatima to serve dinner immediately. I had hoped I would not have to ride that horse again today."

"Can't wait to get at a corpse, can you?" Emerson inquired, baring his large white teeth. "Dismiss the idea, Peabody. It can wait until tomorrow. He isn't going anywhere."

As Ramses explained during dinner, the determination of sex and race had been arrived at because of the scraps of clothing found with the bones. I expressed my surprise at the deductive powers of the police official, and at his request for Nefret's services. He could have spared himself considerable trouble by disposing of the remains without bothering to mention them to the British authorities.

"He's a new broom," Ramses replied. "The old chief tottered off into retirement a few months ago. Ibrahim Ayyad is young, ambitious, energetic, and canny enough to avoid stirring up trouble until he's certain of his conclusions."

I had reached certain conclusions of my own, but like the admirable Mr. Ayyad, I was canny enough not to commit myself. If the others shared my suspicions they did not say so.

I had intended to pay a quick visit to the dahabeeyah before accompanying Nefret to Luxor, but it did not prove necessary. Sethos arrived at break of day. Informed of his presence by Gargery, I hastily finished dressing and went to the veranda, where I found that Fatima had brought him coffee. He looked reasonably respectable in flannels and tweed coat, which Nasir must have pressed for him. The bruises had faded to a greenish yellow, and the beard was now well developed.

"Breakfast will be served shortly," I informed him.

"So Fatima told me, with apologies for the delay. Sit down, Amelia, and let us watch the sunrise together. You will no doubt appreciate the symbolism."

Pale clouds of rose and amber washed the cerulean blue of the heavens. It was the same sight I had watched so often with Abdullah, from a greater height. The symbolism did not elude me.

"You have made your peace with Maryam, then?"

"We had quite an emotional few hours," said Sethos, at his ease. "She's a moist young woman, isn't she? I don't recall her weeping so much."

"She has had cause for tears."

The tone rather than the words themselves conveyed the reprimand I intended. His eyes avoided mine. "My remark was in poor taste. You have reason to believe me a poor parent, but I did spend time with the child whenever I could. I don't . . . The truth is . . . Confound it, Amelia, I felt as if I were speaking with a stranger—a pretty, mannerly young woman so unlike the rebellious child I once knew that I found it difficult to believe she was the same person."

"The change is for the better, isn't it?"

He nodded without speaking, his face still averted. "Children change a great deal as they become adults," I said. "One might say that they do become different people. Just look at Ramses!"

He looked up, his strangely colored eyes brightening from pale hazel to paler gray as the light caught them. "A most encouraging example, it is true. Oh, we got on quite well, avoiding by mutual consent such delicate subjects as her mother's career as a murderess."

"You will have to face that subject sooner or later." I spoke rather sharply. Cynicism was his defense against emotion, but it was high time—in my opinion—he dropped those defenses against his daughter. "Get it out into the open and set her straight. I doubt she has heard the true story."

"She did seem chastened. She spoke gratefully of you."

"All the more reason to clear the air. I will do it if you shirk the task."

"Better you than I. You are very good at setting people straight."

"I will find a suitable opportunity," I promised. "So you took her back to the *Isis* last night?"

"Yes. The old lady had retired, so I did not present myself. I am to fetch Maryam and her belongings, such as they are, later today, and bring her back to the dahabeeyah."

"It would not be proper for her to stay there with you."

"For God's sake, Amelia, she's my daughter!"

"Do you want everyone in Luxor to know that?"

Sethos scratched his chin. The scruffy beard and the healing cuts itched, I supposed. "I am becoming weary of inventing new identities and preposterous plots, Amelia. So far as her employer is concerned, I am an old friend of her father. Maryam says the old lady is a trifle vague, so she won't ask awkward questions; the busy gossips of Luxor certainly will, however. I have decided to be Major Hamilton again. Retired, of course. There's an outside chance that someone may remember Maryam as Molly, and that's the easiest way of explaining my interest in her."

"Hamilton was red-haired," I said, with a critical look at his streaked hair.

"I'm going gray. Sad, isn't it, how the years take their toll?"

"Hmph," said Emerson, appearing in the doorway. "Er—everything all right with the girl?"

"Yes, quite," I said, for I knew he did not want explanations, only assurance that he wouldn't have to do anything. "Is breakfast ready?"

"Yes. I assume," said Emerson morosely, "that it would be a waste of breath to ask you not to come to the zabtiyeh."

"You are correct. It would be advisable for Sethos to join us, since he was well acquainted with the corpse."

Sethos's only response to the news of Martinelli's death consisted of raised eyebrows and a silent whistle. I did not elaborate on the bare facts, nor was the subject discussed during breakfast. Evelyn asked after Maryam, Walter made several unsubtle attempts to find out Sethos's real name, and Ramses, in an effort to divert us, described Selim's fascination with the aeroplane. "He stroked the dirty canvas like a lover, and asked the lieutenant how hard it was to drive."

Most foreigners had nothing to do with the native police. They were not subject to the laws that governed Egyptians, and preferred to deal with occasional cases of theft and extortion through their dragomen or tour agencies. In Cairo the police—like everything else in Egypt—was headed by a "British adviser," but for the most part the provincial police were under the jurisdicion of the local mudir. I had visited the zabtiyeh (police station) in the past, and I was pleasantly surprised at its changed appearance. The broken stairs and windows had been repaired; two constables, in smart white uniforms and red tarbooshes, stood at attention at the door, instead of sleeping on the steps as they had been accustomed to do. It was a sign of the changing times, of the new wind that was blowing through Egypt, and the young man who rose to his feet when we were shown into his office was another symbol of those times. Taller than most Egyptians, his sable beard and mustache trimmed close, he had the smooth dark skin of a Sudanese and the manners of a Frenchman, though when he respectfully kissed the hand I offered, I detected a glint of irony in his keen black eyes.

"This is an honor I had not expected, Sitt Hakim," he said.

Taking this as the subtle rebuke that was intended, I replied in my best Arabic, "I could not resist the opportunity of meeting one whose praises I have heard sung."

"With you be peace and God's mercy and blessing," Emerson added. The formalities having been concluded, so far as he was concerned, he went on, "You have met my son. This is my daughter-in-law—a genuine Sitt Hakim—and—er—"

"A friend," said Sethos, bowing. "Sabah el-kheir, effendi."

Ayyad's eyes rested on him for a moment and then returned to Nefret. "I thank you for coming. I have ordered the objects to be brought here. The mortuary is not pleasant for a lady."

Nefret might have reminded him that her acquaintance with unpleasant cadavers was almost certainly greater than his, but she recognized the courtesy and acknowledged it with a smile.

The room was fairly large and crowded with shabby furniture—a red plush settee, several chairs of European style (the cushions worn and faded), a large desk, and two battered wooden cabinets. Under the windows on the east wall was a long table, covered with cotton sheeting. Without ceremony Ayyad whisked it off.

In Egypt one inevitably thinks of mummies. However, a body left unburied has little chance to dry out before predators get to it—vultures, wild dogs, jackals, and, after them, a varied collection of insects. There was nothing left of this one but pale bones, splintered and gnawed and disarticulated. As Nefret bent over the unsavory ensemble, her face absorbed, Ayyad said, "They were widely scattered, and some we did not find, though we searched far."

She heard the defensive note in his voice and gave him the compliment he wanted. "You've laid them out in the right order," she said, without looking up. "I'm impressed that you found so many. The small bones of hands and feet are missing; that's not unusual, in such cases. Some of the ribs . . ." As she spoke, she took a tape measure from the pocket of her skirt. "Without the feet I can only estimate his height."

"How estimate?" Ayyad asked, edging closer.

"There are tables of proportions. I can show you someday, if you like."

"You say 'his.' How do you know that?"

"But you knew that." She gave him a comradely smile, as one professional to another. "From the clothing. Scraps of European-style trousers and coat and waistcoat, we were told."

"Yes, they are in that box. But there are other ways—from the bones themselves?"

She gave him a little lecture, to which he listened attentively, his head close to hers. "The skull also indicates a male," she finished. "You see these ridges of bone over the eye sockets? In most women they are not so prominent, and the angle of the jaw is more rounded."

"Age?" Ayyad rapped.

"Not a boy, not an old man. That's just an educated guess. Based primarily on the teeth. The four back molars have erupted and show signs of moderate wear. I can't tell you much more. The damned jackals haven't left me enough to work on."

She had spoken English, and he had replied in the same language, so absorbed that he spoke to her as directly as he would have addressed a man. I sympathize with the desire of any person to improve his understanding, but time was getting on, and Emerson was beginning to fidget.

"Enough to determine his identity," I said, forestalling another question from Ayyad. "It is Martinelli. Look at his teeth."

Stained brown and yellowish green, the chipped lower incisors bared by the fleshless lips, they grinned up at us.

THE SCRAPS OF THE CLOTHING confirmed my identification. The faded shepherd's plaid was the same pattern as that of the trousers Martinelli had worn the night he disappeared. The only other objects in the box were a few buttons and metal fasteners from various articles of dress. His ostentatious stickpin and his pocket watch and chain were not there. Needless to say, neither were the gold bracelets and the pectoral.

Sethos stepped in to relieve us of the problem of what to do with the bones. Declaring himself to be an acquaintance of the dead man, he manfully struggled to conceal his shock and distress at the bad news. "How often have I warned him of the dangers of those long, solitary walks of his," he murmured, passing a clean white handkerchief over his eyes. "His heart was weak; he must have collapsed and died, out there in the waste, under the cold, uncaring moon, and it would not be long before . . ." He shuddered. "He is at peace now."

I was tempted to give him a hard poke with my parasol, but he prudently stayed at a distance.

After promising to collect the bones and notify the proper authorities, we left the office. Zabtiyeh Square was an ecumenical area, with a mosque and a Roman Catholic church and two modern hotels as well as the police station. Pretty gardens filled the center; the color and scent of the blossoms were especially refreshing after the sight we had seen.

"This certainly puts a new complexion on things," I remarked. "Martinelli never left Luxor. He must have been killed the same night he disappeared."

"You don't know that it was murder," Emerson muttered. He knew my conclusion was correct, he just didn't want to admit it.

"A man of his sort was not in the habit of taking long solitary walks," I retorted. "Some individual took him out there, by force or by guile, and left him dead. In my opinion that is a strong presumption of murder. As for his weak heart, you invented that, didn't you?"

My brother-in-law met my gaze with a shrug and a smile. "There was no need to confuse the issue. So far as the authorities are concerned, it was a sad accident. How did he die, Nefret?"

She started slightly when he addressed her, and turned troubled blue eyes toward him. "You don't miss much."

"You have a very unguarded, expressive face, my dear. Something about the neck bones, wasn't it?"

"There was some damage. I couldn't swear to it under oath, but he might have been strangled. Or," she added sourly, "he might have had his head bashed in—impossible to tell whether the breaks were post- or pre-mortem—or been fed poison, or stabbed or shot!"

I took her hand and patted it. "Shall we stop at the Savoy for a nice cup of tea?"

"Good Gad, no!" Emerson increased his pace. "I have work to do. Cyrus will have to be informed. I leave that to you, Peabody."

"If theft was the motive for his murder . . ." I began.

"What other motive could there be?" Emerson demanded. "The fellahin who found the remains would have taken anything of value, but it is much more likely that he was robbed by someone to whom he had been fool enough to display the jewelry while he was swanking round the cafés and bars. The value of the prize was fabulous enough to move even a cautious Luxor thief to murder. The portmanteau he carried is probably at the bottom of the river, filled with stones. That's how I would have disposed of it," Emerson concluded. He took me firmly by the arm and hurried me on past the shops that lined the esplanade.

His obvious disinclination to continue the discussion did not prevent me from speculating. His theory (ours, I should say) was probably correct, but then what had become of the princesses' jewels? Were they still in the house of the thief, in a secret hidey-hole like the one old Abd el Hamed had excavated under the floor of his house? Had they been sold to one of the Luxor dealers? The latter seemed to me unlikely. The jewelry was distinctive, its ownership and origin well known; were it to be offered to a buyer, we would hear of it sooner or later, and Emerson would come down on the unlucky dealer like a thunderbolt. Perhaps our original theory had been the right one: The treasure had been taken to Cairo, though obviously not by Martinelli.

Later that afternoon I sat alone on the veranda awaiting the arrival of Sethos and his daughter. I was grateful for an interlude of reflection. Shortly the entire family—et quelle famille!—would be upon me, and although I seldom have any difficulty keeping track of a plethora of problems, I found myself unable to concentrate. My thoughts fluttered as randomly as a butterfly from one thought to the next, some important, some utterly inconsequential. What to wear to the fantasia certainly fell into the second category, and so did the dinner menu, which I had already settled with Fatima, and the ostracon I had found that afternoon—another part of the one that had caused Ramses such embarrassment. The disposition of the lower limbs in this bit was really quite astonishing, but Ramses had refused to discuss the matter with me.

With an effort I forced myself to fix my thoughts on more important matters. I had not had the opportunity to tell Cyrus about Martinelli. I was in no hurry to see the Vandergelts, since we had yet to decide what to tell Cyrus about Sethos. All three of them knew of his relationship to Emerson. Selim was the only other person in Luxor who knew, but Selim was unaware that the drab companion was Sethos's daughter. Or was he?

My head was aching. It was Emerson's fault, for dragging me back to the dig before I could pin my elusive brother-in-law down. We had left him in Luxor, where, as he explained, he hoped to acquire a few basic necessities before collecting his daughter. They were to come directly to us, and I had expected them before this. Matters might not be so easily settled as Sethos had assumed. Mrs. Fitzroyce might reasonably make a fuss, and Justin was almost certain to do so.

Emerson was the first to join me. "Where is everybody?" he demanded.

"They will be here soon, I expect. All of them."

They were. All of them except Sethos and Maryam. The children began clamoring for tea, so I told Fatima to serve.

"Shouldn't we wait for our guests?" inquired Sennia.

My poor head gave a great throb. I had forgotten about Sennia, bright as a new penny and as " 'quisitive" as the elephant's child. How much had I told her? How much should I tell her? She had met Maryam when Maryam was Molly. She had encountered Sethos, not as Major Hamilton but as "Cousin Ismail" . . . I gave it up.

"How do you know we are expecting guests?" I inquired feebly.

Sennia was a trifle vain and always insisted on dressing in her best for tea. She smoothed her ruffled skirt and rolled her eyes. "Fatima told me. Who are they? Is one of them Mr. Badger from the aeroplane?"

"It is a surprise," I said, since I had not the least idea what Sethos would look like or what he would call himself. Surely she wouldn't remember or recognize "Cousin Ismail."

Knowing Sethos's penchant for dramatic epiphanies—the aeroplane was certainly the most impressive to date—I might have expected he would wait until he had a large audience before he presented himself. We saw the carriage coming some distance away; it was the best of those for hire at the landing. It drew up with a flourish in front of the house, and Sethos got out. Then he swooped like a hawk on Davy, who was scuttling as fast as his fat legs could carry him toward the motorcar. The child was absolutely uncanny. I had just that moment opened the door.

Sethos held the little boy up so that their eyes were on a level. "And who is this adventurous young man?" he inquired. Davy giggled.

The little rascal had got us over the first awkwardness. Sethos handed Davy over to Ramses and helped Maryam out of the carriage, while the rest of us fended off the other children. They immediately gathered round Sethos; Davy was captivated by his new acquaintance, and the little girls responded as all females did to his calculated charm.

"What happened to your face?" inquired Evvie, leaning against his knee. "Did someone hit you?"

"Three someones," said Sethos, without missing a beat. "Three large, cruel men. They were about to hurt a poor cat. I made them stop."

The twins chirped approvingly and Evvie batted her lashes at him. "Where is the kitty?"

"At my house. I am calling her Florence. She has black stripes and a white front."

"That was very noble of you, sir," said Dolly.

Sethos's face softened a trifle as he looked at the little boy. "You must be young Abdullah. I knew your great-grandfather well. He would have done the same."

"Why don't you all draw a picture of Florence?" I suggested, glaring at my inventive brother-in-law. Abdullah had hated cats.

The pack dispersed, except for Sennia. "Was that a true story?" she asked, fixing Sethos with a questioning stare.

"Not a word of it," said Sethos promptly.

Sennia chortled. "You are funny. Who are you, really? Are you her father? I remember her; she was here a long time ago."

She gestured at Maryam, who was sitting next to Evelyn. The girl was wearing the hat I had given her, and a new frock—the best Luxor had to offer, one must assume—of pink mousseline de soie. Papa had taken her shopping.

"Why don't you go and introduce yourself?" I suggested.

General conversation was impossible with so large a group. It did not take Sethos long to maneuver himself into a tête-à-tête with me, while Maryam responded shyly to Evelyn's kindly questions, and the children set to work on innumerable drawings of presumed felines. The tête-à-tête was immediately expanded by Emerson, who squeezed himself onto the settee next to me and fixed stern sapphirine orbs upon Sethos.

"You are awaiting my report, I suppose," the latter said.

"I am awaiting elucidation of precisely who everyone in Luxor believes you to be," I replied. "What did you tell Mrs. Fitzroyce?"

"I did not meet her." Sethos leaned back and crossed one leg over the other. "Two husky lads intercepted me at the head of the gangplank. When I handed over my card I was informed that the Sitt was resting but that the other lady was expecting me. I wasn't allowed onto the boat. Maryam appeared with her pathetic little bundles and we left."

"Then you did not meet Justin?"

"I caught a glimpse of him, peering out from the doorway to the cabins. At least I assume it was he; he appeared as wary as a timid animal, so I pretended I hadn't seen him."

"What card did you leave?" I asked.

"That of Major Hamilton, of course. I always carry a selection."

"Ha," said Emerson. "The Vandergelts know your real identity."

"I suppose there is no way of avoiding them," Sethos said with a martyred sigh.

"I don't see how you can be ready to leave Luxor for a few more days," I said. "The Vandergelts are giving a soiree on Sunday, and Selim will expect you to turn up for his fantasia tomorrow."

Sethos groaned theatrically. "Must I?"

"You sound like Emerson," I said, wondering if he was doing it on purpose to annoy. "It would be advisable to give the impression that this is an ordinary visit from an old acquaintance. Your habit of popping in and out in various bizarre costumes, like the Demon King in a pantomime, makes things very difficult."

"But much more interesting, Amelia dear."

WE LINGERED OVER FATIMA'S EXCELLENT dinner, for everyone was on his or her best behavior, and Sethos exerted himself to be agreeable. I was about to suggest we withdraw to the parlor when a visitor was announced. I had been half-expecting him, for nothing is a secret in Luxor.

"Show Mr. Vandergelt into the parlor," I said to Gargery. "And make sure there is plenty of whiskey."

Cyrus was too much of a gentleman to forget apologies and greetings, but even these held an element of reproach.

"I figured the fella in the aeroplane was you," he said, shaking Sethos's hand. "I'd have called earlier, if anybody had bothered to tell me you were here. What are you gonna do next, ride in on an elephant?"

"Whiskey, Cyrus?" I inquired.

"I reckon. Thank you." He tugged fretfully at his goatee and turned reproachful eyes on me. "How come I have to hear all the news secondhand? Don't you folks trust me anymore?"

"Er, hmph," said Emerson, busy with the decanters. "The fact is . . . er . . ."

"There hasn't been time," Nefret said. She perched on a hassock beside Cyrus and put a caressing hand over his. "You've heard about the identification of the bones? Don't be angry, Cyrus dear. We would have notified you at once if we had found the princesses' jewels."

"You think I'm pretty selfish, I guess," Cyrus muttered. "That poor devil, out there all this time, and me thinking the worst of him . . ."

"This discovery alters neither the circumstances nor your assessment of Martinelli, Cyrus," I said. "He took the jewelry, there can be little question of that, and although we may never know his motive for doing so, he had no right to remove it without your permission."

"You're sure it was him? Where was he found?"

"If you are thinking of conducting a search of the area, I beg you to abandon the idea," Ramses said; like myself he had seen the stubborn glow of archaeological greed in Cyrus's eyes. "Believe me, Cyrus, I would have done so myself if I believed there was the least likelihood of finding the jewelry. It was Martinelli, all right, but if he wasn't murdered and robbed, the men who found the body would have taken anything of value."

Cyrus knew he was right, but he was not the man to abandon hope so easily. He kept asking questions and proposing theories. His final appeal was to Sethos.

"Can't you do anything?"

The corners of Sethos's mouth twitched slightly. "Not much use having a master thief as a friend of the family if he can't help out, eh?"

"I didn't mean—" Cyrus began.

"Of course you did. Quite right, too. I will make further inquiries, but don't get your hopes up."

"Sure appreciate it," Cyrus said, his hopes obviously rising. "Well, I better get on home. Sorry for busting in on you like this." He had avoided looking directly at Maryam. Now he went to her and held out his hand. "Good to have you back in the family, young lady. We will see you at our soiree on Sunday, I hope."

His tact and kindness brought a becoming flush to her cheeks. "Thank you, sir. I don't know . . ." She glanced at her father, who said easily, "We accept with pleasure. Please convey my thanks and regards to Mrs. Vandergelt. I look forward to seeing her and her son again."

"Oh, say, that reminds me." Hat in hand, Cyrus turned to me. "Katherine told me to ask whether some of you folks might want to stay with us at the Castle. We've got plenty of room, and you must be getting a mite crowded here."

Such was certainly the case. I had had to move Sennia out of her pleasant little suite of rooms and give them to David and Lia and their children. She was in David's old room, with the one next to it serving as a schoolroom. Evelyn and Walter occupied the guest rooms at the other house. What with additional offices and storage rooms, both houses were full up, and I had been forced to ask Sennia to share her schoolroom with Maryam, an arrangement that did not please Sennia. I would have consigned the Luxor gossips to the devil and sent Maryam to stay with her father on the *Amelia,* but she needed a little more time to be comfortable with him. Besides, I wanted her with me, where I could keep an eye on her. The girl had been attacked once already, and that incident had yet to be explained.

I was tempted to send Sennia to the Castle, along with Basima and Gargery, whose constant surveillance was beginning to get on my nerves. However, Horus would have had to accompany them, and he had no manners, particularly with regard to the Vandergelts' cat Sekhmet.

I was about to tell Cyrus I would think it over and let him know, when Evelyn spoke up. "That is very good of Katherine, Cyrus. If you are sure, Walter and I will take advantage of your kind offer. I will speak to Katherine about it tomorrow."

Evelyn was the mildest and most accommodating of women, but when she spoke in that decisive tone I never attempted to differ with her. I waited until after Cyrus had left us before venturing to ask what had prompted her decision.

"Having houseguests for a protracted period becomes inconvenient" was her smiling reply. "Ramses and Nefret would never say so, but I am sure we are putting them out. Katherine and I enjoy each other's company; she has been feeling a bit neglected, I think."

Ramses leaned over the back of the sofa and put his arm round her shoulders. "You needn't be so tactful, Aunt Evelyn. Being in the same house with my children is enough to drive anyone into a nervous collapse."

He was laughing and she laughed too, as she looked up at him. He was standing between her and Maryam; the girl shifted position slightly.

"Very well," I said. "It will be a nice rest for you, Evelyn, being away from the little darlings for a while. The accommodations at the Castle are quite luxurious, and you will be waited upon like a queen."

Somewhat belatedly, it occurred to me to ask Walter what he thought about the scheme. The little darlings had not bothered him, since he was deaf and blind to all distractions while he was working. Nudged by his wife, he said absently, "Certainly, my dear, whatever you say. I will take the papyrus with me. It is proving to be most interesting."

"I'm afraid it is my fault that you are all being put to so much trouble," Maryam murmured.

"Not at all," I said. "This will work out nicely for everyone. You can move into the other house tomorrow. I expect you are tired; come along and I will show you where you are to sleep tonight."

The schoolroom—no longer to be referred to as the day nursery—was not directly connected to Sennia's bedroom—not to be referred to as the night nursery. The doors of both rooms opened onto the courtyard behind the house. A cot had been moved in, and Fatima had made certain all was neat and tidy, but I had not realized how shabby the room looked. The calico curtains, moving gently in the night breeze, were threadbare, and the tiled floor bore certain indelible stains—ink and paint and the evidence of feline visitation.

"I am afraid it isn't very elegant," I said apologetically. "But it is only for one night."

She said something under her breath—something about "no better than I deserve." Since I believe in striking when the iron is hot, I decided to take the bull by the horns. I motioned her to sit down. "I have been wanting to talk to you about your mother, Maryam. She was an unfortunate woman who behaved very badly and who died violently—but not at our hands, or at those of your father."

She gasped as sharply as if I had struck her, and looked up into my face. "You don't believe in beating round the bush, do you?"

"There is no sense in that. I don't know what you have heard about her, but I intend to set the record straight and remind you that you are in no way accountable for any of her actions."

"My father was not present when she . . . when she died?"

"No. Shall I tell you what really happened that day?"

She nodded, her eyes wide.

"Her—er—association with your father followed other—er—associations of a similar nature," I said. "I am giving you the bare facts, Maryam, without attempting to explain or excuse them, though you must bear in mind that she had no chance at a better life. That is tragically true of many women, but Bertha was not the sort to submit meekly. She formed a criminal organization of women and was, in a somewhat unorthodox way, a supporter of women's rights. She came to dislike me because she believed—er—"

"That my father was in love with you."

"In essence, that is correct," I said with a little cough. "Such is no longer the case, if it ever was, but jealousy drove her on several occasions to try to kill me. The final attempt occurred on the day of which I am speaking. She had taken me prisoner the previous afternoon. Thanks to your father, I was able to escape; but when I came out of the house of my friend Abdullah, where I had found refuge the night before, she was lying in wait for me. I was saved by Abdullah, who threw himself in front of me and took in his own body the bullets meant for me. Several of the men who were present—friends of ours and of Abdullah—had to wrestle her to the ground in order to get the gun away from her. I do not know—I doubt anyone knows—who actually struck the fatal blow. My full attention was on Abdullah, who lay dying in my arms. They did not set out to kill her, Maryam; they were mad with anger and grief, and she would have gone on shooting if they had not prevented her."

"Abdullah," she repeated. "Little Dolly's great-grandfather? Selim's father, and the grandfather of David . . . You all loved him very much, didn't you?"

Her composure worried me. It was unnatural. "Yes, we did."

"They were present—Selim and David?"

"Why, yes. So were . . . See here, Maryam, if you suspect Selim or David of striking the fatal blow—"

"That was not what I meant."

"Good Gad," I exclaimed in horror, as her meaning dawned on me. "Are you suggesting that one of them—one of us—blames you for your mother's actions and wants revenge? That one of them—one of us—hired an assassin to attack you? Nonsense, child. Aside from the fact that none of us would perpetrate such an act, your true identity was unknown to us until after the event. Get it out of your head this instant."

The curtains flapped violently. Maryam let out a little scream and I let out a muffled swear word as a portly form climbed laboriously through the window. Once Horus had been able to leap through it. Age and weight had taken their toll; now he had to scale the wall. Poised awkwardly on the sill, he looked round the room, spat, and vanished into the night.

"He was looking for Sennia," I explained. "I hope you are not frightened of cats."

"I like them very much. I never had one."

"Don't waste your time trying to make friends with Horus. He detests all of us except Sennia and Nefret. He won't bother you again tonight. Can you sleep now?"

"Yes." Impulsively she put her hand on mine. "Thank you. You have cleansed my mind of some very ugly thoughts."

It was a pretty gesture and a pretty little speech. "You do believe me, then?" I asked. "It is a sad story, but we must not judge others or feel guilt for their actions. Each of us has enough on our consciences without taking on the guilt of others."

FROM MANUSCRIPT H

Emerson's hopes of resuming his full work schedule were doomed from the start. Only he, as his wife acerbically remarked, would have trotted blithely off to Deir el Medina when so many duties, domestic and investigative, took precedence. Immediately after breakfast she intended to help Evelyn and Walter pack for their removal to the Castle, and arrange for Maryam to move into their rooms. Lia was ordered (it was couched as a request, but no one doubted it was an order) to go through her wardrobe to see if she could find something for Maryam to wear. A long monologue, to which Ramses listened with only half an ear, explained her reasons—something about relative sizes and the absence of practical garments in the girl's wardrobe. At the last minute Nefret received an urgent summons to the clinic; the word of its opening had spread and her services were increasingly in demand.

Emerson listened openmouthed to this ruthless depletion of his work force. "Curse it," he exclaimed. "The fill is piling up, Peabody. How long is it going to take you to pack a few clothes?"

"You know nothing about it, Emerson, so kindly refrain from putting your oar in." Obviously pleased with this bit of slang, she added, in a more amiable voice, "I will be along later, perhaps. You can have Ramses and David, if you like."

"Good of you," muttered Emerson. "Let's go, boys, half the morning is gone."

It was just after 7 A.M.

Despite Emerson's complaints they had managed to make some progress in deciphering the plans of the various shrines north of the village and the Ptolemaic temple. Some were better preserved than others, but all had been damaged by time and amateur diggers, and it required skill and experience to untangle the original plan. Bertie, the best draftsman of the group, had been faithful in his attendance. He arrived soon after they did, apologizing for his tardiness, and produced the latest of the plans he had been working on for over a week.

"Ha," said Emerson, studying it. "Yes, that seems to be acceptable, so far as it goes. I want to identify the deity to whom this structure was dedicated." He took out his pipe and stabbed at the incomplete outline of what appeared to be a smallish chapel.

It was, in Ramses's opinion, a futile task. The little private shrines had not been constructed of stone but of mud brick, plastered and painted. By now the plaster had flaked off and disintegrated. They hadn't found a flake larger than a thumbnail.

He took the liberty of pointing this out to his father. "A votive stela," said Emerson dogmatically. "That's all we need. Even an ostracon inscribed with a prayer. Something may yet turn up in the area we haven't finished clearing. Anyhow, the plan isn't complete. Where's the back wall? Selim!"

Selim hadn't been listening. His head thrown back, he was staring at the brightening blue of the sky with a bemused expression. Looking for another aeroplane, Ramses thought, with inner amusement. Emerson had to call him twice before he responded.

Emerson's luck was proverbial. They found his votive stela, or part of it, dedicated by the workman Nakhtmin to the deified king Amenhotep I and his mother, Ahmose Nefertari. Emerson carried it off in triumph to the shelter while Selim's crew went on clearing the sanctuary.

"Where the devil is your mother?" Emerson demanded, delicately brushing encrusted sand from the brief inscription. "The rubble is piling up!"

She arrived a little before midday, bringing the hamper of food Emerson had forgotten, and accompanied by Lia and Sethos. Emerson hurried to meet them.

"The rubble," he began.

"Yes, Emerson, I know. You may as well stop for luncheon now. As you see, we have a guest."

"Ha," said Emerson, studying his brother's elegant tailoring and spotless pith helmet. "He can help you with—"

"Not today," said Sethos amiably. "I only came along to keep the ladies company and have a look round. There's not much here to interest an enthusiast," he added, with a disparaging survey of the monotonous grayish-brown foundations and scattering of stones.

"We have just found evidence that Amenhotep the First and his mother were worshiped here," Emerson exclaimed. "A stela fragment."

"How exciting," Sethos drawled. "If it had been a statue—"

"You'd try to steal it," said Emerson, glowering.

"*Your* finds are safe from me," Sethos said, emphasizing the pronoun.

Emerson wisely decided not to pursue this. "Where is everybody?" he demanded.

His wife began unpacking the hamper. "Where I told you they would be, Emerson. Evelyn and Walter are settling in at the Castle, Nefret is tending to a patient, and the children are running wild as usual. I was under the impression that you meant to spend more time with them."

The blow was expertly calculated. Emerson closed his mouth, rubbed his chin, and looked self-conscious. "Never mind, never mind." He raised his voice to a shout that made everyone jump. "Selim! Rest period. A quarter of an hour."

They were still eating when another rider approached. It was Cyrus Vandergelt, urging his reluctant mare to a trot and waving a large envelope. He dismounted with more haste than grace and ran toward them.

"Just got this from Lacau," he panted. "It has to be a list of the objects he wants. Look at the thickness of the envelope! I came here for moral support, didn't have the nerve to open it."

"Get a grip on yourself, man," said Emerson, taking the envelope from him and ripping it open.

The sheaf of papers inside was indeed depressingly thick. Emerson scanned the pages. "He wants the coffins and the mummies. Well, we expected that. The robe Martinelli restored, the storage chests with the rest of the clothing, the canopic jars—"

"All of them?" Cyrus cried in anguish.

"Hmph," said Emerson in acknowledgment. Concluding that it

would take less time to read out the objects Lacau did not want, he proceeded to do so. "Half the ushebtis—his choice, naturally—three small uninscribed cosmetic jars, an ivory headrest . . ."

Everyone waited with bated breath until he finished, "Two beaded bracelets and two rings."

Cyrus groaned and dropped onto a stone column base.

"Rotten luck, Cyrus," Ramses said sympathetically, while his mother patted the afflicted American's bowed shoulder.

"He says he is being excessively generous," Emerson reported, after reading the enclosed letter. "By rights the Museum ought to keep everything. Except for Tetisheri, this is the only royal burial that has been found, and the Museum has few pieces from this period."

"It's a reburial, though," Bertie said. "Doesn't that change the terms?"

"Lacau defines the terms. He requests that we begin packing the objects. He is sending a government steamer for them."

"Why not ship them by train?" Bertie asked.

"Too rough a ride," Ramses replied. "They will be jostled less in the hold of a boat. When will the steamer arrive?"

"He doesn't say."

"Let him send his damned steamer," said Emerson through his teeth. "He can sit here twiddling his thumbs until we have finished the job, which we will do at our leisure."

"No." Cyrus rose slowly to his feet. "What's the use? May as well get it over with, the sooner the better. I can count on your help, I know, Amelia."

"I commend your fortitude, Cyrus," she said. "We will all help, of course."

Emerson's black brows drew together. "Now see here, Peabody!"

"No one expects you to assist in such menial tasks," she informed him. "It is woman's work, as usual. At least this will be one thing off our minds. I believe we still have the packing materials we used when we transported the objects to the Castle. I will begin tomorrow morning, with Lia and Evelyn, and Nefret, unless she has a patient."

"You've got it all worked out," David said with a smile, while

Emerson mumbled discontentedly. "What about me, Aunt Amelia? I'm fairly good at this sort of woman's work."

"Yes, my dear, you are. Very well. Sennia too; under supervision, she can handle the less fragile objects. And Maryam, if she is willing."

"Come back to the Castle with me now, Amelia," Cyrus begged. "We can make a start, anyhow."

"I have another appointment this afternoon, Cyrus. There is the little matter of the bones of Martinelli."

CHAPTER NINE

W e have to do something with him," I pointed out, after Emerson had run out of expletives. "It would be indecent to leave him lying round the police station. I asked Father Benedict to make the arrangements, and to meet us at the cemetery this afternoon. Since Martinelli was Italian, I assume he was of the Roman Catholic faith."

"I doubt he believed in anything beyond his own gratification," Sethos murmured.

"He may have repented at the end," I said firmly. "We must give him the benefit of the doubt. The rest of you need not attend, but I feel obliged to be present."

"I don't know how you do it, Aunt Amelia," Lia said, shaking her curly head. "I admire your energy and goodwill, but I think I will beg off."

"I suppose I ought to be there," Cyrus said. "Should have made the arrangements myself."

The only other volunteer was Sethos. At the last minute Cyrus—guided by a few gentle hints from me—decided he was not obliged to pay his last respects to the man who had robbed him so callously. He had only offered because he did not want me to go alone. "You'll keep an eye on her," he said to Sethos. "And don't let her dash off on some private expedition. She does that."

"Why else would I go?" Sethos inquired rhetorically.

The small Christian cemetery, on the road to Karnak, was somewhat more seemly than it had been when I attended my last funeral there. Distressed by the neglected graves and the feral animals who made it their home, I had formed a committee. My friend Marjorie, who headed it, had done her best to improve matters; the graves were clear of weeds and the headstones were straight. Not much could be done about the animals. If driven off, they returned as soon as the guards departed. One had to watch out for droppings and gnawed bones. It was a dismal place, despite—or because of—the wilting flowers on the graves of those who had friends or kin in Luxor. Flowers did not last long in the heat. The shade of my parasol was welcome. It was black—not for mourning, but for practicality. The parasol was one of the heavier ones.

The good father awaited us, his bald head bared to the bitter sunlight. He did his best, but he could not do much except repeat the formal prayers. Afterward, Sethos, who had not spoken except to acknowledge a distant acquaintance with the dead man, took out a handful of money.

"I beg you will add to your kindness by saying a few Masses for his soul," he said. Not until we had turned away, followed by the dismal drumbeat of soil landing on the simple coffin, did he add, "If anyone is in need of them, it's Martinelli."

I did not respond. I was thinking of certain other graves in that cemetery—reminders of several of our earlier encounters with crime. Poor young Alan Armadale and Lucinda Bellingham. I had been unable to save them, but I had avenged them. (With a certain amount of assistance, in the latter case, from Ramses.) There was another such burial, and when Sethos would have headed for the entrance I took his arm and led him back, to the far end of the cemetery. A feral dog, sprawled across the untended grave, rose as we approached and backed off, snarling. It was a female, heavy with young.

"Fitting," said Sethos. "Why did you bring me here, Amelia?"

"You have never visited her grave?"

The arm I held was rigid. "Once. I wanted to convince myself she was really dead. I suppose it was you who erected the headstone. Only her name? Couldn't you think of a fitting epitaph?"

"There is one." I knelt and pushed the dusty weeds away from the base of the stone. Under her name were the carved words, "May she rest in Peace."

"Oh, God." He pulled me roughly to my feet and and put his arms round me. "You are unbelievable, Amelia. She tried to kill you and murdered one of your dearest friends. How can you forgive that?"

It was a brother's embrace, not that of a lover, but I detached myself as gently and quickly as I could. Bertha would not have made the distinction, and although I do not share the ancient Egyptian belief that the soul lingers near the mortal remains, I preferred not to take the chance.

"Our Christian duty requires us to forgive those who have injured us," I said. "It is easier to do that, I admit, when the individual in question is deceased."

He let out a choked laugh and passed his hand over his mouth. "Does Maryam know her mother lies here?"

"I have no idea. Will you tell her?"

"No. I don't know. Damnation, Amelia, don't you ever weary of prodding people's consciences? I can forgive Bertha for what she did to me—I assure you, you don't know the half of it—but not for what she did to you and to Maryam. May we go now, or have you more to say?"

"Not to you." I took his arm and we turned our backs on the desolate grave. "I believe I will have a few words with Maryam."

He kicked at a clump of weeds. "Do you believe she is responsible for the accidents that have plagued you?"

"The possibility had of course occurred to me after the affair of the Veiled Hathor," I said, fudging the truth just a little. Maryam had not been on my original list. "She was one of a number of females who might have believed herself badly treated by Ramses—"

"Good Lord." Sethos came to an abrupt halt. "You never told me. Must I call Ramses out for seducing my daughter?"

"You can hardly suppose Ramses would take advantage of a fourteen-year-old girl," I exclaimed indignantly. "*She* made the advances to *him*. I should not have to tell you that he behaved impeccably."

"No, he's a gentleman," Sethos agreed, with a cynical twist of the lips. "Well, that is most interesting, but it isn't as strong a motive as seeking revenge for her mother's death."

"I have already discussed that with her, and I believe I am safe in asserting that she has reached—or is on the way to reaching—a proper understanding. Moreover, it would have been impossible for a girl that age to carry out such a complex scheme. She certainly could not have been Hathor, since the most recent appearance of that lady occurred when Maryam was with Ramses, and Mrs. Fitzroyce told me she was here in Luxor when Hathor made her first appearance."

The carriage we had hired was waiting for us on the road. I accepted the hand he offered to help me in. In my opinion it is not a betrayal of one's feminist principles to accept such gestures graciously.

"We will discuss this later," I went on, as the carriage rattled into motion. "With everyone present. It is time for a council of war!"

FROM MANUSCRIPT H

Emerson sent the men home earlier than usual that afternoon. His wife had not returned, nor had Nefret turned up.

Ramses went at once to the clinic. There were two people in the waiting room, a very pregnant girl of about fourteen, and a child racked with an incessant dry cough. Nisrin was with them, looking very professional in a tightly wound white headcloth and a man's gala-beeyah that had been shortened at the hem and the sleeves. "Nur Misur is very busy, but I will let you go in," she announced.

"Kind of you," Ramses said, and went through into the surgery.

To his surprise, the patient was Daoud. He gave Ramses a sheepish smile and Kadija, standing over him with folded arms, said, "Marhaba, Ramses. Tell this stubborn man to show Nur Misur his hand. I had to make him come to her."

Finding himself outnumbered, Daoud obeyed.

"It needs to be stitched," Nefret said, inspecting the ugly gashes that ran across his large palm and the insides of his fingers. "How on earth did you do this?"

Daoud mumbled something. Kadija said, "Someone left a hegab—a charm—lying in front of the house, and Daoud, fool that he is, picked it up."

"It was a fine hegab," Daoud protested. "Large and silver, with red stones. I would have asked who had lost it. But when I closed my hand over it, it cut me."

"What did you do with it?" Nefret asked.

"I buried it," Kadija said. "It was a holy thing, but broken. Sharp as a razor along two sides."

Nefret selected an instrument and bent closer. "It's a good thing you did. There's something metallic deep in the wound. Hang on, Daoud." She exchanged the probe for tweezers and before long she had it out—a needlelike bit of metal half an inch long. "Good heavens, Daoud, this must have hurt badly. Why didn't you come to me right away?"

"I put the ointment on it," Daoud said defensively.

That was obvious. His palm was green.

"That probably prevented an infection," Nefret said, with a nod at Kadija. "Well, now we know why the owner discarded it. Let me make sure there are no other broken pieces embedded."

Daoud sat like a large brown statue while she cleaned the cuts and put several neat stitches into them before bandaging his hand.

"Change the dressing every day," she said to Kadija, giving her a box of bandages. "I don't have to tell you what to watch out for."

"No, Nur Misur. Thank you."

"How does it feel to be back in harness?" Ramses asked, as Nefret cleaned her instruments and put them away.

"Wonderful. I should have done this ages ago. Nisrin, show in the next patient, please."

"Have you been at this all day?" he asked. "Can I help?"

"No, thank you. If you want to do something useful, go and play with the children."

That puts me in my place, Ramses thought. Baby-tender. The children were gathered in the courtyard. His advent was greeted with cries of relief from the adults who were present, and cries of welcome from his daughter, who ran to him holding out her arms. He picked her up. She jabbered imperatively at him, her black eyes bright and demanding.

"Mama has been busy with a poor sick man," he said, assuming that was what she wanted to know. Apparently that was only part of it; she tugged at his shirt and dug her knees into his midriff. He had learned to interpret that gesture. He helped her climb up onto his shoulders.

"High time you got here," said Lia. "As usual, you men left us to do the hard work."

"Not me," David protested. He was on his hands and knees, giving Evvie a ride.

"Everybody but you," Lia said.

The women looked as if they had had a hard time. Lia's hair was in wild disorder, and Evelyn was leaning against the back of the sofa, her eyes half closed. Sennia was conspicuous by her absence. He couldn't blame her; it wasn't fair to expect her to play nursemaid. Maryam had been pressed into service, though. She seemed to have suffered less than the others, perhaps because she had concentrated her attention on Dolly. He sat close beside her, with her arm around him. She looked up from the storybook from which she had been reading, and smiled at Ramses.

"Where is everyone?" he asked.

"Katherine was here for lunch," his aunt replied in a faint voice. "She helped entertain them for a while, but she finally gave out. Walter is playing with his papyrus, your mother is attending a funeral and so is Sethos. I presume your father is still at his cursed dig."

"An undeserved denunciation," said Emerson, coming out of the house. "I am shocked to hear you use such language, my dear Evelyn."

He made sure the door was firmly shut before he turned to meet the assault of the children. Charla was among them; she rappelled herself to the ground as soon as her grandfather appeared. "Have you had a good time?" he inquired.

Evelyn said carefully, "The children have been very active. Very."

"They do seem a trifle restless," Emerson conceded, gazing benevolently at the twins, who were clutching at his legs while Evvie tried to pull Charla away. "You have kept them cooped up too long. Young children need to run about and be kept busy."

Emerson never needed as much rest as a normal person. His blue eyes were unshadowed and his smile broad and cheerful. He seemed to be unaware of the fact that several hostile looks were focused on him.

"Thank you for pointing that out to us, Emerson," said his sister-in-law, snapping the words out. "No doubt you have a suggestion."

"Hmmm. What do you say to a nice donkey ride?"

The shouts of approval of the children were not echoed by the adults. This activity would demand as much effort as their earlier exhausting supervision. However, Emerson swept all before him, and the affair was underway when his wife and Sethos returned.

"High time you lent a hand," said Emerson, addressing both of them. "What took you so long?"

"I stopped by the clinic to see if Nefret needed my assistance," his wife replied.

Sethos's gaze had gone to his daughter, who was trotting along beside Evvie, holding on to the child. Evvie did not want to be held on to and said so, at length. Maryam laughed. "Don't go so fast, then. I'll not hold you if you let the poor donkey slow down to a walk." She seemed to be having as much fun as the children, and Sethos's hard mouth curved slightly as he watched.

The donkeys were the first ones to show signs of disaffection. "Enough," Emerson declared, lifting Davy off his steed. It had come to a complete standstill and refused to move. "Run along and have a little rest before tea, eh?"

"They won't, but I intend to," Lia declared. "David?"

"I promised Maryam a riding lesson," David said. "She's been wonderful with Dolly."

"He's a dear little boy," Maryam said, blushing prettily at his praise. "Reading to him is such a pleasure, he listens so intently and asks intelligent questions. I don't deserve to be rewarded, and you must be tired, and . . ." Her smooth cheeks turned pinker. "To be honest, I'm a little afraid of horses."

"All the more reason to become accustomed to them," said her father. "Don't you agree, Amelia?"

"By all means" was the brisk reply. "Our horses are pefectly gentle and well trained."

"I'll give her a lesson, if you'd rather, David," Ramses said. "You've been with the little dears longer than I."

David grinned and ran his fingers through his disheveled curls. Evvie had used his hair as reins. "I won't refuse. You're a better rider than I am, anyhow. She can take Asfur."

"I haven't the right clothes," Maryam demurred.

"Don't let them bully you into riding if you'd rather not," Lia said pleasantly. "But you are welcome to borrow one of my outfits. I don't know what to do about boots, your feet are so tiny. Perhaps Sennia's would fit you."

Ramses stopped by the kitchen and then went to the stable, where he found his father and Sethos inspecting the horses. "They are superb creatures," said the latter. "Would you consider selling one?"

"To you?" Emerson asked suspiciously. "What for?"

"So I can ride it," his brother explained.

Before Emerson could think of a sufficiently withering response, the girls joined them. From pith helmet to boots—Sennia's, Ramses presumed—Maryam was properly attired and looking very pretty.

However, she was not pleased with Asfur. "It's so big," she said, stepping back as David's mare turned mild eyes toward her. "Isn't there a littler one?"

Emerson, who had gone with them to the stable, made soothing noises and looked as if he wanted to pat her on the head. Even Sethos's smile lacked its usual touch of cynicism. "Arabians are smaller than most breeds," Ramses explained. "And Asfur wouldn't bolt if you lit a fire under her."

"What about this one?" Maryam asked, moving down the line of stalls. "It's very pretty."

The filly, a granddaughter of the original pair, poked an inquiring nose over the bars. She was pure white, like the fabled unicorn, and, like all the other Arabians, as friendly as a domestic cat.

"I don't know," Emerson said doubtfully. "She's young and still a bit frisky. What about Moonlight?"

"Can't I have this one?" Maryam let out a little giggle as the filly nuzzled her shirtfront. "She likes me."

"She's looking for a treat," Ramses said, handing her one of the sugar lumps he had got from the kitchen. "It's all right, Father, I trained Melusine myself. She can use Nefret's saddle."

The stableman, who had watched with amused condescension, helped them saddle and bridle Risha, the filly, and Emerson's gelding for Sethos, who had decided to join the party.

It was he who gave the girl a hand up and a few casual reminders. "Loosen up on the reins and relax. She's accustomed to a light hand—isn't that right, Ramses?"

They walked the horses up and down a few times, and then took the road to Gurneh. There were quite a few people about at that time of day, some on foot, some on donkeys or driving carts. Maryam let out a cry of alarm as a camel lumbered toward them, its long face set in the ineffable camel sneer.

"Keep the reins loose," Ramses instructed. "She knows about camels, she'll go round it. You're doing fine."

The camel having been successfully circumnavigated, Maryam relaxed. "This is fun. Can we go faster?"

"Not in this mob," Ramses said. The closer they got to Gurneh, the more people they met. They obligingly moved aside, waving and calling out. Sethos had dropped behind. Suddenly Maryam cried, "Look! That man—"

She pointed. Before Ramses could identify the man she meant, the filly bolted.

It took Ramses several seconds to gather his wits and go after them. Melusine had left the path, striking off to the left, across the open desert. She was in full gallop, but Risha had no difficulty in catching her up and keeping pace with her. A quick glance told Ramses Maryam had dropped the reins and was clinging to the pommel. He leaned sideways and caught her round the waist.

"Get your feet out of the stirrups!" he yelled.

She'd already lost them. He lifted her up and onto his saddle. Responding instantly to his touch, Risha slowed and stopped. The gelding thundered past; having seen that his daughter was safe, Sethos went on in pursuit of the filly.

"You're hurting me," said a faint voice.

Ramses let out a long breath and loosened his tight grip. "Sorry. I had to."

"I know." She leaned back against his shoulder and raised a face rosy with heat and smeared with dust. Her eyes were red-rimmed, but there were no tears. "Thank you. Is the horse all right?"

"Your father has her. Maryam, I'm terribly sorry; I can't imagine why she bolted, she never has before."

"I must tell you something. I never have a chance to talk with you alone—" Feeling him stiffen, she went on in a rush of words. "No, no, it's not what you think. I wanted to ask your forgiveness for the day I came to your room and tried to . . ." A darker flush of color ran up from her throat to her hairline. "I embarrassed you and made a fool of myself, but I was only fourteen and I know now that . . ."

He tried to help her out. "That I wasn't worth all that fuss."

"Oh, no. You're a wonderful man; any woman would be proud . . . You're teasing me, aren't you?"

"A little. It's forgotten, Maryam."

"Now that I've seen you and Nefret together, I know you were meant for each other." The long lashes fell, half veiling those extraordinary hazel eyes. "I'd like us to be friends. Cousins. Can we?"

"We are."

Sethos came up, leading the filly. "All right, are you, Maryam?"

"Yes, sir. Thanks to Ramses."

"Yes, it was quite a spectacular performance," said Sethos. The smile was the one that always made Ramses want to hit him.

"She seems calm enough now," Ramses said, inspecting the filly. "I can't imagine what spooked her."

Sethos directed their attention to a trail of blood on Melusine's right flank. "That's what. A sharp object piercing her side."

Maryam's hand went to her mouth. "The man. I saw him, just before she ran away with me. The same man who attacked me before."

⊃⊂

"ANOTHER INCIDENT TO ADD to the list," I said. Our council of war had convened. I had insisted that everyone attend, in case one of them could contribute information others had missed. Fatima sat uneasily on the edge of her chair. She would much rather have been trotting round offering food. The only one not present was Kadija. She would not have spoken up in company anyhow.

"So now we have an aborigine with a blowgun?" Ramses was pacing irritably up and down, his hands clasped behind him.

"A projectile, propelled by any one of a number of means," Sethos corrected. "The object was sharp as a tack and it penetrated less than an inch."

"So what do we have?" I took a refreshing sip of my whiskey and read the list aloud.

1. The theft of the jewelry and the murder of Martinelli
2. The Veiled Hathor of Cairo
3. The sinking of the boat
4. The initial attack on Maryam
5. The second appearance of Hathor
6. The second attack on Maryam

"It's not complete," Emerson said, chewing on his pipe. "We agreed, did we not, to include every unusual incident, even if it seemed to have a logical explanation?"

"Well done, Emerson," I said, with an approving nod. "That is why I wanted everyone here, to make sure we had neglected no possibility. Give vent to your imaginations. Do not be deterred from the wildest sort of speculation. Anything at all, no matter how far-fetched it may seem."

Once I had got them on the track, the suggestions came thick and fast. The shot that had just missed Selim, Daoud's wounding by the hegab, the scorpions in his house—even the cobra at Deir el Medina.

"Goodness gracious," I remarked, examining the revised list. "Either our imaginations have run away with us, or we have been singularly obtuse. I confess, however, that I fail to see a consistent pattern."

"Do you?" David had taken out his pipe. "Supposing we are correct in assuming that all these incidents are related, one thing stands out: The only ones who have been physically attacked are Daoud, Selim, and Maryam."

"How extraordinary," I exclaimed. "As a rule, such attacks are directed at us. Of course we are affected by danger to any of those we love . . ."

Reader, are you familiar with the sensation of trying to capture an elusive thought—an idea that hovers just on the edge of awareness? I feel certain you are. I was attempting to pin the thing down when Emerson spoke.

"It's a blow, isn't it, Peabody? Your favorite method of catching criminals is to provoke them into attacking you. We've all got off scot-free in this affair; even the Veiled Hathor only wanted—er—that is to say—"

"But what can be the connection between Maryam, Daoud, and Selim?" Ramses, glancing self-consciously at his wife, was quick to change the subject.

"I confess I cannot find a common denominator," I admitted. The vagrant thought had escaped, back into the murky depths of the subconscious. I did not attempt to pursue it. "Let's try another method. What do we know about the enemy?"

"He has access to a rifle and is a good shot," Ramses said. "That suggests a man, but the Veiled Hathor was obviously a woman. I fear it's another dead end, Mother; there may be a number of people involved."

"A gang," I murmured. "How annoying. I much prefer dealing with individual criminals."

"How can you all speak so coolly?" Maryam's eyes moved from one of us to the other. She was sitting quite close to her father, in a posture that would have prompted most men to put a comforting arm round her shoulders. Sethos had not done so, but he seemed more at ease with her. She had acquitted herself well that afternoon, remounting Melusine (who had behaved like a lamb all the way home) and making light of her aches and pains. Being thumped down onto a hard saddle, with an arm like a steel vise gripping one round the ribs, leaves bruises in sensitive areas.

"That is just Mother's little way," Nefret explained lightly. "She expects all of us to demonstrate a stiff upper lip. Maryam, are you certain you can't think of anyone who means you harm? I don't want to pry into your private affairs, but—"

"The answer is no," Maryam said. Her eyes locked with those of Nefret. "If you would like me to relate my experiences of the past two years in detail . . ."

"No," Sethos said harshly.

"No," I agreed. "We are looking for a common denominator, a motive that would also explain the vindictiveness against Daoud and Selim. Maryam has not even been in Egypt for the past . . ."

There it was again, darting like a shadow into my head and out of it again. The others took advantage of my silence to go on with the discussion. It didn't get very far, even with David making suggestions as to how to rearrange the facts we had—or thought we had. One such "pattern" eliminated possible accidents, but we were still left with a series of apparently unconnected occurrences which could not be dismissed so easily: the Veiled Hathor, the theft of the jewelry, the murder of Martinelli, and the deliberate damage to the boat—which, as Emerson optimistically pointed out, might have been aimed at someone other than Daoud. Another pattern eliminated the theft and murder as an unrelated, coincidental criminal act; still another would remove Hathor from the equation, supposing her to have been motivated by what David delicately referred to as personal feelings.

Ramses did not like this pattern. He had taken to pacing again. "We can't eliminate her or Martinelli," he declared vehemently. "Neither of those theories makes more sense than any other. There has to be a connection. We haven't found it yet, that's all."

"Well, I sure don't see it," Cyrus declared. "All right with you, Amelia, if we call it quits for now?"

"Yes, run along. If you think of anything we have overlooked, make a note of it."

"We've got everything in that list except the finger I cut on a piece of paper," Cyrus said.

He was mistaken—as was I. We had overlooked one "peculiar incident," which would prove to be the key to the entire mystery. If my more astute Readers have spotted it, allow me to deflate their self-esteem by pointing out that they are sitting at ease reading this journal—not trying to deal with four active children, an unpredictable brother-in-law, an archaeological dig, and a thousand household chores. Not to mention Emerson.

FROM MANUSCRIPT H

As they walked along the shadowy path to their house, the leaves of poinsettias and mimosa stirred, rustling as if they were conversing in some unknown language. Rather like the twins, Ramses thought.

The Great Cat of Re marched ahead of them, taking the lead as cats will without regard to their convenience. Every now and then he would stop without warning and stare into the shadows. Sometimes the stare was followed by a sudden leap and a frantic rustle of activity in the shrubbery; sometimes he just sat there until they stumbled over him.

"We need more lights here," Nefret said, catching hold of his arm.

"Or a better-trained cat. Damn it, he's got something. I hope it isn't a snake."

"They're all tucked up in their little holes for the night," Nefret said. "Don't bother yelling at him, Ramses, he'll ignore you with magnificent disdain."

"Stop for a minute."

"Why?"

He showed her why, drawing her into his arms and holding her while his mouth drifted across her face until it reached her lips. They parted, welcoming and warm, and her hands slid into his hair. After a long moment she whispered, "Don't start something unless you're prepared to finish it."

"I can finish anytime, but let's sit here for a while. It's a beautiful night, and Lord knows we don't have many chances to be alone."

He picked her up and sat down on a nearby bench, holding her on his lap. The breeze lifted a strand of her hair. It brushed his cheek like a caress. Between kisses he told her all the things he felt but seldom said, and she responded with the murmured endearments only he had heard.

The cry that broke the spell was sharp and high and human. Ramses sprang to his feet and lowered Nefret to hers, pushing her behind him as he turned to face the thrashing in the shrubbery.

"Who's there?" he demanded, reaching for his knife and realizing he didn't have it.

"Don't, don't hurt me! I'm sorry!"

She came out from behind a rosebush, an unidentifiable shadow in the darkness—but he had recognized her voice. At his shoulder Nefret said, "Hell and damnation!"

"I'm not going to hurt you," Ramses said in a strangled voice. He would almost have preferred armed attack to the embarrassment that flooded hotly through him. How long had the wretched girl been hiding and listening?

"It was the cat," Maryam said apologetically. "I was just taking a walk, it's such a beautiful night, and he jumped at me, and I was startled and . . . I'm so sorry."

The Great Cat of Re had followed her, his tail waving triumphantly. He had flushed an impressively large prey this time.

"No harm done," Ramses said. "But you shouldn't wander round alone at night."

"I'm sorry. I won't. I only wanted—"

"Good night," Nefret said.

"Good night." She fled, stumbling, her hands covering her face.

The Great Cat of Re brushed against Nefret's foot, inviting admiration and praise. "Oh, yes, well done," she said. "How much did she hear, do you suppose?"

"She'd have heard more if the cat hadn't taken a hand," Ramses muttered. "And seen more. I feel like a blithering idiot."

"You didn't sound like a blithering idiot, darling," Nefret said. "But we may as well go in now."

"Yes. Damn cat," he added unfairly.

"He is a gorgeous creature, though."

The Great Cat of Re preceded them into the house, taking his time, so that they had to wait, holding the door for him, and then headed toward the kitchen.

"Yes, he's beautiful. And the most useless cat we've ever owned. D'you want a nightcap or a glass of milk?"

A yawn was his answer. He laughed and encircled her waist with his arm. "Come to bed, then. I'm ready to finish what I began, despite the interruption, unless you're tired. I almost wish you hadn't opened the clinic, you've been working too hard."

"I love it, you know that. But dear old Uncle Sethos wears me out."

"I thought you liked him." He closed the door of their room. Nefret sat down at the dressing table and began taking pins out of her hair.

"I do. But when he's around I feel like a cat in a Cairo alley, trying to look in all directions at once. What was that saying of el-Gharbi's? He walks among naked daggers—and they follow him wherever he goes."

"The same could be said of us. He's walked into our nest of daggers this time."

She didn't answer. The quick, hard stroke of her hairbrush, and the way the long golden locks clung to her fingers told him she was in no mood for reassurance or reason.

"When this is settled," he began. A small silent voice in his head jeered, Oh, no trouble at all. Solve the murder of Martinelli, locate the missing jewelry, identify the bastard who sank Daoud's boat and the crazy woman who thinks she's Hathor . . .

"When all this is settled," he went on, after a slight pause, "why don't we get away for a few days, just the two of us?"

"And leave the children?" Nefret opened a drawer and took out a nightdress.

"They've got a dozen people looking after them."

At that inopportune moment a hair-raising shriek split the silence. Nefret started violently and dropped the nightgown. Ramses snatched up the shirt he had removed and slipped into it. "I'll go," he said. Charla was having one of her nightmares. The cries twanged directly into a parent's nervous system.

The children's nursemaid, Elia, slept in the same room. She was a competent young woman and the children both adored her; but she couldn't get through to Charla when the child was in this state. She was at the door when Ramses got there, wringing her hands in distress.

Ramses caught the screaming child up off her cot and held her tightly against him. She clung to him with hands like small claws, and the screams turned into sobs. "Sssh," he whispered. "It's all right, sweetheart, I'm here."

He had left the door open. Hearing hurried footsteps he turned, expecting to see Nefret. It was Maryam, her face drawn with concern. She hadn't paused to put on a dressing gown. The clinging silken nightgown must be one of Nefret's; it wasn't the sort of thing one would find in the wardrobe of a lady's companion.

"What's wrong?" she asked. "I heard her—the poor little thing—what can I do?"

"Nothing," said Nefret, pushing past her. "Go back to bed, Maryam, or put on some clothes."

Her voice was, it seemed to Ramses, unnecessarily harsh. He smiled at Maryam. "It was kind of you to rush to the rescue. As you see, she's all right now."

Nefret went to Davy, who was sitting up in bed, his fair hair ruffled and his hands over his ears. He was a heavier sleeper than his sister and he resented being awakened by loud noises. When he saw his mother he took one hand from his ear and pointed at the window.

"Something she saw?" Ramses asked. "Something looking in the window?"

He knew he wouldn't get an intelligible answer from either of them, but he kept hoping. It was only at times like this that the twins' slowness to speak really bothered him. Dream or not, the terrifying thing she had seen was real to her, and he could have dealt with it more effectively if only she could tell him what it was.

Davy was twittering helpfully and Charla, sobs reduced to snuffles, began to wiggle. She was over the worst of it now; the tight grasp and crooning reassurances were what she wanted. He laid her back on the cot. Elia, smiling in relief, handed him a handkerchief. He wiped Charla's eyes and nose and brushed the tangled curls off her face.

"Tell Papa what it was," he coaxed.

She told him, at length and with gestures. Something to do with the window. Her cot was under it, but surely she must have been dreaming; the aperture was barred and curtained.

Ramses drew the curtain aside and looked out. The window was unglazed, covered only by a loose netting to keep out insects. Moonlight bathed the distant cliffs and whitened the sandy waste that faced that side of the house. Nothing moved.

"All gone," he said, bending over his daughter. "I made it go away, and it won't come back, ever. Nothing can hurt you. Go to sleep now."

He got a damp kiss (she was still leaking at eyes and nose) and a squeeze round the neck from Davy, who was now wide awake and ready to be sociable. He hugged his mother and held out his arms to Maryam.

"May I?" she asked timidly.

"Yes, of course," Ramses said. "I'm sorry you were disturbed."

"I shouldn't have intruded," she murmured. "But her crying was so pitiful. I responded without thinking. Good night, darlings."

All she got from Charla was a sleepy grunt. Davy was in a mood for conversation, but he submitted to having his mouth and eyes buttoned shut with the chuckles this game always induced.

The nightmares had begun only recently. According to Ramses's mother—the ultimate authority—a number of children suffered from them at this age, and got over them eventually.

Which was all very well, but Ramses realized there wasn't much chance of a romantic holiday while the nightmares lasted. He didn't flatter himself that he was the only one who could comfort Charla; it just happened that he had been first on the scene every time, and Elia, for all her admirable qualities, didn't understand that a tight grasp and a firm, reassuring voice was what the little girl wanted. His father or David—or his mother—could probably act as effectively. However, it wouldn't be fair to ask any of them to sleep in a neighboring room while he and Nefret were absent.

It took a while to get Nefret back into the mood that had been interrupted, not once but twice. She was upset about something—he had learned to know the signs—but he couldn't think what.

THE FANTASIA WAS NOT DUE to begin until evening, but even Emerson glumly conceded that there was no use going to Deir el Medina that morning. Selim and Daoud and the others were determined to put on the most extravagant performance ever given in Gurneh. The whole village had been buzzing, and no one had the least intention of working that day. The motorcar stood in front of the house, shining like jet. Selim had spent all evening scrubbing and polishing it.

After breakfast his mother rallied her troops and took them off to the Castle to begin packing the artifacts. She declined Emerson's half-hearted offer to join them—"You'll only stand round grumbling and lecturing"—and Sethos said he had business in Luxor. Cyrus was ready for them; the packing materials they had used before had been taken out of storage and brought to the display room, and a local carpenter was nailing the wooden cases back together. Ramses understood why Cyrus wanted to get the job done. It was pure torment to see the magnificent assemblage and know it was lost to him. In theory Ramses agreed, as did his father, with the idea that Egypt's treasures belonged in Egypt, but Cyrus's hangdog looks made him wish Lacau had been a little more generous.

They started with the smaller and less fragile objects—the stone and metal vessels. Even these were wrapped in cotton wool or waste fabric, with layers of straw under, between, and over them. When a packing case was full, Bertie and David nailed it shut. Cyrus trusted no one except themselves in that room. Ramses was assigned to the task of making lists of the contents of each case, with Lia to help.

In some ways the job was easier this time, since they had done it before, but additional precautions were necessary for a more prolonged trip—and, Ramses feared, more careless handling. Cases containing the more breakable objects, of faience and pottery, would be fastened with screws instead of nails.

Maryam hadn't seen the display before. Awestruck and breathless, she moved from one table to another, her hands tightly clasped behind her back like a child who is afraid she will be tempted to touch. As it would any woman, the jewelry held her longest.

"How can you bear to let it go?" she asked naively, gazing up at Cyrus.

"I haven't got any choice in the matter, my dear. Take your time; you'll never see anything like this again."

"I think it is very unkind of him not to leave you more."

"I think so too," Bertie said with a rueful grin. He straightened up and stretched. "Which piece of jewelry do you like the best?"

"Oh, goodness!" Unconsciously she moistened her lips with a pink tongue. She put out her hand, glanced guiltily at Bertie, and pulled it back. He laughed indulgently. "You can touch them, they won't break. What about these earrings?"

"They're beautiful, but so big." Timidly one finger indicated a ring. "This is pretty."

It was one of the least impressive of the lot, a gold band with a flattened bezel on which the figure of a seated crowned woman had been somewhat clumsily inscribed.

"Try it on," Bertie said. He took her hand.

"Oh, no, I couldn't!"

"You have tiny hands and slim fingers. You won't hurt it."

Ramses noticed that his mother was watching the pair with an enigmatic smile. She had been critical of Bertie's "moping" over Jumana—not because she disapproved of the relationship, one-sided as it was, but because she disapproved of moping. Katherine had made no secret of her hope that Bertie's interest in the Egyptian girl was only a temporary infatuation. Ramses wondered if she would be less prejudiced against the illegitimate child of a master thief and a murderess. Not that he blamed Bertie for indulging in some harmless flirting. Maryam was a pretty little thing, and she was obviously enjoying the young man's attentions. She held up her hand, admiring the ring.

"It's not as pretty as some of the others," remarked Sennia, who had also had the two under close observation. "I like this one, with the carnelian cat. But I would never try it on."

"Why not?" Cyrus exclaimed suddenly. "Why the dickens not? Try 'em all on! Amelia—Lia—all you ladies. They'll be stuck away in dusty museum cases from now on, never again gracing a pretty hand or neck. Give 'em a last treat."

"Cyrus, you are a sport," Ramses said.

"And a poet," Bertie declared. "Sennia, here's your cat. Mother, what's your choice?"

Ramses supposed that for Cyrus it was an act of defiance, a final gesture of possession. The women converged on the table, behaving as if they had been suddenly and simultaneously infected with the same benign fever, one that brought color to their cheeks and a glitter to their eyes. Even his mother, who claimed that baubles did not interest her, bent her head and allowed Cyrus to hang a magnificent pendant around her neck; it was a three-dimensional lapis ram, crowned with gold and reclining on a golden plinth. He'd noticed that jewels had a strange effect on women . . .

. . . Noticed, and forgotten. How long had it been since he gave Nefret a piece of jewelry? She had her own money and could buy whatever she wanted, gems more expensive than anything he could afford. But from time to time she still wore the cheap gold bangle he had given her when they were children, and there had been her little joke the other night about the bracelets . . . If it was a joke. In vino veritas? She seemed particularly interested in several of the remaining bracelets, and he went to help her fasten a massive hinged cuff around her wrist. David was laughing as he bedecked his wife with pectorals and bracelets. Then he insisted she and the others pose for photographs.

"We'll never dare show them to anyone outside the family, though."

"Never mind," Lia said. "We will gloat over them from time to time, and remember a wonderful experience. Thank you, Cyrus."

The fever had passed. Slowly and with obvious reluctance the women began to divest themselves of the jewelry. Though the pieces had been skillfully restored and mended, they required to be handled gently. Ramses went to help his mother remove the heavy pendant, which depended from a necklace of gold barrel beads.

"Suitable for a God's Wife—the ram is Amon-Re, of course—but I wonder if she ever wore it in life," she remarked, rubbing the back of her neck. "I wouldn't care to do so. Well, we have enjoyed a jolly time, but we had better get to work. We must stop early today in order to prepare for the fantasia."

THEY HAD DISCUSSED WHETHER OR not to take the children. The very idea of the three younger hellions running around in the dark, among open tomb shafts and blazing torches and half-savage dogs, made Ramses's hair stand on end, and he was relieved when his mother put an end to the discussion with a decided, "Out of the question. Dolly will accompany us, but not the others."

"Isn't that a little unfair?" Nefret asked, while Lia looked apprehensive—no doubt picturing Evvie's response.

"It would be unfair to Dolly to do otherwise. He should not be punished because the younger children cannot be controlled. It is not their fault, they are just like little animals at this age."

This appraisal did not go over well with either Lia or Nefret.

His mother had invited the Vandergelts to come by the house beforehand. No alcoholic beverages would be served at the fantasia, and Cyrus enjoyed a preprandial nip of whiskey. They drove up in style, behind the matched grays that drew Cyrus's carriage. Cyrus and Bertie and Walter were on horseback, dressed in their best to do Selim honor. That left room in the carriage with Katherine for several of the ladies, as Cyrus pointed out, adding a delicately phrased compliment about their small size and slimness.

"We could take—" Emerson began.

"No, Emerson, we cannot," his wife said sharply. "You promised

Selim he could drive it." She ran an appraising eye over the group and settled the matter in her usual brisk fashion. "Evelyn and Sennia and I will go in the carriage."

"As I have already demonstrated, I am not a good horsewoman," Maryam said, eyes downcast. "I hope I am not inconveniencing anyone. Perhaps I should stay with the children."

"No, no, my dear, you will enjoy it," Emerson said, responding with his customary chivalry. She looked up at him, her long lashes fluttering, and smiled.

Her father paid no attention. He was talking to Cyrus. His luggage must have arrived by train; he was wearing well-cut tweeds and riding boots, and his hair was now grayish brown. It would, Ramses suspected, continue to gray at an unnatural but measured speed.

They waited until the sun set and the calls of the muezzins had faded into silence before preparing to leave. Sennia, who had taken to wearing a somewhat unorthodox version of Egyptian dress, preened herself in a robe Nefret had helped her design; she looked unnervingly like a miniature Hathor sans ears and crown, draped in white and bedecked with glass beads. Dolly, very spruce in his best coat and trousers, was to ride with his father.

"Where is Selim?" Emerson demanded. "Has he changed his mind about driving the motorcar? We could take—"

"No, Emerson! He has it all worked out. He wants to make a grand entrance."

Their own entrance was not without éclat. Their hosts had sent torchbearers to meet them midway, and a gaggle of children accompanied them up the hill. Selim and Daoud were at the door to greet them and escort them into the house, where an elaborate meal was ready. Selim's wives, Rabia and Taghrid, must have been cooking all day. Dolly sat cross-legged next to his father, watching his every move. He had been instructed in the proper etiquette and was determined to make no mistakes. The Vandergelts had attended other such affairs, and even Katherine used her fingers neatly and with smiling good humor. Walter's glasses kept steaming up.

When they had eaten more than was good for them, they went outside. Torches and bonfires lit the scene as the darkness deepened.

Daoud's house, which had once been Abdullah's, faced onto one of the few open spaces in the village. As honored guests, they were shown to a row of chairs in front of the house and the show began.

Dancers and singers, musicians and magicians performed in turn. Selim caught Ramses's eye, winked, and withdrew. The most famous storyteller in Luxor launched into a tale.

A hand plucked at Ramses's sleeve. Maryam was sitting behind him. "What is he saying?" she whispered.

The flames gave her face a rosy glow and danced in her eyes. She looked as if she were enjoying herself; he didn't have the heart to hush her, although talking during the performance was frowned upon. "It's just a little fairy tale about a princess and a magician. I'll translate it for you later, all right?"

"Thank you." A shy, charming smile. Then her hand went to her mouth. "Oh . . . what's happening?"

The storyteller must have exceeded his time limit. Daoud hurried into the center of the space, gesturing and calling out orders. The audience moved back. Some of them were in on the secret; grinning and jumping with excitement, they helped Daoud clear the area, thrusting children into the arms of their mothers and hauling goats and donkeys out of the way. One of the drummers sounded a beat and the others joined in, accompanying the rising roar of the engine as Selim sent it racing up the path.

Ramses thought, "He's going too fast," but he never knew whether it came just before or just after the awful screech of tortured metal. Premonition or recognition, he was on his feet and running when the crash came.

The motorcar was upside down, halfway down the slope, jammed against a ridge. One of the lamps was broken but the other had miraculously survived; its light shed a sickly glow over the scene. Selim lay on his back, flattened, unmoving. His robe was torn and stained.

Ramses was the first to reach him. He searched for a pulse in the limp wrist. It was slippery with blood and his hands were shaking. He couldn't find one.

Nefret shoved him out of the way. "Don't anybody touch him.

Stay back. Get out of the light, damn it! Ramses, make them back off. Keep Rabia and Taghrid away, they mustn't see him like this."

He could hear Selim's wives keening and begging to go to him; his Aunt Evelyn was reassuring them, her voice calm and authoritative. His mother, of course, was already on the scene, shining a torch onto the broken body. She was the only one who'd had the sense to think of it. Ramses could almost have wished she had not. In its direct beam the bloodstains sprang to life, wet and red and glistening.

"What do you need?" Ramses asked.

Nefret didn't look up. "Your coat. Yours too, David. Splints. Bandages. For starters."

"Thank God," Ramses whispered. He had been afraid to ask. "He's alive?"

"So far."

Naturally enough, Selim's two young wives wanted him brought to their house. Nefret overruled them, curtly and coldly. The burden was on her now, and Ramses, aching with sympathy for her, knew she was desperately afraid. She had always agonized over losing a patient. Losing this one would devastate her.

Carrying the litter on which Selim lay wrapped as rigid as a mummy, Emerson and Daoud started along the road home. Cyrus had offered the carriage; Nefret had refused in that same chilly voice. The patient must not be jolted, and the two strongest men could move him more gently than any other means of transportation. Subdued and anxious, the Vandergelts left, taking their guests and Sennia and Dolly with them. Nefret didn't wait for the rest of them. She mounted Moonbeam and headed her down the hill.

"Do you want me to stay?" Ramses asked.

Selim was lying facedown on the table in her examining room; it had been scrubbed and covered with a white sheet. The lights glared down on his naked body, still clotted with blood where it wasn't dark with bruises.

"Yes," Nefret said. "Scrub and put on a gown. You too, Mother. Everybody else out."

His mother nodded and began rolling up her sleeves. "Selim will have a fit when he finds out we undressed him," she said calmly.

It was precisely the right note—her unquenchable optimism and her "little joke." Nefret's tight lips relaxed a trifle.

"He's got several cracked ribs, plus cuts and bruises. Not too bad. But . . ." She ran a gentle hand over Selim's black head. "Mother, put your fingers here."

His mother complied. "Fractured skull," she said evenly.

"Depressed fracture. Probably bleeding in the brain."

"You will operate, then."

"Mother, I can't! I've only performed the procedure once, and that was years ago."

"There is no surgeon of your competence closer than Cairo," his mother said remorselessly. "Would he survive the journey? Would not his condition worsen with delay?"

The answer was engraved on Nefret's white face.

⊃⊂

CHAPTER TEN

The sun rose behind me as I climbed, and my long pale shadow leaped ahead, racing me to the summit. Abdullah was waiting for me in the usual place, at the top of the rocky slope behind Deir el Bahri. Instead of offering a hand to help me, he stood with folded arms, his bearded face grim.

"Will he live?" I gasped, collapsing onto a boulder.

"Thanks to the goodness of God and the skill of Nur Misur. You could have prevented this, Sitt Hakim."

The cruelty of the charge brought me to my feet, shaking with anger. "No, but you could have. Why didn't you warn me?"

"There are many futures. The final shape is not known until it takes place." His thin lips curled. "I never thought to see you behave like a woman, Sitt."

"I'm not sure I want to know what you mean by that."

"Tending babies, ordering food to be prepared, beds to be made ready, while a web of evil is woven round you."

Behind him the path, white in the dawn, went on across the tumbled rocks of the plateau toward the Valley of the Kings. It was a well-traveled path, but in these dreams there was never a human form but ours. A scorpion rattled over a stone, its envenomed tail raised. A long brown shape, thin as a rat's tail, left a twisted trail through the sandy dust.

"As usual," I said bitterly, "you talk of danger but not how to prevent it."

Abdullah let out a little sound of exasperation. "I am not allowed. I have told you before—in attempting to prevent one danger, you may run headlong into another. You must work out the pattern for yourself. There is a pattern, Sitt. You will see it if you try. Come," he went on, in a kinder voice, "let us look across the valley."

I let him draw me to the spot where the path plunged down. "The sun is born again from the womb of night," he said. "See how the light spreads, remaking the world."

The shapes of mountain and sown land, ruined temples and homely houses seemed to spring into existence out of the nothingness of the night. He was trying to tell me something, but I was cursed if I knew what. My black mood lifted a little, though. His hand was as firm and warm as that of a living man.

"So you have become a poet as well as a saint, Abdullah?"

"Ah, that." Abdullah looked pleased, but he shook his head. "It is part of the pattern too, Sitt. Go now. Be careful on the path—not only this one, but the one you must follow."

He had never descended with me, not even a few steps. Always his path led toward the west.

EVEN EMERSON WAS IN NO fit state of mind for work the next day. None of us had got much sleep; it had been impossible for anyone to seek repose until I brought the news that Selim had survived the operation. Further comfort than that I could not honestly offer at the time, but Nefret, who had stayed with him all night, turned up for breakfast to report that he was holding his own, and indeed seemed a little better.

"I must get back," she went on, looking with distaste at the heaped plate Fatima promptly set before her. "Kadija is with him now, but—"

"Eat something and then go to bed," I said firmly. "You cannot risk falling ill. Kadija and I will look after him."

"He will be all right, won't he?" Sennia raised tragic black eyes.

"Yes," I said.

"He wouldn't dare die with your aunt Amelia and Nefret looking after him." The speaker was Sethos, who had just entered, after snatching a few hours' sleep on the dahabeeyah. He patted the child's curly black head and glanced at his daughter, but contented himself with a nod and a smile.

I put my serviette on the table and rose. "I am going to Selim now. Get some rest, Nefret. I will notify you at once if there is any change. You can trust me to do that, I presume?"

"Yes, Mother."

"The rest of you carry on. Keep busy."

"Yes, Mother," said Ramses.

"And you, Emerson," I began.

"Yes, Peabody," said Emerson, with only the slightest note of irony. "Are you certain *you* can trust *me* to carry out an investigation without your assistance?"

"In this case," I conceded, "you are probably better qualified than I."

"Good Gad," said Emerson. "Probably?"

FROM MANUSCRIPT H

They had been too worried and distressed the night before to discuss what had caused the accident. Anyhow, it would have been unproductive to speculate before they had all the facts, and the wreckage could better be examined in daylight.

In the end, six of them rode to Gurneh. Walter would not be left behind—although, to the best of Ramses's knowledge, he knew very little about the workings of motorcars—and Bertie turned up as they were leaving, to offer what assistance he could. They spent a little time with Selim's wives, who went about the conventional gestures of hospitality with better spirits than Ramses had expected. They knew Selim had got through the operation.

"The Sitt Hakim sent Daoud to tell us," one of them explained.

Of course, Ramses realized, she would think of that. He hadn't.

Guiltily, praying he was not holding out false hope, he added additional reassurance. "He is better this morning. She says he will live."

They had never doubted it. Not with the Sitt Hakim's magic working for him. Nur Misur was loved and trusted, but a little magic never hurt.

Half the village followed them to the scene of the crash. Nothing had been touched. Emerson had left orders.

In bright sunlight the wrecked motorcar looked even worse than it had the night before. It had gone off the path to the left, fallen onto its side, and slid down before it turned over, leaving a wide swath of disturbed soil littered with broken glass and bits of metal before crashing into the ridge. If that outcrop had not been there, it would have rolled on down to the bottom of the path—and if Selim had not been thrown out before it fell he would almost certainly have been crushed in the wreckage.

Almost all the structural damage was on the left side of the vehicle: the door ripped off its hinges, the windscreen bent and shattered. One wheel was missing; the wooden spokes of the other were splintered and the tire was flat. The radiator had burst and the petrol tank had been ruptured. By now the petrol had evaporated, though the smell lingered.

"Here's the wheel," David called from farther up the hill. They scrambled to join him. Emerson swept the area with an eagle eye, measuring distance and trajectory.

"If it came off as a result of the impact, it would be under the car, or lower down," he muttered.

"The lug nuts are missing," Ramses said. "All six of them." Even though he had expected this, he felt slightly sick. "They must have been deliberately loosened. The car toppled over when the wheel came off."

"It wasn't an accident?" Bertie looked as sick as Ramses felt.

"Not a chance of it," Emerson replied grimly. "Selim is a first-rate mechanic, and he kept the cursed thing in top condition."

A murmur arose from the watching audience. Some of them understood English; they were passing the news on to the rest. A slender black-robed woman picked up the child playing at her feet and hushed it. One of the squatting men lit a cigarette. Otherwise no one stirred. Intent dark eyes followed their every movement as they went over the vehicle inch by inch. Emerson insisted that it would have taken a man's strength to loosen the bolts. Ramses wasn't so sure of that; a long-handled wrench might have done the job if it were in the hands of a determined woman who knew something about motorcars.

"When was it done?" he asked.

Emerson fingered the cleft in his chin. "We put the wheel back on day before yesterday. It was the wheel on the front right—not this one. The job must have been done that night. If I had put the damned car in the stableyard, as your mother kept telling me to do . . ."

The lines around his mouth deepened. "It wouldn't have made any difference," Ramses said. "The stableyard is easily accessible and Ali sleeps like the dead. Loosening the lug nuts would take only a few minutes."

"He, whoever he was, counted on the wheel coming off when Selim hit a steep stretch," Sethos said musingly.

"The car was bound to turn over once it lost a wheel," Ramses argued. "Wherever that happened. He had to keep up a fair speed, that's the only way to drive over rough terrain."

"Agreed. But the damage, to Selim and the vehicle, would have been considerably less if it had happened on a level stretch. It was a gamble—supposing that murder was the intent."

"Just like all the other cases," Ramses muttered.

Emerson looked round. "Daoud. I want the motorcar brought back to the house. Collect every scrap."

"It's a total wreck, sir," Bertie exclaimed. "You'll never repair it."

"Do you suppose I give a curse about that?" Emerson demanded.

Daoud flexed big brown hands and nodded vigorously. "It shall be as you say, Father of Curses. Selim can repair the motorcar. You will see."

Emerson's features twisted into a painful grimace. His voice was hoarser than usual when he replied. "You are right, Daoud. He can and he will."

"And," said Daoud placidly, "you will find the man who did this and give him to me."

"Inshallah," said Sethos under his breath.

Daoud repeated the word and, after a moment, so did Emerson.

⋙⋘

I HAD SENT WORD TO Katherine and Cyrus that morning, for I knew they would want the latest bulletin. Shortly thereafter they came in person.

"We won't stay unless we can be of use, Amelia," Katherine assured me, seating herself next to me and taking my hands. "What can we do to help? Is he really better?"

I had just left the sickroom, where Kadija sat like a large ebony idol, her very presence reassuring. "He is still unconscious, but his breathing is easier."

"It must have been horrible for Nefret," Katherine murmured, with a little shiver. "The knowledge that the life of someone she knows and loves was in her hands . . ."

"She has always come through when she had to," I said. "Cool and steady as a machine. She will break down eventually, but not before she is certain he is out of danger. You will stay for luncheon, won't you?"

Fatima, who had been trying to force me to eat again, let out a murmur of pleasure and hurried into the house. Cyrus stopped pacing—he had been up and down the length of the veranda a dozen times—and put his hand on my shoulder.

"Sure we won't be in the way?"

"Not at all," I assured him. "We could use some help with the children. I am very grateful to you for getting Dolly and Sennia away so quickly, but they all know something is wrong and they are, of course, behaving like fiends."

"How well I remember." Katherine rose. "Where are they?"

"Lia and Evelyn have corralled them in Sennia's courtyard. At least I hope they have."

She hurried off. I motioned to Cyrus, who was still pacing. "Sit down, Cyrus. The men will be back soon. They went to Gurneh to inspect the motorcar. Will you wait for them here? I promised Nefret I would sit with Selim while she got a little rest."

She was in his sickroom when I hastened in, bending over the bed. Guiltily I began, "I am sorry, Nefret. I was only away—"

She looked up. Her eyes were luminous. "He's conscious. Kadija came for me."

I dropped to my knees beside the bed. Selim's eyes were open. He saw me; he recognized me. His lips parted.

"Don't speak," I said gently. "Don't move. You had an accident and were badly hurt, but Nefret has taken care of your injuries. You are in her clinic and you are going to be fine."

I thought that answering the most obvious questions would keep him quiet, but he had something else on his mind.

"Did my father tell you—"

"He told me you would live."

"Ah." It was a soft, relieved sigh. I have long been convinced that the mind affects the body in ways we cannot define. With that assurance Selim had gained additional strength and will to live. Who could deny the wisdom of a saint?

Nefret's fingers were pressed to his wrist. "You have a number of broken bones and your head was hurt," she said. "You must not move it. I will give you something for the pain now."

Selim's eyes opened wide, the whites showing all round the pupils. "A needle? No! I do not want—"

"All right, no needle," Nefret said quickly. "Don't get excited."

Selim grunted. Then his expressive orbs rolled in my direction. "Who took my clothes off?"

Nefret began to laugh. It was the sort of laughter that is often followed by tears, so I was relieved when the door opened and Ramses looked in. "What—" he began.

"He asked who undressed him," Nefret gasped. She turned blindly into Ramses's arms, her face streaked with tears.

"I did, Selim," said Ramses, over her bowed head. His voice was steady, but his black eyes shone suspiciously as he gazed at his friend. "With you be peace and God's mercy and blessing, my friend."

"No needle," Selim whispered.

"Not if you behave yourself," Ramses said. "Sleep now."

Selim's lids snapped shut. I looked at Kadija. She smiled her beautiful, kindly smile, and nodded. I noticed that under the bandages Selim's shaven head was green.

WE HAD A GENUINE CELEBRATION, for even Nefret admitted to cautious optimism about her patient. She looked exhausted but radiant, the violet smudges under her eyes intensifing their blue. "There is always danger of a relapse, but his recuperative powers are astonishing. If I believed in miracles . . ."

"Miracles be damned," said Emerson predictably. "It was your skill that saved him. Well done, my dear girl."

"Well done indeed," Katherine agreed. "I sent messages this morning, postponing our soiree."

"Right. How could we hold a soiree without Selim to waltz with the ladies?" Cyrus demanded. "We'll have a real party once he's fully recovered—and the villain who tried to kill him is dead or in prison."

"Are you sure Selim was the intended victim?" Sethos asked.

Naturally the same question had occurred to me. "A number of people knew that Selim meant to drive the motorcar to the fantasia," I replied. "However, the miscreant could not be certain Emerson would not take it into his head to operate the thing before Selim did."

"Just as the miscreant who sank the boat could not be certain who would be harmed," Ramses said thoughtfully. "There's a nonchalance about all this that is extremely strange. If the fellow is trying to commit murder, he's not very good at it."

Fatima came in with another platter of her famous spiced lamb and rice. Sethos leaned back and folded his hands over his flat stomach. "Thank you, Fatima, but I have already eaten more than I ought. I will be getting stout if I stay much longer."

"How long will that be?" I asked. Maryam, who had eaten in silence, head bent, looked up.

"However long it takes to find your antagonist" was the reply. "You lot are exhibiting less than your usual efficiency. What's the difficulty? I'd have expected Amelia to come up with a suspect or two long before this."

"The difficulty is that we don't know which incidents are relevant and which are accident or coincidence," I replied indignantly.

"It is like finding the original pattern in a jumble of loose beads," David added. "Some of which belong to another piece of jewelry altogether."

Sethos's curiously colored eyes studied him. "An interesting analogy. You are something of an expert on restoration, David; how would you go about separating the disparate elements?"

"Lay them all out on a table, examine them, and try them in different arrangements" was the prompt reply. "After long experience, one acquires an instinct for such things."

"Like Amelia's instinct for crime," said Walter eagerly. "And—er—that of—er—"

"Mine?" Sethos's brows rose. "You forget, Walter, that I have investigated fewer crimes than I have committed. However, I have no intention of leaving you without my protection."

Emerson growled.

SELIM CONTINUED TO IMPROVE. HE was able to sit up for short periods and his appetite was good—though no one, not even Daoud, could have consumed all the food Fatima tried to force on him. He ought to have been a pathetic sight, encased in sticking plaster, with a miniature turban of bandages covering his shaven head; however, his cherished beard had been left intact, and that seemed to cheer him a great deal. At first his speech was a trifle slurred, but that did not prevent him from asking innumerable questions, most of them about the motorcar.

"It was not your fault," said Emerson, who had been allowed to visit Selim for a few minutes. "Someone deliberately loosened the bolts on the front wheel. As soon as you are fit, we will repair it. By that time we will have found the man responsible."

"Daoud is looking after your family," I added, "and so are we all. You are not to worry about anything except getting well."

"The excavations," Selim said. "You must not allow——"

"Don't worry about that either," Emerson said. "We will carry on as best we can until you are back on the job."

Knowing how trying it would be for a man of Selim's energy to remain quiet, I arranged a schedule of entertainment. In my opinion Emerson was not a soothing companion for a sick man, but Ramses and Bertie came by every day to report on the excavations, and Sennia and Evelyn read to him. I knew he was on the road to recovery when he gravely asked Evelyn to read from a manual on the maintenance and repair of motorcars.

Never suppose, Reader, that my attentions to our friend had kept me from other duties. Unfortunately and infuriatingly, the most imperative of those duties took very little of my time. Emerson brooded morbidly over the wreckage of the motorcar, which had been transported to the stableyard. Even he admitted there was nothing more to be learned from it. Daoud instigated another, more intensive search for Maryam's first attacker, and dragged several quaking strangers to the house to confront Maryam and Ramses. Neither was able to make an identification.

To say that we were watchful and wary is to understate the case. Fatima went through both houses several times a day brandishing a broom, on the lookout for venomous creatures. Kadija and two of her daughters took up permanent residence, sitting with Selim and keeping the children under close surveillance. I refused to allow Emerson to go alone to the dig, which provoked him into furious protests—though he insisted I follow the same precaution. The inevitable result was that everyone became twitchy and irritable, especially the children.

We got on with packing the artifacts. As Emerson continued to point out, with increasing acrimony and inventive swear words, Lacau would damn well have to sit and wait until we finished the job, but I had reasons of my own for wanting it completed before he got there. One of them—I feel no shame in admitting it—was that I had no intention of mentioning the stolen jewelry, or of allowing the others to do so. Lacau was unlikely to demand that the carefully packed cases be opened. He would have his lists and his inventory, and would doubtless go over them painstakingly when he unpacked the cases in the Museum. If at that time he realized several pieces were missing . . . sufficient unto the day is the evil thereof, as Scripture so wisely reminds us. We would confess if we had to, but not until we had to— and there was still a chance, however unlikely, that we might yet find the thief and murderer. In fact, as Emerson would have expressed it, we had bloody well better find him, before he decided to strike again.

At least the packing process kept us occupied. Everyone pitched in with a will, including Maryam. She had a delicate touch, and demonstrated a genuine interest in the precious things.

"You can help me with this, if you will," I said, indicating a painted chest. "I really do not know what we are going to do about packing materials. I have used up all the fabric and most of the cotton wool, and even so I fear the garments in this chest will shatter when it is moved."

"What does the writing say?"

"It is a list of the contents—gloves, sandals, two robes, and a few other articles. Ramses has already copied and translated it. He reads hieratic as easily as he does English."

"I would like to learn more, so that I can help with your work. Perhaps he would give me a lesson?"

"If you are truly interested, we can arrange for you to study the subject." I added, with a laugh, "Though it will take more than a few lessons. You have already been very useful, Maryam. I have been meaning to thank you for your help with the children."

"I want to be useful. And I love being with the children." The next words were so soft I had to strain to hear them. "I am very happy here. I will be sorry to go."

"That won't be for a while. We must have you here for Christmas, at least."

"And afterward? I know it is a great deal to ask. But . . . could I stay with you for a while? You have all been so good to me, and I think I could be useful—with the children, even on the dig, if you will teach me."

It was not only that she was happy with us; she was still uncomfortable with him. I had wondered what on earth he meant to do with her. He traveled a great deal, and so did Margaret. They had no permanent establishment where she could receive the attention she needed. And how in heaven's name would Margaret respond to the role of stepmother? Not well, if I knew Margaret.

"I will discuss it with your father," I promised, though I felt like an overburdened donkey who has just had another sack of grain added to his load. "Perhaps something can be worked out."

FROM MANUSCRIPT H

Ramses was sitting with Selim reading from the motorcar manual (his aunt Evelyn having admitted defeat) when the door opened and Sethos put his head in. "Are visitors allowed?"

It was the first time he had seen Selim since the accident. Selim's black eyes brightened and his hand went to his beard. It was certainly more impressive than that of Sethos, though the latter's was coming along nicely. His face was almost back to normal except for a few faded bruises.

"Yes, come," Selim said eagerly. "You are still here!"

Leaning against the doorframe, a picture of sartorial elegance in well-cut tweeds, Sethos gave him a friendly grin. "You didn't suppose I would abandon the family at a time like this? With you out of commission, they need all the help they can get."

"That is true," said Selim, starting to nod and then remembering he wasn't supposed to.

"Thank you both for your confidence," said Ramses.

"You are too honorable," Selim explained. "He is not."

Sethos threw his head back and shouted with laughter. "Right on the mark, Selim. Is there anything I can do for you?"

"Tell me about the aeroplane," Selim said eagerly.

"Another time. Fatima said I wasn't to stay. She's bringing your dinner."

Selim groaned. "She brings me food, Rabia and Taghrid bring me food, Kadija brings me food. Soon I will be fat."

"So what are you after, really?" Ramses asked, as they strolled along the path toward the main house. "Visiting the sick isn't your style."

"How cynical. I like Selim." Sethos paused to sniff at a pink rose. "You're right, though. It was you I was after. Would you care to join me in a visit to the gay and glamorous night life of Luxor? Lovely spot, this," he added, gazing sentimentally at a vine covered with blue flowers. "Perhaps when I retire I'll settle down in Luxor. The whole family together, eh?"

Ramses refused the bait. "Why?"

"To pass my declining years in the company of my nearest and dearest. Oh—you mean why go to Luxor. I think I may be on to something."

He refused to elaborate, claiming that he wanted an independent judgment. His announcement of their intentions was met with raised eyebrows, but without comment, at least not at dinner. When Ramses went to change, Nefret went with him.

"What is this about?" she asked.

"He says he's on to something."

She watched curiously as he selected the suit he intended to wear. "Black tie? Where are you going?"

"He wouldn't say."

"Someplace respectable, at least," Nefret said, "That's a relief. Are you going to take your knife?"

"It doesn't go with evening kit."

She did not return his smile. "It goes with Uncle Sethos. Please."

THE SO-CALLED NIGHT LIFE of Luxor ranged from the repellent to the respectable. The cafés and drinking establishments that catered to tourists were located along the corniche; a few were relatively harmless, but evening clothes would have been glaringly out of place in any of them. The hotels, especially those of the top category, were the centers of social activity for upper-class visitors and residents. The tourist steamers and dahabeeyahs drawn up along the bank formed a narrow floating residential street. Lights shone from the decks and saloons.

Their first stop was the Winter Palace, where Sethos was obviously known and welcome. He was choosy about which table to select, and when the waiter hurried up to take their order he said, "Nothing tonight, Habib. But there will be baksheesh for you if you tell the Brother of Demons what you told me."

"About the Italian gentleman and the lady?" Habib asked, with a nod of greeting for Ramses. He extended a thin brown hand.

They visited two other hotels, the Savoy and the Tewfikieh, on the road to Karnak, and got the same story, though not the same description of the "lady." At the latter establishment, which claimed the optimistic designation of "Grand-Hotel," Sethos ordered whiskey and invited Ramses's comments.

"One Titian-haired, one dark, one fair," Ramses said. A breeze rustled the leaves of the arbor over their heads. "Martinelli was quite a ladies' man."

"Come now," said Sethos, with a grin.

"The same woman?"

"He acquired female acquaintances in other places. I've already eliminated them, and a damned tedious chore it was. This one was different. A lady, well-dressed, quiet and very retiring. Except for the hair, the descriptions were the same. Approximately five feet three inches, shapely figure, young."

"None of the waiters recognized her?"

"They all claim they had never set eyes on her before. But I think you have."

"Hathor?" Ramses thought it over. "The description fits, such as it is."

"It must be the same woman. This is the connection between two seemingly unrelated parts of the pattern, and it explains how Martinelli was lured to his death. He'd follow a woman anywhere."

Ramses ran his fingers through his hair. It was late, and he was tired, but several other pieces of the pattern were falling into place. "So he 'borrowed' the jewelry in order to impress her. Offered it to her, perhaps, in exchange for favors she had withheld. He had no intention of paying so high a price, though. It would have meant the end of his lucrative job with Cyrus, and the police on his trail. What a dirty little swine he was."

Sethos lifted his glass and set it down again, making a pattern of interlocking rings on the table. "A moralist would say he got what he deserved. She agreed to sell her favors, with no more intention of carrying out her share of the bargain than he, and he went panting after her, too blinded by lust to wonder why she was leading him into a remote part of Luxor; and in a dark, verminous alley his doom awaited him, as Amelia might put it. He was probably dead before he knew what had happened."

"They bundled him up and tossed him over a donkey and carried him out into the desert." Ramses continued the story. "They took the jewelry, and everything else that might have identified him, and left him for the jackals."

"It was as easy as taking candy from a child," Sethos said, bland and unmoved. He sounded almost admiring. "Brilliantly planned, really. One had only to look at the poor bastard to know he had had no success with the sort of woman he wanted. No woman of taste would have touched him with a barge pole. He was ripe for the plucking, and she plucked him like a goose."

"Why? If it's the princesses' treasure she's after . . ." He wondered why he hadn't thought of it before. "Could that be it?"

"Why ask me? I'm a reformed character," said his uncle virtuously. "If I were after it—and don't give me that fishy stare, I'm not—I wouldn't go about it in such a disorganized fashion. I certainly wouldn't arrange a series of haphazard attacks; they've only succeeded in putting you on the qui vive. No. What I'd do is bide my time, lull you into a sense of false security, and then strike. I could break into that locked room in sixty seconds, and with a dozen well-trained villains helping me, clear out everything that's portable and be away from Luxor before morning."

"I'll bet you could, at that," Ramses muttered.

"It would be an attractive challenge," Sethos mused. He leaned back and lit a cigarette. His face took on a dreamy expression. "Transport arranged in advance . . . ready admission to the Castle for a trusted friend . . . servants asleep in their wing of the house . . . Cyrus gently escorted back to his room and locked in, with his wife . . ."

He sighed regretfully and blew out a wobbly smoke ring.

"It must be quite a temptation," Ramses said, with unwilling amusement. His uncle's expression was that of a man remembering a particularly successful romantic interlude. "How you must miss the good old days, before Mother reformed you. Or has she?"

"Mmmm." Sethos put out his cigarette and leaned forward, elbows on the table, no longer smiling. "Believe this, if you can. I swore to her I would never interfere with their work again. That goes for Cyrus too. I don't steal from my friends."

"Does that mean—"

"We had better go. Your wife will be sending out search parties."

His evasive response roused certain dire suspicions. It wasn't the first time they had entered Ramses's mind. What had Sethos been doing in Jerusalem when he was supposed to be in Constantinople? Since the war the former battlegrounds had been in turmoil, and the preservation of antiquities was undoubtedly low on the list of the occupying powers. It was a perfect opportunity for a picker-up of unconsidered trifles, and Sethos was an expert picker-upper.

There's nothing I can do about it, Ramses told himself, even if it's true. And I can't prove it is.

The colored lanterns began to go out as they left the hotel and started back along the road above the embankment. Ramses loosened his tie. "So if it isn't the treasure, it's something else she wants. Was Martinelli's death part of the plan?"

"He had made a few enemies," Sethos said noncommittally.

"While he was working for you?"

"Then, and when he was working for other people. Given his weakness for women, it isn't impossible that he—er—offended one of them. Tracking him down would be easy. Everyone in Luxor knew he was working for Cyrus." His uncle was a shadow beside him. They passed the Savoy and the Hotel de Karnak, now dark except for a few lamps next to the entrances. Bats flapped and swooped between the trees. A long, piercing whistle began and grew louder—the night train from Cairo, several hours late as usual.

It was drowned out by a roar of sound. The black sky to the east reddened and quivered.

"My God," Ramses gasped. "What was that?"

Sethos's head was raised like that of a pointer sniffing the air. "It's near the railroad station. Come on."

CHAPTER ELEVEN

None of us heard the explosion, which was a good thing, since certain of us might have been worried enough to investigate. When a loud noise is juxtaposed to the absence of Ramses, one naturally assumes he had something to do with it. As Nefret told me later, he did not return until almost three in the morning. His attempt to undress without waking her did not succeed, and when she lit a lamp the sight of him almost made her drop it. His best evening suit was a complete ruin—torn, smeared with blood and ashes and other unmentionable substances, and his hands were, to quote Nefret, a bloody mess. The rest of us did not learn of the matter until breakfast.

"I wasn't hurt and neither was Sethos," Ramses insisted, trying to get a firm grip on his fork. "We were a half mile away when the blast went off. I cut myself up a bit digging people out of the rubble. Damn it, Nefret, I don't need all these bandages. You always—"

"What happened?" My voice was, perhaps, a trifle loud.

Ramses picked up a sausage in his fingers. "They tried to blow up the train station, just as the express from Cairo was coming in. Mercifully they didn't make a good job of it. The tracks weren't damaged, and only part of the station went up. One man was killed and half a dozen others were injured—all of them Egyptians. The European waiting room and the platform were unscathed."

"They," Emerson said. "Who was responsible?"

Ramses had bit off a chunk of sausage. He shrugged.

"The peasants are revolting," said David. His lips twisted. "The damn fools!"

Ramses swallowed. "That is the assumption. The rioting last spring included similar acts of sabotage."

"Damnation." Emerson took out his pipe.

"Don't sprinkle tobacco on your eggs, Emerson," I ordered.

"I've finished," said Emerson, sprinkling tobacco on the remains of his breakfast and the surrounding area. "I suppose we can expect a contingent of troops from Cairo. What a bloody nuisance. David, perhaps it would be advisable for you to—er—lie low for a while."

David's finely cut lips straightened. "I won't run away, sir. I had nothing to do with this and they can't prove I did."

"The military doesn't need proof," Emerson muttered.

"Yes, by God, they do," Ramses said vehemently. "David is a British citizen, and some of the biggest guns in the government will vouch for him."

"Including me," said Sethos, posing in the open doorway. "Am I too late for breakfast, Fatima?"

"Can't you ever enter a room without making a theatrical production of it?" I inquired.

"It's a habit," Sethos explained.

"Let me see your hands."

He held them out. "Clean enough?"

"You were digging too," I said, observing the broken nails and scraped knuckles and scorched palms. "Come to the clinic and I will—"

"Well, of course I was digging. Did you expect me to stand idly by while Ramses was being heroic?"

Ramses let out a sound like a softer version of his father's growl. "We were both extremely heroic," Sethos said soothingly. "Don't fuss, Amelia, I applied half a bottle of whiskey—and even a little soap and water." He took a chair next to Maryam and Fatima hurried to set a place for him.

"Are you all right, sir?" Maryam turned a pretty, anxious face toward him.

"Quite. Why are you all getting worked up? This was an isolated incident, and at present the cause is unknown. I telegraphed Cairo to that effect first thing this morning. Unless something else occurs I believe they will be content to leave the investigation in my hands and those of the police."

"I hope so. Candidly," I declared, "at this moment I don't give a curse about riots and insurrections, and the explosion cannot have any bearing on our other problems."

"Problem," Sethos corrected. "There is a common cause, and last night Ramses and I . . . Oh, thank you, Fatima. That looks delicious. Last night we discovered one of the links. Have you told them, Ramses?"

"Haven't had a chance," Ramses said curtly. "Your discovery, anyhow."

I will confess, in the pages of this private journal, that my first reaction to Sethos's account was chagrin. I ought to have thought of it myself. Is not "cherchez la femme" a favorite axiom? Not with me, however, and in a case of presumed strangulation a female does not immediately leap to mind.

"Well done," I conceded. "Though, if I may say so, certain of your conclusions are based on unsubstantiated extrapolation. I do not . . . I beg your pardon, Emerson? Did I hear a reference to pots and kettles?"

"I would never express such a trite aphorism, Peabody."

"Hmm. As I was about to say, I do not see that this gets us much further. We had postulated a gang, had we not?"

"But now we know—" Catching my eye, Ramses amended the statement. "We may reasonably assume that the appearances of Hathor are not extraneous to the pattern we have been trying to establish. There is a woman involved."

"A young, beautiful woman," Nefret murmured.

"Quite," said Ramses. He snapped off another bit of sausage.

"But what was the purpose of those ridiculous appearances?" I cried in exasperation. "And who the devil is she?"

"A permanent resident of Luxor or a tourist who arrived in Luxor over a month ago," said Sethos.

"A month?" I asked.

"I've made a timetable," Sethos explained, with a superior smile at me. He knew I had not, or I would have said so. "Martinelli disappeared over three weeks ago. Give her a week or so before that to become acquainted with him. If it is the same woman, she made a quick trip to Cairo when you did, and then came back in time to arrange to sink Daoud's boat and stage her second appearance. There is every reason to believe she is still here."

"That limits the number of suspects, surely," David said thoughtfully. "Most tourists stay for only a few days, and there aren't that many permanent residents who are female."

"And young and beautiful and—er—no better than she should be," I agreed. "It can't be one of that group. I know them all, and I assure you one of my acquaintances would have informed me if a newcomer had settled here."

"She's right about that," said Emerson to the group at large. "Those females are always quick to relay the latest gossip."

"Still, there is no harm in inquiring," Sethos said. He had taken advantage of the lull to empty his plate, which Fatima immediately refilled. "No, Amelia, not you; a direct question to one of your friends would arouse curiosity, and we must avoid that at all costs. I will make my availability for social functions of all sorts known to the good ladies of Luxor society. A new face is always welcome, and there is no man more welcome than an eligible bachelor."

"You had better do something to your face if you intend to attract the ladies," I retorted. "That beard—"

"I've been waiting for it to grow out," Sethos explained, stroking his chin. "Just wait, Amelia; once I've had it trimmed and touched up a bit—and made a few other changes—the mere sight of me will cause you to swoon with admiration."

"Bah," said Emerson. "All you will learn is that there are several women in Luxor—I name no names, Peabody—who would stop at nothing to marry off their spinster daughters. The woman you're after won't come anywhere near you."

"I think she might," Sethos said, his smile fading. "I am known to be a friend of Mr. Cyrus Vandergelt, am I not?"

"In short," said Ramses, after a moment of silence, "you intend to set yourself up as bait."

Maryam let out a little cry, and her father turned to her with a reassuring smile. "It's perfectly safe, Maryam. I doubt very much that she would try the same trick a second time. If she does, I promise I won't follow her into a dark alley." He looked round the circle of sober faces and shrugged. "It's our best lead and it ought to be pursued."

"It would be nice if we could clear the matter up soon," I said. "The Christmas season is approaching. I have never allowed a criminal to interfere with my holiday celebrations, and I don't intend to begin now."

"Christmas!" Emerson exclaimed, eyes bulging. "Now see here, Peabody, I have never objected to the unnecessary effort you expend on what is essentially a pagan holiday with accretions from an equally nonsensical superstition—"

"We certainly can't disappoint the children," Lia said. "I must confess I hadn't given it much thought."

"I have," I said. "But we still have a few weeks."

"There is another matter," said David, glancing at his father-in-law. "The Milner Commission is due in Egypt shortly, and the British attitude is already known. The Protectorate will continue. Zaghlul Pasha has sent word that the commission is to be boycotted entirely. There will be strikes and demonstrations all over the country."

"How do you know that?" Lia asked.

"I read the newspapers," David said somewhat impatiently. "I hope Sethos is right, but I have a feeling that Cairo is going to take the explosion at the railroad station more seriously than he anticipates."

"It has nothing to do with us," Ramses said, watching his friend with a furrowed brow. "Stay out of it, David. You promised you would."

"We will keep him out of it," I said firmly. "Good heavens, haven't we enough to worry about without that?"

Fatima came in. "There is a patient for you, Nur Misur. Will you go?"

"Of course." Nefret rose.

"And the rest of us must return to our labors," I declared. "Who is going to the Castle with me?"

"Not I," Emerson growled.

"No one expects you to, my dear. Cheer up; we will have finished the job in a day or two and then we can get on with our investigation."

"What investigation?" Emerson demanded. He pushed his plate away with such violence that it knocked over a glass. Water spilled across the cloth. "Curse it," Emerson shouted. "I am sorry, Fatima. It was your fault, Peabody, your bland optimism drives me wild! There is nothing to investigate. We've come to a dead end. You know perfectly well we can't do a bloody thing except sit round waiting for another bloody attack!"

"That is not quite correct, Radcliffe," said Walter, adjusting his eyeglasses. "Er—Sethos's scheme—"

"Is posturing without purpose," Emerson snarled. His hard blue stare moved from one of his brothers to the other. Sethos grinned appreciatively and Walter, who had known Emerson even longer, calmly buttered another piece of bread.

WHEN I ARRIVED AT THE Castle, I found Cyrus pacing up and down the display room, tugging at his goatee. Katherine trotted alongside, patting him and emitting breathless phrases like "Now, Cyrus," and "Cyrus, dear." He was going at a great pace and my dear Katherine was a trifle stout; she let out a gasp of relief when my appearance brought Cyrus to a halt.

"Now what?" I demanded. "Katherine, sit down, my dear, and catch your breath."

Cyrus turned remorsefully to his wife. "Sorry, Cat. I was so het up I wasn't paying attention."

He was holding a crumpled paper—a telegram, by its color. "Is that what got you het up?" I inquired. "Let me guess. Another message from M. Lacau? What does he want now—everything?"

"Not so bad as that." Cyrus smoothed out the telegram and tried to fan his wife with it. "I don't know why it got me so mad. The tone of it, I guess. He left Cairo yesterday—took over twenty-four hours for the telegram to be delivered, as usual. He expects to arrive on Thursday, and he wants to load up in one day—can you believe it? Only he didn't say expect and want and will you please. Do this and do that was more like it."

"Telegrams are not the medium for polite circumlocutions," I replied. "What got him so het up?"

"He did say something about that." Cyrus read the words. "'Rumors unrest alarming. Stop. Safe arrival Cairo artifacts paramount. Stop.'"

"Wait till he hears about the explosion," David murmured. "He'll be all the more determined to leave Luxor in a hurry."

"He's got his goldurned gall suggesting the artifacts aren't safe here," Cyrus snapped. "They're safer than they would be in that dodblasted Museum . . . Oh, shucks. You don't think he found out about the stolen jewelry, do you?"

"I cannot imagine how he could have," I replied. "He is just being officious and overly fearful. This really doesn't change anything, Cyrus; we will have his precious artifacts ready for him and he can load up and go to the devil, as Emerson might say. If we make arrangements in advance for bearers he may actually be able to accomplish it in a single day."

By midday we had run out of straw and cotton wool. We had dealt with most of the smaller objects; there remained only the coffins, the mummies, and the beaded robe.

"I am sure I do not know how we are to pack that," I declared. "I would be afraid to roll it or fold it again, and if we insert pins to keep it from shifting around as it is moved, the pins may do even more damage. David, have you any suggestions?"

"There isn't much we can do," David said regretfully. He brushed straw off his shirt. "Except cover it closely with a clean sheet and wrap bandages round the whole ensemble, with additional layers of padding above. If it is gently handled—"

"It won't be," I said with a sigh. "Ah well, what cannot be mended must be endured. We have done our best. I believe we can finish tomorrow if we can find more packing material."

"I'll go over to Luxor," David said. "There must be some seller of fabric we haven't cleaned out."

"Shall I come with you?" I asked.

"That isn't necessary. I'll try to locate more clean straw too, while I'm about it."

He picked up his coat and went out before I could reply. His haste and his refusal to meet my eyes made me wonder if he was up to something. David hardly ever did anything underhanded (unless he was egged on by Ramses), but in his own quiet way he was as stubborn as my son. His disclaimers to the contrary, I suspected he had not entirely severed his connection with the Nationalist movement, and this latest outbreak obviously worried him.

I ran after him, calling his name. He pretended he didn't hear, but I caught him up while he was saddling Asfur. "You are going to the railroad station," I panted. "Aren't you?"

David had never been able to lie to me. Moral force, established at an early age, is irresistible. (It had never been completely successful with Ramses, but he was an exceptional case.) David looked down at me with an attempt at sternness and then caved in, as I had known he would. "Confound it, Aunt Amelia, how do you do it?"

"It is well known in Luxor that I am a magician of great power," I replied with a smile. David did not return it.

"I only want to see the damage for myself."

"To what purpose? David, please don't go alone. Get Ramses or Emerson to go with you."

"Take the Father of Curses away from his excavations to play bodyguard? What can possibly happen that I can't handle? This is Luxor, not Gallipoli."

I let out a sigh of exasperation. Masculine ego is a frightful nuisance. "I am in no mood for argument or explanation, David. Just do as I say. Ramses is at the house working on his ostraca. That isn't far out of your way. And don't swear at me," I added, for I saw the word forming on his lips.

They drew back into a shape that was at least partially caused by amusement. "All right, Aunt Amelia, you win—as always. You are finished here for the time being, I expect. Shall I give you a lift back to the house?"

He mounted and offered me a hand. I backed away. "No, thank you, dear boy, I have enjoyed that romantic but uncomfortable experience too often. Tell Fatima we will be lunching here. And eat something before—"

He gave me a grin and a mock military salute and rode off. Thoughtfully I returned to the workroom.

FROM MANUSCRIPT H

Once Ramses would have been happy to be left to work on the inscribed material, but he was unable to concentrate. He knew why his father had not insisted on his presence that morning. They had not discussed it; there was no need. Selim was still helpless and the children were vulnerable, and if an adversary wanted to get into the sprawling, unguarded house, there was no one to stop him except the women and Gargery. The dear old idiot would die to defend any one of them, but that was about all he could do—if he didn't shoot himself first.

After the others had gone to the Castle, Ramses wandered rather aimlessly around the perimeter of the grounds, ending up at the clinic. The waiting room was full. Nefret's reputation had spread; but the need was so great, the lack of decent medical care so extensive that any halfway competent physician would have more than she could handle. Ramses felt the same helpless rage Nefret must feel every day, every hour, when he saw the suppurating wounds and runny eyes, the sickly babies and the swollen bellies of girls in their early teens. Obstetrics was and would be a large part of Nefret's practice.

Nisrin came out of the surgery. Blood spattered the front of her white gown, but she greeted him with an unperturbed smile. "Do you wish to see Nur Misur? She is sewing up this patient now."

"No, I can see she's busy. Unless there is something I can do to help."

She waved him away with the patronizing air of a trained nurse dismissing male incompetence, and he went to see how Selim was getting on. Sennia was with him, devouring honey cakes and discussing the Second Intermediate Period. She was doing most of the talking. Glancing at Ramses, she said indistinctly, "We are up to the Hyksos."

"So I hear," Ramses said. A paw, claws fully extended, shot out from under her chair. Ramses skipped aside. Horus's filthy temper hadn't mellowed, but he was slowing down physically. "Are you sure Selim wants to hear about the Hyksos?"

Sennia swallowed. "He is very interested in Egyptian history. Aren't you, Selim?"

Selim rolled his eyes and grinned. "The Little Bird is a good teacher."

"I am good at taking care of sick people too," Sennia said complacently.

"And the food here is excellent," Ramses said, as she reached for another honey cake. "You seem to be getting on nicely. Don't tire him, Little Bird."

"I am tired of lying here," Selim said. "I feel well. Tell Nur Misur she must let me get up."

The subject of his telling Nefret what to do was one he preferred not to pursue. He left.

His next stop was in the courtyard, where the children were playing. After a quarter of an hour Fatima made him go away, saying it was time for their luncheon and he was getting them too excited. The shrieks of protest that followed him did sound more vehement than usual. According to his mother, children were sensitive to atmosphere; the uneasiness of the adults was probably affecting them.

Having exhausted all means of entertainment, he went back to the study, and had just begun working when Gargery came in.

"There you are, sir," he said accusingly. "We have been looking all over for you. Mr. David—"

"You needn't announce me, Gargery," David said.

"Are you lunching, sir? We did not expect you. May I ask—"

"No," Ramses said. "Run along, Gargery, and tell Fatima—"

"Tell her not to fuss," David said. "A sandwich will do."

Gargery "ran along," sniffing. Ramses leaned back in his chair. "May I ask . . ."

"I'm off to Luxor. We ran out of cotton wool and cloth. Aunt Amelia made me promise to take you along. But if you're busy—"

"You aren't going to get out of it that easily." Ramses pushed the papers aside. "I've been translating that horoscope text for Mother. Couldn't concentrate on anything more difficult. What made her suppose you needed me to come along?"

"I'm going to the railroad station."

"And?"

"And nothing. I hope."

"You think there will be trouble?"

David smiled slightly. "I have a foreboding."

It was more than an idle premonition, it was the knowledge of how easily a group of idlers could turn into an angry mob. A crowd would certainly gather, inspired by curiosity and the hope of scavenging. Ramses blamed himself for failing to follow the current news, as David had. The situation was already volatile. The slightest provocation, real or fancied, could start a riot.

And David would try to stop it. Damn it, Ramses thought, we don't need this. "I'm with you," he said. "Whenever you're ready."

By the time they reached the station it was early afternoon, and the temperature was in the nineties. They heard the uproar some distance away.

An irregular line of police held the crowd back from the tracks and the station, where several men in khaki were standing guard over the wreckage, ignoring the curses and waving fists with admirable British aplomb. How the soldiers had got there so quickly Ramses didn't know; Allenby must have taken the precaution of dispatching mobile columns into potential hot spots. The police officers in their shabby uniforms didn't look happy. Many of them were in sympathy with the protesters. Someone was waving a banner with a rude (and incorrectly spelled) description of the Inglizi. The sun beat down like a furnace and dust fogged the air, kicked up by the shuffling feet.

"Stop a minute," Ramses said, catching hold of David before he could plunge into the thick of it. "They're just letting off steam. What's going on?"

The man he addressed wore a ragged galabeeyah and a dirty rag wrapped round his head. He turned with a snarl on Ramses, recognized him, and turned the snarl into a propitiatory smile. "We only wanted to take away the broken wood and the nails and bricks, Brother of Demons. What harm is there in that? But the accursed—uh—the British stopped us."

"They want to find out what caused the explosion," David said. "You will be allowed to remove the wreckage when they have finished. Tell your friends to go home."

"I? What sort of fool do you take me for? They are angry."

"And enjoying themselves," Ramses said to David in English. "Nothing like a jolly riot on a hot day to alleviate boredom."

"Someone is haranguing them," David said, trying to see over the field of bobbing turbans, with an occasional red fez for contrast.

The fellow was no orator, but he was loud and indignant. Words like oppression and injustice—and the name of the exiled patriot Zaghlul—started an angry muttering. David swore and began to force his way through the close-packed bodies.

Ramses followed, shoving even harder and making suggestions. "Go home, you fools. Get away from here. Think of your wives and children. Do you want to be shot?"

They made way for him, and a few took his advice to heart, but the orator was still screaming and the front ranks of the mob surged forward. The police weren't armed, but the soldiers were. Hoping none of them would mistake him and David for rioters, Ramses dodged the hands of a hot-eyed protester who was reaching for his throat and kicked the fellow's feet out from under him. The men in the front rank were the bravest, or, to look at it another way, the ones with the least sense. David flattened a few of them, fighting with the cool efficiency Ramses remembered so well. The ones nearest the victims began to have second thoughts. They backed off, leaving Ramses and David in the empty space before the beleaguered policemen.

"Where is the bastard?" David panted, referring, Ramses assumed, to the orator.

"Faded into obscurity, it would appear. See if you can yell louder than he."

David raised both arms and yelled louder. After a few sentences the audience settled down to listen. Egyptians were peaceable souls, on the whole, and they enjoyed a good speech. Nods and sheepish looks acknowledged David's impassioned appeal. That it came from the heart Ramses did not doubt. "Violence will only bring harm to you and your families, my brothers. Does not God forbid killing except in self-defense? Be patient. Freedom will come. I know this is true. I have fought for it and I will go on fighting."

He was the hero of the moment. Fickle as all mobs are, they surged toward him, the men who had resisted him before now trying to embrace him. Ramses, who admitted to being more evil-minded than his friend, had been scanning the jostling bodies and excited faces with a cynical eye. He saw the raised arm draw back and shoot forward, saw the stone hurtle through the air, and threw himself at David. He was a half second too late.

AFTER CONSIDERING THE MATTER, I concluded we might as well stop for the day. There was no hurry. Most of the more valuable objects had been packed. I had not decided what to do about the beaded robe and the rolls of the Book of the Dead. The former had suffered since Martinelli treated and unfolded it; the color had darkened perceptibly, and the fabric looked as if it would shatter at a touch. With a regretful sigh I acknowledged what I had suspected from the first; we were bound to lose it, no matter what we did. So why not let M. Lacau bear the ultimate responsibility? If he demanded we prepare it for transport we would, and then he could amuse himself in Cairo picking out loose beads and scraps of linen.

As for the Book of the Dead, I was in hopes of persuading M. Lacau to leave it with us for the time being. Softening and unrolling the brittle papyrus was a task at which Walter was particularly skilled.

I doubted there was anyone in Cairo who could do it as well, and of course he was one of the world's leading authorities on the ancient texts.

After I had reached this conclusion and explained it to the others, we enjoyed one of Katherine's excellent luncheons and dispersed— Evelyn to take a little rest, Walter to his papyrus, and Lia back to the house.

"Where are you off to?" Cyrus asked, watching me draw on my gloves and adjust my hat.

I decided I might as well tell him the truth. "I thought I would pay a little visit to Abdullah's tomb before I go home."

"Not alone," Cyrus declared, beckoning the stableman to saddle Queenie.

"I don't know why you assume I am in need of an escort, Cyrus. You let Lia go off alone."

"I trust her and I don't trust you," said Cyrus, tugging at his goatee. "Is that all you're going to do—call on Abdullah and maybe ask for some advice?"

"We are in need of advice, don't you think? I assure you, I have no other aim in mind."

"I'm comin' anyhow," said Cyrus.

The climate of Egypt is very dry, but a temperature in the nineties is hot, whatever the humidity. The shade of the little monument was welcome after our ride across the baking desert. Cyrus paid the assiduous Abdulrassah his dues and sat down, fanning himself with his hat and courteously looking elsewhere, while I entered the tomb.

I did not kneel or pray aloud. Leaning against the wall, I closed my eyes and thought of Abdullah. I don't know what I expected. He had never come to me when I was in a waking state, and I had no reason to suppose he would respond to my silent appeal now. To be honest, it was not so much an appeal as an irritable demand. What was the use of having an informant on "the other side" if he could not or would not inform me?

The blackness behind my closed lids swam with little specks of color, spirals and whirls of light. Sounds intensified: the shuffle of

Abdulrassah's sandals, the swish of the broom, the flap of birds' wings under the cupola, distant voices . . .

A hand touched my shoulder. I opened my eyes and saw Cyrus's face close to mine. "You were wobbling like a top when it starts to slow down," he said. "What were you trying to do, put yourself in a trance?"

"Entering a trancelike state when one is perpendicular is not very sensible," I said. "Nor do I consider myself psychic, in the usual sense of the word."

"You believe in your dreams, though." He gave me his arm. Abdulrassah propped his broom against the wall and sat down in a pointed manner beside his begging bowl. I added a few coins and answered Cyrus's implied question.

" 'Believe' is not precisely the right word. I accept them. I suppose you are a skeptic."

"I dunno." Cyrus helped me to mount. "I've seen a lot of strange things in my time, and I'd sure like to set eyes on good old Abdullah again. Did you have any luck?"

"I didn't see him, if that is what you mean. I thought . . . I may have been mistaken, but I thought I heard his voice. 'You are at the starting point, Sitt. Now go on, and watch where you step.' "

"What does that mean?" Cyrus asked.

"Cursed if I know, Cyrus."

OUR ATTEMPT TO BEHAVE NORMALLY at teatime, for the sake of the children, was not entirely successful. The patch of sticking plaster on David's brow could not be ignored. The other children accepted his assurances that it was the result of an unlucky accident, but David John kept pressing wet kisses on his nose and brow and ears until I finally lured all of them into their barricaded corner with handfuls of biscuits. (Desperate times justify desperate measures.) We were just beginning to settle down when Sethos appeared at the door demanding entrance. He must have been lunching in Luxor, for he was rather foppishly attired in a greenish tweed suit, with a regimental tie to which I felt sure he was not entitled. Beard and hair were now iron-gray and his well-cut features had assumed their normal proportions. The only discordant note was a scowl as formidable as one of Emerson's.

"Good afternoon," I said, admitting him.

Instead of replying, he fixed the scowl on David. "What the devil do you think you're doing?" he demanded.

"You heard?" David inquired mildly.

"Of course I heard. It's all over Luxor, and by tomorrow at the latest it will be all over Cairo that you fomented a riot today. You bloody young fool—"

"Please!" I exclaimed. "The children!"

"He didn't foment a riot, he prevented one," Ramses said, returning the glare with interest. "There were British soldiers present. They heard."

"They heard a 'native' talking Arabic." Sethos threw up his hands. "They didn't understand a word. Nobody is going to believe what the Egyptians tell them. He was already under suspicion—"

"He was trying to save lives," Lia said. She was sitting up very straight and her cheeks were bright pink.

"I don't give a damn what he was trying to do. I've done my best to lull official suspicions, but if he persists in putting his nose in—"

Several persons burst into indignant rebuttal. Emerson's voice was the loudest and the most incoherent. I smiled to myself and remained silent. I had seldom seen Sethos so angry. It was a touching demonstration of concern.

In the lull after the verbal storm a soft voice made itself heard. "I beg your pardon—er—Sethos—"

"You agree with me, Walter." Somewhat surprised, but expecting support, Sethos turned to him. "Tell your impetuous son-in-law to back off."

"No, I will not do that," Walter said.

Having silenced us all by this surprising statement, he went on in the same gentle, hesitant voice. "A man must follow his own conscience. I was wrong when I demanded that David do otherwise. His is a powerful voice for restraint and for peaceful means of protest. I—

er—I believe in his cause and I will support him to the extent of my ability."

"Hmph," Emerson exclaimed. "Well said, Walter."

"Thank you, sir," David murmured. His eyes shone with tears, and so did those of Evelyn.

"Oh, Father." Lia went to him and embraced him.

"Oh, blast." Sethos sat down and loosened his tie. "I didn't intend to start a huge emotional orgy. If anyone cries I shall walk out."

"No one is going to cry," I said, with a stern look at Maryam, who looked as if she was about to. "I am well aware that your anger was caused by your affection for David, but it is somewhat alarming to those who are unaccustomed to the outbursts of temper that characterize the men of the family."

"Quite," said Ramses, still resentful of Sethos's criticism of his friend. "It would be more helpful if you tried to ascertain what started the trouble. You claim to have connections in the highest levels of intelligence. Don't they have informants in the radical movement?"

"Unfortunately we lost our best agents when you and David retired," Sethos said. "Are you suggesting that this disturbance was instigated by outside agitators?"

The compliment was wasted on Ramses. He was not proud of his expertise in deception. "I am telling you that it was. I saw several strangers in the crowd. I thought I recognized one of them—the man who threw the stone. David?"

"I didn't get a good look at him," David admitted. "But I suppose it might have been . . . You mean that fellow François, the boy's bodyguard? But he—"

"He's a Parisian apache," Ramses interrupted. "At least he fights like one. What do you know about him, Maryam?"

She shrank back, her hands fluttering at the throat of her dress. "Nothing. Honestly. He was with the party when I joined them. No one ever told me where he came from. I—I'm afraid of him. I have always been."

"Did he ever—er—bother you?" Emerson asked fiercely.

"Oh, no, nothing like that." His chivalrous indignation on her behalf produced a smile. "I can't believe he would be involved in any cause, he's not that sort of man. Justin is his cause, if you like; he is fanatically protective. But he does hold grudges. Are you sure . . ." She hesitated. "Are you sure he was aiming at David when he threw the stone?"

Her suggestion made a certain amount of sense, which the image of François as a revolutionary did not. If he had been drawn to the scene by curiosity he might well have taken advantage of the opportunity to get back at someone who had injured him—and, even more infuriating to a person of his temperament, defeated him. Ramses admitted he had simply assumed the missile was aimed at David.

"This is unacceptable," I declared. "I would rather have nothing to do with any of them, but if that vicious French person is going around throwing things at people he dislikes, he must be stopped. Good heavens, Emerson, you may be next."

"That would suit me admirably," said Emerson, his sapphirine orbs brightening. "I will just pay a little call on the old lady, and if I should happen to run into François—"

"You will do nothing of the sort, Emerson."

"But, Peabody—"

"I will talk to her, if you like," Maryam said diffidently. "I have been thinking I ought to call on her and see how Justin is getting on. It is the least I can do, after leaving them without notice."

"An admirable sentiment," drawled Sethos. "I will go with you. Perhaps the old lady will allow me to pay my compliments."

"I doubt she will," Maryam said.

She went to get her hat and I took Sethos aside. "Why must you jeer at the girl? She is doing her best, and you are not trying at all to be—er—"

"Fatherly," Sethos supplied, his lips twisting. "I am trying, Amelia, believe it or not."

"You are afraid to allow yourself to care for her."

Sethos caught himself on the verge of a shout. He glanced over his shoulder at the others and said through tight lips, "Don't do that, Amelia. I am sufficiently aware of my motives and feelings. I don't need you to explain them to me."

It was probably not a good time to mention the principles of psychology. I contented myself with a forgiving smile, and after a moment he said irritably, "Very well. I will take her to dinner in Luxor, how's that? I had intended to dine with your friend Mrs. Fisher, who knows every lady in the area, but I will send regrets."

"That would be very nice," I said.

Immediately after dinner Emerson went to his study, ostensibly to "set the rest of you a good example" by bringing his excavation diary up-to-date. The others also retired, though probably not with any intention of emulating Emerson. David's courageous act and Walter's unexpected commendation had brought a renewed awareness of that affection which is too often taken for granted; as Walter led his wife to the waiting carriage she clung to his arm and there was the old firmness in his stride. When I returned to the sitting room after seeing them off, Lia and David had already gone and Ramses was on his feet.

"We will say good night too, Mother," he said.

"Are you sure you wouldn't like another cup of coffee?" I suggested. "Or a little chat?"

"He needs to rest," Nefret said, taking the hand Ramses offered and rising. "He's had rather a long day. Good—"

"Indeed he has. I feel obliged to remark, Ramses, that in giving David his well-deserved praise, we slighted you. You saved David from serious injury and risked yourself, as you have always done, for the sake of friendship and the cause of—"

"Don't make a speech, Mother." He was laughing, though, and he bent his head to give me an affectionate kiss on the cheek. "You'd have done the same, and probably more effectively. One glimpse of that parasol and the mob would have fled, screaming. Oh, I almost forgot. I translated a few pages of that papyrus for you. They are on your desk."

"Thank you, dear boy. Nefret, how is Selim getting—"

"I will look in on him before we go to bed," said Nefret fondly but firmly. "Good night, Mother."

I did not feel it necessary to wait up for Maryam; it just so happened that I was sitting on the veranda, enjoying the peace of the quiet night, when they returned.

"Good evening, Amelia," Sethos said, helping his daughter out of the carriage. "Since you have waited up, like a conscientious chaperone, I will not stay. Good night, Maryam."

Maryam would have gone on her way through the garden had I not opened the door in a pointed manner. "Sit down for a moment," I said pleasantly. "Did you enjoy your dinner with your father?"

"Yes, it was very nice." My expectant silence evoked additional comment. "I didn't realize he was so popular. A number of people stopped to talk to him. A friend of yours—Mrs. Fisher, I believe—sent her best wishes."

"After extracting an introduction to you, I expect. Newcomers to Luxor are always of interest. Did she remember having met you some years ago, when you were here with your husband?"

"Did I meet her? I don't recall. It was a long time ago, and I have changed a great deal since then."

The door to the house opened and Emerson peered out. "What are you doing out here? It is time for . . . Oh. Er. Hullo, Maryam. Did you have a nice evening?"

"Yes, sir, thank you."

"What about that scoundrel François?" Emerson inquired. "Did you see him?"

"Yes, sir, I did. Mrs. Fitzroyce called him to the saloon after I told her about the stone-throwing. He . . . I . . ."

"Don't stutter, child," Emerson said kindly. "He denied it, I suppose."

"No, sir, he didn't." She raised her eyes to his face. "He said terrible things, about Ramses and you. He hates you."

"Not to worry," said Emerson cheerfully. "If he shows his face round here I will deal with him."

"He won't. She spoke to him very sternly—threatened him with dismissal if he did anything like that again. That is the worst punishment he could receive, to be separated from Justin."

"Nevertheless, we will watch out for him," I declared.

"It won't be for long," Maryam said. "They are leaving for Cairo in a few days. Justin has been unwell."

■ ■ ■

EMERSON HAD HOPED TO FIND an excuse to fight with François, but the next two days passed without a sign of him, or of any other trouble. The treasure was packed and ready to go, except for the items I had decided to leave, so I soothed Emerson by returning his staff to him and allowing him to get on with his excavations. The discovery of several nice votive statues and stelae which had been overlooked by earlier diggers enabled him to ascribe one group of broken-down foundations to an Eighteenth Dynasty shrine, and Bertie finished his plan of the Amenhotep I temple. While digging out the cellar of a house in the village Ramses came across another collection of ostraca. He translated one of the most interesting for us over luncheon one day.

"It falls into the category of what might be called Letters to the Dead," he explained. "This appears to be written by a widower to his deceased wife. 'To the excellent equipped spirit Baketamon: What have I done to you that you have caused evil to come to me? I took you as wife, I did not put you away, I brought many good things to you, and when you sickened I caused the chief physician to come to you; I wrapped you in fine linen and gave you a good burial, and since that time I have not known another woman, though it is right that a man like myself should do so. Yet you torment me and bring evil upon me!'"

"Does he say what sort of evil?" Nefret inquired, her arms clasped round her raised knees.

"No. Presumably he had a streak of bad luck."

"And blamed it on her," Lia said with a little laugh. "Don't say it, Aunt Amelia."

" 'Just like a man,' you mean? Persons of both genders and all cultures fall into that error," I admitted generously. "It is comforting to ascribe misfortune to demonic influence, since one may hope to avert it by magical means instead of being forced to accept it as inevitable."

"Or as one's own fault," Lia said. "It does seem to me that he wouldn't have picked on her—poor dead woman—unless he knew he had done something to deserve her anger. Not that he would admit it."

"He couldn't," Ramses said, placing the fragment carefully in a padded tray. "He says he's going to file a complaint against her in the Tribunal of the Gods. This is a formal appeal—a legal document, in a sense."

"Like taking the Fifth Amendment in American law," Bertie said with a grin. "One wouldn't expect him to testify against himself."

Emerson, who had listened with only half an ear, ordered everyone back to work.

Sifting rubbish does not require one's full attention if one is as experienced as I. The Reader will no doubt anticipate the tenor of my wandering thoughts. Less perceptive individuals might have been reassured by the relative peace of those days, without a single incident that could be viewed as hostile. To me, it was highly suspicious—the calm before the storm, the lull before the battle. Something was brewing, I felt it in my very bones. But though I had gone over and over the facts we knew, the pattern yet eluded me.

Having been left one evening with no one to talk to, I went to my own little study. The weary workers had dispersed, Walter and Evelyn to the Castle and the others to their rooms, and Emerson to his own office. My desk was piled high with work in progress, including my own excavation notes, but I was diverted by three sheets of paper covered with Ramses's emphatic scrawl. It was the translation of part of Walter's horoscope papyrus he had promised me; I hadn't had a chance to look at it before.

It began with that memorable entry concerning "the children of the storm." Memorable and seemingly significant, but as I glanced through the remainder of the pages I found nothing of interest. "It is the day of Horus fighting with Set" was followed by "It is the day of peace between Horus and Set." Not surprisingly, the first was designated as "very unfavorable," and the second as "very favorable." Neither could reasonably be said to have any bearing on our situation.

After all, what had I expected? Deciphering Ramses's handwriting always gave me a headache. I put the pages aside. Under them was one of my lists—the names of the women with whom Ramses had been involved. Guiltily, I wondered if he had seen it. He had. At the bottom of the page was another entry in that same emphatic scrawl. "Shame on you, Mother."

I began idly sketching on a blank sheet of paper. I do not draw well, but I had learned the rudiments, as all archaeologists must, and I had found this mechanical operation to be conducive to thought. When the hands are busy the mind is free to wander at will. Never before had I been at such a loss to find a solution to a criminal case.

I drew a rather nice little jar and added a few elements of decoration—lotus blooms, a hieroglyphic bird or two, a winged scarab. They reminded me of the jewelry with which we had bedecked ourselves. Vanity is a sin, but I had enjoyed it as much as the others! I tried, without great success, to sketch the horned ram of Amon which had rested with such heavy import on my breast. It was one of the simpler ornaments, despite the complexity of the beautifully sculpted animal; much Egyptian jewelry is made up of many different elements, like the pectoral that had been stolen, with its central scarab and row of lotus blossoms below and the two flanking cobras. I drew them and added nice little white crowns to their heads; and as my pencil moved randomly across the paper, my mind moved as randomly, mentally fingering the disparate elements of the pattern we had attempted to establish, arranging them and rearranging them. Had not Abdullah assured me the pattern was there? I was inclined to believe I had really heard his voice that day, for it was like Abdullah to throw out a tantalizing, equivocal statement instead of giving me a direct answer. "You are at the beginning . . ."

My fingers clenched so tightly on the pencil that the point broke off. "That too is part of the pattern," he had said once before, when we talked of his elevation to the role of sheikh. And his tomb was the beginning . . . I stared at the uncompleted sketch of the pectoral, and I knew there was one pattern we had not considered—and one avenue of information we had not explored.

Inspired and revived, I sprang to my feet and hastened out of the house.

My peremptory knocking went unanswered for some time, but I persevered. Not until Ramses himself opened the door did I realize how late was the hour.

"Oh dear," I said. "Did I wake you?"

"I wasn't asleep." He tied the belt of his robe and ran his hand over his tumbled curls. "What's wrong? Come in and tell me."

"No, no. I am sorry to have disturbed you. I have only a single question."

When I asked it, his drowsy eyes opened wide and his jaw dropped. "I don't remember. Why on earth—"

"You had heard the name of the place, though?"

"I may have done. Father might know. Have you asked him?"

"I prefer not to mention the subject to your father. Try to remember. I could telegraph Thomas Russell, but time is of the essence."

He shook his head. "It's been several years, and I don't understand why—"

"Ah well, perhaps it will come to you in the night, when your mind is on something else," I said helpfully. "That is how memory works. Do not hesitate to come to me immediately, whatever the hour."

He was wide awake now, but he had learned not to persist in questions I had no intention of answering. His lips curved in an expression that might have betokened amusement, though I rather doubted it.

"I wouldn't want to wake you, Mother. Or disturb you when your mind is on something else."

"Don't worry about that, my dear. I am a light sleeper."

"If you say so. Come, I'll walk you back to the house," Ramses said, stifling a yawn.

"No, thank you, my dear. You ought not go out of doors barefoot, and by the time you found your shoes you might wake Nefret."

"She's awake. Am I to take it that you don't want me to mention the subject to her either? See here, Mother—"

"Until later, then," I said, and got away before he could object.

Most of the lanterns along the path had burned out. The area seemed much darker now than it had when, sped by the wings of discovery, I had traversed it earlier. Something larger than a mouse or a shrew rustled in the shrubbery. I knew it was probably one of the cats, but I am not ashamed to confess that I moved as fast as I dared.

It was somewhere around three in the morning when I was aroused by a scratching at the window. Emerson did not stir; he can sleep through a thunderstorm. I made sure my nightdress was modestly buttoned before I went to the window and leaned out. We always kept a lamp burning in the courtyard. By its light I recognized the tall form of my son. His posture and the tilt of his head indicated a certain degree of vexation.

"You have remembered?" I whispered.

"Yes. It came to me," Ramses added in an expressionless murmur, "when I was thinking of something else. The place is about thirty miles south of here, on the West Bank. I presume there is no point in asking you why—"

"You will learn the answer tomorrow. I want you to come with me. And don't tell your father."

"Or Nefret?"

"No."

I glanced over my shoulder. Emerson had turned over and was muttering to himself. When he reaches for me and I am not there he becomes agitated. "I will make the necessary arrangements," I hissed. "Go now, your father is stirring."

Emerson sat up. "Peabody!" he shouted. Ramses vanished into the darkness.

GETTING AWAY WITHOUT EMERSON'S KNOWLEDGE was not easy, but I managed it by telling him he could have Lia and David with him that day.

Emerson said, "Ramses—" and I said, "He promised to finish a translation for me this morning. We will be along later."

Emerson wisely decided to take what he could get, and swept Lia and David out of the house as soon as they had finished breakfast, for fear I would change my mind. Nefret and Maryam were not at the breakfast table. I assumed the former was with a patient and at that moment I did not care where Maryam had got to, as long as she was not in my way. Like me, Ramses was attired as he would have been for a day at the excavation, so we did not have to delay to change. As we left the house I selected a particularly sturdy parasol.

I had not seen the train station since the explosion and was surprised to find so little damage. Business was going on as usual. We were recognized, of course, and had to answer a number of friendly questions and listen to the latest gossip. The train was an hour late, which was not unusual. It was a local, with only second- and third-class carriages; as Ramses helped me into one of the former, I saw a familiar form on the platform. Catching my eye, Dr. Khattab swept off his fez, placed a fat hand on his embroidered waistcoat, and bowed. I concluded he must be meeting someone, since he did not board the train.

The aged carriage jolted and clanked along the rails and a fine sandy dust blew in through the open window. Ramses put a steadying arm round me and offered me a handkerchief.

"You didn't bring your knife," I said.

"Are you expecting trouble? You might have mentioned it."

"I do not expect it, but I believe in being prepared. Never mind, I have my belt of tools and my parasol."

"That should suffice," Ramses agreed. "You told everyone who asked where we were going."

"I also left a message for your father. Should we fail to return—"

"Damn it, Mother!" The train hit a bump. I bounced, and he tightened his grip. "I beg your pardon. Are you going to confide in me now?"

In the cold light of morning my brilliant inspiration did not shine as brightly. I rather regretted wasting an entire day on a far-fetched idea—and bouncing up and down on the hard seat was cursed uncomfortable. "It will all be made clear to you at the proper time," I said, hoping it would be made clear to me as well.

Ramses said another bad word. This time he did not apologize.

■   ■   ■

FROM A DISTANCE THE VILLAGE looked quite picturesque, set in a grove of palm trees, with a pretty little minaret poking up through the branches. Experience had taught me that close up the effect was less picturesque than nasty, and as we approached, the village looked no different from dozens of others I had seen: the same flat-roofed, plastered mud-brick houses; the same chickens and pigeons pecking at the dirt under the trees; the same pack of children dashing toward us with outstretched hands, asking for baksheesh; the same black-clad women pausing in their work of grinding grain or kneading bread to stare curiously at us.

However, as the small predators gathered round, I noticed that their half-clad (or unclad) bodies were healthily rounded and their eyes free of infection. Even the dogs skulking behind us were not so lean as most. There were other signs of prosperity: rows of gracefully shaped water jars baking in the sun outside the potter's house, several webs of woof threads stretched between the trunks of palm trees, with busy weavers at work. I left Ramses to deal with the predators, which he did by promising baksheesh, much baksheesh, if they would take us to the house of the man we sought.

Before we had gone far along the narrow lane we saw a man hurrying toward us, his hands outstretched, his face wearing a happy smile, as if he were coming to greet old friends. He was young and well-set-up, though running a trifle to fat.

"God's blessing be upon you, Brother of Demons!" he cried and threw his arms round Ramses. "Welcome. How good it is to greet you again!"

"Greetings to you, Musa," said Ramses, freeing himself with a rather peremptory shove. "This is—"

"Ah, but who would not know the Sitt Hakim!" The fellow flopped down onto the ground and kissed my dusty boots. "It is an honor. My lord has heard of your coming, he eagerly awaits you."

He dismissed our youthful entourage with a few words, and to my surprise they dispersed without argument. The house to which he led us was built of stone—probably pilfered from ancient monuments—and surrounded by trees and a nice little garden. In the mandarah, the principal reception room, a pleasant chamber furnished with low tables and a cushioned divan, el-Gharbi was waiting.

I had heard of him many times, but this was the first time I had set eyes on him. Instead of the women's robes and jewels he had once affected, he wore a simple caftan of blue silk and a matching turban, but his round black face was carefully painted. Kohl outlined his eyes, and lips and cheeks were reddened with henna. A sweet, pervasive aura of perfume wafted round him.

"Don't get up," I said, watching in some alarm as he writhed and wriggled.

I had spoken English. He understood, but he replied in Arabic. "The Sitt Hakim is gracious. Alas, I am old and even fatter than I once was." He clapped his hands, and Musa trotted off. "Be seated, please," the procurer went on. "We will drink tea together. You honor me by your presence, you and your illustrious son. Beautiful as ever, I see."

He leered amiably, not at me, but at Ramses, who replied equably, "And you are flourishing as ever. The village seems prosperous."

El-Gharbi rolled his eyes and looked pious. "I cannot see children go hungry and the old and sick left to die. I have helped—yes, I have helped a little. One must make one's peace with God before the end, and atone for one's sins."

Neither of us was rude enough to say that he had quite a list for which to atone, but he must have known what we were both thinking. His black eyes twinkled and his large body shook with silent laughter. "Is it not written, 'Whoever performs good works and believes, man or woman, shall enter into Paradise'?"

The quotation was correct, and his was not the only faith that implies there is salvation for a repentant sinner. At least the Koran demanded good works instead of a desperate, last-second mumble of belief.

Musa returned with several servants carrying trays. They were all men, all young, and all quite handsome. Tea was handed round and fresh-baked bread offered, while el-Gharbi carried on a polite conversation. "And your lovely wife is well? May God protect her. And the Father of Curses? Ah, how kind he was to me. The motorcar I—er—

procured for him several years ago was satisfactory, I presume? And the forged papers? I was so happy to do those small services for him. May God protect him!"

The whole performance had a certain element of parody, but it would not have been courteous to interrupt. Finally he gave me my opening by asking us to stay and dine that evening. "Musa will show you the village. You will admire it, I think."

"You are most kind, but I fear we cannot stay," I said. "We must be back in Luxor tonight. I came only to ask you a question."

"One question? All this way for a single question?" He put his fat hands on his knees and nodded benignly. "I live only to serve you, Sitt Hakim. What would you ask?"

Now that the moment had come, I had to force myself to speak. Ramses was watching me intently, and so was the procurer.

"You sent us a warning once," I said. "You said, if I remember correctly, that the young serpent . . . er . . ."

"Also had poisoned fangs. I remember, Sitt. I hope the warning came in time."

"That remains to be seen," I said, avoiding the astonished gaze of my son. "She is staying with us now. I have no reason to believe she means us harm, but I must know what prompted your words. Her marriage to the American gentleman ended badly, and she is—"

"Marriage? American?" His eyes widened until the kohl rimming them cracked.

"You must have known of it," I said. "You are reputed to know everything."

"I knew. But, Sitt Hakim, it was not that one I meant. It was the other one."

CHAPTER TWELVE

Nefret did not learn of her husband's deception—as she viewed it—until midday, when her father-in-law burst into the surgery. The patient was a woman, whom Nefret was treating for a breast lesion. She let out a squawk of offended modesty, and Emerson backed out as quickly as he had entered. "How much longer will you be?" he shouted from the next room.

"Not long." She sent the woman away with a little pot of ointment and went into the waiting room. Emerson was stamping up and down, swearing.

"Read this." He thrust a crumpled paper at her. None of the chairs in the waiting room was occupied; if there had been other patients, they had beat a hasty retreat. "No man dares face the wrath of the Father of Curses."

Wrathful he was, blue eyes snapping, teeth bared. "Well?" he demanded. "Do you know anything about this?"

Nefret's own anger rose as she read the brief message. "'Ramses and I have gone off on a little expedition. We will be back this evening. In the event that we have not returned by tomorrow morning you may look for us at a village called El-Hilleh, approximately three miles south of Esna, on the West Bank. I consider this contingency highly unlikely, however. À bientôt, my dear Emerson.'"

"Damn him," Nefret said, closing her fist over the paper.

"Ah," said Emerson, in a less accusatory voice. "They didn't tell you either."

"No. She considers it highly unlikely that they will fail to return, does she? What is this village?"

"The name means nothing to me." Emerson took out his pipe, remembered that she didn't allow it in the clinic, and started for the door. "Let us ask Selim."

"No!" Nefret whipped off her gown and tossed it onto a chair. "I won't have Selim worried. Come outside, Father."

A feathery tamarisk tree gave partial shade to a wooden bench which had been placed there for the accommodation of patients when the waiting room was full. Emerson sat down and filled his pipe. "Now, now, my dear, don't be upset. She does this sort of thing all the time, you know."

"He doesn't. He swore to me he would never go off on his own again." Nefret tucked a stray lock of hair under her cap. Her fingers were shaking.

"He's not alone," Emerson pointed out. "Don't blame Ramses; if I know my wife, and I believe I do, she insisted he keep it a secret."

"He could have refused. There are other loyalties." The knowledge that Ramses was with his mother did not give her the comfort Emerson had intended. "She's as bad as he is," Nefret burst out. "The two of them together . . ."

"Hmmm, well, er." Unable to refute this, Emerson smoked in silence for a few moments. "They must have caught the southbound train. There isn't another until this evening."

"We could take the horses. How far is this place?"

"Over thirty miles. It sounds as if they expect to catch the after-noon train back to Luxor. Hmph. That would give them only a few hours in the cursed place. I wonder what . . ." He shook his head in exasperation. "There is no sense in speculating, or in following them. If the northbound train is on time, they will be on their way back by the time we get there."

"How can you be so complacent? Aren't you angry?"

"I was briefly put out," Emerson admitted. "However, I should be accustomed to Peabody's little tricks. We've played this game for years, each trying to be the first to solve a case. She cheats, you know."

"Then there's nothing we can do but wait," Nefret muttered.

"That's how I see it. I may as well go back to work for a few hours. Let me know if they turn up."

Nisrin put a cautious head out the door. Emerson, who hadn't noticed her before, gave her an affable smile. Emboldened, she ventured out. "Nur Misur, there is a sick one who has come back. And this message."

"From Ramses?" Emerson asked expectantly.

"No." The curving, ornate handwriting was unfamiliar. Nefret ripped the envelope open. "It's from Dr. Khattab—Mrs. Fitzroyce's physician. Justin is ill. He asks if I will have a look at the boy."

"I will go with you."

"That's silly," Nefret said impatiently. "What possible harm could come to me in broad daylight, with hundreds of people around? I'll deal with my patient—it's probably that old hypochondriac Abdulhamid wanting more sugar water—and be back in a few hours."

By the time she set out for Luxor she was in a calmer frame of mind. Ramses couldn't be in serious trouble; she would know, as she had always known, if danger threatened him. She would have a few words to say to him when he got back, though, on the subject of promises broken and trust betrayed; but in a way she didn't blame him. His mother was an elemental force, as hard to resist as a sandstorm.

As Nefret approached the *Isis* she saw signs of unusual activity and deduced that the dahabeeyah was preparing to get underway. The doctor was waiting for her at the head of the gangplank, his hat in his hand. His waistcoat was particularly resplendent, glittering with gold threads. "My dear lady, how good of you to come." He grasped her hand and would have kissed it had she not pulled it away.

"What's wrong with him?" she asked.

"A fever." The broad smile with which he had greeted her was replaced by a worried frown. "I have tried without result to bring it down. Our departure is imminent, as you have no doubt observed, but it will take several days to reach Cairo, and my mistress wants to be sure all possible ways of relieving the boy are taken before—"

She cut him off. "Then let's not waste time talking. Take me to him."

"To be sure. Follow me."

He indicated the shadowy passage that led between the cabins to the saloon. The doors lining it were closed, so that the only light came from the open entrance through which they had come.

"After you," said the doctor, bowing. "It is the last door on the right."

His vast shadow enveloped her, and a hand took her by the elbow as if to guide her steps. He was close behind her, she could hear his quick breathing, and she stopped, resisting the pressure on her arm, seized with sudden panic. Too late. His arm gripped her, pinning her arms, and his hand clamped over her mouth. She struggled, but he had her in a hold that was impossible to break, the great bulk of his body as impervious to blows as a feather bed, the big fat hand covering half her face. She kicked back. Pain shot up her ankle as her heel slammed into his shin, and with a grunt of annoyance he pinched her nose shut, cutting off the last of her breath. Her darkening vision swam with purple and green lights and her legs gave way. When he took his hand from her face she could only gasp, sucking in air, while he opened one of the doors and pushed her into the room beyond. She fell to hands and knees. The door slammed, leaving her in total darkness.

Nefret rolled over onto her back and lay still for a time, getting her breath back and trying, not so successfully, to get her thoughts in order. She had made a bad mistake, but that didn't matter now. What mattered was what they meant to do with her—and how she could prevent it.

A wry smile touched her bruised lips. She had found her mother-in-law's gang, and by the method favored by that estimable lady. How many of them were involved? The entire crew, almost certainly; the doctor couldn't take her captive without their knowledge. It was possible that the boy and his grandmother were unwitting dupes, used by a group of criminals for their own purpose. Neither of them was mentally competent. Maryam was not incompetent, though, and she was her mother's daughter.

The floor under her vibrated more strongly as the beat of the engines increased. Khattab hadn't lied about that. The boat was getting underway. She started to stand up, and then made herself remain on her knees. She had no idea how large the room was, how high the ceiling. The blackness was palpable, she could almost feel it pressing against her eyeballs, her face, her body. The air was hot and close with a strange metallic tang. Fighting the temptation to close her eyes and curl up into a fetal position, she edged forward, arms extended.

She had found a wall and was following it, trying to get some idea of the dimensions of her prison, when the door was flung open. Even that much light was welcome after the claustrophobic darkness, but she couldn't see much, for the opening was blocked by several bodies. The doctor's familiar, hateful voice said, "A companion for you, my dear lady, and a patient as well."

Justin, was her first thought. But there were two men carrying the limp body. They dropped it unceremoniously onto the floor and backed away as Nefret flung herself down beside Emerson, sinking her teeth into her lower lip to keep from crying out. His eyes were closed and one side of his face was smeared with blood.

"Bastards," she gasped. "What have you done to him?"

"Such language from a lady," the doctor said with a high-pitched giggle. "I regret the necessity, but he is as hard to stop as a charging elephant. I don't believe he is seriously injured. Take care of him."

"Wait," Nefret said desperately. The door was closing. "I need light—water—my medical bag . . ."

"You surely don't expect me to hand over that bag with its nice little collection of scalpels and probes." Another giggle. God, she thought, the man is as mad as Justin. Madder. He's reveling in this.

"Please," she whispered.

"I suppose I could leave you a lamp," the doctor conceded. "There is water here. You will have to manage with that until we can make other arrangements. We weren't expecting him, you see."

He issued a low-voiced order in Arabic. One of the men put the lamp down on the floor. The door closed.

Nefret looked wildly round the room. There was a jar, presumably containing water, in one of the corners she had not reached in her blind exploration, and a crude clay cup next to it. She didn't look for anything else. Splashing water into the cup, she wet her handkerchief and went back to Emerson.

"Father. Father, please say something," she whispered.

The blood came from a single cut, which had bled profusely, as scalp wounds do. Her fingers probed the spot, finding only a rising lump. Anxiety hardened her touch, and Emerson stirred.

"Hell and damnation," he remarked.

"It's me, Father." She heard herself laugh, as insane a sound as the doctor's. "Oh, Father, are you all right?"

"I am," said Emerson, flat on his back and scowling like a gargoyle, "a bloody fool. Rushing in where angels fear to tread. Peabody will never let me hear the end of this. Nefret, my dear, are you crying? Don't cry. I can't stand it when you cry. Did they hurt you?"

"No. I'm sorry, Father, I'm just so relieved that you aren't . . ."

"Takes more than a bump on the head to kill me," said Emerson with satisfaction. "I am the one who should apologize. I walked right into it, like a rabbit into a snare, and now they've got both of us. What sort of place is this? Let's have a look."

"Don't move yet." Her handkerchief was saturated. She threw it aside and began unbuttoning her blouse.

"Time to tear up some extraneous garment or other," said Emerson coolly. "Not your garments, though, your mother would not approve. My shirt. It's too cursed hot in here anyhow."

She bandaged the cut, but Emerson refused a drink. "Better not. It may be drugged. Let us see what we have here."

He got to his feet, steadying himself with a hand on the wall as the boat dipped. "They were prepared for you," he said, looking round. "Or for someone. This isn't a stateroom, it's a prison."

The small room had been stripped of all furnishings except a piece of matting, six feet long and several feet wide, the water jar, and another, larger vessel. The windows were covered with heavy boards. The nailheads, fresh and unrusted, shone in the light.

"They might have left an airhole," said Emerson, running his hands over the boards. "Have you anything we could use to prize up these nails?"

Nefret shook her head. Emerson unfastened his belt. "Not strong enough," he said, examining the buckle. "But we may as well give it a try. Tell me what happened. Did you see the boy or the old lady?"

"No." She knew what he was doing—keeping her mind active and her hopes up, and, at the same time, searching for some clue that would help them. "The damned doctor met me and brought me straight here. Justin and Mrs. Fitzroyce may not know what is going on, but Maryam must. The attacks on her are the extraneous parts of the pattern. They were staged. She stabbed poor Melusine herself, with a heavy needle or a nail."

"Hmmm." The metal rasped like a file as he dug away the wood around one of the nailheads. "But what about the second appearance of Hathor?"

"Perhaps she hired some local girl to play the part. That incident was designed to provide her with an unbreakable alibi." Nefret sat down cross-legged on the mat. There was nothing she could do but watch, and as her eyes moved over the impressive form of her father-in-law her spirits lifted. It did take more than a knock on the head to kill Emerson, or discompose him for long. He began to hum under his breath. She recognized the melody, though it was horribly off-key. " 'She never saw the streets of Cairo; she never saw the kutchy-kutchy . . . ' Curse it," said Emerson. He tossed the broken buckle aside and sat down beside her.

Nefret wrapped both hands around his upper arm and laid her cheek against his shoulder. "I'm not glad you're here, Father, but there's only one other man on earth I'd rather have with me."

"Well, now," said Emerson self-consciously. "Not my ingenious brother?"

"He's good," Nefret conceded. "But he's not you. Or Ramses."

"He's charming, though," Emerson said gloomily. "I'm not."

"I think you are."

"Your mother doesn't."

"Father, that's not true." She squeezed his arm, comforted by the feel of the hard muscles under her hands and by his monumental calm.

"I've been behaving like a boor," Emerson muttered. "Ever since he arrived. He brings out the worst in me. And rouses the direst of suspicions."

At first she thought he was referring to his long-held jealousy of his brother. Then she let out a gasp. "He can't be a party to this."

"I wish I could be sure. Nefret, that little girl cannot have planned this business, it's too devilish and too complex. There's someone else behind it, and some motive stronger than revenge for a long-past death."

"What?"

"It is a fatal error," said Emerson, obviously quoting, "to speculate without sufficient data. We've quite a bit of data, though. Speculation helps pass the time."

"Is that what you and Mother do when you're shut up in a place like this?"

"Generally we argue about whose fault it was." Emerson chuckled as if he didn't have a care in the world. "Come, my dear girl, think. What motive leaps to mind where Sethos is concerned? What was he doing in Jerusalem? Not working for the War Office, Smith made that clear. Someone gave him a beating, which I do not doubt he well deserved—because he had tried to interfere with their business arrangements? Since the war, Palestine and Syria have become a paradise for looters and tomb robbers. What is in that room at the Castle, neatly packed and ready to be transported?"

It hit her like a blow in the stomach. "The treasure. Good Lord! No, I don't believe it."

"Lacau will arrive tomorrow and load the cases onto the steamer," Emerson said, inexorably logical. "It won't take him long. He'll go straight back to Cairo. The *Isis* is a modern vessel with a large crew—easily large enough to overpower the guards on the government steamer and unload the cargo. There is unrest in Egypt because of the arrival of the Milner Commission. The theft of the treasure will be put down to radicals."

"They'll have to kill the witnesses," she said numbly. "And sink the steamer."

"Not necessarily. Sethos is not a violent man. But there is no one better equipped to get a load like that into the marketplace."

The lamplight flickered. Their shadows rushed back and forth, as if frantic to escape. She felt his lips brush her hair, and then he gently detached her hands and got to his feet. "If Sethos is the ringleader, you've nothing to fear. He wouldn't harm you. Better get hold of that lamp before it falls over. We are picking up speed."

The motion of the ship was more pronounced. Emerson began going through his pockets. "Went off without my coat," he said, removing a handful of motley objects and inspecting them. "No pipe, no tobacco—and no matches."

"No gun, no knife," said Nefret, trying to emulate his coolness.

"They overlooked these." Emerson picked half a dozen nails out of the mess and shoved the rest of it back in his trouser pocket. "Did they search you?"

It came back to her then, the sensation of hands moving over her body. Big, fat hands. She grimaced. "Superficially. He was looking for a weapon. I didn't have one."

"Take these." Emerson handed her three of the nails. "And hide them. Not in your pocket; they may decide to search you again." He went back to the window and began scraping. "That fellow spoke of other arrangements," he said over his shoulder. "If they separate us—"

"Oh, no," Nefret whispered.

"If that happens . . . Well, my dear, a nail isn't much of a weapon, but a sharp jab in the region of a man's kidneys, or—er—elsewhere, will certainly give him pause. Not to worry; I'll get you out of this somehow. It's my fault. If I hadn't been such a bloody idiot, there would be help on the way now."

Nefret took a deep breath and steadied herself and her voice. "If you're a bloody idiot, so am I. I ought to have suspected something when he brought me here."

"Could you have done anything if you had?" Emerson inquired reasonably.

"Maybe not. He's as strong as a bull, and even if I could have overpowered him, I'd have had to evade the crewmen. They must be in on this."

"No doubt about that. Three of the bastards jumped me as soon as I was on board. Admittedly, my demeanor was not that of a gentleman paying a social call."

Nefret hugged her knees and laughed, picturing him charging up the gangplank, fists clenched, shouting out accusations. "Stop blaming yourself. If you had delayed to get help, the boat would probably have sailed. Why did you come after me?"

Emerson went on chipping. "Well, you see, it suddenly came to me. When I was thinking of something else. I remembered who it was who lived in El-Hilleh, and why it— Damnation. Shove those things out of sight and come here."

There was only time to push the nails into the tops of her shoes before the key turned in the lock and the door opened a crack.

"Stand back," the doctor said. He sounded nervous. "I have a gun."

"Very nice," Emerson said. He stood in front of Nefret, seemingly relaxed, but she had seen him, and his son, in that pose before. They could both move with the speed of a charging lion.

"We all have guns."

Someone pulled the door back. The opening looked like the entrance to the infernal regions, blocked by hulking bodies and redly lit.

"Don't risk it, Father," Nefret whispered, taking hold of his arm. She knew Emerson's temper only too well and as her eyes adjusted to the light she saw that there were at least three of them in addition to the doctor.

"Hmph." Emerson settled back on his heels. "They're bound to hit something in this confined space. Might be you."

The doctor took a step forward and then thought better of it. Obeying his curt order, two of the men edged cautiously into the room. Both held pistols and one carried a lantern. The doctor remained where he was.

335

"Leading your regiment from behind, I see," remarked Emerson. "Now what?"

"Move forward. Slowly. One step at a time. Hold out your hands. No, madame, not you. Remain where you are."

His voice shook, and so did the hand that held the pistol. There was nothing for it but to obey. The odds were too great and they were both weaponless. Emerson shrugged.

"You should have done this before you tossed me in here," he pointed out, as one of the men fastened a pair of handcuffs over his wrists. "Saved yourself all this fuss and worry. Poor planning. Who's in charge here anyhow?"

"I hate talk like that!" The doctor's voice rose into falsetto. His lips drew back. "I hate you damned British, with your supercilious sneers and your superior airs! How dare you condescend to me? How dare you look at me that way? Don't look at me that way!"

His hand lashed out. The barrel of the gun caught Emerson across the face. He fell back against the wall, his knees buckling.

"Please," Nefret said. "Please don't hurt him again." Her hands were clenched, her nails digging into her palms, but if the man wanted her to beg, she would.

"You have better sense than he," the doctor muttered. "You two, get him out of here."

The men he indicated exchanged dubious looks. Coming within arm's reach of an angry Father of Curses, even when he was barely able to stay on his feet, was not a job a sensible man relished. One of them got up sufficient nerve to grip Emerson's left arm. The other jabbed the gun into his ribs.

"Go with them, Father," Nefret said. "There's no use resisting."

Emerson raised his hands and wiped blood off his chin. "I wasn't resisting," he said in an injured voice. "Meek as a lamb."

"Out!" The doctor shrieked. "Take him out of here!"

Emerson submitted without further comment to being led toward the door. I can't let him go like this, without a word, Nefret thought. I may never see him again. To hell with stiff upper lips.

"Father, I—"

"Yes, my dear, I know." He gave her a quick glance over his shoulder and smiled. "À bientôt."

That said it all, really. Not good-bye. See you soon. "À bientôt," Nefret said.

⋙⋘

EL-GHARBI BADE US FAREWELL with unconcealed glee. We were deeply in his debt now, and I knew it was only a matter of time before we received a demand, couched as an obsequious request, for recompense. We cut his courtesies short and hurried away. I did not want to miss the train. Trains are always late when one is on time, and on time when one is late. I kept telling myself there was no need for haste but I failed to convince myself. Our discovery had altered the entire picture.

We arrived at the station at Esna in ample time. The train *was* late. There were only a few English persons on the platform—students, to judge by their youth and their casual clothing. The vendors of fake antiquities identified us at a glance (those who did not know Ramses personally recognized my parasol and my belt of tools) and left us alone. Other merchants were selling water, fruit, and vegetables. I took a seat on the single bench, next to a gray-bearded gentleman holding a rooster. The gentleman bared a mouthful of brown teeth and greeted me effusively. The rooster cocked its head and gave me a hot, mad glare. Ramses paced up and down, circling groups of squatting Egyptians who were accustomed to such delays and who whiled away the time nibbling on sweetmeats and gossiping. I too was accustomed to such delays, but as the sun sank into the west and the shadows lengthened, the knowledge we had gained that day lay more and more heavily on my shoulders.

The rooster stretched out its neck and gave me a sharp peck on the arm. I accepted the apologies of its owner but I could no longer sit still. Rising, I joined Ramses, who had stopped to chat with a small party consisting of a man and a woman and a babe in arms. The young mother was unconcernedly suckling her infant, while her husband talked with Ramses and scratched his stomach.

"Are you hungry, Mother?" he asked. "They have kindly offered to share their dinner."

The man fished a chunk of gray bread out of the basket beside him and offered it to me. His hand and the bread were both extremely dirty, and I felt sure he was covered with fleas, but his generosity and his smile were so gracious that I would have taken the bread, and my chances with fleas and disease, had I not suspected that there was not much food in the basket. They were very young and their garments were threadbare.

I explained in my best Arabic that I thanked them for their kindness, but that I had just eaten, and drew Ramses away.

"Can you give them some money?" I whispered. "Without offending them?"

"Poverty does not allow a man the luxury of pride," said Ramses, with a twist of his lips. "I will take care of it, but if I start handing out baksheesh openly, everyone else will ask."

The train tracks stretched emptily into the distance, shining in the sunset. "Curse it," I burst out. "Where is the cursed train? We are going to be very late, and your father will be fuming."

"So will Nefret. But they will forgive us—inshallah!—when they hear. Mother, we're within a few hours of ending this business. Be patient."

"Emerson will be knocked into a cocked hat," I agreed, not without a certain relish.

Ramses's face relaxed. "I don't think you mean that, Mother."

"It is the wrong expression? I am endeavoring to improve my command of current idiom," I explained. "Some of the new slang words are extremely expressive. Never mind, you know what I meant."

"Quite." A pigeon flapped between my feet, and he took my arm. "I was knocked for a loop too. Who could have suspected that Bertha had two children?"

"The children of the storm," I mused. "Is it only an odd coincidence that Set was the god of storm and chaos?"

"Yes," Ramses said curtly.

"Quite. I believe you have never known me to succumb to— Oh, thank heaven, there is the train at last."

FROM MANUSCRIPT H

Nefret had wrapped a bit of cloth round the head of the nail. It served as some protection, but her fingers kept cramping. The wood was soft. She had scraped away enough to expose a half-inch length of the shaft. It moved a bit when she tried to wriggle it, but it was too deeply sunk to be pulled out with her fingers and she had nothing to use as a lever.

The lamp had long since expired. It seemed long, but there was no way of measuring time in the stifling darkness. Her throat was dry and the slosh of water in the invisible jar was a constant temptation.

She knew now that she wouldn't break down. Being with one of the Emerson men—and at least one of the women—even briefly, was like a shot of adrenaline for a faltering heart. She couldn't imagine what Emerson could do, but he had promised he would get her out of this and against all reason she believed him.

The others wouldn't be idle, but it might take them a while to put two and two together—her absence and that of Emerson, the departure of the *Isis*. At least they knew where she had gone; Nisrin would tell them. Emerson might not have bothered to inform anyone. He had come after her as soon as that mysterious memory returned—on the road to Deir el Medina, since he had been only a few minutes behind her.

If they hadn't been interrupted, she would know what it was he had remembered, and why it had sent him rushing after her. If the village of El-Hilleh was the key, Ramses and/or his mother must know too, and if the knowledge was so important they might also be in danger. She thought of her husband, picturing him in her mind—the tall strength of him, the curling black hair he kept trying to flatten, the smile that warmed his lean brown face—reaching out, stretching the mental sense that bound them together. She had always known when he was threatened with death or injury. There was no such feeling now.

She wiped her stinging eyes on her sleeve. Perspiration, not tears, she told herself.

Maryam. It all came back to Maryam. Emerson refused to believe the girl was the one primarily responsible, but that was only because he was soft-hearted and sentimental. Nefret dug viciously into the wood. The nail slipped, digging a long ineffectual gouge, and her numbed fingers lost their grip. She heard the nail hit the floor and bounce. She knelt and felt around for it. No luck.

I'll just rest a little, she thought, slumping against the wall. Rest and try to think. Emerson, soft-hearted and sentimental . . . And jealous. Jealousy was responsible for the case he had constructed against Sethos. It had sounded convincing when he stated it, but the case against Maryam was even stronger. She knew something about disguise, enough to fool a vague old woman and seduce a vain man. Her mother had been deeply involved with the criminal underworld. Bertha had even formed her own group, a criminal organization of women. Enlisting prostitutes had been one of Bertha's brighter ideas; exploited and mistreated, they had unique opportunities to gather information that could be used for blackmail or murder. What had become of those women? Women like Layla, who had in the end turned against her leader and saved Ramses's life; women like the formidable female, strong and sturdy as a man, who had been Bertha's aide-de-camp in several of the latter's crimes.

The stories had become part of family legendry, told and retold, wild as any romance and embroidered with the passage of time. There had been equally preposterous stories about Sethos in his unregenerate days, and about Bertha, who had been Sethos's mistress after she left the man known as Schlange . . . another of the innumerable enemies the parents had encountered . . . what a long list it was . . .

Her head dropped with a jerk, bringing her back to consciousness. Breathing was an effort. Swallowing was impossible. There was no air in the room, only darkness and heat and thirst. She knew she would have to risk a drink soon or fall into a stupor that could end in death. Perhaps that was what they intended. No marks on the body, no signs of violence.

It was impossible to think of oneself as a body, a thing, the thinking mind, the laughter and loving obliterated forever, to imagine the world going on without one. She thought of her children, and anguish wrenched her. But they were so young, so surrounded by loving care; in a few years she would be nothing more to them than a face in a faded photograph. Ramses wouldn't forget, any more than she could ever forget him. But there would be other women. She couldn't expect him to remain celibate forever, not Ramses. He would marry again, if only for the sake of the children.

The thought of him holding another woman in his arms, kissing her upturned face, gave her energy enough to pull herself to her knees. If he does, I'll come back and haunt him, she thought. Like that woman whose husband wrote asking what he had done to offend her, that she continued to torment him after death. Maybe she only wanted to make sure he wouldn't forget her.

She crawled along the wall, feeling for the water jar. Her fumbling hands found it at last—lying on its side in a pool of water. It had cracked when it fell.

She was lying flat, sucking up the tepid liquid, grit and all, when suddenly there was light. She raised herself on her elbows and turned her head. Even those few drops of water had helped, and so did the air, cool and fresh as a night wind by comparison to the noxious mixture she had been breathing. The light was dazzling to eyes long accustomed to darkness. She could see only an outline, standing motionless in the doorway. Then the glow behind it strengthened, shining on a halo of golden curls. She tried to speak, but could only croak like a frog.

"Hello, pretty Mrs. Emerson," said the clear, sweet voice. "Would you like to come out now?"

❧❧

DARKNESS HAD FALLEN BEFORE THE train arrived in Luxor with a series of self-satisfied chugs and congratulatory blasts on the whistle. So they sounded to me, at any rate; I had taken a strong personal dislike to the train, as if it were deliberately dawdling in order to annoy me. I could hardly wait to tell Emerson that I had solved the case.

341

As the car slowed and the platform came into sight I peered out the window, braving the smoke and dust. I fully expected I would see Emerson in the forefront of the waiting passengers, arms akimbo and brow threatening. In vain did I seek that unmistakable form. Someone else had come to meet us, though. Catching sight of me, he waved and began running alongside the car.

"It's David," I said. "I wonder why Emerson sent him instead of coming himself."

Ramses glanced out the window. "He's got something on his mind. I don't like the look of this, Mother. Stay with me."

I followed close on his heels as he shoved and pushed toward the end of the car, so that we were first in line to exit. The train stopped with a shudder. Ramses swung himself out without waiting for the steps to be put in place, and reached up to lift me down.

"Thank God!" David exclaimed. "We hoped you would take this train. I've been waiting for over an hour."

I did not have to ask if something was wrong. The deep lines of anxiety on his face, the hard grip of his hand as he seized mine were signs anyone could read.

"The children," I cried, remembering Abdullah's warning. "Has something—"

"No, they're all right. And will be, I've taken precautions." He didn't stop moving, but went on, almost at a run, toward a waiting cab. I had to trot to keep up, which, you may well believe, Reader, I did.

Ramses said softly, "Nefret?"

David knew better than to try to spare him. "Gone. So are the Professor and Maryam. The *Isis* sailed six hours ago."

Without haste, but with a tighter grip than was strictly necessary, Ramses helped me into the cab. "Six hours ago. What have you done about it?"

David collapsed onto the seat opposite us and waved the driver on. "We didn't realize they were missing until a few hours ago. The Professor had gone back to the house, or so we assumed, but he wasn't there, and—"

The lights of Luxor flashed past, and the carriage jolted alarmingly. "Take it slowly, David," I said. "You are becoming incoherent. And tell the driver to slow down. I believe he is whipping the horse. You know we never permit that."

Ramses said, "Go on, David. Take it in order. Father wasn't at the house . . ."

David's voice rose. "None of you were there! When nobody turned up for tea I thought you might be at the Castle, so I sent Ali to inquire. So much time wasted . . ."

He covered his face with his hands. I jogged his elbow. "Self-recrimination is fruitless, David. I cannot see that you acted irresponsibly. Go on."

David pushed his hat to the back of his head, took a deep breath, and resumed in a calmer voice. "The Vandergelts came, with Mother and Father. They were concerned; said none of you had been there. We started counting heads. That was when we realized Maryam hadn't been seen since last night, nor Nefret since midday. We found the note—your note—in the surgery, so at least we knew where you two had got off to. We had to track Nisrin down, she'd closed the clinic and gone home; it was she who told us Nefret had been sent for by the doctor on the *Isis*. The boy was ill, he said."

Still at full gallop, the horse turned onto the corniche and I fell heavily against Ramses. He put me back onto my seat with hands as cold and hard as ice.

David shouted at the driver and our headlong pace slackened. There was enough traffic on the road to make this expedient; it was still early by Luxor standards, and the tourists who sought pleasure rather than edification, and those who catered to them, were out in full force. The cold white light of electricity shone from the hotels, the mellower glow of candles and lanterns from shops and houses.

"As soon as we learned where Nefret had gone, we crossed to Luxor, Bertie and I. That's when we found out the *Isis* was gone. The vendors and shopkeepers along the street had seen Nefret go on board. She didn't come off."

"And Emerson?" I inquired, straightening my hat.

"You told me to take it in order," David replied. "Are you all right, Aunt Amelia?"

"Perfectly." There was a lump the size of a cannonball in my stomach, and I wanted to scream at him.

"Almost there," David said, glancing out the window. "Well, shortly after Nefret boarded, along came the Professor at a dead run. He went pelting up the gangplank, and that was the last anyone saw of him, or Nefret. A short time later the gangplank was hauled in, and the boat sailed."

"We had been seen visiting the *Isis*," I mused. "The watchers would have no reason to suppose anything was wrong. Which way did it go?"

"We're working on that." The carriage stopped. David jumped out and handed me down. "I'll tell you about it in a minute. Sabir is waiting with his new boat."

Tourist steamers lined the bank, all atwinkle with lights. There was no gap in the line. The *Isis*'s berth had been taken by another boat. When Sabir saw us coming he stood ready to cast off.

"What, then, is the current situation?" I asked, stepping into the boat.

"We decided Bertie should go back to the house to tell the others while I waited for the train. The *Isis* headed downstream, we learned that much; Bertie said he'd telegraph the police at Hammadi and Qena to watch out for her."

Motionless as a statue, his hands clasped, Ramses said, "Useless. All she has to do is pull in to a landing somewhere, dowse her running lights, and make a few alterations under cover of darkness. A new name, another flag at the stern, and she'd be difficult to spot."

David was no more deceived by that cool voice than I was. "Ramses, I'm sorry. I should have—"

"Done what? It wasn't your fault. It wasn't anyone's fault."

When we reached the house it was buzzing like a beehive and shining like a Christmas tree, every lamp alight and—as it appeared—a goodly portion of the population of Gurneh mounting guard. Some were pacing up and down, all were talking, and a few brandished rifles. It was illegal for Egyptians to own them, but the authorities tended to turn a blind eye when the owner was a responsible individual. Though I do not generally approve of firearms, I found the sight comforting.

Evelyn was the first to burst out of the house. She flung her arms around me. "Thank God you are safe, Amelia."

"I was never in danger, my dear," I replied, putting her gently away. "There is no time for that sort of thing now. We must have . . . Ramses, where are you going?"

"I won't be long."

I watched him move away with long, measured strides, and had not the heart to call him back. No assurances are as convincing as the evidence of one's own eyes. He was going to the children.

The others were in the sitting room. Cyrus and Katherine and Bertie, Walter and Lia, Gargery, Daoud and Kadija and Fatima, and . . .

"Selim!" I cried. "Go back to bed at once."

His brown face was a little paler than usual, but he was fully dressed and his neatly wound turban concealed the bandages. "Lie in bed while Emerson and Nur Misur are in danger? My honored father would rise up from his tomb."

"It is true." Daoud nodded. "Now you are here, Sitt Hakim, God be thanked. You will tell us what to do."

The hard knot in my interior softened a little as I looked round the room. No woman could have had more valiant allies than these. I did not protest, for I knew I would have to have Selim tied to his bed to keep him there. He had a knife at his belt and so did Daoud. Cyrus, too, was armed, with a holstered pistol. I didn't know whether to laugh or cry when I saw that Evelyn was gripping my sword parasol. They would obey my slightest command. If only I knew what command to give! I had preserved my outward calm, but inwardly I was in such a confusion of rage and worry I couldn't think sensibly.

Stalling for time, I took a chair and asked, "Where is Sethos?"

"Somewhere around," Cyrus replied. "Said he couldn't sit still, and durned if I blame him."

Ramses and Sethos must have met outside, for they came in together. "Ah, there you are," said the latter, nodding at me. "Hasn't anyone offered you a whiskey and soda?"

Cyrus let out a multisyllabled American exclamation. "Jumping Jehoshaphat, I should have thought of it. How about you, Ramses?"

Ramses shook his head. "What we need is one of Mother's famous councils of war."

Everyone looked expectantly at me. "First," I said, taking the glass from Cyrus, "tell us what steps you have taken. You telegraphed, Bertie?"

Bertie nodded. He looked absolutely miserable.

Sethos had helped himself to a whiskey. I suspected it was not his first. "That step was necessary, but it may not be of much use. I have taken the liberty of dispatching a number of your fellows to alert the villages between here and Nag Hammadi, and upstream, as far as Esna, in case she changes course. The word will be passed on."

"A regular Pony Express," Cyrus said, with an approving nod.

"Donkey express," Sethos corrected. "And a few camels."

"That's all very well and good," said Walter peevishly. "But I do not understand why we are sitting round drinking whiskey and not acting!"

"What else can we do?" I asked.

Walter banged his fist on the table. His mild countenance was no longer mild; his eyes glittered. "Go in pursuit! We have the *Amelia*, have we not?"

Sethos put his empty glass on the table and the rest of us gaped at Walter. "I wondered if you would think of that."

"You had, I suppose?" Walter demanded.

"Selim had. That's why he's here. We will need him. There's only a skeleton crew on board, and it would take too long to get Reis Hassan and his engineer back."

"Hmph," said Walter, only slightly appeased and sounding as warlike as Emerson. "Then why haven't we started?"

"Because," said Sethos, in his most irritating drawl, "we cannot start before morning. Aside from the danger of navigation at night, we could go right past the *Isis* in the dark. And because we were waiting for Amelia and Ramses. And, most importantly, because we need to gather all the facts and plan our strategy before we charge ahead. Suppose we do catch her up, then what? Board her, swords in hand?"

Walter jumped to his feet. He looked twice the man he had been when he arrived in Cairo, and for the first time I saw the resemblance between him and the man he confronted. He snatched his eyeglasses off and threw them across the room. "Damn you, er—Sethos, are you making fun of me? If swords are required, I will use one!"

Sethos said in quite a different tone, "I beg your pardon . . . brother. I know you would. We had better pray it won't come to that. Sit down, I beg, and let us discuss the situation calmly. Amelia, would you like to take charge of the discussion?"

Before I could begin, Selim rose carefully to his feet. "I am going to the *Amelia* to begin overhauling the engines. I will have her ready to sail at daybreak."

"I will go with you," Walter declared. "What the devil did I do with my glasses?"

"Here." Evelyn handed them to him. "Walter, dear—"

He knew what she was about to say. Adjusting the eyeglasses, he took her by the shoulders and smiled at her. "Perhaps I can be Selim's hands or run errands for him, if I can do nothing more."

"I too," said Bertie. "I know a little something about engines."

"Selim, I strictly forbid you to let that horse gallop," I called after them. "Walter, make sure he obeys."

"Losing control of your subalterns?" Sethos inquired. "I am your willing slave, as always. What orders have you for me? Another whiskey, perhaps?"

"I am in no mood for humor," I informed him.

"Only trying to relieve the tension, my dear. The fact is, I believe we have matters under control here. The children are all in the main house, and it is surrounded—men every ten feet, all aroused and looking for trouble. The women and children will be safe—"

A united outcry from every female in the room silenced him. "If you think I am staying here," Lia began.

"Or me!" Evelyn cried, brandishing the parasol.

"You will both do what you are told," I said. "By me. We must decide how our forces can best be employed. Someone must remain to deal with M. Lacau. He is due tomorrow."

"He's here," Cyrus said. "Got in this evening. How can you worry about him at such a time as this?"

"For one thing, he may be persuaded to join in the hunt for *Isis*."

"Not very likely," Cyrus said. "He'll be too worried about his consarned treasure. What about the other tourist boats?"

"I could not in conscience ask a party of innocents to take an active part. We could ask the cruise boats to keep an eye out for the *Isis*, but I expect by morning she will have altered her appearance. Since our enemies have departed en masse, I doubt there is danger to anyone here—"

"An assumption we dare not make," said Sethos. "We believed the immediate family had not been targeted. That is what we were meant to believe. Now they have taken Nefret. They didn't plan on Emerson, but now they've got him they aren't likely to let him go. We know the motive now. It applies equally strongly to the rest of you—and to me."

He went to the sideboard again and splashed whiskey into his glass. I could have used another myself. We had skirted round the subject, but it could no longer be avoided.

"I am sorry," I said haltingly. "I had hoped she was innocent."

Sethos swung round to face me. "She looks so innocent, doesn't she? Those childish freckles and wide hazel eyes . . . She took me in, too, Amelia, if that is any consolation."

I saw the pain his controlled countenance endeavored to conceal, and so did my dear Evelyn. Going to him, she embraced him like a sister. "She may be a prisoner, dear—er—"

The tenderness of her manner, and the stumble over his name, were too much for him. Affection and laughter choked his voice. "Dear Evelyn. Would you like me to tell you my real name?"

"You need not tell me if you would rather not."

"Seth."

"What?" I cried. "Not Gawaine, or George, or Milton, or—"

Visibly amused, Sethos lifted his glass to me. "What an imagination you have, Amelia. Where do you suppose I got my nom de guerre? My parents gave me a perfectly respectable biblical name, but when I realized how close it was to that of an ancient Egyptian pharaoh I couldn't resist. And how appropriate! Sethos, the follower of Set, god of storm and chaos, deadly enemy of his noble brother—" He broke off with a snap of his teeth. "Ramses, will you for God's sake have a drink, or say something, or at least sit down? You make me nervous planted there like a bloody granite statue. We'll get her back."

It might have been the thought of the other young woman, the loving daughter Sethos would never get back, that broke Ramses's stony control.

"I'm sorry," he began.

Sethos snarled at him. "I don't want your pity. I want information. There is nothing we can do for several more hours, so we may as well talk. I don't suppose anyone intends to sleep. Is there any longer the slightest doubt as to what has motivated this string of extraordinary occurrences?"

"No," I said. "Once I realized that revenge for Bertha's death was the motive, every incident fit snugly into the pattern. The first, which I flat-out missed until recently, was the death of Hassan—or rather, his sudden turn to religion. What had he done that he should feel the need of forgiveness?"

Ramses nodded. "That's what Selim said, in almost those precise words. I missed it too. Hassan was one of the men who was with us that day at Gurneh, when Abdullah died and Bertha . . . Are you suggesting that it was Hassan who struck the blow that killed her?"

"I think that if he did not, he believed he had, or claimed the credit—for creditable it would have seemed to those who revered Abdullah and held the old tribal beliefs—an eye for an eye, a death for a death. Do you remember the letter Ramses read us, from a man to his deceased wife? I would not be surprised if Hassan did not hold the same view about ill fortune—that it must be due to a malevolent spirit. Hassan had lost his own wife, and he had begun to suffer the effects of old age. Guilt and the hope of forgiveness made him seek the protection of a holy man—even if he had to invent one himself! Most of the other men are dead, except for—"

"Selim and Daoud," David breathed. "Good God. She would have no trouble murdering Hassan—poison in one of the dishes of food he was brought—but I can't believe—"

"Selim and Daoud," Sethos said, in a hard flat voice, "were next. She played with them like a cat with a mouse. None of the incidents proved to be fatal, but any one of them might have been. She staged her own misadventures to allay your suspicions. Martinelli would seem to be an aberration. I don't know why she went after him. To the best of my knowledge, she never met him."

"There are a number of things you do not know," I said. El-Gharbi's revelations had been overshadowed by the magnitude of the catastrophe that had befallen us, but they were vital to the case. Evelyn and David had voiced a hope, a doubt, which must be present in the minds of the others. It was hard to picture that fresh-faced girl as capable of murder.

"It is important that all of us understand precisely what we are up against," I went on. "It is not a—er—disturbed young woman with a crew of venal cutthroats. There is at least one other individual involved, a hardened criminal with the same motive as Maryam's. Maryam is not Bertha's only child."

For almost the first time since I had known him, Sethos lost his composure. His face went white. "No," he said hoarsely. "No. Not another of my . . . Who told you that?"

"El-Gharbi," Ramses said. "That was where we went today, to his village, where he had been exiled. Mother remembered something he had said—about the young serpent also having poisoned fangs. Why she didn't see fit to mention this to anyone else—"

"I forgot," I admitted. "It was so vague, like one of those Nostradamus predictions that can be interpreted in many different ways. We were at that time involved with that vicious boy Jamil, who could certainly have been described in those terms. Emerson also knew, but like myself he forgot or dismissed the warning. Not until last night, when I finally began to see the pattern we had been seeking, did I realize el-Gharbi might have information we did not."

"You ought to have told us," Evelyn said accusingly.

"It is easy to see what one ought to have done after the event," David said quietly. "I want to know more about this second child."

Lia let out a cry. "Justin. Is it Justin? But he's even younger than Maryam, he cannot be more than fourteen. He——"

"He," I said, "is a young woman. The short stature, the beardless face, the high-pitched voice should have alerted us. She was in her late teens when el-Gharbi knew her in Cairo. One of the more—er— exclusive, I suppose I should say—houses of prostitution was owned by an older woman, a European, who also had a hand in various illegal operations. She and el-Gharbi were never in competition; they operated, so to speak, on different levels, but he was familiar with her activities. Her customers included the highest officials and the wealthiest, most fastidious tourists. Justin was her protégé, and her able assistant in every criminal activity, from drugs to murder."

"Not mine, then," Sethos said in a ragged whisper. "Not mine."

I understood his feelings. If the information gave him any comfort, I was ready to give it.

"According to el-Gharbi's sources, her father was an Englishman named Vincey, the man with whom Bertha lived for several years before we exterminated Vincey and Bertha went to you. No. You are not her father. She and Maryam are half sisters. How they met and when I do not know, but Justin is unquestionably the ringleader. She is the elder, and unlike Maryam she has lived all her life with criminals."

"That doesn't absolve Maryam," Sethos said. Except for the perspiration that beaded his forehead, he might have been talking about a stranger. "She was a willing participant from the start. The attack on her was staged; the result was that Ramses 'rescued' her and brought her to you—with well-feigned reluctance that gained your sympathy and support. She's been spying on you and reporting back to the others."

"She may be under duress," Evelyn said.

"Give it up, Evelyn," Sethos said. "She is a true child of her mother—and God help us, of me."

CHAPTER THIRTEEN

The boy wasn't ill. She ought to have known it had been a ruse. He stood lightly poised, swaying with the motion of the vessel, and his face was as pretty and bland as a wax doll's.

"Were you lapping the water like a dog?" Justin asked.

There was a note in his voice that sent alarm bells jingling through Nefret's head. She tried to speak, but produced only a rusty croak.

"A nice cup of tea is what you need," Justin said cheerfully. "Can you walk, or shall François carry you?"

The last hope faded when she saw he was not alone. What part he played in this she could not yet determine, but at best he was useless, incapable of understanding and too frail to resist. François had to be one of them, though. He reached for her, grinning unpleasantly. Nefret staggered to her feet, pushing his hand away.

"As you like," Justin said. "Come with me."

Nefret followed him along the passageway and into the saloon, with François close behind her. Smiling sweetly, Justin indicated a chair, and Nefret sank gratefully into it. Tea was set out on a table, a handsome service of silver, but there was no one in the room except herself and the boy and his attendant. Her eyes moved to the windows. It was dark outside. And the boat had stopped.

"Drink your tea," said Justin, pouring. "You must be very thirsty."

Something about the gesture, the turn of his wrist, caught Nefret's attention. She watched him as he lay back against the cushions of the divan, one hand behind his head, the other gracefully limp.

"Who are you?" she demanded.

The light peal of laughter, a tone higher than Justin's, was the final clue. My God, how could I have missed it? she wondered. "His" coat was open and the thin shirt clung to the curves of a woman's breasts, now unconfined.

"My name, you mean? I have had a number of them. You may continue calling me Justin. It sounds a little like Justice, and that is what I am about to deal out."

Nefret shook her head dazedly. "Why are you doing this? What do you want of us?"

"Justice. For a dead woman and her children. Come now," she said impatiently, as Nefret stared openmouthed. "How stupid you are. Your family took my mother's life and would have left me to die, unprotected and exploited, had it not been for her friends and my own talents."

"Your mother," Nefret echoed. She picked up her cup and burned her tongue on the scalding tea. "Who . . . ?"

"It shouldn't be that difficult. How many women have met their deaths at the hands of your virtuous family?"

"None. Not even . . . Oh, good Lord." Nefret gasped. "Bertha? You are her child? But—but that's not fair, we didn't even know you existed. Mother and Father would have helped you. They would help you now."

"I don't want help. What I want I will take, as my due, not as charity."

Nefret couldn't think what to say. In all their theorizing, they had never anticipated this. She sipped the tea, stalling for time until she could get her wits back. "What have you done to the Professor?"

"Not as much as he deserves." François had taken up a position beside his . . . mistress. His scarred face twisted. "He is only chained and locked into that room. She wouldn't let me—"

"I did not give you leave to speak." The light voice pierced like a sword blade. François recoiled, and then dropped to his knees and began mumbling apologies.

"It really would serve him right," Justin said, ignoring her groveling servant. "He has thrown all our plans into disarray. Would you like to know what they were, and how they have changed? François, where are your manners? Offer our guest a biscuit."

"I'm not hungry," Nefret said. "Tell me."

Justin lay back against the cushions, her hands under her head, breasts lifted.

"Hathor," Nefret said in stunned disbelief.

"On both occasions, yes. You suspected Maryam, didn't you? I did it for her. She wants your husband. If the Professor hadn't interfered today, she'd have got him."

"Never," Nefret said steadily.

"Oh, I think her chances were excellent. You see, our original intention was to get you aboard and then, wearing your clothing and hat, I would have gone ashore and strode briskly off into the alleys of Luxor. When I returned it would have been as myself. By the time your friends came looking for you, the *Isis* would have sailed and a dozen gaping witnesses would have reported you had left the boat."

Watching her, Nefret was reminded of something Ramses had once said about the art of disguise. It wasn't so much a matter of physical change as of demeanor and gesture, speech and movement. She had played a boy's role well, but she couldn't have pulled it off if they had not thought of Justin as not quite normal. No wonder she had reacted so vehemently to being touched. She might bind her breasts and wear loose boy's clothing, but her body was a woman's.

"But now that's out of the question," Justin went on briskly. "Those same gaping witnesses saw both you and the Professor board the boat; they had told him you were here and he was prepared to tear the place apart to find you. We had no choice but to move up the time of our departure and take both of you along." She sighed. "Poor Maryam. She can't go back and pretend innocence now."

"Where is she?" Nefret asked.

"Sulking in her cabin. She's been complaining all day," Justin added contemptuously.

Nefret's eyes wandered to the window. It opened onto the deck. The shutters had been thrown back. She could see stars, and the dark outline of land not far away. Her heart sank at the idea of abandoning Emerson, but if she could get onto the deck . . .

Nefret made a dash for the window. Her legs were still shaky, so it wasn't so much a dash as a series of stumbles. François was after her the moment she moved. He twisted her arms behind her and held her.

Nefret shook the straggling hair out of her eyes. Knowing you look like a fright, dirty and sweaty and disheveled, has a demoralizing effect on any female. The woman lounging on the couch knew that; smiling, she ran her hands caressingly over her body. She made a very pretty woman with that head of crisp curls, bright as gold shavings, and that slender young body.

Nefret tried to stop herself, but it was no use. She had to know. "Why did you take Ramses prisoner? What would you have done to him if he hadn't got away?"

"It was a test, of sorts, to see how well my people performed," Justin said, stretching like a cat. "And I was curious about what Maryam saw in him. Then—well, I saw. I thought it would be fun to have him make love to me."

"You're insane," Nefret said. "You couldn't have made him do that."

"Oh, yes, I could, if I'd had a little more time. I quite looked forward to it. I enjoy men, and he is a particularly handsome specimen—in every way. Maryam doesn't appreciate that sort of thing. She only married that vulgar American because she wanted his money. She thinks she's in love." The tone was one of pure disgust.

"You've never been in love?" Nefret asked. She was following one of the family's basic rules: Keep the other person talking, watch for a slip of the tongue or a moment of carelessness. One never knew what might turn up! And there was a horrible fascination in the conversation. She had never encountered a woman like this. But then, she reminded herself, I never knew Bertha.

"In love?" The pretty mouth curled. "I wanted him, though, and I'd have had him if he hadn't got away from me. I may succeed yet. I generally get what I want, and I expect he'd be willing to do anything to keep me from hurting you."

"Not anything," Nefret said. "And you'd be a fool to let him get close to you when he's angry."

"What an innocent you are," Justin murmured. "There are ways . . . I know most of them."

She was baiting her prisoner, only too successfully. Nefret swallowed the sickness rising in her throat. "What are you going to do with us?" she demanded.

"Nothing just yet" was the careless reply. "We may need you."

"What for?"

"Wait and see." Laughing, Justin sat up and clasped her hands. "Wouldn't you like to freshen up before dinner?"

The room to which François took her was a distinct improvement over the other. The shutters over the windows were closed, and barred from the outside, but the gaps between the wooden slats admitted air. There were a bed and a washbasin and even a lamp, hanging on a bracket by the washbasin. An impromptu prison, this, not as formidable as the other, but they had left nothing that could be used as a weapon or a tool. Bed and basin were bolted to the floor; they had even removed the stout wooden bar on the inside of the shutters.

Nefret moved purposefully around the room, looking into the cupboard over the washbasin and under the bed. The water pitcher was not a heavy earthenware vessel but a delicate bit of china, painted with pansies. It was part of the usual set. The other vessels were just as dainty; hitting someone over the head with one would only irritate him. The soap dish held a bar of scented soap. Apparently that diabolical woman really did want her to tidy up before . . . dinner? A towel and washcloth had been provided too.

Why not? She could at least wash face and arms. The tepid water felt wonderful against her hot cheeks.

It would have been heavenly to take off her clothes and sponge the dried sweat off her body, but there was no way of locking the door from the inside. She compromised by removing her filthy shirt and washing her upper arms and throat. The chemise that had been so fresh and white that morning was just as grimy as the rest of her clothing. The thin cotton stuck to her breasts and ribs. In a moment of purely illogical, utterly feminine weakness, she compared her body to the graceful form on the divan, and snatched up her shirt. How old was the damned woman? Younger than she by a good ten years. Maryam was even younger. Neither of them had borne two children.

And neither of them had Ramses, she reminded herself. She began taking the pins out of her tangled hair, remembering how his hands had stroked it over her shoulders. She had been a fool to let jealousy sour her mind and sharpen her tongue. He wouldn't rest until he had found her, and her formidable mother-in-law would be hot on Emerson's trail by now. She thought of Emerson, sweltering in the dark hold of her former prison, manacled and injured, and her jaw set. I'll ask if I can see him, she thought. I'll beg. On my knees, if the bitch wants that.

She looked for a comb, without success. They were taking no chances. Sharp teeth, even of celluloid, could rake painfully across a face. Philosophically she began running her fingers through her long locks, smoothing them as best she could. She stood up and tucked her shirt in. When the door opened she was behind it, the dainty pitcher raised. One must do one's best, whatever the odds!

The door was flung back, flattening her painfully against the wall. The pitcher fell and shattered. A hand reached round, gripped her wrist and pulled her out of concealment.

"You have spoiled the set," the doctor said, studying the pink-and-blue shards. His fingers squeezed like pincers.

He maintained the painful grip as he led her along the passageway to the saloon. A table had been drawn into the center of the room, covered with white damask and spread with china and crystal. Flowers filled an epergne in the center. There were four places set, but only two of the chairs were occupied. Nefret stopped, rubbing her aching wrist. The men who stood at attention behind the chairs didn't look much like waiters. François was one of them.

She realized now what had been wrong with the room. It was as contrived and unreal as a stage setting, a recreation of stuffy respectability. Its artificiality was emphasized by the bizarre occupants—the heavily muscled, hard-eyed attendants, and the woman she knew only as Justin.

The name was particularly inappropriate now; she wore the robes of Hathor, complete with black wig and artificial cow's ears. Maryam sat at her right. Her eyes were fixed on her plate. One of the companion's loose black dresses made her look almost as shabby as Nefret felt, but the stolen pectoral gleamed on her breast, deep lapis blue framed by the gold curves of the two serpents.

"Where are the bracelets?" Nefret asked steadily.

"My, my, what admirable sangfroid," Justin murmured. "Show her, Maryam."

Maryam raised her hands, but not her eyes. The bracelets were clasped round her wrists.

"Sit there," Justin directed. "At my left. That will be all, Khattab."

"The good doctor isn't dining?" Nefret asked, settling into the chair the waiter held for her.

"He's no doctor, he's a cheap abortionist who worked for me in Cairo," Justin replied with careless contempt. "Hardly a social equal."

Khattab's shoulder blades twitched. He left the room without replying and slammed the door.

"Not that you are a suitable dinner companion," Justin went on, inspecting Nefret critically. "Was that the best you could do?"

"Under the circumstances, yes." Nefret was past caring about the woman's taunts. "If you find my presence so offensive, why am I here?"

"Two reasons. We hadn't finished our little chat. I enjoyed watching your reactions. You have such an open, uncontrolled face. And there is still such a lot you don't know."

"And the other reason?" She didn't turn her head to look at the windows. The draperies had been drawn, but she could hear sounds of activity outside, on the deck.

"To join us in our celebration," Justin said. She pulled off the heavy wig and tossed it to François. "Tomorrow—or next day, at the latest—we will complete our mission. It has been a year in the making, but it will be worth the wait."

The only thing Nefret could think of was the family—her children, Ramses, her mother-in-law—all the others, friends and kin—caught up in the same web that had entangled Emerson and her. She told herself it was impossible to strike at all of them at once. Some of them, then. Which? And how?

Involuntarily she looked toward the windows. Some heavy object had fallen, thudding onto the deck; a round Arabic curse burst out, followed by a hissing adjuration to silence.

Justin laughed gleefully and clapped her hands. "Plain as print, that face of yours. Why don't you just ask what they're doing? I don't mind telling you."

"What?" Nefret asked.

"By morning the *Isis* will be a different boat—fresh paint, a new name, the Stars and Stripes waving bravely at the stern."

Nefret nodded. "Clever, but not good enough. Where are we?"

"I don't mind telling you that either. We're at anchor near an island just south of Qena."

Only a few hours downstream from Luxor. He was only a few hours away. She tried to imagine what he—and the others—might be doing, how long it had taken them to realize what had happened to her—and Emerson. Then she remembered her mother-in-law's complacent statement: "I do not expect that such an eventuality will occur," and icy fingers traced a path down her spine. If they had been detained, by force or accident, at that obscure village, Ramses might not yet know she was missing.

"You are thinking of him, aren't you?" Justin cooed. "I can tell. So far as I know, he's in no danger, dear, and I feel certain he will rush nobly to your rescue. But don't get your hopes up. They will have to follow by water, and they can't have put two and two together before dark. We are far ahead and they will have to be very clever to find us before we've accomplished our aim. Even if they do, they won't dare interfere so long as we hold two hostages. You are also hostages for each other. If you don't behave yourself, the punishment will fall on him."

"Is he hurt?" Nefret asked. "May I see him?"

Justin's lips curled into a tight-lipped smile, as enigmatic as that of an archaic statue. "Say 'please.'"

"Please."

"Later. Perhaps. He's not seriously injured, but he isn't very comfortable."

Maryam hadn't moved a muscle or uttered a sound until then; the movement was slight, only a jerk of her slim shoulders.

"Then I take it he won't be joining us," Nefret said. She too had flinched at the gloating malice in Justin's voice but she was trying to live up to Emerson's standards. "Who is the fourth? Someone I know?"

"Yes and no," Justin said. "I wonder what's keeping her. Waiting to make a grand entrance, I suppose. François, go and tell—ah. Finally!"

The woman who entered was tall and thin. Her wrinkled face and white hair bore the uncompromising marks of time, but her step was firm and her shoulders were straight. She had abandoned her veils and widow's weeds; her black dress was severely practical, with no concession to vanity, not even a ruffle of lace.

Justin pushed her chair back and rose, followed more slowly by Maryam. Nefret had been taught to stand up when an older woman entered the room. She remained seated.

"A criminal organization of women," she said. "At least you're not another of Bertha's get."

The old woman, whose name was almost certainly not Fitzroyce, passed a caressing hand over Justin's bright curls. Then the same withered hand administered a sharp slap across Nefret's face, the sort of slap a governess might give an impertinent pupil.

"Your manners are not so pretty as your face. Stand up in the presence of your elders."

With a slight shrug, Nefret obeyed. The old woman went to the head of the table and seated herself. "Thank you for waiting, my dear," she said to Justin. "François, you may open the wine now."

"What took you so long?" Justin asked.

A cork popped and foam bubbled up over the bottle. "Clumsy

oaf," the old lady snapped. "Pour it and don't spill any more. Where was I? Paying a little call on the Professor. It was hard to tear myself away."

"Is he all right?" Nefret asked. Champagne slopped into her glass.

"No, he isn't all right. He has a vile temper and the strength of an ox, and I'm taking no chances on his getting away. Now join me in a toast to our success." She raised her glass.

"You can hardly expect me to drink to that," Nefret said.

She expected a reprimand, if not another slap, but the old woman only smiled. Her collection of wrinkles looked like a map of Cairo, with its curving lanes and intersecting alleys. They were the result, Nefret thought, of weight loss in a woman who had once been stout and strong. She was by no means feeble, though. Her hand was all bones and sinew.

"I could have François pinch your nose and pour it down your throat," her hostess said. "But that would spoil the effect. Maryam— Justin . . ."

Ceremoniously they raised their glasses and drank.

The first course was soup of some kind. It was tepid and overfla-vored with onion. Even the cook must be one of the gang, Nefret thought. The wine was excellent, a pale hock, and Nefret allowed her-self a sip. The sounds of activity outside were more muted now.

"What was it I didn't drink to?" she asked. "And who the hell are you? Bertha's avenger?"

"Do you suppose I would go to so much trouble for the sake of revenge?" The old woman leaned forward, withered hands planted on the table. "Sentimentality is a weakness of the young. I had no objec-tion to Justin arranging her cunning little accidents and epiphanies. She only succeeded in killing one of the men who had murdered Bertha, but some of the others were seriously inconvenienced and she enjoyed your fear and confusion. I stopped caring about such things a long time ago."

"If it's money you want," Nefret began.

"I want it and I intend to get it. This is an expensive operation," she went on, in a voice as practical as a banker's. "It took every penny

I had saved and all the money Maryam inherited from her doting old husband. I believe it will prove a worthwhile investment."

The waiters removed the soup plates and replaced them with fish, white-eyed and dry as a mummy. Nefret was glad she had forced herself to finish the soup. She didn't think she could deal with that dead fish, and she definitely needed to keep her wits about her. She said, in the same matter-of-fact voice as the old woman's, "Perhaps we can come to an agreement. I can match—"

"Perhaps you could, though I doubt it." "Mrs. Fitzroyce" glared at the fish. "Disgusting. Take it away. Money isn't all I want. I am not, it appears, as impervious to emotion as I had believed. Three of you were primarily responsible for the death of the woman I loved like a daughter and admired as my leader. Not the poor fool who struck the actual blow; the ones who had tormented and foiled her. The satisfaction I felt when I beheld one of them in my power at last, helpless and suffering as she had suffered, took me by surprise. It would give me even greater pleasure to lay my hands on the others."

A calloused brown hand slapped a plate of beef down in front of Nefret. Blood formed a repulsive puddle around it.

"You were one of Bertha's aides," Nefret said slowly. "A member of her notorious organization of women. You took it over after she died. You must be . . . I've forgotten your name."

"It was a nom de guerre. We never met formally, but you may remember the nurse who was in attendance on a pregnant lady. Pregnant with that one," she added, frowning at Maryam. Her eyebrows squirmed like blind white caterpillars. "Sit up straight, girl. What are you sulking about? The failure of your romantic fantasy? I trust you aren't having second thoughts."

"It wasn't a fantasy," Maryam said sullenly. "It would have worked." Her wide hazel eyes moved from the old woman to Nefret and back.

"Nonsense. In any case, it's too late now."

"Matilda," Nefret breathed. "That was the name. Mother told us about you. It's she you want. Mother and—"

"The man who abandoned my girl for her. Her lover."

"They were not lovers," Nefret said indignantly.

The old woman cackled with laughter. "No? The more fool she, then. I took rather a fancy to him myself, but of course he never gave me a second look. I wonder . . . Would he be willing to exchange himself for you, little Maryam? Then you can have your precious Ramses, supposing you are woman enough to win him."

Maryam's mouth tightened. "He wouldn't agree. They must know now I'm as guilty as you."

"We can think of something," Justin said eagerly. "I'd like to know him better. Much better."

"Control yourself," Matilda said severely. "Revenge is all very well, but it must not interfere with our primary aim."

Nefret didn't have to ask what that was. Emerson had been right. There was only one way they could recoup their "investment"—by seizing the princesses' treasure.

"How are you planning to capture the steamer?" she asked casually.

Matilda grinned at her. "Clever girl. Since you're so clever, you figure it out. It will give you something to occupy your mind for the remainder of your stay with us."

WE WERE ON BOARD BEFORE daybreak. I do not believe anyone had slept, despite my admonitions. I know Ramses had not. The dark stains under his eyes looked like smears of charcoal. Waiting with forced patience for that moment when there was enough light to distinguish a black thread from a white, I stood at the railing looking toward the outline of the western mountains and reviewing our preparations to make sure nothing had been overlooked. The messengers were on their way to villages down- and upstream; signals had been arranged, so that any news could be immediately relayed to us. We had a crew of twenty, all thirsting for blood; we might have had fifty, had there been room for so many. Cyrus had brought his entire arsenal of pistols and rifles.

The greatest difficulty had been persuading some members of the family to remain behind. My orders had less effect than Ramses's appeal.

"If something goes wrong, the children mustn't be left without all their parents and grandparents. Lia—Aunt Evelyn—promise you will look after them."

At this point Gargery burst into tears.

"You too, Gargery," Ramses said resignedly.

"With my life, sir, with my life," Gargery sobbed. "But, sir, don't talk so discouraged-like. You'll come back."

"Not without her," Ramses said. He turned away.

I loved Nefret like a daughter, but it was of Emerson I thought in those last dark moments before sunrise. If I knew my spouse—and I did—they could not have taken him without a struggle. Did he lie even now wounded and suffering in some hastily contrived and horribly uncomfortable prison? Or had they already . . . No. I would not think that.

Our force consisted of Cyrus and Bertie, both of whom were good shots, Ramses, who was even better when he overcame his dislike of firearms, David, Selim and Daoud, Sethos, our twenty loyal men, and of course myself. I was fully armed, with pistol, knife, belt of tools, and the sword parasol I had retrieved from Evelyn. My blood was up, and I hoped I would have a chance to use the last item. Only hand-to-hand combat would satisfy my righteous wrath.

Ramses joined me at the rail. "You are grinding your teeth," he remarked.

"My blood is up," I explained. "I am going to tell Selim we are ready to push off."

"You don't have to tell Selim anything." The breeze freshened, blowing the hair back from his brow; we were in motion, gliding gently away from the dock. "I only wish we had a helmsman. Bertie and David know a bit, and so do I, but you had better pray we don't go aground."

The sun peeped over the eastern hills, blood-red, as suited my mood. Gradually the temples of Luxor faded into the morning mist.

If the Reader has a map before her (or, as it may be, him) she will see that the Nile does not run directly northward from Luxor, but in a gentle curve to the northeast. After approximately sixty miles it swings westward, in a sharper curve. What the Reader may not see are the innumerable smaller bends, curves, and bays—or the islands and sand-banks that interrupt the smooth flow of the river. A feature that looks small on a map occupies hundreds of yards on the ground. The vessel we sought might be concealed anywhere—or it might be miles ahead, steaming at full speed toward some unknown destination.

The wind tugged at my garments. The *Amelia* was capable of a fair turn of speed, especially downstream. How satisfying it would have been to race in pursuit, the rapidity of our progress keeping pace with our raging anxiety! It was a luxury we could not afford. We had to watch for signals from our scouts along the bank, and for the missing dahabeeyah.

After a time Sethos came to stand beside me. "Nasir has made coffee. Shall he bring you a cup?"

"Yes. No. Nasir should not be here. He is no fighter, he is only a steward, and not a very good one."

"Fatima sent him. Along with enough food to nourish a regiment for a week."

"Each of us serves in her own way," I murmured gratefully.

"Quite. Now, Amelia, gripping the rail in that white-knuckled fashion isn't going to help. I'll be right back."

When he returned, Nasir was with him, trying to balance a tray. I rescued the cup before it slid off, and thanked him—amd observed with alarm that the boy had strapped to his narrow waist a knife as long as my forearm.

"Oh dear," I said to Sethos, as Nasir staggered off. "We must keep him from engaging in combat."

"Be honest, Amelia." Sethos leaned forward, arms resting on the rail. "You would sacrifice Nasir or anyone else if it were necessary to save Emerson."

"Yes," I said.

Neither of us looked at the other. Our eyes were fixed on the shoreline. Nestled in the shelter of palm groves, amid the green of growing crops, were the whitewashed houses of a village. Above the rooftops rose the minaret of the mosque. Two black-robed women bearing jars on their heads descended the bank toward the river.

"Why are we slowing down?" I demanded.

"Looking for our first signal," Sethos replied. "That insignificant hamlet is Tukh. The channel is close to the West Bank here, and when a vessel is spotted all the local entrepreneurs take to their boats, hoping to sell some piece of junk to the tourists."

We all crowded to the left side of the boat (it is properly termed starboard, I believe, or perhaps port). A water buffalo wallowed in the shallows, and above it, on the bank, were several figures capering up and down, waving a banner. It was bright green.

"They saw her," I cried. "She passed this way. But when?"

"Green means yesterday," Sethos said coolly.

"Not much help," I muttered, waving away the platter of bread Nasir shoved under my nose.

"We're two hours down from Luxor," Sethos said. "That means she passed here late in the afternoon. And we know we're going in the right direction. There was always a chance she'd turn and go upstream."

"But they are at least six hours ahead of us, even if they stopped last night."

"They must have done," Sethos said impatiently. "Don't be such a pessimist, Amelia, it isn't like you. No captain would risk his boat trying to navigate this river after dark."

"Then she would have to put in last night . . . where?"

"Somewhere around Qena," Ramses replied. "Three hours away, at our present speed. We daren't go faster, none of us knows the river well enough. Eat something, Mother."

I took a piece of bread, since Nasir would not leave me alone, and went back to my post on the other side of the boat.

Sunlight sparkled on the water. Our speed had increased, once we were in mid-channel. I could not take my eyes from the passing scene, and I wished I had another pair of them in the back of my head. We had men stationed at the prow and the stern and along both sides, watching as keenly as I, but that wasn't enough for me; I felt I could trust no eyes but my own. The water, which looks so clear and sparkling at a distance, was a muddy brown and as littered as a Cairo alley. The river constantly shifts, eating away at one bank or the other;

we passed a once-flourishing grove of palm trees, some precariously balanced on less than half their root base, others already fallen, their leaves trailing in the water. Withered palm fronds and dead branches floated past, with an occasional dead animal for interest. I am sure I need not tell the Reader that my eyes followed each such object with morbid dread, and each time I held my breath until I had identified it.

The river was not the populous thoroughfare it had been during my early years in Egypt, when it had been the only means of travel and transport. The railroad was cheaper and quicker, except for short distances. In Middle Egypt one would still see barges carrying sugar cane to the factories, but below Assiut only small local boats and an occasional tourist steamer used the river. We came up on one of the latter, flying the British flag, and I recognized one of Cook's vessels, the *Amasis*. We passed her so close I could see the pale, staring faces of the passengers standing at the rail—too close for the captain's taste, apparently, since he waved his fists and yelled at us.

Ramses came to me. He had lost his hat and his hair blew wildly about his face. "I let David take over," he said. "I hope he can do better than I."

"We are going too fast. That was a good-sized island we passed. Shouldn't we have investigated the other side of it?"

Ramses turned to face me, one arm resting on the rail—but his eyes, like mine, continued to scan the banks. "We cannot circle every island and sandbank, there are too many of them. With an inexperienced hand at the tiller there's a good chance we would run aground. That would slow us even more."

"What is the point of this pursuit then?" I demanded.

"Could you have remained in Luxor, knowing that every minute, every hour was taking them farther away?"

A flush of shame warmed my face. He and I were the ones most deeply affected, and he was taking it better than I—externally. I was not deceived by his impassive countenance and cool voice.

"No more than you," I said.

His expression did not change. "There is relatively little traffic on this part of the river, and it's possible, even probable, that a conspicuous vessel like the *Isis* would have been observed. What I'm praying for is that she ran aground. Though it's more likely that we will. Mother, you will wear yourself out standing here. Come to the saloon and have something to eat. Nasir keeps cooking; I can't stop him."

"I will wait until we reach Qena. How is Selim?"

"I can't stop him either," Ramses admitted. "He won't leave his engines. He seems to be all right."

Another hour passed. I counted off every minute, willing the hands of my watch to move faster. There might be news at Qena. A rotten log floating by had the exact shape and size of a human body.

Cyrus was the next to approach me. "Come and have luncheon, Amelia," he said, covering my clenched hand with his. "We've got a dozen people keeping watch, you can't do any good here."

"Soon. We are nearing Qena, I believe. That is Ballas, on the West Bank."

Qena is a prosperous town, set in a well-cultivated countryside and noted for the quality of clay in the area. All along the bank lay row upon row of pottery vessels, round-bellied pots and tall water jars, ready for transport. Beyond the rows of pots a banner was raised, held high on long poles by two men. It was white. The *Isis* had not been seen.

The other men had gathered round. Bertie let out a muffled oath, and Daoud invoked his god. "Does this mean the boat did not come this far?" he asked.

"Not necessarily," Ramses said. He leaned out over the rail, squinting against the sunlight. Water traffic was heavier here, vessels coming in to load, and departing with their cargoes of pots, a steamer slowing for the landing ahead, where tourists would disembark for a visit to the temple of Denderah. Feluccas glided like large white butterflies around the larger boats. One of them appeared to be heading straight for us.

Ramses let out a shout. "Stop! Tell Selim to stop the engines."

The boat *was* heading straight for us. Standing upright, one hand on the mast, the other arm waving in emphatic gestures, was a man whose face and sturdy frame were oddly familiar. His bearded face split in a grin when the *Amelia* began to slow. The little craft came neatly alongside. The man grasped one of the hands that reached down for him, and scrambled nimbly on board.

"Reis Hassan," I cried. "How did you—"

"The word has gone down the river with the speed of a flying bird. We have been watching for you. What have you done to my boat?"

"Nothing yet, but we had a few close calls," Ramses said, with the first genuine smile I had seen on his face for hours. "Marhaba, Reis Hassan—welcome and thrice welcome. Something told me we might see you here."

"Nothing told me," I admitted. "Yet I ought to have known. Thank you, my friend, worthy son of your father."

He shrugged my thanks away. "This is not a time for talk. What is the plan? Where do you want to go? And who"—his voice cracked—"who is steering my boat?"

FROM MANUSCRIPT H

Nefret had asked for more oil for the lamp. She hadn't got it. They had also refused her request to see Emerson, but she knew where he was—in the room next to hers. As they led her along the passageway she had raised her voice in a string of swear words, and got an immediate, equally profane, response. The doctor added a few curses of his own before he pushed her into her room.

At least she knew he was still alive and conscious, and she had been able to reassure him about herself. The lamp was burning low. It wouldn't last much longer. She examined the wall that separated the two rooms, inch by inch, and could have laughed aloud when she heard a steady scraping sound at the base of the partition. Lying flat on the floor, she retrieved the last of the hoarded nails from her shoe.

At the first sound from her, the scraping stopped. Three soft knocks sounded. She knocked back, three times, wondering what system of communication he had in mind. Tapping through the alphabet would take forever.

Apparently Emerson came to the same conclusion. The scraping resumed. Her ear against the panel, Nefret located the source of the sound and began digging with her nail. The wood of the partition was thin, but neither of them had a proper tool; it seemed like, and probably was, hours before a sharp point jabbed into her hand. She pulled it back, and heard splinters snap as Emerson enlarged the hole. When she heard his voice she lay flat and pressed her ear to the small opening.

"Nefret, my dear. Can you hear me?"

"Yes. Father, are you hurt?"

"Perfectly fit, my dear. Pay attention, time is running out on us. It will be light before long. They had me in that room for a bit earlier on. I believe you can lift the bar on the outside of the shutters."

"I haven't anything to use as a lever. I tried to steal a knife at dinner, but—"

"Pay attention, I said. There's a lamp bracket next to the washbasin. I managed to loosen it a trifle. If you keep bending it back and forth, it ought to come off. Do it now."

"Yes, sir."

The last of the oil flickered out as she wrenched at the metal strip. It came away from the wall so suddenly, she staggered. She had to feel her way back to the hole.

"I've got it," she reported. "As soon as I get out of here I'll come to your window and—"

"As soon as you get out of there you will go over the side. I don't know how far we are from land. Are you willing to risk it?"

"Risk be damned. I won't leave you here."

Their faces were close together. She felt his breath warm on her cheek. "You can't get me out. Even if you could, I would find it a trifle difficult to swim with fifty pounds of ironmongery attached to me. Are you crying? Don't cry, curse it! Do you know what they're planning?"

"Yes. That horrible old woman told me, at dinner. But I can't . . ."

She knew he was right, though. She couldn't free him, and she was no good to him as a fellow prisoner.

"She told me, too. Or rather," said Emerson complacently, "she confirmed my deductions. I could have dropped—if I hadn't already been recumbent—when she told me who she was. It just goes to show that one should never leave old enemies lying carelessly about. Go on, now. Er—"

"À bientôt, Father."

"Er—yes. My dear."

She was afraid to speak again, for she knew her voice would betray her. The faint slits of light at the shutters guided her. It took all her strength to force the blunt end of the bracket into the crack between shutter and window frame, and for a while she didn't think she could exert enough pressure to force the bar up. It gave all at once, and Nefret's heart stopped as it swung free, striking the shutter with a sound that seemed to her as loud as a pistol shot. Emerson heard it; he began to yell and bang on the door, making enough racket to drown out louder sounds than the ones she made climbing out the window. There was no one in sight on the narrow stretch of deck.

She felt as if some other entity had taken control of her body, blocking off emotions she couldn't afford to feel. Smoothly and quickly, she closed the shutters and replaced the bar before she climbed over the rail and lowered herself into the water.

The shock of immersion took her breath away. Clinging to the side she looked round, trying to get her bearings. The moon was on the wane, a thin sliver of silver, but the stars were the bright stars of Egypt. Behind her, not far away, a low, dark bulk blotted out a section of sky. An island, and not a very big one—just long enough to hide the *Isis* from one direction.

Bare feet thumped on the deck, only a few inches over her head. Emerson's outburst must have drawn some of them away from their posts temporarily. They had silenced him now.

Nefret drew in a deep breath and pushed herself away from the boat in a long glide. When she was forced to come up for air she turned onto her back and paddled gently with her hands. Now she could see the ghostly outlines of the cliffs of the high plateau. They looked awfully far away. West bank or east? She floated, letting the current carry her for a few yards downstream. The cliffs were those of the West Bank, then. Maybe the eastern shore was closer. Something bumped into her, something squashy and vile-smelling. Nefret fended it off, fighting revulsion. There were always dead animals in the Nile. She didn't want to see what this one was. Turning over again, onto her front, she started swimming toward the island.

It was only a sandbank, less than sixty feet long and a few yards wide, but reeds had rooted themselves and weedy plants struggled for sustenance. Nefret pulled herself out of the water and looked round. The eastern shore looked just as far distant. If there was a village on either bank, it showed no lights. The villagers couldn't afford to waste oil. She looked in vain for a familiar landmark. Emerson would have found one—he knew every foot of the river—but to her the cliffs looked all alike. To her left—north, downstream—she could see what appeared to be other small islands.

One thing was certain. She couldn't stay here. Once her absence was discovered they would look for her, and the reeds offered no concealment. She sat down and began struggling with the wet laces of her boots. It cost her a fingernail before she got them off. Hastily she stripped off her wet shirt and trousers, flattened them into a bundle, and used her belt to strap them onto her back. Silly, perhaps, but if she was fortunate enough to reach shore she didn't relish the idea of showing herself to a group of conservative villagers in wet, skimpy underclothing.

The sky over the eastern cliffs had paled. Dawn was near. She waded through the weeds, slid into the water, and started swimming toward the eastern shore, downstream, with the current and across it.

She had known everyone used the Nile as a trash depository, but it was one thing to know, and quite another to be in the middle of the mess, nose to nose with rotting vegetation and dead branches and other things she preferred not to think about. Organic objects that had sunk rose when the gases of decomposition swelled them. She had heard her first lecture on that interesting subject from her mother-in-law, years ago; Emerson had been absolutely scandalized . . .

The thing came at her from behind, floating downstream. It struck her upraised arm a numbing blow and caught her again on the shin as she went under, her mouth filling with water. She fought her way back to the surface, her lungs heaving. The thing was beside her, turning idly in a little eddy—a section of palm trunk, with a few fronds still attached. Dizzy with pain, and half-drowned, Nefret caught hold of a handful and with the last of her strength pulled herself far enough forward to throw one arm over the rounded trunk. Swimming was out of the question, her right arm hurt and her stomach was in knots and she was tired. So tired. She hung on, letting the impromptu raft draw her along with it, saving what was left of her strength, expending only as much energy as was necessary to keep her head above water. The sky began to brighten. Her left arm ached. Everything ached. Ankle, leg, right arm, back.

A sudden jar broke her numbed hold. Her head went under water and her feet jolted against a solid surface. She stood up, wobbling on one leg, and pushed the streaming hair out of her eyes. The log that had been both disaster and savior had run up against a muddy bank. It was not either of the river banks—just another damned island.

A wave lapped her ankles. The log dipped, as if nodding a courteous farewell, and floated away. Nefret leaned over and threw up.

Once she had rid herself of the rest of the water she had swallowed, and all of the meal she had eaten, she realized she was ravenous. A brief, hobbling survey of her current position offered no hope of relieving her hunger or her thirst. This island was a little larger than the other, but not much, and she was still in the middle of the river, no closer to either shore than she had been, though she was some distance downstream. The only other inhabitants were birds, snowy white egrets, and a few kingfishers. She startled a nesting goose, which rose flapping and honking. In the strengthening light Nefret considered the clutch. No, she wasn't that hungry. Not yet.

She sat down and examined her bare leg. It hurt like the devil, but there was no break, just a bruise the size of her closed fist. Swearing and wincing, Nefret probed the injured arm, and diagnosed a bruised bicep. She wouldn't be using that arm for a while. But there would be boats on the river soon. She ought to be able to hail one of them, making damn good and sure before she did so that it was not a dahabeeyah the size of the *Isis*.

It did not take her long to discover that the main channel was too far away for her faint calls to carry. She grew hoarse from shouting. Against the gray-green reeds her body was essentially invisible. She had nothing bright to wave, no way of starting a fire.

When the sun was high overhead, she saw the *Amelia* go past. She went on waving and calling until it was out of sight, and then sank down and hid her face in her folded arms.

>=<

I DECIDED I COULD ABANDON my post for a short time, and summoned the others to the saloon. No one was hungry, but it is necessary to keep up one's strength when strenuous endeavor may lie ahead.

"You mean a fight?" Cyrus asked. "I sure would like one, but has anybody figured out what we're actually going to do if—when—we catch up with them?"

"Run them aground," Selim said. It had taken a direct order from me to remove him from his engines. He allowed me to take his pulse and feel his brow for signs of fever, but refused to let me do more; and indeed there was not much more I could do. Black smears of oil stained his clothes, from his turban to the hem of his galabeeyah, but so far as I could tell he was holding up well.

Daoud scooped up a portion of chicken and vegetables with a bit of folded bread and popped the whole thing neatly into his mouth. He nodded in agreement.

"Let's see where we stand," Sethos said. He had finished eating. Now he reached for the map Nasir had pushed aside when he served us. "The *Isis* was seen at Tukh yesterday afternoon. Reis Hassan swears she didn't pass Qena today. If we take his word, and I gather you are all inclined to do so, there are only two possibilities. She has changed her name and her appearance, or she is lying low somewhere between here and Tukh."

"Why?" The question came from Ramses, who was standing at the window, looking out, his hands clasped behind him. He swung round. "Why should they delay? What are they after? Would they have collected all of us, one by one, if Father hadn't spoiled their plans? Or did he? Goddamn it, we're sitting here studying maps and timetables, and Cyrus is the only one who's asked a sensible question. Supposing we do catch her up. Then what? Fire a cannon across her bows? That would be entertaining, if we had a cannon. Board her, with cutlasses between our teeth?"

He broke off, breathing hard. I went to him and slipped my arm through his. "That has always struck me as an impractical procedure," I said. "One would have to have extremely hard teeth and strong jaw muscles, and even then an involuntary movement might easily result in the loss of teeth and jaw."

For a moment I feared my attempt at a little joke had been misplaced. His black eyes blazed with anger. I said, "I too am very worried."

The hard lines around his mouth softened. He bowed his head. "I'm sorry, Mother. It's selfish of me to be glad that Father is with her, but . . ."

"I am also glad of it," I said. It was partly true. "I don't know what it was that made Emerson realize Nefret might be in trouble, but it is just like him to go rushing to the rescue all by himself. One good thing has come of his impetuosity. The villains know we will be hot on their trail. Whether it was their original intention or not, they will not . . . they will keep them as hostages."

Walter coughed. "I have been thinking," he said.

"Yes, Walter?" I gave him an encouraging smile. He was so anxious to be of use, poor man, but he had only succeeded in getting in everyone's way. Selim had politely but firmly rejected his further assistance after he burned his arm on the heated metal of the engine, and his attempt to use the sounding stick had almost got us run onto an invisible sandbar.

"I'm not good for much else, you see," Walter explained matter-of-factly. He adjusted his eyeglasses. "We have been operating on the assumption that revenge is the motive for this."

"What other motive could there be?" I asked.

"The *Isis* is an expensive operation," Walter said. "And revenge loses its force after so many years. They are after something more rewarding. What else could it be but the princesses' treasure? And if that is the case," he went on, raising his voice a trifle to be heard over Cyrus's oaths, "it alters our entire strategy. Let us say that M. Lacau finishes loading the artifacts today. If he is in sufficient haste, he will try to get a few miles downstream before nightfall. I think the *Isis,* under a new name, will intercept the steamer tonight, under cover of darkness."

"Suppose Lacau doesn't leave until tomorrow morning?" David asked.

"Then they will strike tomorrow night. The point is—" Walter raised an admonitory forefinger—"that they don't know his schedule either. They will have to lie in wait for the steamer and follow it until it stops for the night, whichever night that may be. We must turn back. We may not be able to identify the *Isis* in her new guise, but we can't miss the government steamer, and if I am right, the dahabeeyah will be nearby."

"What if you're wrong?" I asked, half convinced but reluctant to abandon the pursuit. "We would never catch them up if they have gone on ahead."

"I think he's right," Sethos said. He gave Walter an approving nod. "There is definitely a streak of larceny in the family. I'm ashamed I didn't think of it myself. I vote for heading back upriver."

"No," Ramses said. He went back to the window.

I looked at David. He had seen it too, the increase of tension to such a point that Ramses was beyond reason. The idea of retracing our route was unbearable.

David took him by the shoulders and spun him around. Ramses's eyes were dead black, without a spark of awareness. He swung at David; David dodged the blow and struck back, hard enough to set Ramses back on his heels.

"It takes a blunt instrument to stop him when he's in this frame of mind," David explained coolly.

Ramses's eyes came back into focus. He rubbed his cheek and blinked at David. "Did you have to do that?"

"My friend, you have been half out of your mind for hours. Stop and think. Father's theory provides the first rational motive we've found. Everything fits, don't you see? Even blowing up the railroad station. An armed assault on the steamer will be attributed to terrorists. We have to gamble, but this is our best hope. If we start back straightaway, we can reach Qena before dark."

Ramses nodded. "All right."

"I'll tell Reis Hassan," Walter said happily, and trotted off.

"All right," Ramses repeated.

My heart ached for him. "What about a nice whiskey and soda?" I suggested.

"If you would like one, Mother."

I was afraid I would have to administer another therapeutic smack on the face. However, Ramses is a true son of his father (and me). He passed his hand over his mouth, gave himself a little shake, and managed a smile.

Everyone joined us except Selim, who could not be extracted from his engines. Reis Hassan got us turned round in a series of maneuvers that inspired several breathtaking close calls and a lot of bad language from the persons thus inconvenienced. The white sail of a felucca passed so close it filled the entire window aperture. But finally we were headed south again.

It was late in the afternoon and the sun was setting when Bertie came into the saloon to report that someone was hailing us. "Looks like a local fishing boat."

"Probably hope to sell us something," Cyrus grumbled.

"We had better see what they want," I said. "They may have news."

We followed Bertie onto the deck. The sun was low in the west. A flotilla of small boats raced toward us, their white sails flapping like the wings of a flock of birds. The occupants were all shouting at once. It was impossible to make out words.

"Good heavens," I said. "It is a miniature armada—every boat in that small village, by the looks of it. Tell Selim to stop the engines. They must have news for us."

In my understandable agitation I caught the arm of Ramses, who stood next to me. He shook me off with absentminded force and raised both hands to shield his eyes against the glare of the sunset. Then his rigid body sagged forward across the rail and his breath came out in a long, shuddering sigh.

My vision is not the equal of his, but I believe I was the next to see her, standing in the nearest boat, supported by one of the men. The coronet of golden hair was unmistakable, but so unbelievable and so welcome was the sight I refused to credit the evidence of my own eyes until the little boat came alongside and the grinning crewmen lifted her up into Ramses's outstretched arms.

"It is a miracle," Walter said reverently. He removed his eyeglasses and wiped them on his shirttail.

"Miracle be damned," said my other brother-in-law. "Nefret, I am unspeakably relieved to see you, but—"

"Give them a minute," I said. Ramses's arms held her close and his face was hidden against her hair.

Nefret raised her head and turned in the circle of his arm. She held out her hands to me. "He is alive, Mother. I spoke with him early this morning. I didn't want to leave him, but he—"

"You did the right thing, my dear," I said. The situation was still grave, but I felt as if an enormous weight had been lifted off my shoulders. "Now come and rest, and eat something."

"I'm not hungry," Nefret said. "They fed me and washed my clothes and dried them. They—"

David had been talking with the boatmen. They were so pleased with themselves they were reluctant to go, but after we had showered them with praise and thanks, and all the money we had in our pockets, they tore themselves away. Ahead the lights of Qena shone through the gathering dusk.

It took a little while for us to get underway, since every man on the *Amelia* had to see Nefret and touch her before they could believe she was safely back. Nasir burst into tears and flung himself at her feet. The sight of Selim, oily, weary, and smiling, brought a cry of protest from his physician but he would not let her examine him.

"Tell us," he said. "Everything."

After Nasir had been restored, he stumbled round lighting the lamps and the rest of us crowded round Nefret, who was seated on the divan, with Ramses's arm round her. I am not ashamed to admit that the whiskey flowed freely. Nefret shook her head when Cyrus offered her a glass.

"My stomach is still a little queasy, and you know how the stuff affects me. I'll tell you everything in due time, but you must hear this first. They are planning to take the princesses' treasure!"

The announcement fell a little flat. "Curse it," Nefret said. "You knew? How? I didn't find out until last night."

"Walter figured it out," said Sethos. "Do you know when they plan to strike, and how?"

"No."

"Damnation. If Lacau has already left Luxor, they could seize the steamer tonight."

"I've been thinking," Walter said.

This time his announcement got more attention. "Yes?" Sethos said respectfully.

"Certain of my initial assumptions may have been in error," Walter explained in his precise schoolmaster's voice. "One takes it for granted that dastardly deeds are done under cover of darkness, but they cannot travel at night, can they? Surely they would want to get under-way as soon as they are in possession of the treasure."

"It would take 'em a while to unload the cargo," Cyrus said, stroking his goatee.

"No, no," Walter said excitedly. "Why should they do that? It would, as you say, take a great deal of time, and the dahabeeyah is cer-tain to be seen, however she changes her appearance. Every craft on the river would be on the lookout for her. The government steamer, on the other hand . . ."

"Of course," I breathed. "They will board the steamer—massacre the crew—sink the *Isis* . . . Oh, my. What will they do to poor M. Lacau?"

No one seemed especially concerned about poor M. Lacau. Sethos shook his head. "I've been out of the business too long. Lost my touch. It's a pity Walter is an honest man. What a partner he would make!"

Walter beamed. "You think I am right, then?"

"I know you are right." Sethos slammed his fist into his palm. "That's exactly how I would have planned it, supposing I were cold-blooded enough to murder a dozen innocent men. We've got until morning, then. Someone must go ashore at Qena and try to find out whether Lacau has left Luxor, and if so, when."

"I'll go," Ramses said. It was the first time he had spoken since he took his wife into his arms, and his face was still alight with joy and disbelief.

"We must hear Nefret's story first," I said, with a fond smile at the pair. "She may have seen or heard something that will affect our plans. Start at the beginning, my dear, if you will be so good, and don't leave anything out."

It was, to say the least, an absorbing tale. The faces of the listeners reflected their feelings—surprise, indignation, admiration—but no one interrupted until she described the transformation of Mrs. Fitzroyce.

"Good Gad," I cried in chagrin. "I never suspected her."

"No wonder she avoided me," Sethos said grimly. "I knew the—I knew her well. That explains Martinelli. They were bitter enemies. That isn't good news. She was one of Bertha's most ruthless assistants."

"Justin is equally ruthless," Nefret said. "He—she—isn't quite normal."

She went on to describe her last conversation with Emerson, and his insistence that she leave him. "I would never have made it if he hadn't been there," she said simply. "It was impossible not to live up to his faith in my abilities and my nerve. But I did come close to breaking down when I saw the *Amelia* pass by earlier today."

"It must have been horrible," I said sympathetically. "Where were you?"

"On one of the islands in midstream. I was trying to swim to shore when I was struck by a floating log. I managed to hang on to it until it came aground, but my shoulder was hit—"

Ramses took his arm away. "Why didn't you tell me when I grabbed hold of you? Did I hurt you?"

She touched his cheek. "I didn't even feel it. I never dared hope I would see you so soon, even after I finally managed to attract the attention of a fisherman from the village. Once I had identified myself, they couldn't do enough for me. Late in the afternoon they got word that the *Amelia* was heading back this way, and the whole village piled into their boats, they were so anxious to be the first to give you the news. Now tell me what happened after I left the clinic. Is everyone—are they—"

"Oh, my dear," I said. "I ought to have reassured you immediately. The children are safe—they are all safe—and the house is well guarded."

"So," said Daoud, who had been listening with interest but with increasing signs of impatience, "now we must think how to rescue the Father of Curses."

CHAPTER FOURTEEN

After Ramses had gone ashore, accompanied by Reis Hassan, I persuaded Nefret to rest for a while. She declared she was too keyed-up to sleep, but as soon as her head touched the pillow her weary eyes closed. I stood looking down at her, watching the lines of pain and worry smoothed by the benevolent hand of Hypnos, and thanking Heaven for her preservation. She had made light of her own suffering and struggle, but I knew what she must have gone through. I dared not think of what Emerson was still enduring.

The rest of us sat talking in low voices, so as not to waken her. Daoud had, with the acumen that sometimes marked him, hit the nail square on the head. We might be able to find the *Isis* before she way-laid the steamer, but while Emerson was a prisoner we were powerless to prevent an attack.

"I'd give up the whole goldurned treasure rather than see him come to harm," Cyrus declared.

"That is very noble of you, Cyrus, considering that the treasure isn't yours to dispose of," I retorted, and immediately repented my rudeness when I saw his hurt expression. "Forgive me, Cyrus. I did not express myself well. What I meant to say was that M. Lacau may not share your sentiments."

"That's okay, Amelia, I understand."

"We cannot allow them to take the steamer," I went on. "And we cannot attack the *Isis* openly until Emerson has been freed."

"Attack?" Bertie echoed. "What with, a few rifles, when they are probably armed to the teeth? I don't like the odds, Mrs. Amelia. Cyrus is right, let 'em take the confounded treasure. They won't get away with it. We'll track them down."

"It is not the treasure I am thinking of, but the lives of the men on the steamer."

Bertie's brow furrowed. "Oh, Lord. They wouldn't really kill all those people, would they?"

"I am convinced of it. I remember Matilda well; she was a worthy disciple of her mistress. In my opinion, the young woman is even more dangerous. She has exhibited evidence of severe mental disturbance."

"Then there's my dear little daughter," said Sethos. He reached for a cigarette. His hand was steady. "What a pretty trio they make."

An uncomfortable silence followed. Cyrus looked away, and Bertie bit his lip. I had observed his increasing interest in Maryam. It is painful for a young fellow to think that a young lady's interest in him may have an ulterior motive. In fact, I considered the girl less culpable than the others, but to say so would not have comforted her father. Guilty she unquestionably was, and what we were to do with her if we succeeded in capturing her I could not imagine.

And at that moment she was the least of my concerns. "We will have to get onboard the *Isis*," I said. "Unseen and undetected."

"That is right," said Daoud, nodding approvingly.

The others reserved their commendations. "What a good plan," said Sethos. "How do you propose we go about it?"

"I have a few ideas . . ."

Ramses did not return until close to midnight. He had had to wait at the telegraph office for replies to his urgent telegrams. (He did not explain how he had persuaded the clerk to remain on duty past his usual hour, and I did not ask.) Lacau was still in Luxor, but he had finished loading the treasure and was expected to depart in the morning.

That was not all he and Reis Hassan had accomplished. Ramses had had a few ideas of his own. Runners—donkey riders, to be more precise—had been dispatched south from Qena and northward from

Luxor. Scouts would be in position by morning, and the same signal system would be used. Any private dahabeeyah would be reported.

"You seem to have thought of everything," Sethos said grudgingly. "Except how we can get to Emerson without being seen. The *Amelia* is somewhat conspicuous."

My warning shake of the head stopped Ramses on the verge of a hot retort. He swallowed and looked at Nefret. She had awoken instantly when he entered and was curled up on the divan, watching him as he paced to and fro. "I have thought of that too, sir. We're taking a small boat in tow. She's a miserable-looking craft, so the crew of the *Isis* won't be surprised when we appear with our sail trailing. While the rest of you entertain the observers by screaming poignant appeals for rescue—which you are not likely to get—I'll swim to the *Isis*."

"And I with you," said Sethos.

"How far can you swim underwater?" Ramses inquired gently.

"Far enough."

"No. I," said Ramses in the same quiet voice, "am running this show. Anyone who won't accept that can damn well stay here. The boat will hold four. It will be the job of the others to distract the crew while David and I get to the dahabeeyah. After that . . . well, it will depend on what transpires, and that is likely to be unpleasant."

Naturally they all wanted to go. Daoud rumbled hopefully. Ramses smiled and shook his head.

"Impossible to disguise you, Daoud—or you, Cyrus. Selim isn't fit enough. The rest of us will wear the usual rags. Myself, David, Bertie—and you, Sethos, if you promise to follow my orders."

I sat very quietly in the corner, my hands folded in my lap. Ramses said, without looking in my direction, "No, Mother. Not a chance. Did you hear what I said?"

"Certainly, my dear. I heard every word."

"THERE SHE IS, RIDING AT anchor near the West Bank." Ramses raised one arm and gave the signal to Reis Hassan.

The sun was still low over the eastern cliffs and the lovely flush of sunrise had not completely faded. We were south of Qena, approaching the stretch where, according to Reis Hassan's deductions, the *Isis* was most likely to be lurking. There were only a few villages in that area and traffic on the river was minimal.

"Has she seen us?" I asked.

"I don't think so. Thank God for Reis Hassan," he added, as the *Amelia* came to a grinding halt and began to reverse. "He can make the *Amelia* jump through hoops. Time to go."

Our anchor went over the side and the small boat was drawn up. It was a pitiful craft, the sails patched on patches, and we were an equally hapless-looking crew. Ramses and David wore a minimum of clothing, in preparation for swimming. The rest of us were attired in ragged galabeeyahs.

When I appeared on deck in my hastily assembled disguise Ramses was rude enough to shout at me. Naturally I forgave him, since I knew he was under something of a strain.

"Don't talk to her as if she were a woman, Ramses," Nefret said.

"She is a woman! She's my mother! I won't let her—"

I raised my voice just a trifle. "You said, back in Luxor, that you would not return without Nefret. I will not go back without your father."

"You can't stop her," Nefret said. She stroked his bare arm, as one gentles a restive stallion. "You haven't the right."

"You're on her side," Ramses groaned.

"Of course. If it were you, I'd be in that boat myself."

"A compromise," I said helpfully. "I won't take my parasol."

On Ramses's countenance amusement struggled with anxiety and anger, and I knew I had won. "All right, Mother. But please—not the eye patch."

"It helps to hide my face," I explained. "I neglected to bring a beard."

The others had wisely refrained from joining in the discussion. Cyrus gave me a hearty embrace and helped me into the boat. "We'll be waiting for your signal," he said. "Good luck."

David cast off and raised the sail. Sethos caught hold of me and pulled me down on the seat beside him.

"You are an infernal nuisance, Amelia, do you know that?"

"I believe I can be of some use," I replied modestly.

I was the recipient of an extremely ambiguous glance from my son, who was at the tiller. "Get out the oars," he said.

The prevailing wind swelled the sail but the current was strong. With Bertie and Sethos rowing, we made good progress, and finally Ramses said, "They've seen us. David, start playing wounded duck, but get well upstream of her before you drop the sail. Bertie, if anyone makes a hostile move or points a rifle at you, make sure you shoot first."

We had two rifles, wrapped in oiled cloth, and extra ammunition. We would have had three if anyone had listened to me, but Ramses would not let me have one. Now he went on, "Mother, for God's sake, stop staring, you don't make a very convincing male Egyptian—even with an eye patch."

I raised one arm so that my full sleeve covered my face, but I peered out from over it. We flapped on past, close enough to see the faces of the crewmen, who had gathered to jeer at our erratic progress. Several of them were armed, among them Dr. Khattab, who appeared to be in charge. I ducked my head and heard him call, obviously in answer to a question. "It is only a fishing boat, madame. About to capsize, if I am any judge."

Then we were past. "Here we go," Ramses said, and fell overboard with a startled cry and an impressive splash. The boat rocked, the sail collapsed, and David slid into the water. The rest of us were making as much noise as possible. Sethos cupped his hands round his mouth. "Throw us a rope," he shrieked. "Help, we will all drown. For the mercy of God!"

There was no mercy on those hard faces. Laughing, one of them pointed at a pair of arms and a distorted face that rose above the water between us and the dahabeeyah. The arms waved pathetically and disappeared. Bertie was paddling wildly in circles. The audience found this even more amusing. They began offering advice, all of it rude, some of it quite vulgar. My arms over my head, I swayed and whimpered. My breath came hard and my heart was pounding.

Sethos's cries cut off abruptly. Peering round the hem of my sleeve, I saw two other people at the rail. Justin was wearing male clothing, but everything else about her—the way she stood, the gesture with which she pushed back her windblown curls—was so obviously female that I wondered how I could have been deluded. She had her arm round Maryam, who gripped the rail with both hands and stared fixedly at us.

Justin's pretty face wore a frown. "Bring them on board or sink them," she called, in idiomatic and accented Arabic. The accent was that of a Cairene.

One of the men raised a rifle; clearly he found the second alternative more interesting. Maryam whispered something to her sister. After a moment Justin nodded. "I suppose you're right. Gunfire might attract attention." She went on in Arabic, "Do not fire. Throw them a rope."

Bertie caught it on the second try. The men on the dahabeeyah made no effort to help; one of them had fastened the other end of the rope to the rail, leaving it to us to pull ourselves in—if we could. "Now what?" Bertie whispered. "Won't she recognize you?"

"Me and the lady with the eye patch," said my brother-in-law in an equally subdued voice. "Pull us in. When we are within ten feet, grab the rifle and start shooting."

Bertie's lips tightened. It went against the grain for him to fire first, but he knew there really was no sensible alternative. We had to disable as many of them as we could before we boarded. At least the lad wouldn't have it on his conscience that he had fired at a woman. Justin and Maryam had left the deck.

Squatting in the bottom of the boat, Sethos unwrapped the rifles. I reached for the little pistol I had concealed under my rags. The next ten minutes would tell the tale: victory or defeat, life or death.

FROM MANUSCRIPT H

Ramses came up on the far side of the dahabeeyah and hung on, gasping for breath. He looked wildly around for David, and could have shouted with relief when David's head popped up a few feet away. He reached out a hand and pulled his wheezing friend to his side. David had lost his turban. His black head, sleek as a seal's, streamed water. Ramses removed his own dripping turban and pushed his hair back from his face.

There was no need for discussion, they had worked it out beforehand, trying to cover all possible contingencies. Ramses gripped the rail and pulled himself up till he could see the deck. There were three windows on this side, all open or ajar. None was the window to his father's cell; according to the plan Nefret had drawn, it was on the opposite side of the dahabeeyah. The deck was deserted; the show had drawn the crewmen to the other side. He could hear their yells, and the agitated shrieks of his cohorts. Then he heard a voice he recognized, issuing orders that made him hurl himself up and over the rail. David was close behind him. Fighting the instinct that demanded he go to his mother's help, whatever the odds, he climbed in the nearest window. They hadn't started shooting. It was small comfort, but he had to stick to the plan. Their best and only hope was to take a hostage of their own.

The cabin was a woman's. Various female garments were scattered about, and the hat his mother had given Maryam hung on a hook by the door. Without pausing he went to the door and listened before easing it open. Then he heard the sound he had been dreading, that of rapid rifle fire, and abandoned caution, bolting straight down the corridor toward the saloon, with David close on his heels.

They were there, all three of them—the old woman, Justin, and Maryam. And the doctor. Ramses left him to David, heard a grunt and a thump, and caught Justin by the throat. "Order them to stop firing," he panted. "Maryam, tell them I'll kill her if they don't surrender."

Without a word or a look, Maryam darted out. After a moment the firing stopped. Ramses loosened his hold, feeling like a brute. She stood quiet in his grasp; her throat was soft and slender, and her blue eyes were reproachful.

"You wouldn't hurt me, would you? Your pretty little Hathor?"

"You've lost," Ramses said. "It's over."

She laughed at him, showing even white teeth. David was standing by the old woman, who hadn't moved from her chair. She looked contemptuously at the knife David held to her throat.

"Put that away, boy. Neither of you would harm a woman, and we hold the ace in this little game. If you want the Professor back in one piece, you will surrender to us. Once we have what we are after, we will set you ashore, unharmed."

"You're lying," Ramses said. "Give me the keys to his room."

"They are in the drawer there."

He started toward the bureau and Justin laughed again. "They won't do you any good. The Professor is not alone, you see. François is with him, and if anyone opens that door without giving the agreed-upon signal, he will cut your father's throat. He can't defend himself," she added brightly, "because he is chained hand and foot."

Ramses couldn't think. The sounds on deck had subsided, but Maryam hadn't come back, and his mother might be . . . Torn in two by conflicting filial concerns, he was about to tell David to go out and see what had happened when the curtains at the window were pushed aside and his mother poked her head in. She had lost her turban, her hair was straggling around her shoulders, and there was blood on her face—but the eye patch was still firmly in place.

"Ah, there you are," she said, brandishing her pistol. "I presume everything is under control."

"Well, no, not exactly," Ramses said, struggling for breath. "Mother, are you . . . Sethos and Bertie—"

"Both wounded, but not seriously. They have subdued the crew." His mother climbed nimbly through the window. "This isn't my blood," she added. "My dear boy, you are white as a sheet. You weren't worried about me, were you?"

"Worried? About you?" He ran out of breath again.

"Thank God," David exclaimed. "But the Professor is—"

The pound of feet along the passageway stopped him. Emerson burst through the door. "I heard gunfire. Where—damnation, Peabody, I knew it was you! Why are you wearing that idiotic eye patch?"

She dropped the pistol, and Ramses, dizzy with relief, was treated to the spectacle of his eminent parents, both of whom resembled survivors of a small war, rushing into each other's arms. Their incoherent remarks were, he realized, completely in character.

"How dare you do this to me, Peabody? Ramses, why did you— never mind, you couldn't have stopped her. My darling Peabody, are you injured?"

Interspersed were her own comments. "Another shirt . . . Oh, my dearest Emerson, what have they done to you?"

"And what has happened to François?" Ramses asked. "They told us you were shut in with him."

"Well, I had to kill the bastard, didn't I?" Emerson detached himself from his wife's embrace and ran a bloodshot eye over the room. Unconquerably Emerson, he gave the old woman a stiff bow. "Good morning, er . . . Matilda."

The old woman sat with a face like death. "So you have won. The last battle."

"Have we won, Ramses?" Emerson inquired.

"Yes, sir, I believe so," Ramses said. "But how—you were chained and locked in, weaponless—"

"I didn't need a weapon for a piece of scum like that," his father said magnificently. "I did have one, though. And she had freed me, early this morning. When they put François in with me, I had to—"

"She? Who?"

"Little Maryam, of course. I told you the child was . . . But where is she? She was following me."

"And where," said his wife, "is Justin?"

She had taken advantage of their distraction to slip away, and so had Khattab. They found Maryam lying in the corridor. She had been struck unconscious—it wasn't hard to guess by whom—but she was beginning to come round, and when Emerson lifted her, she caught hold of him and tried to speak. "Quick . . . You must go. She has lit the fuse."

⧏⧐

MATILDA JUMPED UP AND RAN for the door. She was quite agile for an elderly person; the prospect of imminent death, I have observed, lends wings to the feet. Ramses was quicker. He took her by the shoulders and shook her, none too gently.

"Where has she gone?"

She tried to twist away from him. "It's in her room. She loves dynamite. You can waste time trying to break the door down, if you like, but let me go! God knows how much time we have, if she has shortened the fuse."

"She is right," I cried. "This is no time for bravado, or chivalry. Hurry!"

Bertie and Sethos were holding the disgruntled thugs at gunpoint. Several bodies lay sprawled on the deck. Sethos's eyes moved from Emerson to Maryam, but before he could speak, Emerson bellowed, "Abandon ship! Everyone! She's about to blow!"

Thugs rained into the river like beetles shaken from a branch. Sethos limped toward us. He had taken a bullet in the leg and a trail of blood spots followed him. "The boat," he said. "Get the women into it."

The little craft was tied to the side. Matilda was the first to reach it; she scrambled into it and started to untie the rope. "Hands off, Matilda, or I will shoot you where you sit," Sethos said. She backed off, cursing him. Emerson shoved me in and handed Maryam down to me. "Now you," said Emerson, turning to his brother. "And Bertie. Get in and row like hell. Ramses, David, over the side with you."

I will say this for the members of my family that they know when argument is inexpedient. Everyone moved as quickly as if they had rehearsed the procedure. Bertie was grinning, oblivious of the spreading bloodstain on his side; he had always wanted to take part in one of our little adventures. I sincerely hoped that he would survive this one.

I pushed Matilda out of my way and sat down, holding Maryam, who appeared to be in a state of shock; her eyes were blank and unfocused, her body limp. Bertie and Sethos snatched up the oars, and Emerson untied the rope. As we moved away from the doomed vessel, aided by the current, I saw Ramses and David treading water and looking back at Emerson, who was leaning over the rail.

"Who the devil do you think you are, the captain?" I shrieked. "Get off there this minute."

Emerson climbed up on the rail and dived. The boys converged on him, but he was not in need of their assistance, as his vigorous strokes made evident.

Ten feet . . . twenty . . . My eyes were glued on the *Isis*. She looked so peaceful riding there at anchor, her decks deserted. Thirty feet. Swimming strongly, the men had almost caught us. Bertie held out an oar and was royally cursed by both Sethos and Emerson. "Keep rowing," the latter bellowed. Forty feet.

The *Isis* blew. The roar of the explosion deafened me. Bits of wood and rail, metal fittings and miscellaneous debris were hurled into the air. The boat rocked wildly as the shock waves reached us. When they finally subsided I realized we were still afloat and that the dahabeeyah was ablaze. She burned quietly and beautifully, the bright flames swaying above her like a curtain.

We sat transfixed and, in my case at least, filled with profound and humbling thoughts. I believe I was the only one to have seen, among the floating debris, a mutilated but recognizable shape. If she had meant to escape the boat before the dynamite exploded, she had waited too long.

I bowed my head and murmured a little prayer—for our faith offers hope of redemption for even the worst of sinners. I added a brief prayer of thanks for our survival, and then looked up to make sure I had not been premature. Yes, they were all there, safe and more or less sound. And beyond them, coming toward us at full speed, was the *Amelia*.

They took us on board and even Reis Hassan abandoned his post to join in the congratulations and questions. Cyrus clasped his son in an impetuous embrace, to Bertie's great embarrassment; Nefret ran to Ramses, and Selim embraced everyone in turn.

I was about to suggest that we defer further celebration until the wounded had been attended to when I saw something that caused me to call out and point. Bruised and battered, dripping with water and blood, the survivors of that incredible adventure stood gazing in silence as the government steamer sailed sublimely past, on its way to Cairo and safety.

OUR UNEXPECTED AND, NEED I say, welcome arrival in Luxor several hours later evoked considerable excitement. No one had known precisely where we were, and everyone was in a fever of anxiety about us. A triumphal procession gathered as we made our way from the dock to the house, where we underwent another round of embraces. Having allowed Evelyn and Lia—and Gargery—to vent their emotions, I put an end to the flood of questions.

"We will tell you all about it at teatime. We are all in need of a bath and change of clothing, and some of us are in need of medical attention. Cyrus, go home and bring Katherine back with you for tea. Daoud, take that woman to the storage shed and lock her in—with the necessary comforts, of course. Selim, Bertie, off to the clinic with Nefret."

"Sethos, too," said Nefret. "I want to get that bullet out of him."

He had not let go his hold on his daughter since Emerson told him that he owed his survival to her—and, in fact, the success of the entire enterprise, since we could not have prevailed while he was in danger. What she had told her father after they went off together for a long private conversation I did not know, but of course I expected to find out in due course. It had been sufficient to bring about the long-delayed and total reconciliation.

Now he said, with almost his old irony, "I would rather leave it there. I have been the subject of Nefret's medical attentions before."

Naturally I overruled him. He and Maryam followed Nefret. Her arm supported him and his was round her shoulders.

"As for you, Emerson," I began.

Nefret had cleaned him up as best she could, but he was still a horrible sight. The only one whose clothing would fit him was Daoud, who had no extra, so he was still attired—more or less—in the garments he had worn when he rushed in pursuit of Nefret. There were bits of bandage all over him, and quite a number of bruises. His breezy dismissal of François's attempt to murder him deprecated the magnitude of that struggle, against an opponent without scruple or mercy.

"And as for you, Peabody," said Emerson, folding his arms, "I have not finished telling you what I think of your reckless, inconsiderate behavior. Come along with me."

"Yes, my dear," I said.

∎ ∎ ∎

WE WERE, IN MY OPINION, entitled to a celebration. Fatima, whose sentiments were usually expressed with food, piled the tea tables high. Daoud was there, and Kadija, and even Selim, who had refused to go back to bed. The family, including the Vandergelts, Sennia and Gargery, both cats (who were completely indifferent to our misadventures, but who knew Fatima had prepared fish sandwiches), and the dear children—all of them. They were making enough racket to wake the dead, but I felt that they were entitled to be with their parents. The only ones not present were Sethos and Maryam.

Some of us had preferred whiskey and soda to tea.

"Let us drink to another resounding success," I remarked, raising my glass.

"I'm not sure how many more of these resounding successes we can afford, Peabody," said Emerson, shifting uncomfortably in his chair. "I don't mind admitting that I feel a trifle fatigued, and Sethos and Bertie were—"

"Deuced lucky," said Bertie, with a broad smile. The brave lad was so pleased with himself that he had actually ventured to interrupt Emerson. "My injury was only a scratch, nothing to speak of, and Nefret said Sethos would be back to normal in a few days. I wouldn't have missed it for the world."

"It did have its moments, didn't it?" I said, returning his smile. "I have always wanted to hear someone say 'She has lit the fuse.' Or, as the case may be, 'He has lit the fuse.' "

"You couldn't resist the eye patch, either, I suppose," said Emerson, grinning.

"Another of my great ambitions in life is to have boarded a pirate vessel," I confessed.

"Too bad about the cutlass in your teeth, Mother," said my son.

"Ah well, one cannot have everything. Davy, have you quite finished kissing everyone's wounds? Thank you, dear boy. Now go and draw pictures with Evvie and Charla. They are about to have words over that purple crayon, I believe."

"Now, for pity's sake, Amelia, tell us," Katherine begged. "Cyrus and Bertie refused to talk about it, they said they would leave it to you."

"We are only waiting for Sethos and Maryam," I said.

When Sethos joined us, he was alone. "I persuaded her to rest," he said. He looked us over and smiled slightly. "She hasn't yet acquired the family resilience."

"Perhaps that is just as well," I said. "Sit down and put that leg up. Emerson, will you—oh, thank you, Walter."

He had already pressed a glass into his half-brother's hand.

"We are waiting, Amelia," Evelyn said.

"Where to begin?" I took another sip. "It is a complicated story."

"Like most of them," Cyrus said.

"I suppose that is true. Perhaps I should begin by going over my list of Extraordinary Incidents—which I happen to have with me—and explain how each event fits inexorably into the pattern our adversaries attempted to establish in order to deceive us as to their true motive."

"I think we've all worked that out, Mother," Nefret said. Confirmation came in the form of nods from the others.

"Oh," I said. "Including Justin's masquerade as Hathor? The second incident was designed to clear Maryam of suspicion, and it was rather cleverly arranged. Justin was wearing her boy's clothing under that clumsy robe; all she had to do was slip out of it while Maryam and the others distracted you four. The scrap of fabric Emerson found—"

"Was planted," Ramses interrupted. "Excuse me, Mother, but we've worked that out too."

"Oh. Hmmm. The plot began to take shape when Matilda learned of the princesses' treasure. She was at that time running a house of—er—in Cairo, and engaging in various other illicit activities. It was Matilda who had, several years earlier, told Maryam a pack of lies about her mother and induced her to run away. Maryam was young and rebellious—the two are practically synonymous—and she was thrilled to discover that she had a sister and a motherly protector. Matilda arranged Maryam's marriage to a wealthy man—and, I suspect, disposed of poor Mr. Throgmorton once he had made a will leaving everything to Maryam. I am sure Maryam had no hand in his demise."

"He was good to her," Sethos said. "She was fond of him. Not until sometime after his death, when she had returned to Matilda, did she begin to suspect foul play."

"What I don't understand," Cyrus said, "is how they intended to get the artifacts unloaded. They couldn't have gone on to Cairo with them."

All eyes—even those of Emerson—turned to none other than Walter. A modest but pleased smile illumined his scholarly countenance. "I have been thinking about that, Cyrus," he said. "I believe— and this can easily be confirmed—that they planned to tie up somewhere between Qena and Hammadi—they might have had to wait at Hammadi for the bridge to be raised, which would have placed them under close scrutiny—and unload under cover of darkness. The heavier objects could be temporarily concealed in an empty tomb or cave, to be retrieved later, when the—I believe the expression is, 'when the heat was off.' A few of them would have taken the steamer on downstream next day and abandoned or destroyed her."

"I am sure you have the right of it, Walter," I said. "But if you will forgive me, we are getting off the track here."

"My fault," said Cyrus, grinning. "Sorry, Amelia. Go on."

The story of our visit to el-Gharbi was new to some of them, and if I may say so, I told it well. (I saw Daoud, lips moving and eyes abstracted, and knew he was memorizing everything I said, to be repeated, with embellishments.) "It came as a complete shock to me," I admitted handsomely. "I went to el-Gharbi because I had deduced that Maryam's misadventures were, so to speak, the pieces that did not fit into the puzzle, but all I expected to learn was more about her past history. She overheard me talking to Ramses; she had got in the habit of walking in the garden at night. Her reasons do not concern us," I added, with a little cough.

Nefret glanced at Ramses, who was studiously not looking at anyone, and moved closer to him. She looked weary but very beautiful, her face shining with a new contentment. She had learned one important lesson: that the marriage of true hearts does not alter when it alteration finds, and that love is not time's fool—as Shakespeare so nicely puts it. I nodded affectionately at her and went on.

"Maryam realized when she heard me mention el-Gharbi's village that he would tell me about Justin—and that that information would put the entire party on the dahabeeyah under suspicion. I believe I may confidently assert that my explanation of the true facts surrounding her mother's death, as well as the kindly reception she received, had altered her feelings for us. At first light she went to Luxor and attempted to dissuade Justin and Matilda from carrying out their plans—at least the part of those plans that depended on the abduction of Nefret. She swore she would not betray them, but apparently her agitation was so great that they decided they could not trust her, so they locked her in her room and sent Khattab to the railroad station to see whether Ramses and I actually took the train. Exposure was imminent; however, they knew we could not return before evening, so they had only to move up the time of their departure by a few hours. When Maryam was forced to attend that incredible dinner party at which Nefret was also an unwilling guest, she put on a show of submission and acquiescence."

"She certainly deceived me," Nefret admitted.

"It was necessary that she deceive them, so that she might remain at liberty. Upon hearing of Emerson's capture and Matilda's vindictive intentions, she realized that she was the only one who could save him. With great courage and at considerable risk to herself, she stole the keys last night, crept into his room, and freed him from his shackles. She tried to persuade him to escape that same night, but he refused. Like the confounded fool he is," I added.

"I had some hope of preventing the attack on the steamer," said Emerson, smoking placidly.

"Single-handedly?" I inquired with raised brows.

"I rather expected Matilda to pay me another call," Emerson explained. "She so enjoyed the first. Then, you see, I would have taken her hostage and forced the others to surrender to me."

"An excellent plan," said Sethos, with excessive politeness.

"Well, curse it, I didn't expect them to shove François in with me. When I heard them at the door I rearranged my shackles so that I appeared to be still confined and put on a show of weakness. I hoped to get more specific information from him, about the timing and method, but all the bas—er—fellow did was sit glowering at me and fingering his knife. I had about decided there was no point in waiting any longer when I heard gunfire. I had just finished dealing with François when Maryam came back to let me out. She is a brave little girl, and risked a great deal for us."

"More than you know," Sethos said. He rose stiffly to his feet. "Look after her, will you, Amelia? I must catch the night train to Cairo."

"Out of the question," I exclaimed. "You should not be using that leg, and anyhow, your first duty is to your daughter. Tell Mr. Smith to go to blazes."

"I am perfectly fit," said Sethos, sounding alarmingly like Emerson. "And this duty takes precedence over all others. You are on the wrong track, Amelia. Evelyn had the right idea after all."

"She *was* under duress," Evelyn exclaimed. "I knew it. What hold did they have over her?"

"The most powerful hold you can possibly imagine." He smiled at me with something of his old mockery, but there was a light in his eyes. "Some might declare there are enough small children in this adventure already . . ."

"Can never have enough of them," declared Emerson sentimentally. Then his jaw dropped. "What do you mean? Oh, good Gad! Do you mean—"

"I have just been informed that I am a grandfather," said Sethos. "The child is a boy. He is a year old, and Matilda has had him in her hands since shortly after he was born."

"Good heavens," I cried, leaping to my feet. "In the hands of that vicious, unprincipled . . . We must go at once! Er—where?"

"I know where," Sethos said. "I had a little chat with Matilda just now. Sit down, Amelia, and have another whiskey. You won't be needed. I must catch that train, though. I promised I would bring him back to her as soon as is humanly possible."

"Of course," I murmured. "How she must have suffered!"

Emerson knocked out his pipe. "I'm going with you. You aren't fit to travel."

Neither was he. Ramses looked from him to Nefret, whose hand rested in his. "No, sir, I'll go."

"What about me?" Bertie asked.

"You have done enough," I said affectionately.

"No, ma'am, not really. The rest of you chaps . . ." His kind brown eyes moved from Ramses to David to Emerson to Walter. "The rest of you want to be with your wives. I—er—I'd like to go. If—er—Sethos will have me. Just to—er—lean on now and then, you know."

They had formed a bond, I believe, during those last desperate minutes, when Bertie, firing as coolly and accurately as Sethos, had eliminated four of the armed men who stood at the rail before they realized what was happening. While he and Sethos fought their way onto the deck I paused only long enough to tie the rope to our little boat before joining them. The struggle did not last long. As I always say, hired thugs are not reliable.

Sethos said, "Thank you." Which was, for Sethos, a remarkable concession.

We saw them off, with hearty good wishes and packets of sandwiches forced on them by Fatima. Dusk softened the dying light and the stars shone in the sky over Luxor.

"That reminds me," I said. "It is high time I started my Christmas shopping. What a celebration we will have this year!"

"Hmph," said Emerson. It was a soft hmph, though, and he offered no further objections.

"Did you catch de lady?"

For a moment I thought the childish treble was Evvie's—but Evvie never abused her diphthongs in that fashion. I had only known one other child who did. We turned as one. Peering at us over the barricade of boxes was Charla.

"I don't want her to come to de window anymore," she said.

Ramses made a leap for his daughter and snatched her up. "What did you say?"

"I don't want de lady wit' de yellow hair to—"

"You're talking. She's talking!" Ramses shouted.

"I told you she would when she was ready," I said, anticipating with resignation several years of mutilated diphthongs. Just like her father. At least her vocabulary appeared to be that of a normal child. Unlike her father.

Ramses collapsed into a chair and put his arm round his daughter. "What did the lady do to frighten you?"

"She whispered things." Charla's eyes were round and fearful. "Things that happen to bad children. She said I was bad. Once she tried to put a snake in de window, but you came and she ran away."

"Oh my God," Ramses whispered, holding her close and bowing his head over hers. "You aren't bad, sweetheart. You're good and wonderful and brave. The—the lady is gone, she'll never come back."

Charla was pleased, but not entirely convinced. "Is she dead?"

"Yes," I said firmly. "She is dead. The dead do not come back."

"It was Justin, wasn't it?" Nefret said, her voice unsteady. "Another of her little games. To torment a child like that!"

"Your premonitions were correct, you see," I said. "She *was* a threat to them."

Nefret ran her hand caressingly over the two curly black heads. Then she sauntered, with seeming casualness, toward the barricade.

"Davy?" she said tentatively.

The little boy looked up and showed his four teeth.

Nefret held out her arms. "Will you come and talk to Mama?"

"If you don't mind, Mama, I would prefer to be called by my full name from now on," said David John, articulating with hideous precision. "What subject would you like to discuss?"

I sank into the nearest chair. "Emerson," I said faintly. "Emerson—another whiskey, please."

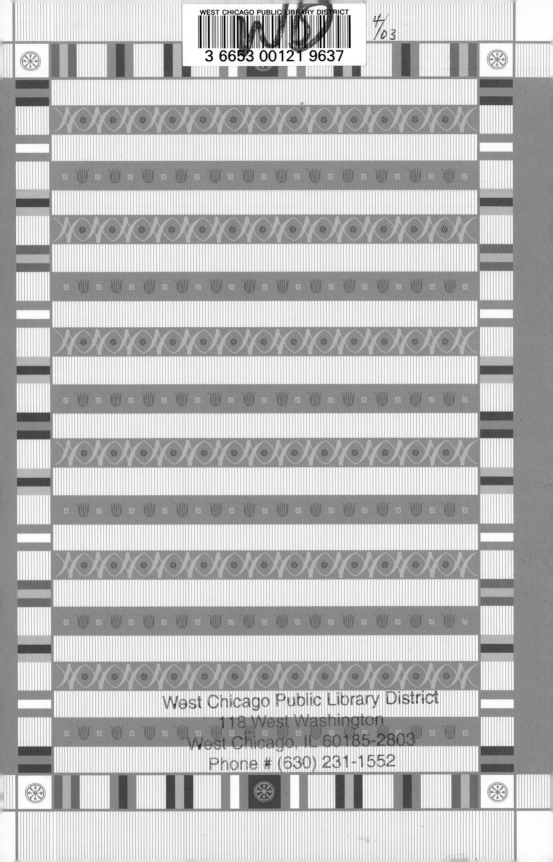